To Charlotte
from Chef John 2017

Roadside Sisters

'. . . robust, funny . . . the jokes run through her books like a constantly bubbling, refreshing stream.' —*Age*

'An Australian Thelma and Louise without the violence . . . warm, witty and enjoyable.' —*Herald Sun*

'A heart-warming read from the wonderfully insightful Wendy Harmer.' —*AussieReviews.com*

'*Roadside Sisters* is easy and light, perfect for the beach, or with a cocktail on a hot, summer night.' —*Publishers Weekly*

'Wendy Harmer is one of Australia's most enduring comediennes and it is clear from the wit and warmth of this novel why it is she has such broad appeal.' —*South Coast Register*

'The pace is brilliant . . . never a dull moment . . . what a talent is Wendy Harmer.' —*Sunshine Coast Sunday*

'The strength of Harmer's story lies in the warmth she shows for her subject and her brutal honesty about female friendships.'
—*Illawarra Mercury*

GW00370735

WENDY HARMER is one of Australia's best-known humorists. She has enjoyed a highly successful thirty-year career in journalism, radio, television and stand-up comedy.

She has written for newspapers, been a regular columnist for magazines and is the author of five books for adults, two plays, three one-woman stage shows and a libretto for the Australian Opera. Her bestselling children's book series 'Pearlie in the Park' has been translated into ten languages and is the subject of an animated television series.

Wendy lives on Sydney's Northern Beaches with her husband, two young children, and (at last count) fifteen chickens and three ducks.

Wendy Harmer

Roadside Sisters

ALLEN&UNWIN

This edition published in 2010

First published in 2009

Allen & Unwin
83 Alexander Street
Crows Nest NSW 2065
Australia
Phone: (61 2) 8425 0100
Fax: (61 2) 9906 2218
Email: info@allenandunwin.com
Web: www.allenandunwin.com

Cataloguing-in-Publication data is available
from the National Library of Australia
www.trove.nla.gov.au

ISBN: 978 1 74237 231 0

Set in 11.5/18 pt Sabon by Bookhouse, Sydney
Printed and bound in Australia by Griffin Press

10 9 8 7 6 5 4 3

For my three fellow travellers—
Brendan, Marley and Maeve

One

'This is your half-hour call. Technical crew, performers, front of house—theatre doors are now open. This is your half-hour call.'

The announcement from the tinny speakers on the walls of the dressing rooms at the Athenaeum Theatre stirred everyone into frenzied activity. Meredith leaned towards the make-up mirror and attacked her black spikes of gelled hair. 'Has anyone seen Corinne yet? Where the hell is she?'

'I'll check the other dressing rooms,' Nina volunteered. 'Oh God! I feel sick. I've been to the loo five times already! And wearing this thing . . .' she flapped the purple batwings of her gospel robe, 'it takes twice as long. You want anything from the Green Room? I'm getting something.'

'White wine. Thanks.' Annie, sitting on the threadbare carpet, held up her plastic cup for another refill. Nina took it and hoisted her hem. She stepped over Annie's splayed legs.

'Haven't you had enough already?' Meredith gave Annie an evil-eyed reverse squint through the illuminated mirror.

'Tonight's not a rehearsal! Every one of us has to be on-song, note-perfect.'

Annie rolled her eyes. Praise be to Sister Meredith for restating the bloody obvious. 'Wait, Nina, I'll come with you.' She leapt into the hallway and sniffed the air—a lean-limbed whippet at the entrance of a rabbit burrow.

'ANNIE! I want everyone back here in five minutes!' Meredith bellowed after her.

Backstage was a dimly lit labyrinth connected by narrow wooden stairs. The sounds of last-minute rehearsals issued from every dressing room door Annie passed by. She noted the odd tootle from a trumpet, the chorus of a song accompanied by a strummed guitar, stray punchlines to half-heard set-ups—and judging by the anatomical detail of the gags, it sounded as if a good many of them tonight would be about Ronald Reagan's colon surgery.

In the mid-eighties it seemed as if everyone in Melbourne wanted to be up on stage to be a part of this 'New Wave' of entertainment. Almost overnight, a crop of stand-up comedians, sketch comedy ensembles, punk magicians, circus acts and tap dancers (with or without small dogs) had sprouted from fallow suburbs to perform with rented sound systems set up in every empty corner of the city.

And if the organisers of the 'venue' wanted to call the night a 'cabaret', they also booked a musical act. Hundreds of musicians and singers formed and re-formed into groups, like mounds of tzatziki on a plate shovelled by grilled flat bread at a Greek café. A jazz ensemble was piled into a big band, then separated into a ukelele, polka or cowboy band, a musical parody duo, trio or quartet (often with hilarious costumes), and finally what remained was scraped into a gospel choir. If you couldn't play an instrument, weren't funny or a natural performer or had no charisma whatsoever, you could always find yourself a place in a gospel choir.

In the Green Room Annie shook the cardboard box of Coolabah to drain the last drops of riesling into her cup. She sidled up to Nina, who was piling her paper plate with wholemeal pita bread and brown rice salad.

'I'm going for a smoke,' she whispered and headed for the stage door. There would be comedians and musicians out there in the laneway—cigarettes, filthy jokes and laughter. She vaulted up the stairs in high-heeled boots, dragging her Drum Blue tobacco out of the back pocket of her jeans as she went.

'Don't be long! Meredith says . . .' Nina's voice trailed away as she saw Annie disappear. She turned her attention back to her towering plate and saw, with some guilt, that she had enough food to feed a family of starving Ethiopians. She crammed cold rice into her mouth. Nina always ate when she was nervous. Or depressed, or happy, or bored.

On the way back to her own dressing room, Nina knocked on the door of the cubbyhole next door and peeked inside. She saw, through a thick, silvery haze of dope smoke, Genevieve and Jaslyn sitting back in plastic chairs with their bare feet up on the bench. Jasyln's silver toe rings glinted, catching the light as she crossed chunky, hairy ankles. Genevieve idly picked at the threads of tobacco on her tongue.

'You seen Corinne?' Nina fanned at the pungent cloud. They shook their heads in reply. Nina groaned. 'Bloody hell! Meredith will have a heart attack if she doesn't get here soon.'

'She needs a manipulation,' drawled Jaslyn. 'Her Vishuddha chakra is blocked. Or I could give her a reflexology massage.' Nina dutifully returned to Meredith and relayed the message.

'The last thing I need now is Jaslyn's hippie bullshit!' snapped Meredith. 'We've got twenty minutes until showtime. The biggest agent in Australia is going to be watching us out there. We've got no Corinne, Annie's half pissed, Briony's still sticking those damned anti-nuclear leaflets on windscreens in Collins Street and I can smell Genevieve's joint from here!'

Meredith reached for the garish-hued gown hanging on a coat hook. It was an appropriate enough garment for tonight, she reflected. If they screwed up their performance they might as well be singing at their own funeral.

'Just go and get Annie. She should be dressed by now,' Meredith instructed as she pulled the voluminous shroud over her head.

Nina flew out the door and wondered why it had been left to her to round everyone up . . . again. She located the stage door, shoved it open and fell into the laneway. She found Annie there doubled over with laughter in the middle of a group of blokes in scruffy tuxedos whom she recognised as members of the comedy tuba quartet, also on tonight's bill.

'Annie,' Nina flapped her robes in urgent semaphore, 'Meredith wants you to come now.'

'Ah,' said Annie, pointing at Nina's improbable get-up. 'Mother Superior's calling me for vespers. I'll catch you guys later. Have a good one!'

Annie paused at the doorway, turned, crossed herself with a grand comic flourish and sang loudly: '*Gloria Patri, et Filio, et Spiritui Sancto.*' She blessed those assembled with the tossed remains of her ice cubes.

☼

With five minutes until curtain-up, the six of them were now squeezed into one dressing room. Meredith paused, mascara in hand, and checked her watch. She hurled the brush at her reflection. 'We'll just have to assume Corinne isn't coming.'

'No!' gasped Briony, pausing with her fingers plunged up to the second knuckle in a jar of glitter hair gel. 'She's got all the solos and—'

'I know that!' Meredith interrupted. 'We'll have to share them around. I'll take the first one. Nina, you can take—'

'I couldn't. I just couldn't!' wailed Nina. Her curling wand clattered onto the bench. 'Ohmigod! I have to go again . . .' Nina pushed her way through to the door and hurtled into the hallway.

'We've got two options,' said Meredith. 'We either get out there and give it a go, or give up.'

'Let's just fucking do it,' came Genevieve's muffled reply from inside the bundle of fabric Annie was now forcibly dragging over her nodding skull.

Meredith poked at the spikes of hair which were threatening to slump into flat, soft petals. The second last thing she needed was directions from Genevieve. She reeked of marijuana and would be lucky to find her way to the stage, unless they all held hands like preschoolers and led her through the dark.

'*Ladies and gentlemen . . . Welcome to the Athenaeum Theatre for this night of stars . . .*' the PA system popped, crackled.

The activity in the dressing room stilled and became a religious tableau painted by Caravaggio. Each head turned to the speaker on the wall, as if the Voice of God was to be heard there. With the first round of applause from the capacity audience in the auditorium, the tiny dressing room erupted in a riot of elbows, knees and metres of noxious purple polyester. Nina returned and squashed in. They jostled for space to peer at their reflection by the stark light of the naked globes.

'SHOOSH!' commanded Meredith. She turned and raised her arms to her small congregation. 'Look, we're the last act in the first half. That gives us thirty minutes to get it together.'

'She's right,' declared Briony, still red-faced from grappling with a thousand windscreen wipers and her canvas bag of fluorescent orange A4 flyers. 'We're wimmin! Sisters Are Doin' It For Themselves!' She sang the Eurythmics hit they all knew from FM radio.

Jaslyn shook out her dreadlocks and slapped two large hands on her thighs. 'We can do this! Yes we can! I threw the I Ching this morning and it said—'

'Let's just find a place to rehearse,' Meredith ordered, and charged out the door with her robes flapping behind her like the wings of an avenging angel.

The six of them stood outside on that cold April night and did their best to 'get it together', even as they kept an eye on the stage door, hoping that the apparition of Corinne would appear and lead them to salvation. It was not until the stage manager gestured for them to follow him through the dark to the wings that they knew for sure they'd been abandoned.

Huddled in the velvety blackness, they twined their arms around each other's waists and swayed to a silent hymn. Just metres away microphones were illuminated in celestial spotlights. Meredith was suddenly reminded that this was how people described a near-death experience—you were drawn towards a blinding radiance that was the font of all love and understanding. Then, if it wasn't your time to go, you were sent back to earth, with gratitude, to live again. At least, that is what Meredith hoped it would be like—she had no desire to die out there and end up in cabaret purgatory. Each woman prayed to her own god for deliverance.

'Ladies and gentlemen,' announced the MC, resplendent this evening in a powder blue velvet suit with embroidered lapels, 'please welcome seven—' Meredith hissed at the stage. The MC turned and peered under the brim of his black cowboy hat to see her upheld fingers—'no, six women tonight with heavenly voices. Melbourne's favourite gospel choir . . . Sanctified Soul!'

Two

It was Nina who picked up the phone and rang Meredith and Annie to suggest the three of them should have dinner to honour the twentieth anniversary of the night the group disbanded. She'd only put the dates together when she was sitting at the dining table sorting through a box of photographs. More raw material to feed her latest mania for scrapbooking. She'd found a poster, gnawed by silverfish, advertising their performance at the Athenaeum in April 1987. There was Sanctified Soul, listed in a stellar line-up of comedians, singers and bands. Nina recognised all the names. Some of the comics now had respectable jobs working on ABC radio, while others had become actors, writers or were in the 'where are they now?' file. The musical performers had likewise met various fates— one of them was in fact teaching Nina's eldest son guitar on Saturday mornings.

The keeping of the Sanctified Soul mythology had fallen to Nina, Annie and Meredith. As the three of them went about their business in the city they would sometimes drive past a pub, restaurant or town hall where they'd performed. Some of the spaces had been rebirthed as poker machine lounges or cocktail bars. Once Annie had been standing at the cash register of a Prahran noodle shop and suddenly remembered they had played a gig in the spot now occupied by a despairing giant crab in a fish tank.

When Nina, Annie and Meredith had last met—was it a year ago?—they shared a guilty laugh about who had made the least fortuitous escape. They choked on blueberry brioche as they realised the joke was on them. They were the ones still living in Melbourne. All these years later and they still lived within a fifteen-kilometre radius of where they'd sung that final night.

There had been seven of them back then—a goodly number for a heavenly choir. Genevieve had long since been claimed by a heroin overdose; Briony was now hostage to the tourism industry in Cairns; Jaslyn was working with UNICEF in Afghanistan. And Corinne? Corinne Jacobsen was in Sydney and was the one who had apparently 'made it'. After years of hosting morning television she was now a 'household name'—in the same way you knew the brand name of your favourite bench wipes and chose them at the supermarket, someone had cattily observed. How many of the performers from that night, Nina wondered, had walked out of the theatre and never, ever appeared on a stage again? Like Nina, Annie and Meredith.

✵

A week after that phone call the three of them were sitting around a linen-covered table in a quiet corner of an Italian restaurant in East Melbourne.

'Remember the time the sprinklers came on at that crappy motel in Shepparton and drenched us just before we were supposed to leave for the gig?' asked Nina.

Annie and Meredith laughed. They did remember. And a lot more besides.

'It can't be twenty years ago.' Meredith shook her head in disbelief. It was the fifth time she'd said this since they sat down. 'You were a baby then, Annie. A baby. I can't believe we took you on the road with us when you were, what? Eighteen?'

'Nineteen. Yup! Fresh off the farm.' Annie grinned. She reached for her wineglass and scraped back her trademark tumble of amber curls. 'I came to the city to "find myself" and I found all of you instead. I never knew women like you existed!'

'So, you must be coming up to the big four-oh—' Nina had been doing her sums—'and you've still not remarried. No kids. That's a shame.'

'Knock it off, Nina, you're sounding like my mother.' Annie drained her glass and poured herself another. Nina registered the rebuke, but couldn't help noticing that Annie had hardly touched her veal cutlet. But she'd drunk most of the bottle of Barossa red. Was that how she stayed so slim? What a shame to see all that good meat going to—

'Nina was always the motherly type.' Meredith patted the sleeve of Nina's lilac knitted cotton cardigan and turned to

Annie. 'She was always nagging us to have breakfast before we got on the mini-bus.'

'Nothing's changed,' Nina grimaced. 'But I'd swap nagging six grown women for three teenage boys and a husband any day. They never listen to anything I say. I feel like the invisible woman. But then I look in the mirror and wonder how they could possibly miss me. I think I've put on a kilo for every year since the choir broke up.'

'Come on, you still look fine.' Meredith waved away her concerns. She was reminded that Nina had always moaned about her weight, even when she had been a curvy size twelve. 'I remember back then you were on the Israeli Army Diet.'

'Oh, my God! I was too,' squealed Nina. 'Two days apples, two days cheese, two days chicken and two days salad!' She counted on her fingers. 'I got as far as cheese and then went on to biscuits.'

Annie reached for her glass again. 'Christ, imagine naming a diet after the Israeli army these days! About as politically correct as the Palestinian Refugee Camp Diet.'

'What's that? I might give it a try.' Nina found her spoon and scraped up the last of her tiramisu. Annie was reminded that her musings always went over Nina's head.

'What I mostly remember,' said Meredith, 'is battling Corinne for time in front of the mirror. And Briony with her disgusting bircher muesli—containers of curdled yoghurt and grated apple stashed in her vile canvas backpack.'

Annie spluttered into her glass. 'That's right! I had to share a motel room with Jaslyn and her stinking patchouli incense sticks! I'd never seen a woman with dreadlocks before. All I could think of were the dags on a sheep's bum!'

And then it was Nina's turn: 'Do you ever think of poor Genevieve, with her Indonesian clove cigarettes and God-knows-what-else she was on?'

There was a pause as they all remembered Genevieve, dead now for twelve years, but still alive in their minds, swaying with her hands on her heart singing 'Asleep in Jesus'.

Asleep in Jesus! Blessed sleep,
From which none ever wakes to weep;
A calm and undisturbed repose,
Unbroken by the last of foes.

Asleep in Jesus! Oh, how sweet,
To be for such a slumber meet,
With holy confidence to sing
That death has lost his venomed sting!

Five of them had sung that song at Genevieve's funeral. They could only hope that she had indeed found peace at last.

'So, Annie,' Nina paused to lick her spoon—and her fingers—'how's the real estate business going?' Nina thought things must be going rather well, judging by the size of the diamond dress-ring Annie was wearing and the price of the wine she'd ordered ($60!).

'It's all good. Got a cute little place by the beach in Port Melbourne. One bedroom. Nothing like Meredith's palatial ranch out east, of course.'

'Yee-hah!' Meredith swung her napkin over her head like a cowgirl riding a $10,000 Miele range oven and five-burner cooktop. 'I've just finished another round of renovations. The "ranch" is looking fabulous. You must come and see. And come into the store if you're looking for something special for the home. In fact, I've got my latest full-colour catalogue right here. I'll give you a discount.'

'So you're still in the house-porn business,' said Annie as the catalogue was waved in front of her. Meredith dropped it back into her bag. She'd forgotten how sharp Annie's comments could be. Cutting. Right to the bone. Always delivered with that winning, country-girl 'whaddya reckon?' grin.

'As a matter of fact, Annie,' Meredith leaned across the table and whispered, 'I just got a shipment in from Sweden and I am in possession of some serious objects of desire.'

Annie remembered that Meredith had always been clever, quick-witted. How old was she now? Fifty? And still rail-thin and utterly intimidating. She was all cream suede and pearls this evening. The eighties feminist firebrand in overalls who had scaled billboards in the dark to deface sexist advertising had been spray-painted over. In her place was a tasteful mantelpiece portrait of carefully understated eastern suburbs affluence.

'Ooooh, Swedish appliances!' Annie teased and pouted glossy red lips. 'Anything with studs and rubber? Maybe I will stop by.'

Nina had been reading the menu in search of one last treat and had missed most of this exchange. 'I love your hair. It really suits you,' she said, admiring Meredith's slim face framed by sleek silvery layers. 'When'd you stop colouring it?'

Meredith ducked Nina's outstretched hand. 'Six months ago. Not long after Donald left. I needed a change. How much of a cliché is that? "Husband walks out, wife runs to hairdresser." Let's order coffee.' Meredith turned away and looked for the waiter.

Nina, as the convener of the occasion and self-appointed cheerleader, was torn. Meredith and Donald had been married for . . . it must be close on thirty years. She needed more information. Then again—Nina checked her watch—it was almost 10 pm. She would just bet that Jordy was still on the bloody computer in his bedroom, that the twins hadn't done their homework and Brad was flaked out on the couch in front of the television. She should probably call home in a few minutes.

'How old are Sigrid and Jarvis now?' Annie asked Meredith.

'Well, that's the big news. Sigrid's getting married in Byron Bay in three weeks. Jarvis is coming back from London for the wedding. He's been working at Sotheby's in Asian art.' The name 'Sotheby's' was offered with some pride. Annie was suitably impressed, although she wasn't sure Nina caught the reference.

'Siggie's getting married? No!' exclaimed Nina. 'I can remember her coming to rehearsals in fairy wings.'

There was a brief silence in which they found themselves in a bare Scouts hall, warm breath visible on a freezing July afternoon. Seven grown women shrieked with alarm to see tiny blonde-headed Sigrid tear off her sparkly wings, and her clothes, and dance across the icy floorboards as her little brother, Jarvis, sitting in his stroller, chortled with delight. The moment came to them as a black-and-white scene from an old movie, cast with people they hardly recognised.

'So she'd be . . . what? Twenty-four now?' Annie was groping her way down the long corridor of the past, trying to make sense of it all.

Nina's congratulations were heartfelt. 'Well, that's wonderful! You must be so proud, Mother of the Bride. Who's she marrying?'

'I have absolutely no idea. All I know is that his name's Charlie. Coffee! Where's that damned waiter?'

Annie and Nina exchanged a second's glance that said it all. They'd better order more supplies and settle in for the duration.

'I'd like a nightcap as well. Something sticky and hideously expensive,' chirped Annie as she swivelled her diamond ring to catch a sparkle in the low light.

'And chocolate-dipped apricots. It says on the menu they make them in-house.' Nina clasped her hands and gave thanks for the imminent blessing of sugar.

※

'Did you know Oprah Winfrey and her best friend Gayle have known each other for thirty years?' Nina leaned across the table. 'And they still call each other four times a day?' She picked at crumbs of chocolate with pink-frosted fingernails. Nina wanted a friendship like that. Half the women in the English-speaking world did. Oprah had declared her unconditional love for her friend so often that her sentiments had mutated into a global epidemic of female inadequacy.

'How hard could it be to get someone on the phone when you're worth more than a billion dollars?' Meredith scoffed.

'They're probably gay,' Annie muttered under her breath as she sipped at her dessert wine.

'And Oprah says,' Nina continued, pausing to insert a nail into her mouth and suck, 'that she feels like their friendship has been designed by some higher power.'

Nina caught the flicker of disbelief telegraphed between her companions. 'Have you ever had a friend like that?' she persisted.

'No, and I wouldn't want to,' Meredith stated. 'I've got enough going on in my life. Who's got the time for all that? It doesn't sound like a friendship to me. It sounds more like some "co-dependent relationship". Doesn't Oprah bang on about that sort of stuff?'

Nina wasn't to be so easily dismissed. 'What about you, Annie? Do you spend much time with your girlfriends?'

Annie tipped her glass in Meredith's direction. 'Same as you. Actually, most of my friends are men. I can't stand the way women judge each other all the time. You meet another woman and she runs her eyes up your whole body—from your toes to the top of your head—like she's doing this inventory. Sizing up a piece of furniture or . . . an overripe avocado.'

Nina guiltily ducked her head. She'd done it. Surveyed Annie's trim figure, checked the size of her diamonds, taken note of the fabric and cut of her sleek black jacket, and her red lipstick, matching finger- and toenails. What had she deduced? That Annie must be looking at her and thinking she'd let herself go to hell. Nina caught her reflection in the mirror and saw that her hair looked like grated cheese piled on top of a baked potato.

'And men don't have this hideous insecurity about their looks and their lives,' Annie went on. 'Or if they do they're better at keeping it to themselves. I couldn't stand having someone constantly ringing and whining for reassurance. It'd be exhausting. Bore the shit out of me.'

Nina chose to ignore Annie's detour sign and ploughed on: 'I was thinking, while I was going through my scrapbooks, that you are the two friends I've known for longest.' She chased flakes of chocolate around her plate with a plump thumb. The rest of the sentence was left unsaid, a silent accusation: *And you never ring me, ask me how I'm going, take any interest in my life.*

Annie thought of her pack of cigarettes in her satin purse. She silently cursed the 'no smoking' signs and raised her hand for a Flaming Sambucca.

Meredith sneaked a look at her watch and peered into her half-full coffee cup. She took a deep breath. 'So, Nina, how *is* everything with you?'

✺

Some time around midnight—over the sound of waiters stacking chairs and clearing glasses from nearby tables—there was an *incident*. It had begun tidily enough as a polite conversation between acquaintances but had quickly slipped into a maudlin, syrupy morass of shared tears and secrets no-one had quite anticipated or was in any way prepared for. The result was—and everyone was hazy on the details of who said what, when, exactly—that they agreed they needed more than a few hours together to celebrate their loving friendship of the past twenty years. The unlikely plan Nina hit upon was to drive all of them in her father-in-law's motorhome from Melbourne to Byron Bay. It was a two-thousand-kilometre journey and she estimated it would take ten days. And if her father-in-law picked up the van in Byron, they could fly back after the wedding and be home in less than two weeks.

When she was later accused of setting up an ambush, Nina was prepared to accept liability . . . up to a point. It was true that she had first brought up the idea because she was the one with the vehicle in her driveway, but it was, in fact, Meredith who had cried. That had been a shock to everyone around the table, no-one more so than Meredith. If there hadn't been tears, they could have made their excuses and moved on. It would also have helped if Annie hadn't taken Meredith in her arms and given that heart-wrenching speech about 'mothers and daughters' and 'once-in-a-lifetime opportunities' and 'eternal regrets', and then brought up her own latest depressing tarot card reading for good measure.

In the end, they were all culpable—including the waiter who had brought the complimentary round of 70 per cent proof grappa and said it was a wonderful 'digestivo'.

When they said their goodbyes that night on the footpath, they had hugged and kissed and squealed with excitement at their forthcoming adventure. No-one dared to voice her misgivings and bear the bad karma of ruining the Oprah *Ah-hah*! So it wasn't until each of them was driving home (after joking that the alcohol in the tiramisu had probably put them over the limit, and deciding to chance it anyway) that all three began to panic and individually consider driving their cars straight off the Punt Road bridge into the Yarra River at the prospect of spending almost two weeks on the road together and talking to each other forty times a day.

Wrestling steering wheels back from the road's edge and checking rear-vision mirrors for flashing blue lights, each began to trawl their memories for the details on how their fellowship had survived the past two decades. Did they even qualify as friends, they wondered? If the length of time they had known each other counted for anything, then they were. But how much did they know about each other's lives, really? The three of them were as unlikely companions as you could find, but they were part of a matched set, like 1950s kitchen canisters of Flour, Sugar and Tea.

Despite their doubts about the pact they had made, they found themselves humming 'Swing Low, Sweet Chariot'. They had crossed the Yarra River—muddy and wide—and were being carried home in their various chariots: Meredith in her Audi Quattro with the pristine chocolate leather upholstery; Nina in the Honda Odyssey, which had twenty filthy football jumpers and thirty-five socks in the back seat; and Annie in her Mini Cooper, its ashtray overflowing, three empty vodka mixer bottles on the floor and now a good three months out of rego.

Three

Annie's phone call came as Nina was standing at her kitchen bench the next morning rereading a particularly inspirational article in O magazine: '*Women's friendships are special. Women friends help us define who we are and who we want to be. They are a touchstone in our lives through family, marriage and childbirth. Female friends offer wise counsel and a trusting and deep constancy.*'

'I was pissed last night. I can't come.'

'OH NO! Annie, why not?' The disappointment came like a head-butt to Nina's midsection. She dumped the magazine on the bench and paced the kitchen with the cordless. All morning she'd been on a high at the prospect of getting away. In her mind she was already lying on a banana lounge by a pool at Byron Bay with a banana daiquiri and the latest Jodi Picoult novel.

'I've got so much on here at work,' Annie sighed. 'I've got three inspections just this afternoon. It's all about time. Who's got the *time* for this?'

'I know that,' Nina countered. 'None of us has the time, but you're the one who was talking last night about "lifelong regrets". We were all remembering the great times with Sanctified Soul when we were on the road. How come we stop doing stuff, having adventures, having fun, just 'cause we're middle-aged?'

The thought of being 'middle-aged' gave Annie a moment's pause. 'But you could go away with Meredith. You don't really need me.'

'Well maybe we don't need *you*, but you need *us*. You're paying total strangers to read your fortune. How crazy is that? What you need is "wise counsel" from female friends. We'll tell you all about your life for free.'

'Yeah, well maybe that's exactly what I *don't* need. And I just had one card reading, that's all. It doesn't *mean* anything.'

This line of argument wasn't getting Nina any closer to backing out of her driveway. She changed gear. 'Look, if you won't do it for yourself, at least do it for Meredith. The whole situation in Byron is going to be really hard for her. She could do with some support and validation.'

'Nina . . .' Annie rolled her eyes at the banal self-help jargon Nina had obviously picked up from daytime TV. 'We'll just be hangers-on. We don't really know any of the family. I wouldn't recognise Sigrid now if I fell over her, and Jarvis was three when I last saw him.'

'Forget about the wedding then. That's just one part of it anyway.' Another smooth gear change. 'Have you ever been to Byron Bay?'

'No.'

'Neither have I, but I've always wanted to go, haven't you? It sounds amazing. All lush and tropical. Beautiful beaches and the water will still be warm. We can walk to the lighthouse. And I hear there's great shopping.'

Nina wasn't sure about the shopping bit, but threw it in for Annie's benefit. She wasn't above telling the odd lie. One of her most celebrated efforts had been activating the car's windscreen washer and telling her three small boys that it was raining when they whined to be taken to the local adventure playground. The boys had been mightily aggrieved when they found out the truth years later, but the story was now part of family legend and Nina went on fibbing when it suited her.

Annie hesitated. It was a silence Nina could almost have driven a five-berth motorhome through. She put the foot down. 'And you never know, Miss Bailey, you might meet some gorgeous men there. There're tons of restaurants and bars right on the beach.'

'Well . . .'

'I tell you what, why don't you come over on Saturday, say midday, and at least have a look at the van. I know you'll love it. You can make a final decision then. Deal?' Nina held her breath. She didn't have anything more to offer right now. She could hardly say to Annie: *If you don't come I might be tempted to drive myself off a cliff, and it will be your fault.*

'OK, deal,' said Annie. 'But don't get your hopes up, that's all.'

Nina replaced the phone and bent for the laundry basket. Two dozen Under-14s football jumpers and shorts to be washed, dried and folded. And there was another fetid pile of Under-16s sports gear in the back seat of the Honda Odyssey. Nina reflected that it was an ironic name for her car.

'Od.ys.sey n: *A long series of travels and adventures.*' Jordy had Googled it the day they brought the seven-seater home. The only long travels she'd taken in that vehicle had been from the house to school, from school to the supermarket, from the supermarket to the house, from the house to the football oval and back to the house. A daily round-trip of tedium.

As for adventures . . . ? The last 'adventure' she could recall was taking her mother, Wanda, to the Brand Smart Factory Outlet in Nunawading. Nina had sideswiped a green Barina in the car park and driven off without leaving a note. For a few kilometres there, she had been tailed by a police car down the Eastern Freeway. The thought that the ding in the Barina might be the first fateful act in an escalating odyssey of mayhem and murder stretching across three states was oddly thrilling and Nina's sweating palms had slipped on the wheel. When she saw the cops peel off at the next exit—despite the pair of huge discount flesh-coloured control briefs Wanda was holding up for her inspection, blocking most of her view of the side mirror—Nina was both relieved and disappointed. It was hardly what you'd call a *Thelma and Louise* moment.

Recalling this episode as she listened to the domesticated waterfall filling the washing machine, she had a vision of herself and Wanda sailing into the void. And as the car somersaulted, end over end until it crashed and exploded in flames at the bottom of the chasm, it was trailed by a spectacular flight of black-and-gold sleeveless polyester-mix football jumpers and massive undies with super-absorbent gussets.

☼

With the first load of washing on, Nina made herself a cup of tea, slapped a chunk of Coon cheese on a Salada biscuit and thought about ringing Meredith. She considered this for a while, fearing that if Meredith knew Annie was having second thoughts she might bail out too. But then . . . if she made a pre-emptive strike?

This sort of strategic thinking was second nature to Nina. She had, after all, spent fifteen years pleading with, persuading, cajoling and threatening her husband and sons to comply with her directions. And if those tactics didn't work, there was always the trio of last resort—flattery, bribery and/or tears. In the end she risked making the call. There were too many details to finalise—including whether she would need a new outfit for the wedding. Finding anything in a size 18 that looked halfway decent on her would take some serious effort.

As it turned out, Nina's fears were well-founded. 'I know I said I'd come, Nina, but I'm flat-out here at the store. If I go away now there will be any number of my ladies utterly furious that I'm off for two weeks at the end of April, and I can't leave it to Caroline to run everything, she's not up to it. That comes to $350.80—shall I put it on credit?'

'Pardon?' said Nina.

'Would you sign here, please? That's lovely, thanks so much. I'll call you when that silverware comes in . . . Bye-bye now.'

'Hello? . . . Meredith, can you hear me?'

'My regulars will be considering themes for winter and eyeing off the pear and apple needlepoint cushions through the front window. And where will I be? Lost somewhere in the back of beyond! They'll kick their Shar-Pei puppies in sheer frustration all the way down High Street. And, truly, who could blame them?'

Nina glanced out her kitchen window to next-door's lemon tree, as if she needed reassurance that she was actually on the same planet as Meredith. 'Really?' she marvelled. 'There are women who actually change their cushions according to the seasons?'

'Oh, don't be daft, Nina, of course there are!'

Nina walked to her lounge room and surveyed the ten-dollar cushions she'd bought years ago from Home Depot. Dark brown corduroy, so they didn't show stains. There were only two seasons in Nina's home. Football and cricket.

'Meredith, you promised!' Nina tried not to sound too needy. She knew that wouldn't cut it with Meredith any more than it had with Annie.

'I don't remember promising anything!' Meredith was indignant. 'I did say it sounded like it could be fun, but—'

'And it will—it will be heaps of fun. Please come. I promise you'll have a great time! You'll kick yourself if you miss out!' This was Nina at her upbeat, pleasing best.

Meredith, however, was scarcely listening. 'That tablecloth is genuine Irish linen. Quite hard to find these days, but you really shouldn't settle for anything less if it's for a christening luncheon . . . Those sheets? Egyptian cotton. Feel them. Superb quality.'

Nina thought of the boys' favourite flannelette sheets covered in a million tiny pills. She spoke up over the clatter of a herd of high heels on the polished floorboards of Meredith's store. 'Annie's coming over on Saturday to check out the van. She's really looking forward to the trip. She's so excited.' Another white lie. All in the good cause of Nina's sanity. 'She really needs a break. And so do you. Why don't you come over as well?'

'Look, I have to go. There's a veritable traffic jam here in napery. Alright, I'll come over on Saturday around lunchtime. But I'm not promising—'

'I know. You're not promising anything.'

'Exactly.'

'Great! See you then.'

Nina immediately put plans into action for her Saturday summit. She was confident she could persuade both Annie and Meredith to come. She was good at this sort of thing. She should have been a member of some kind of delegation to draw up a road map thingy for peace in Iraq.

✹

It was almost midnight when Nina wrestled another container of bolognaise sauce into her freezer. It was a refrigerated shipping container of motherly concern. She wiped wet hands on her T-shirt, dragged damp blonde hair into an elastic and surveyed her handiwork. There were six days worth of meals in there now, all labelled and colour-coded. Blue for weekday dinners, yellow for weekends and green for lunches. Pasta sauces, casseroles, stews, meatloaf—all microwaveable.

She planned to write a list of what could be cooked to accompany what—mashed potatoes, rice, vegetables—and stick it on the fridge door under a 'Batman at Movie World' magnet. She knew the boys wouldn't bother to read it. They would scoop the food straight from the freezer/microwave/dishwasher-safe containers onto toasted Tip Top muffins or white no-fibre bread.

Nina tried to imagine how her sons would cope while she was gone and could only see unwashed hair, unfinished homework and unmade beds. She hoped to somehow get them through it snack by snack, meal by meal. Perhaps every time they peeled back a blue, yellow or green plastic lid, they would remember her. Nina had also stocked up on assorted biscuits, snack bars, chips, powdered sports drinks and instant pot noodles. There were enough instant pot noodles in her pantry to circle the earth, Nina estimated. Enough pot noodles to tie her up from top to toe—around and around, until they suffocated the life out of her.

All that afternoon, as she cooked, cooled and measured the food into containers, Nina had been wondering how she had managed to navigate her boys to a place where the kitchen was a crashed, alien spacecraft, where every domestic dial, switch and appliance was a technology apparently developed by a race of superior beings from a galaxy far, far away.

As she caught herself humming the theme tune to *Star Wars* she reflected that even her innermost thoughts had been colonised by her boys. She was the one who was from an alien race.

Stranded on a planet she didn't recognise, with beings who spoke a foreign language. For fifteen years now she had been trying to understand what was in their hearts. If she had come even close when they were young, now that they were teenagers, it was as if they were spinning out of her orbit. Out past East Malvern to the dark side of the moon.

When Jordan was born, and then the twins, Anton and Marko, Nina remembered being amazed at how they had instinctively imitated every cement mixer and fire truck. 'Brrrmm, brrrmm . . . Woo-hoo.' The next years were accompanied by the 'ch, ch, ch' of Thomas the Tank Engine and the 'thwack, swish . . . aaargh!' as an orc's head was cleaved from its body by Aragorn. It was as if they had been implanted with a silicone sound-effects chip.

In those far-off days when the boys were toddlers, Nina often found herself, at a mothers' group, drawn by the gravitational pull of pink fluff to watch the little girls play. They chattered and cooed like a flock of rosy pigeons, plump fingers carefully placing tiny tiaras on dollies, easing flimsy pantyhose over slender plastic legs and negotiating minuscule buttons. Here was a language she did understand. She wished and wished again that she had been given a daughter.

Watching their bent heads, Nina had felt an almost over-whelming urge to take up a hairbrush and draw it through long hair loosed from ribbons and plaits. Hair the pure, burnished colour of childhood—Snow White, Rose Red and Ebony Black. Hair from a fairytale. Of course, she had never dared to be so intimate with another woman's child.

A screech of pain and a call of 'Nina, it's one of yours!' would jolt her from her Rapunzel fantasy and propel her to the sandpit. She lived in dread that one of her sons would maim a playmate for life. 'Thwack, swish, aaargh!'

When she was gathering her sons to leave and the last misappropriated vehicle or plastic block had been prised from angry fists, the secret longing would insist upon making itself known and Nina would find herself saying aloud: 'I wish I'd had a girl.' She knew that as mothers smoothed and folded tiny pink jumpers against their bosoms, they were congratulating themselves on their own good fortune. Even as they chanted: 'Count yourself lucky. Girls can be such bitches. Wait till they're teenagers, you'll be grateful then. Boys look after their mothers. Girls leave.'

They were hand-me-down mantras from mothers and grandmothers who, generations earlier, had perhaps recognised the particular, exquisite anguish of a woman starved of feminine comfort. But Nina was cursed to live in the New Age, where everything happened for a reason. Every woman created her own destiny. If Nina had given birth only to boys, it was because she had somehow willed it.

Nina slammed the freezer door. She was driving the van to Byron, and that was that. Even if she had to take her sister-in-law Monique instead. Although the thought of Monique packing her crystals, herbal teas, aromatherapy candles and chanting Hindustani goatherder CDs into her straw basket made her shudder. No. There was nothing for it but to get Annie and Meredith to come with her.

She snapped off the kitchen light and then . . . bugger! Nina had lived in this house for ten years and still forgot that if she turned off the light in the kitchen and the boys had gone to bed, she would have to grope her way through the darkened lounge room to the switch at the bottom of the stairs. She felt her way along the edge of the couch with damp fingers and, through the gloom, could just make out the banister.

Twang!

'Ow, ow, ow! Shit, shit, shit!' Nina yowled in pain. She'd stubbed her toe on an electric guitar left lying on the carpet. It hurt like hell. She slumped on the stairs and rubbed her foot. The impact had also jarred her bunion, which was now wailing like a back-up singer to her throbbing big toe.

Marko appeared on the landing, rubbing sleep from his eyes. Nina glanced up and thought he looked like an angel standing on the stairway to heaven. She noted he wasn't wearing his loose cotton pyjama pants. He'd have that rash around his crotch again. Are there mothers in heaven? she wondered. Will they need me then?

Marko picked his sweaty jocks from his bum and grizzled, 'Mum, can you get me a drink of water? I'm thirsty.'

Four

There was simply no way to appreciate the sheer majesty of the RoadMaster Royale without taking a good few steps back. Two, three, four paces . . . right to the nature strip, from where the truly epic proportions of the vehicle were finally revealed. The gleaming white behemoth looked to be firmly wedged in the carport.

'Good lord, Nina, this thing is massive! Are you sure you can even get it out of the driveway?' Meredith retreated further, scraping the heel of her white leather sandal on the bluestone guttering and stumbling onto the street.

'Of course I can get it out,' Nina declared. 'I got it in there in the first place, didn't I?'

This one was a flat-out lie. In fact it wasn't Nina who had backed the RoadMaster down the narrow drive, but her husband Brad. It had taken a good half-hour, many obscene oaths and the life of a prized pink hydrangea.

'The whole idea is ridiculous,' snorted Meredith. 'We should just fly both ways. We'd be there in a couple of hours. We could be sitting down having a cocktail, looking out over the ocean, the same afternoon.'

Nina nodded and marched down the concrete drive, pausing to pat the snub nose of the hulking beast with affection, as if she was approaching a prized milking heifer in a stall, saying: 'There, there, old girl, easy now, easy.' She was fumbling with the key-ring, trying to recall which one of a dozen keys opened the front door, when she heard Meredith's voice from behind. 'Oh-my-good—!'

Nina turned to see her rooted to the spot in front of the truly arresting sight of a giant decal of Elvis Presley rampant— pelvis thrusting, microphone held high. *The King* was plastered from roof to wheel.

'Why?' asked Meredith. She was apparently seeking a logical explanation.

'Elvis. King of the Road. Get it?' said Nina. 'It was something Brad's father had done,' she added lamely. 'I like it. I think it gives the van a bit of personality.'

'If you've got the personality of a rednecked hick!'

'He's always loved Elvis,' Nina said staunchly. 'And it's a good safety thing too. See all the lettering and the jewels on the jumpsuit? They're light-reflective, so you can see the van better at night. You know how the big trucks have lights right down the side so that . . .' Nina hesitated as she saw Annie stalk up the drive, her high heels tapping on the concrete. She stopped and slowly, theatrically, slid her huge sunnies up on top of her head.

'Jesus! You could see this fucking thing from the moon, Nina! You could look out the window of the space shuttle and there it would be, parked right next to the Great Wall of China! You never told us how big it was. You CANNOT be serious!' She lowered her black Gucci frames and folded her arms firmly across her crisp white shirt. Meredith raised her eyebrows at Nina. It sounded like Annie hadn't promised to come after all.

'But, we all agreed . . .' Nina protested.

'It was late, I'd had too much to drink . . . so had you!' Annie accused. 'We can't go in this thing! We'll look like travelling carnie folk. The Beverly Hillbillies. The only thing missing is the Confederate flag.'

'Actually . . .' Nina coughed and walked to the back of the van. Meredith and Annie followed, paused and stared in silence. There it was, in all its red-and-blue starry holographic glory— the rebel flag of the Southern States, unfurled from tail-light to shining tail-light.

The awful moment was interrupted by the bleating of Annie's BlackBerry. She fished it from the pocket of her black trousers, cupped her hand over the device, and spoke in an urgent whisper.

Nina jiggled the key in the lock on the van door and finally wrestled it open. Honestly, she fumed as she stamped up the stairs, who gave a stuff what the mobile home looked like from the outside? The dodgy artwork would be long forgotten when they were all on the road, sitting up front, singing some of the old songs and taking in the vast, arid beauty of the Australian landscape. They would be two thousand kilometres from home and care and responsibility. Nina really wanted to take this trip. More than anything she'd wanted for a long time. She'd been fantasising about it for days—awake, asleep, it didn't matter.

As she spoke into her 'smartphone', Annie sought Meredith's eyes and telegraphed an irritated shrug. How had they let themselves be talked into the madness of coming here to view the monster vehicle? Meredith shook her head. She had no idea either.

Annie terminated her call, in time to hear Nina plead: 'Come inside and have a look, you'll *adore* it.'

Meredith took Annie by the elbow and steered her towards the open door. She had the distinct feeling that if they left now Nina might just stick her head in the . . . Did the thing actually have an oven? She pushed Annie up the metal stairway ahead of her.

Just as Nina had hoped, Annie expressed her surprise when she stepped inside the RoadMaster. It was like a cosy playhouse— everything just slightly smaller and dinkier than in real life. Annie opened cupboards and drawers, pulled curtains, slid screens and expressed a girlish pleasure at the way everything had been configured to pack away so neatly.

'I can't believe this!' she exclaimed. 'There's a toilet, a bath . . . even a place to plug in my hair dryer. Come and have a look, Meredith.' Annie backed out of the narrow bathroom doorway.

Meredith squeezed past and poked her head inside for the briefest of inspections.

'Well, I'd hardly call it a bath. I'd be extremely lucky to fit my backside in there.'

'It's not supposed to be a *proper* bath,' Nina called from behind them with some exasperation. 'Let me in and I'll show you everything.' The three women paused as they considered how they would negotiate this tricky manoeuvre. Annie shuffled forward, Meredith flattened herself against the cupboard and Nina eased her way into the small space and began her spiel. 'It's got shelves behind this mirror, and plenty of space under the sink for all our stuff. Towel racks. A shower. You can even use the toilet when you're driving along. I mean, it's not strictly legal, but it does mean we're not going to have to stop at some spider-infested dunny by the roadside.'

'But there's no window,' observed Annie, examining the smooth expanse of white extruded plastic in the prefab unit. 'It must get really . . . humid in here.' It was exactly the detail a real estate agent would spot.

'You just open this vent.' Nina stood on tiptoe and wound open the cunningly concealed hatch at the rear of the shower cubicle.

'Yeah, that'll work,' Annie conceded. In fact privately she also had to admit that the bathroom was considerably larger and better appointed than some of the ensuites she'd recently encountered in brand-new home units.

'What else could we possibly want?' Nina added with more than a hint of desperation. 'There's a microwave, oven, fridge, freezer, DVD. You just wind up this aerial . . .' Nina again reached for a knob on the ceiling, turned it and then fiddled with the remote. The TV blared. She lunged for the off-switch.

Annie refolded her arms. 'Like I said the other day, it's about *time*. Two weeks away? Meredith will have to leave the shop, I'll have to take holidays. It's crazy! I've got so much on. We should just fly.'

Nina leaned one hip against a cupboard and clasped her hands in front of her. She wanted to snatch up the tartan tea towel on the counter and flick them both to their senses. 'I understand all that,' she said in her most patient tone, 'but getting there is half the fun.'

'Yeah, we could play "Spotto" and sing "Ten Green Bottles",' drawled Annie.

Her sarcasm didn't faze Nina. She was used to these exchanges with her teenage son Jordan. She simply drove around the conversational speed hump. 'Think of what we'd miss out on if we just flew.'

'Mosquitoes, sandflies, spiders, snakes, ants . . .' Annie counted off the bio-hazards of the Australian bush on her fingers.

'That's just silly,' Nina finally snapped. 'You're from the country, you can handle all that. Besides, we'll be travelling in five-star comfort all the way.'

'I'd hardly call this five-star,' Meredith sniffed and plonked herself on a synthetic doona cover festooned with bright orange and yellow hibiscus flowers. 'The décor in here is just . . . appalling.'

Nina saw an opening and jumped at her chance. 'Look, all this can go,' she said, indicating the nasty matching citrus-hued cushions and floral bedsheets. 'You can bring some of your gorgeous stuff in from the shop. Your linens, tableware, crockery. Have it any way you want—give the whole van a makeover.' Nina saw Meredith's eyes brighten at the magic word 'makeover'.

Now, Nina calculated, was the time for the centrepiece of her argument . . . except that the smartphone stowed in Annie's squashy leather handbag squalled again. Annie dumped the bag on the table and rummaged for the thing.

'Annie Bailey speaking,' she smoothly announced, stepping into the bathroom cubicle and closing the door after her.

This time it was Nina who quizzed Meredith with a 'look'. Being with Annie and her dumb phone was like watching a mother let her toddler with Attention Deficit Disorder ruin story time at a playgroup. Meredith nodded in mute agreement.

Nina reached into a cupboard and produced a tablecloth—an Irish linen one she'd bought specially for the occasion—and spread it over the wood-veneer plywood table. She opened the fridge door with a theatrical flourish and presented a sumptuous antipasto platter—zucchini and mozzarella rolls, baked mushrooms with parmesan, potato fritters, roasted peppers with olives, capers and garlic, grilled clams and bacon on the half-shell. A bowl of her famous home-made parmesan cheese and chive biscuits followed.

Annie, her call concluded, stepped outside the cubicle and joined Meredith to lean over the table and coo with pleasure at the feast glistening with virgin olive oil. Nina was a fabulous cook—they'd forgotten that. The freezer gave up a bottle of good chilled Margaret River sauvignon blanc.

With Annie and Meredith both sitting at the table and swooning over the food and wine, Nina continued: 'Just think, you'd have me cooking for you all the way! You could both do with some fattening up.'

Meredith and Annie sensibly ignored this comment. That was Nina's mother, Wanda, talking. But it was true—the food *was* spectacular.

Now that they both had their mouths stuffed full, Nina made one final, heroic effort. 'The thing is,' she said softly, 'I've been thinking about those times on the road with Sanctified Soul and, well . . . they were the best times! After all that, I met Brad, and had kids. It feels like I've been a wife and mother for almost half my life.' Her bottom lip trembled ominously. 'You don't know what it's like living with three teenage boys. It's never quiet. I can't hear myself think, and I'm not sure I'm actually thinking anything anymore. I need to get away, I really do.' She sniffed back tears of last resort. Meredith and Annie set down their knives and forks. Maybe Nina was closer to the edge than they'd realised.

'And I remember you, Meredith,' Nina snuffled, 'leaving Sigrid and Jarvis at home because you knew, even back then, it was important for women to spend some time on themselves.'

'"Self-actualise", they called it in those days,' Meredith interrupted. 'But I think really it was just about getting away from smelly nappies.'

Annie took up her wineglass. 'But you could go away with Brad, or by yourself. What do you hope this whole . . . exercise . . . will *achieve*?'

'I want to be with women friends.' Nina was genuinely passionate on this point. 'People who speak the same language as me. We've known each other all these years, but never spent real time together . . . not . . . you know . . .' Nina gripped the edge of the table, trying to avoid sounding like a cut-rate Oprah.

'If you say *quality* time, I'll hit you.' Annie was only half joking.

'Maybe we'll never have the chance again. Maybe in another ten years' time, when we're almost sixty . . .'

'Hey, I'll only be forty-nine then!' Annie protested.

'Yes, yes, Annie, we all know you're the "baby" of the group.' Meredith was doing her own sums and realised that in ten years' time she *would* be almost sixty. How had that happened?

'Anyway,' Nina continued, 'let's go while we can. We've got the occasion—Siggie's wedding—and we've got the van. Brad's father says he'll pick it up in Byron. He wants to keep going north to Fraser Island, so we can fly back.'

Nina took up her glass, her fingers gripping the stem tightly. If they didn't agree to come right now, she'd have to throw in her tartan tea towel. She had nothing more to offer.

Annie kept her head down, silently tearing at a crust of bread. Meredith sighed loudly. Nina took a nervous sip of wine and watched them both intently. Silence and sighs. That had to be a sign that she was making some headway, surely.

Meredith was almost beaten. She set down her glass and raised one last feeble flag of protest. 'What about that thing?' She pointed accusingly at the wall. It was a gold-framed photograph of Gracelands, Memphis, Tennessee.

'It's gone!' declared Nina. She scrambled over Meredith to pull down the offending item and shoved it in the locker under the bed.

'I can't believe I'm saying this, but . . .' Meredith dropped her head into her hands and pressed her palms into her eyes, 'OK. I'll come. Let's start packing.' Nina whooped and jumped in triumph.

'But when it all goes pear-shaped,' Meredith added, 'remember . . . *I told you so.*'

'Thank you, thank you, thank you!' Nina clapped her hands. 'This will be such fun, you'll see. We should have a toast.' She raised her glass. 'To Byron or . . .'

Annie's leather handbag vibrated with shrill alarm. 'I can't. I'm sorry.' Annie's hand plunged into the depths of her bag. 'It's just . . . impossible.'

Nina lowered her arm. '. . . bust,' she sadly concluded the salutation.

The screen door on the van was wrenched open, banging hard on aluminium. Nina winced at the tinny clang and turned to see her son Anton in the doorway. He was shivering, despite the towel draped around his shoulders. Water was dripping on the black rubber doormat from every angle of his skinny frame.

'Geez, Mum, what are you doing?' he whined. 'You've been in here for ages. I'm hungry.'

Five

Meredith regarded the pile of items she had gathered on the front counter next to the cash register and, once again, saw that her instinctive good taste had not failed her. There were three queen-size doona covers in plain white with a taupe grosgrain ribbon trim; two single covers, contrasting, in the same taupe with white trim; and six oversized continental pillows with cotton covers in a subtle *fallow*.

Meredith liked the name *fallow*. It was a colour a few shades darker than *ecru*—and *ecru* (from the French meaning 'raw' or 'unbleached') had been done to death. It was also lighter than *bole* (rhyming with 'mole'), the shade Meredith had once championed in her interior decorating business.

She had been pleased to inform her clients that *bole* was one of the oldest colour names in the English language, dating from 1386. When children were presented with various shades of brown and were asked to paint the trunk of a tree, the shade they invariably chose was *bole*. Meredith liked knowing these sorts of details. Even if, secretly, she thought *bole* was the ugliest colour on earth.

All her life Meredith had been creative and artistic, and she could often divine what a person's true emotions were through colour. For example, clients would come to her and say they wanted their room decorated in their favourite colour *pistachio*, but Meredith would just know that they needed to let go of the past and embrace something more nourishing, like *moussaka*.

Despite what some people thought, however, she wasn't fixed in her opinions. She could always be swayed by intelligent and rational argument. Actually, for some years Meredith's favourite grey had been *slate*. She had abandoned the shade late last year for *granite*—a shade of flinty determination—and felt the better for it.

Fallow was the hue she was entranced with now. She fingered the soft cotton of a pillowcase and rubbed it against her cheek. There was an honesty here—she could feel that. A rustic energy which demanded a genuine response. Meredith needed to know exactly what she was dealing with. She turned to her computer screen and consulted the dictionary.

'Fal-low *adj: 1. left unseeded for a period of time after ploughing in order to recover natural fertility; 2. currently inactive but with the possibility of activity or use in the future.'*

Meredith was jolted by the description—it was exactly how she felt about her life. Not that Meredith could ever contemplate the idea of being inactive. But, looking past that negative connotation, she had to agree that, when her latest home renovations had finished, a cycle of intense and rewarding productivity had come to an end. And now, with Donald gone, she had to imagine how the rest of her life might unfold.

Many women would have felt depressed about all this, but not Meredith. A friend had once described her as 'indefatigable'—as if she would keep on going when others might fold or fail—so she was looking forward to her regeneration. She would pop up through the soil reborn, in a youthful shade of *pod* or *tendril*.

Next came the crockery and cutlery, all chosen from a new range of summer holiday wares she had imported from Finland. None of it was plastic, which Meredith could not bear to see set on any table, no matter how casual. 'Honestly, Paul Bocuse himself could serve *la Mère Fillioux*—Bresse chicken in a bladder—but if it was on a plastic plate, it might as well be a Big Mac,' Meredith had said more than once.

The china she had picked out was white and chunky, embossed with leaves and berries. These same motifs of plentiful summer bounty were repeated on the cutlery handles and, in a triumph of coordination (which Meredith knew only she would truly appreciate, but then she was used to that), she had discovered a Danish glassware setting for four etched with stalks of wheat.

Meredith turned down the dimmer switch on the store lighting. What could she take with her that might be suitable for her daughter Sigrid's wedding present? She reflected that this, at least, was one benefit of travelling by road. She could bubble-wrap the most delicate, elaborate lamp-base, vase or glassware and feel confident it would arrive in one piece. But would Sigrid appreciate such a gift?

The last time Meredith had been in Sigrid's living space, two years ago, it had been on the top floor of a 1950s block of red-brick flats in Balaclava. Among the jumble of tatty second-hand items—which Sigrid proudly declared she had retrieved from a council skip—there had been some reasons for hope. A lovely vintage embroidered gypsy shawl draped on a corner table; a genuine bamboo bar—from the sixties, by the look of it—set with attractive ruby glass tumblers (although Meredith had counted five glasses and thought one should be disposed of so the set made an even four); and, in the bathroom, a stack of white waffle-weave hand towels. Meredith had paused to arrange them in a pleasing fanned display just next to the duck-egg-blue handbasin. Putting the best complexion on it, Meredith hoped that in the time since she had last seen Sigrid, her daughter had discovered her nascent sense of style and become a Woman of Good Taste. After all, it was in the genes.

Eighteen months? Could it be that long since she had seen her daughter? When Sigrid had announced she was leaving Melbourne to travel north, there had been a fight. Meredith's offer of a junior managerial position in her store, with the possibility of a full partnership in Flair after a couple of years, hadn't appealed to Sigrid. That had been a blow. The time since Meredith had last seen Sigrid had flown by. Mother and recalcitrant daughter exchanged the odd phone call, and Sigrid emailed excuses at Christmas. But even though she was pleased to hear from her only daughter, Meredith just could not stop herself from asking: had Sigrid found a decent job yet? Did she want to come home? Maybe go to university and study? For

God's sake, what was she planning to *do*? And now here they were with this 'Charlie' person wedged between them.

Meredith didn't know if he was a banker or a butcher, a surfie or a used car salesman. The first time she'd heard of him was when the wedding invitation had arrived for a sunset beach ceremony on a *Tuesday*. She's pregnant, was Meredith's first thought. She had immediately rung and felt guilty relief when Sigrid had told her that, no, she wasn't to be a grandmother just yet. But Sigrid had fobbed off her attempts at further interrogation with an airy: 'Just come. You'll see.' Meredith had slammed the phone down and for the last three weeks had been plagued with curiosity and dread in equal measure. Should she go? Should she boycott the whole affair until Sigrid came to her senses? The thought that she had no-one she trusted to discuss this with, now that Donald had moved out, was also vaguely troubling.

Meredith found her reading glasses and peered at the invitation again. Printed on cheap paper and decorated with the ubiquitous yellow frangipani motifs, it didn't hold much promise. Meredith had always imagined her only daughter would walk down the aisle at St Johns, Toorak, at 6 pm on a Friday, in an elegant slip of satin and lace. The invitation would be printed on a thick, gold-embossed card tucked in an envelope sealed with red wax and silk ribbons.

But that was all fantasy. The reality was that once Sigrid had married this 'Charlie' in Byron Bay, there would be no way back. And now she would be the one to shift the mountainous motorhome to visit Mohammed. How could it be almost a quarter of a century ago that she had first held her baby girl in her arms? And Jarvis, away in London this past year—how long since she'd sat him on her knee? Meredith bent her head and sniffed the cover of a continental pillow as if she could somehow conjure the milky custard aroma of a baby's head. Ironing aid—that's all she could smell.

As Meredith activated the alarms and locked Flair's front doors, she also thought of her husband, Donald. Every time she imagined him, his image came to her in a flat brown frame. Not *bole* or *fallow*, just a sort of plain brown. It was frustrating that she could not name the exact shade. *Russet? Bistre? Sepia? Umber?*

Try as she might, she had never quite been able to identify the colour that framed him, but as she looked into the dark street outside the store window tonight it came to her at last. It was as bland as *moth* and as impenetrable as *mud*.

Annie made another call to Nina in the middle of the week. Nina knew it was a Wednesday because Anton and Marko had footy training and she had parked the Odyssey across from the oval to wait for them. She was supposed to be taking the dog for a walk, but instead Metro, the family mutt, was nosing his way through the bushes while Nina was plopped on a bench finishing her Marian Keyes novel and polishing off a packet of salted beer nuts. She checked the carbohydrate content on the back of the packet—3.5 per 100 grams. That was good. She was doing the high-protein, low-carb diet this week in preparation for getting into a bathing suit.

A couple of the school mums reckoned they'd lost three kilograms in five days! Nina had lost a kilo since Sunday. She was constipated and had bad breath, but it was a small price to pay. Only thing was, she was exhausted. She hadn't slept well last night. In her dreams she was driving a baker's van full of loaves and muffins. At 3 am she found herself standing in front of the bread bin in the kitchen, thinking of having just one half of a small dinner roll. She had put it back and walked purposefully upstairs. For the rest of the night—with Brad's long legs intruding into her half of the bed—she dreamed she was tangled in spaghetti carbonara.

'I've decided that I'll come.' It was a female voice.

'Really?' Nina held out her mobile phone and stared at it. As if she had picked up Jordy's phone by mistake and his girlfriend Olivia was telling him she was coming over for an afternoon assignation in his bedroom.

'Is that you, Annie? Are you saying you'll come to Byron?'

'Yep.'

'Really, truly?'

'That's what I said,' Annie replied evenly. It was disconcerting the way Nina swung between being a nagging mum and a wheedling little girl.

'But what about work? You always seem so—'

'Look, do you want me to come or not?'

'Yes, yes I do. That's brilliant, really brilliant!' Nina jumped to her feet and beer nuts spilled onto the gravel path. 'Oh, Annie, that's great, it really is.'

'But I'm telling you, *if it all goes wrong . . .*'

'I know. It will be all my fault.' As if, for the past fifteen years Nina had spent as a wife and mother, it had ever been anyone else's.

☼

Annie wasn't exactly sure why she'd agreed to go to Byron in the ugly bus. Maybe it was as simple as *why not*? She stepped into her compact, shiny kitchen, slid an icy bottle of vodka from the freezer of her side-by-side giant refrigerator/freezer and looked for a clean glass. The shelves were bare. In the sink, slimy cold worms of noodles curled around plastic forks floating on the dull surface of the water. Somewhere under there were glasses.

She swigged from the bottle, lit a cigarette and picked her way through piles of clothes on the floor, back to the bedroom and her empty suitcase. She glanced at her BlackBerry lying dormant on the bed. The demanding little device was dead to the world. And with it switched off, Annie reflected, so was she. If she were to expire right this minute, how long would it be until anyone in her block of flats noticed she was missing? The only clue to her demise would be a letterbox stuffed with Freedom Furniture and Liquorland catalogues. Without the phone's insistent, pitiful cry, there was nothing in particular holding her here.

Annie thought of Meredith's offer of a discount on the price of her designer homewares. Where was home? A pair of standard lamps stood, still swathed in bubble-wrap, on her lounge room floor and she could scarcely recall what colour they were. Brown probably. To match the ultra suede three-seater couch that no-one had sat on in six months. To complement the glass-topped dining table at which no-one had ever eaten a meal.

Perhaps the tipping point had come with the invitation to the five-day conference at Jupiter's Casino on the Gold Coast. The thought of spending almost a week in the company of a couple of hundred other real estate agents from around the country had made Annie's eyes glaze over. She knew exactly how it would go.

There would be the interminable presentations on how to succeed (Be yourself. Stand out from the crowd. Do something memorable for your customers!), how to understand Gen Y (They all want to be individuals. You must be an individual too!), and how to sell to international buyers (They're all looking for a haven from the storm of global realities! Be a Safe Harbour!). There would be the forced jollity of cocktail evenings, fancy dress nights, sports afternoons and formal dinners. There would be an evening when she'd get legless. She would wake next morning to find a double-knit polo shirt and a pair of cargo pants crumpled on the floor of her hotel room and the anonymous, lumpy form of a delegate from Bundaberg snoring in the bed next to her.

It should have been a simple enough task to pack her bag for Byron—a fortnight of shorts, singlets and T-shirts, a good outfit for the wedding. How hard could it be? But Annie was finding it harder and harder to do even the simplest things. Bills were piled, unopened, on the coffee table. Her car was overdue for a service. There was nothing edible in the fridge. The kitchen cupboards were empty. She badly needed her roots done. She hadn't called home in a fortnight.

Annie couldn't help feeling that she was the victim of something as banal as 'bad timing'. Sometimes she recorded episodes of *Desperate Housewives*, only to find that, on playback, she was coming in somewhere after the last commercial break. Sometimes she met a man she liked, only to find that he had broken up with his wife just three months before. Sometimes she woke up with bright enthusiasm about her future, only to find that she was thirty-nine and almost halfway through her life. Her timing was way off and it seemed the problem was cumulative. The older she got, the more it seemed that she was out of step and treading on her own toes.

She kicked over the pile of laundry on the floor in the vain hope there might be a clean pair of black trousers under there which had escaped her notice. No dice. Turning one pair of expensive Italian wool jersey pants right-side-out, she was appalled to see the pink of her palm through a neat round hole. A cigarette burn, right there on the front near the knee. She vaguely remembered jumping up from her bar stool and brushing away a smouldering fag end . . . When had that happened? Thursday, Friday, Saturday night? She cursed and threw the pants into a pile with the other clothes that needed mending. A broken zip here, a missing button there, a hem down. She'd get around to the pile one day. She would go to a haberdashery and buy a sewing kit.

Stowed under her old single bed back at the homestead on the family farm was a cardboard box—covered with floral wrapping paper, lined with tissue and scattered with mothballs—containing all the items Annie had sewn when she was a girl. Dolls' clothes, cushions, doilies, table napkins—even little blouses and jackets for herself. Her mother was keeping them in the hope that one day she would have a granddaughter to give them to. But that would probably never happen now. The box might as well be thrown on a bonfire.

Spying a corner of the conference invitation sticking out from the pile of documents on her coffee table, Annie retrieved the glossy card. She slowly and methodically ripped it into tiny pieces and threw the lot into the air. The multicoloured fragments of the next two weeks of her life floated to the floor.

Cradling her bottle of vodka, Annie crawled into a crumpled nest of bedsheets and blankets. She felt something cold and hard pressing against her left thigh; reaching down, her fingers curled around a remote control. All the smart apartments had them now—very modern, convenient and affordable—so that, from the comfort of your bed, you could set the recessed ceiling and wall lights and table lamps in an infinite number of configurations to match your mood.

In an instant the bedroom was pitch black.

Six

'Did you ever hear that story about a man in America who was driving his brand-new Winnebago on the freeway? He put it on cruise control, got out of the driver's seat and walked through to the back to make a cup of coffee . . .' Annie was telling this tale with her foot on the top stair of the RoadMaster Royale as she carted a half-dozen bottles of Rutherglen merlot through the narrow door.

'Anyway, while he was making the coffee, the van ran off the road and crashed. And then he sued the company because the handbook didn't tell him he had to stay behind the steering wheel!'

'Bloody hell! Is that true?' Nina was kneeling in front of a cupboard with a bottle of aged balsamic vinegar in one hand, and red wine and tarragon vinegar in the other.

'No, no, no! I've heard that story before. It's an urban myth.' Meredith, down the back, was huffing with the effort of stripping off synthetic bed coverings and replacing them with her designer linen.

'Is it? Well anyway, it's a good metaphor for my life.' Annie heaved her provisions onto the table and paused to capture her curls in a hair clip. 'I'm in the back having a drink, and my life is driving itself straight into a concrete crash barrier.' Nina and Meredith's attention snagged on the sharp edge in her voice.

'You can't mean that?' Meredith paused, up to her elbow in a pillowcase.

Nina snapped the cupboard shut. 'I can't imagine you not ever living an authentic life.'

An 'authentic' life? What the fuck did that mean? Annie wondered. Nina was a walking, talking self-help book. Annie wouldn't last the distance with the Oprah of East Malvern spouting these ridiculous platitudes. She briefly and fondly entertained a highlight of last year's real estate conference at Melbourne's Crown Casino when she'd won $500 on the blackjack table. Maybe she'd been too hasty in writing off the entire event. She retreated down the stairs.

'Hey, only joking! Now . . . champagne for all my friends!' she called over her shoulder.

It was 2 pm on Saturday—two hours after the scheduled departure of the RoadMaster from Nina's triple-fronted cream brick home—and the stocking of the vehicle was in full swing.

'Here—take this crockery, and be careful. It's from Finland.' Meredith passed a cardboard box to Nina.

'And then take this—it's from France,' Annie piped up from behind. The van rocked as she dumped another half-dozen bottles on the table.

'Actually,' Meredith began, 'all champagne is from—'

'I know, I know—from the Champagne region, or else it's "sparkling wine". Let's not start arguing now, Meredith. We've got ten glorious days to do that. Let's just get this lot on board.'

'There're bottle shops along the way,' Nina mentioned helpfully as she tried to think where she could possibly store all of Annie's alcoholic supplies. The procession of boxes, suitcases and shopping bags seemed endless. As each one was unpacked, its contents were the subject of a running commentary.

'Dim sum dipping sauce? Satay skewers? Cinnamon sticks? Are you *sure* you're going to use all this stuff?'

'*Seven* pairs of shoes? And you're not really bringing this illuminated make-up mirror, are you?'

'*Cotton* table napkins? What's wrong with a roll of paper towel?'

There was a final swipe from Meredith. Annie had swung by Toorak Road on the way to Nina's and bought herself a couple of new outfits for the trip; now she was stuffing glossy shopping bags sprouting tissue paper under the bed in the rear of the cabin. Meredith watched her, shaking her head in amazement.

'There *are* boutiques in Byron Bay. I'm sure even you'll find a couple of wearable items in the provinces.'

'Yeah? Well, that's what they say about Noosa—and you get there and it's just a load of last year's tat that's been hauled up in the boot of someone's Beemer.'

'Oh, my God! Imagine being spotted in last season's sarong!' Meredith threw up her hands.

'Oh, my God! Imagine having to actually eat off a plastic plate!' Annie countered.

Meredith ignored the comment and retreated to her Audi to fetch one last item. She returned carrying a large box exquisitely wrapped in silver and white embossed paper.

'Now, where will I put this?'

'Oooh, Sigrid's wedding present!' Nina fingered the gorgeous silky ribbons. 'What did you decide on?'

'It cannot—and I repeat, *cannot*—be damaged in any way. There's a thousand dollars worth of Fabergé crystal stemware in here.'

'Lucky Sigrid and . . . what's his name again?' Annie was blithely unaware of the depth of the sorrowful swamp she was wading into.

'Charles Newson. Although it's written as "Charlie" on the invitation.'

'But didn't you say the other night that you've never met him? He might be some scruffy seaweed-head who's never seen crystal in his life. Maybe you should have waited and bought something that suits their house.'

Meredith stiffened. She didn't like this casual intrusion into her private life. She'd revealed far too much over dinner last week and was now regretting it. If she hadn't opened her big mouth, they wouldn't be making this trip in the first place. And she'd *cried*! That was unlike her. It must have been the dessert wine.

She regarded Annie as if she were an errant snail in her *whitlof and pear salade belge*. 'I don't care if he drinks that vile wheatgrass juice or Bollinger—everything tastes better out of Fabergé crystal. And, in the end, it doesn't really matter what their taste is. It's about *good* taste. I'm not going to give them some revolting earthenware mugs, am I? Now where's the safest place to put this?'

Nina led the way down the stairs to the side of the van. The gift box was stowed in a corner of the storage bin with the camp chairs and picnic table. As she turned the lock Nina thought, with weary satisfaction, that at least this was the last of it. There was so much stuff in the van that if they were ever to meet with a natural disaster—stranded by floodwater, say, or lost in the desert—they would be able to survive for months . . . years. Start a new civilisation. Probably even manufacture a range of durable household items. There was not one thing she could think of that they might require that wasn't on board. Saffron strands? Check. Deck of cards? Check. Caramel-scented candle? Check. They were ready for take-off.

Stepping back inside the van, Nina and Meredith were alarmed to see Annie tearing the golden foil from the top of a bottle of champagne. 'This one's cold. I thought we could have a celebratory drink before we head off.'

Nina and Meredith both glanced at the van's wall clock. It read fifteen minutes past three.

'No thanks, I have to drive,' said Nina.

'And I have to navigate,' said Meredith.

'Well, I have to sit here in the back, and I'm not doing it stone cold sober.' Annie popped the cork. It thwacked into the front windscreen. She upended the bottle into an earthenware coffee mug which she'd found at the back of a cupboard and chosen precisely because she knew it would annoy the hell out of Meredith. 'Cheers!' She raised her mug. 'Here's to life on the open road!'

Nina saw Meredith's fists slide up to her skinny linen-swathed hips. 'Yes, yes! Let's get going!' she blurted. 'I'll just say goodbye to the boys and then we're off.'

As she walked through her front door, Nina heard the familiar drone of a televised football game coming from the lounge room. She could scarcely recall a time when her life wasn't punctuated by the exclamations of hyperactive footy commentators: 'Oooh! It's a goal! Millimetre perfect! Richmond ten points in front, going into the third quarter!' Or: 'The Tigers need to score here to even have a chance of staying in the game! Oh, no! He's dropped it. Aaaarggh!'

The only time she noticed the football soundtrack was when it wasn't playing. Last week she'd heard classical music and had raced in from the kitchen to make sure Brad hadn't had a heart attack and expired, remote control in hand, right there in the recliner. Brad had looked up in surprise as his wife flew into the room. Looking at the TV, Nina realised that what she'd heard was an edited montage of the game's all-time greatest marks set to Stravinsky's *Rites of Spring*.

'Did you see that? Absolute screamer!' had been Brad's comment as Nina leaned against the wall with one zebra-striped oven mitt clamped over her racing heart.

This afternoon, as Nina slid open the lounge room door, she found a scene as intensely comforting as it was utterly irritating. The TV was blaring with the usual pre-game blather. Tigers v. Bombers. Brad was in the recliner, boots up on the coffee table.

Anton and Marko were lying on the floor pinging buttered popcorn at each other, and Jordy was curled up on one end of the sofa cradling his mobile.

'Right then, I'm off,' Nina stood at the doorway and announced, half hoping they would all leap to their feet and beg her to stay.

'Shit! Coughlan's gone for the season!' Brad threw the remote across the room.

'Piss off, Marko! Stop it.'

'You started it, you dickhead!'

'Can everyone just shut up? I'm on the phone!'

Nina took a breath and tried again. 'I'm going . . . RIGHT NOW!'

'Oh, OK . . . ow!' Brad hauled himself to his feet, clutching at his lower back, and sidled up to her, eyes still on the screen. 'Boys, say goodbye to your mother.'

They all raised their hands in her direction. 'Bye, Mum! Have a good time! See ya! Bye!' Nina bent over to kiss each cheek and steal a cuddle. She inhaled the familiar teenage-boy aroma of sweaty T-shirts, pimple cream and damp socks. She turned and stretched out her arms to her husband.

'I can't believe it,' he groaned.

'You'll be fine—it's only two weeks,' Nina soothed. They would miss her after all.

'Two weeks? Coughlan's gone for the rest of the year! It's his fucking knee. And we've got Polo out with his shoulder. Hall's done his hip. We've got no chance. The whole year's a total write-off. Christ, my back! I'm the friggin' team manager— I should be there.'

'For God's sake, Brad, I'm talking about ME. I'm the one who's going for two weeks.' As Nina turned on her heel to leave, Brad caught her by the waist and bent to nuzzle her neck. Nina stood for a moment letting 'Kingie', the giant former Richmond full forward, put a smothering tackle on her. 'Everything you need's in the freezer. I've left a note for the rest on the fridge.'

Brad stepped back, sensing the umpire had blown the whistle on the sensitive moment, and took up Nina's bulging handbag. As he hobbled to the front door, he ran through the drill one more time: 'Right. Now remember what I told you. It takes diesel, not petrol. If you're not on a powered site, you switch the fridge to gas and the generator to number 2. Don't forget to check all the latches, vents and windows before you take off. And close down the gas cock. Put the fold-out step up, and secure that hook. Watch out for height limits. Don't panic, it'll only start in neutral. Just jostle the gear stick. If something goes wrong, all the roadside assist numbers are in the glovebox. And don't forget what I told you about the annexe—you have to wiggle that bottom bolt. It's got a mind of its own. And remember what I said: if there's a problem, DON'T TRY AND FIX ANYTHING!'

Nina nodded. She possessed a fully functioning brain, despite what Brad might think. They'd been through the van's routine a dozen times. He'd only driven it once during the school holidays to the campground at Bright but now, apparently, he was an expert on its operation. Nina was confident she was up to the challenge of the mighty RoadMaster. After all, during those years when

Brad Brown—first as 'BB', then as the legendary 'Kingie'—had spent every weekend toughing it out on the oval, she was the one who had been captain of the home team. She had wrangled pushbikes and bouncy castles, skateboards and scooters, kayaks and tents. She had cleared the guttering on the roof, pruned trees and used an electric eel to unblock the drains. The carport was all her work too—she'd drawn up the plans, found the builders, even stapled the shade cloth on top. After shepherding three boys under five, there was nothing a first-grade footballer could teach her about stamina or perseverance . . . or driving a 3500-kilogram motorhome with an inscrutable annexe.

'Just wave me out, Brad. Get out in the street and make sure there's nothing coming,' Nina called from the driver's seat as she adjusted the rear-vision mirrors. Meredith was beside her, making a note in a Japanese silk-covered travel diary as to the exact time of their departure. Annie was in the back, lounging by the table and holding her champagne bottle up to the light to see how many mugs-full were left.

'OK now, turn slightly to the left. No, YOUR left! Yep. Now come straight forward!' Brad was waving wildly, as if he was signalling to his centre-half forward that he was in a position to boot for goal.

'Over a bit! OVER. OVER! You're going too—'

CRUNCH! The sickening sound of torn metal and splintering wood came from the roof.

'OH, NO! Fuck, Nina! The carport! The TV aerial!'

Nina saw Brad limp up the driveway, grimacing in pain and annoyance. She turned off the motor, threw open her door and jumped down onto the concrete. The TV aerial was bent, its head lolling like a snapped sunflower.

'CHRIST! Didn't I tell you to go through the checklist?'

'Don't shout at me! You're making me nervous.'

'I'm making YOU nervous? You're not even out the front gate and you've already caused three hundred bucks worth of damage. God knows what you'll manage in two weeks!'

'Don't talk to me like that! It's just a mistake.'

'It's the six P's, Nina. It's what I tell the boys at training: "Perfect Practice Prevents Piss Poor Performance." You should know better.'

Nina scrambled back into the cabin, slammed the door after her and shouted out the window: 'Jam your six P's up your arse, Brad! If I've broken the TV aerial, I'll fix it. Like I've fixed everything else in the house for years!'

She wrenched the monster motorhome into drive and accelerated. She remembered to release the handbrake. Too late. She clipped the letterbox and hit the bluestone guttering at speed. In the passenger seat Meredith grabbed at the door handle to stop her head from banging into the window. In the back Annie's champagne bottle was flung from the table into the stairwell, its contents gurgling down the steps, under the door and out onto the roadway.

Nina paused for a final word to her husband, standing red-faced by the front gate: 'GO THE MIGHTY BOMBERS!' she screamed, and shook her fist out the window.

The RoadMaster Royale roared up the street, the TV aerial beating time on the roof like a demented metronome. With an echoing, rebellious 'Up yours!' blast on the horn, Nina swerved around the corner into the next street and the King of the Road was gone from view.

✺

The RoadMaster Royale was headed for Lakes Entrance on the south-east coast of Victoria, 319 kilometres from Melbourne. Meredith had estimated the drive would take four hours and they should arrive in time to see a glorious autumn sunset from the famous Ninety Mile Beach, although by now her schedule wasn't worth the organic hand-made paper Meredith had written it on.

Their first stop was unscheduled, only 500 metres away, at the café around the corner where Nina pulled over to fix the infernal banging of the TV aerial. After she'd managed to wind it down and wrestle the mangled vent closed, it was takeaway cappuccinos all round over the table in the back of the van.

'This is bizarre!' said Annie, amazed, as she peeled the top off her hot coffee and peeked through the curtains she'd parted a tiny bit. 'Here we are in our cosy little house on wheels, sitting up at the table. We've got beds and a bathroom, and there are people walking by down the street outside.'

Meredith leaned across the table and pulled the curtains firmly shut. 'For goodness sake! We might see someone we know.'

Annie hooked one side of the curtains back and sneaked another look. 'So what? This is hilarious. Hi!' She knocked on the window, and waved to a startled pensioner leaving the butcher's shop.

Meredith yanked the curtains closed again. 'Don't! They'll think we're a bunch of . . . what do they call them? "Grey Nomads"! Three retirees with dead husbands, who've all gone lesbian.'

'You are mad, Meredith, honestly.' Annie shook her head and slurped at her coffee. 'And that reminds me, I bags the top bed over the cabin. Which, of course, you're welcome to share, girls,' she added with a grin.

'That's not funny, Annie! We've got three decent-sized beds—'

'Two queens and a large single,' Nina corrected. She spoke quietly, head down. She was fighting her way out of a purple haze of anger and regret. She and Brad had parted on such a discordant note. A 'ding' on her mobile phone signalled she had a message. There was probably an ad-break in the football. She was determined not to speak to him until tomorrow morning.

'I thought we agreed,' Annie reminded her. 'Mobile phones off, unless it's for an emergency.' She was already feeling oddly disconnected from the world without the insistent ring of the 'crackberry'. Like she'd dropped her dog off at the kennel. 'If I can do it, so can everyone else.'

Nina and Meredith duly produced their phones. 'One, two, three—off,' directed Annie. A vow of silence was made. They were on their own now . . . with each other.

'So, we should draw straws on the beds,' commanded Meredith, 'although I'd prefer the one down the back. If I had to get out of that top bed in the middle of the night, I'd fall down the ladder. I haven't slept in a top bunk since Girl Guides camp. Nina?' Nina was still brooding over her coffee.

'Come on, darls, cheer up.' Annie threw an arm around her shoulder. 'He shouldn't have shouted at you like that, but he was just being blokey old Brad. My dad still yells at me about my car.'

'Bastard!' Nina wailed. 'He always makes me feel as if I'm some kind of bloody idiot. Like I'm in training, and if I don't perform properly he'll put me on the bench. I'm sick of it.' She wiped her eyes with her sleeve. Damn Brad! She should have been miles down the road by now, speeding past open paddocks, flying free as a bird. Instead she was still earth-bound and pecking through the table scraps of her marriage.

Meredith felt on safe ground here. She was good at this 'tough love' stuff and used it with all her interior-decoration clients when she could see that emotion was standing in the way of clear-headed judgment. 'Well, in that case it's a good thing we're heading off. He'll have a fortnight to think about what life's like without you. And those boys of yours will have to smarten themselves up as well.'

Nina frowned at the mention of her sons. Meredith sensibly caught the warning and moved quickly to explain: 'I mean, they will have the chance to prove themselves as young men. Think of this as boot camp for the Brown boys. In the best-case scenario, you'll come home and they'll appreciate just how much you do for them. You'll have your own life back at last. I always insisted on carving out my own space with my family.'

Annie and Meredith sneaked a sideways glance at each other. Here was Meredith handing out advice as if she had all the answers, but she was alone in her massive house in Armadale. None of them had figured out how to 'have it all' and it wasn't for lack of wanting, or trying. Having it all still meant women had to do it all. And until the world changed around them, it always would.

It was a confirmation of how special women's friendships were—how very, very *special*—that this wasn't mentioned and the coffees were consumed over a spirited round of the drawing of the short satay skewer.

In the end, Annie scored the top bed, Meredith the rear and Nina drew the short skewer for the smaller middle bed which could only be made up when the table was stowed. Nina had expected it. She was, after all, a leading exponent of the 'burnt chop' syndrome, that celebrated condition in which, after the lamb chops have been grilled for the family meal, the mother automatically takes the incinerated one for herself and leaves the perfectly cooked morsels for her deserving brood.

This gesture of the burnt chop could be interpreted in one of two ways. Either it was a demonstration of just how downtrodden a woman really was—and 'Woman is the Nigger of the World', as John Lennon so famously sang—or it showed that a woman was a self-sacrificing martyr who would always put the well-being of her children above her own paltry needs. Nina had always thought of herself as the latter, but did have to wonder how the Nobility of the Burnt Chop had come to be reduced to the Ignominy of the Crap Bed. Was she a doormat for her family *and* her friends, she wondered?

Nina climbed into the driver's seat and rechecked the Melways for the best route out of town. Her mobile beeped, signalling a message. Nina sneakily pressed the phone into service and scanned the screen. The text was from her mother. Barely half a kilometre down the road and Wanda's apron strings were already trying to ping her back, like a floral bungee. She hit 'delete', switched the wretched thing off again and dumped it into the storage well in the van's door.

Soon the 7.2-metre, 3.5-tonne RoadMaster was barrelling down the M1, with the afternoon sun behind it and the warm breeze off the highway funnelling into its four-cylinder 2.2-litre Mercedes engine. The Melbourne skyscrapers were shrinking to Lego-land in the rear-vision mirror but the drive out of town was taking longer than they had expected.

'You know, my father used to say, "I remember when all around here used to be bush",' Meredith marvelled as the van took a rise on the road and another vast expanse of brand-new black-tiled roofs spread across the landscape like a melanoma. 'I can't believe it. It's insane. We've been driving for almost an hour and we're still in the damn suburbs.'

The irony of the charmingly named *Woodland Park*, *Heritage Springs*, *Lakeside* and *Falling Water* housing estates wasn't lost on anyone. There were no woods to be seen here, and bugger-all water either. In the front yards of massive McMansions, reeking of drying paint and PVC glue, strips of newly laid turf were yellowing and curling at the edges like salad sandwiches left out in the sun. The grass, seedlings, shrubs and saplings planted in spring were now, after a blistering summer, merely burnt, crispy offerings, not much more than deep-fried garnish at the edges of concrete driveways. Even the hardest heart could see that out here hopes of a fresh start were withering on the vine.

'Ridiculous place to buy a house.' Meredith reached for her sunglasses. '"Little Boxes". My father used to sing that song about ticky-tacky houses all sitting next to each other and looking absolutely identical. There's not even a decent deli. What were they thinking?' The van sped past a billboard featuring a handsome sun-kissed couple, 2.5 children and a dog. It bore the legend: 'Rather than live someone else's dream, we've built our own.'

'A nightmare, more like,' Meredith crowed. She pointed out the absurdity of the names of the countless streets, courts and avenues that flashed by—*Boronia*, *Wattle*, *Blue-gum*, *Koala*, *Rosella*. 'Apparently you bulldoze the local flora and fauna, and then name a street after it.' Another billboard—bearing the ironic headline 'Natural lake . . . coming soon'—had both Meredith and Nina laughing out loud.

'Well, people have got to live somewhere. And let's face it, Meredith, your lovely leafy suburb once looked exactly like this.' Annie spoke up over the steady hum of the engine. 'Would you like all these mums and dads and their little kids moving into some hideous block of Housing Commission flats?' Annie had come to sit on the step in between the two front seats, despite Meredith's warning that there was no seatbelt and her perch was, in fact, illegal.

'Maybe you'd rather they moved into the snazzy singleton designer apartment next to you?' Meredith shot back.

Nina's fingers tightened on the steering wheel as she tuned in to their bickering. They may have protested that they were 'just having a bit of fun', but she knew very well where that would end—in tears. And she wasn't about to have any of that on this trip. She'd endured years of arguments between her twin boys and had developed a strategy to deal with it. She would create a diversion as cleverly as she had always done. Just like when the boys had been fighting over whose turn it was to have a go on the slippery dip and she had pointed and shouted: 'Look up there! It's a helicopter!'

'My uncle used to have a market garden out here somewhere.' Nina waved her hand vaguely to her left. 'Probably about where that hardware barn is . . . or that homeware supastore. We used to come out here and help him pick vegetables when I was a kid.' The distraction seemed to work, thankfully.

'A miniature Ukrainian babushka!' exclaimed Meredith.

'I can see you on the back of a tractor, in a paisley headscarf and hessian dirndl skirt.' Annie leaned forward and clapped her hands with delight at the image. 'A baby blonde potato dumpling.'

Nina bit her bottom lip and gripped the steering wheel so hard her knuckles whitened. That's how they saw her. As some rotund ethnic Mrs Pepperpot, carting a basket of cabbages. Well, she would show them. She'd lose at least six kilos on this trip. She'd walk every morning and every night. Cut out the starchy stuff and eat only chicken, fish and salads. The twenty kilos she'd gained since she'd married Brad was his fault. There was no way she could have stayed slim when he was playing footy and demanding pasta and potatoes before every match and training session. That's when she'd stacked on the weight. The years of picking at chicken nuggets, chips, and macaroni and cheese from the kids' plates had likewise gone straight to her hips.

Nina thought of Annie's bags of slinky designer clothes stashed in the back. Nina's holiday wardrobe consisted of a few wraparound skirts, baggy shorts, T-shirts and a couple of loose shirts. There was nothing in her size in the smart boutiques of Toorak Road. The last time she had gone shopping—for an evening outfit to wear to last year's televised Brownlow Medal count—she'd barricaded herself in a changing booth with a scrap of beaded taffeta that barely reached around her thighs, and cried for half an hour. The only thing she had bought was a pair of shoes. At least her feet were still the same size as they'd been on her wedding day. She'd cried again when she locked herself in the bedroom and wouldn't come out, despite Brad banging on the door and telling her: 'You're the mother of my kids. I don't care what bloody size you are.'

Nina remembered watching the red carpet arrivals on TV that Black Friday night, the camera zooming in on the footballers' wives and girlfriends in their spangled, low-cut, clingy satin frocks—and howling again. When the chirpy host interviewed Brad 'Kingie' Brown and he lied to a million viewers telling them Nina had been forced to stay home because the kids had measles—and then blown her a kiss—it was only a carton of Cadbury Favourites and a bottle of Yellowglen sparkling that saved her from taking to an artery with a blunt pair of kitchen scissors.

Nina wrenched herself away from the window on the memory. Everything was going to be different from now on. She was determined it would be. 'I did have a headscarf, but it was blue gingham. And my dirndl skirt was embroidered red cotton, not hessian, thank you very much,' she said with as much cheeriness as she could muster.

'But was I right about the tractor?'

'Ha! No prizes for that one, Annie. Every Ukrainian uncle had a tractor. She was green and her name was Vasylna, the Queen of Tractors!'

'Well, there you go. My dad's got a red Massey Ferguson he calls Eric!' said Annie.

'My mum had a Morris Minor she named—wait for it, ladies—"Morris",' Meredith added drily.

There was a welcome round of laughter and with it they realised that, at last, they had hit open country. With every kilometre travelled through the undulating dry paddocks, hearts grew lighter. This was an Australian landscape they knew well from when they were little girls looking out the window of the family car. At the horizon the heat haze dissolved land and sky in an airy confection of yellow and blue fairy floss. Through the middle the road was a flat black licorice strap.

Meredith wanted to shout: 'Look everyone—cows. Real live cows!' The first roadside stall they passed selling bunches of lavender and boxes of lemons, Nina had an urge to stop and buy the lot. Annie couldn't take her eyes off the marshmallow clouds. It was as if she had looked up from the ground to see them for the very first time. They were flying now. Up and away and beyond everything, into the wild blue yonder.

Seven

When the RoadMaster crested the top of the hill on the Princes Highway overlooking the fishing port and holiday village of Lakes Entrance, the April sun was setting. The windscreen framed a scene of old-fashioned beauty that might have been hung on a drawing room wall. The surface of Lake Victoria was a shimmering violet-blue looking glass. The rigging and cables of the fishing boats were strung necklaces, spun gold by the sun's last rays. A ruffle of frothy white lace surged at the neck of the shipping channel; beyond that was the Tasman Sea, which gave way to the vast Southern Ocean, its phosphorescent fabric of aquamarine brilliance fading to dark navy at the horizon.

Nina and Meredith, sitting up front, were stunned by the view. They fancied they were at the end of the earth and, for the first time, the promise of their trip right up the eastern edge of the Great Southern Land unrolled before them like a silken ribbon. A long, slow intake of breath was all Nina could manage.

'It is truly and utterly spectacular.' Meredith found voice for the both of them. '*Evening, When The Quiet East Flushes Faintly At The Sun's Last Look*—that's the title of my favourite Tom Roberts' painting.'

'Fuck Tom Roberts!' Annie muttered as she sat at the table in the rear cabin and poured another glass of wine. She'd forgotten just how tedious long drives through the country could be and had drawn the curtains on the view of endless dreary sunburnt paddocks and scrawny gum trees following the course of dry creek beds. It was hard to muster any affection for this landscape scoured by livestock, ravaged by feral animals and brutalised by the drought.

Annie was dying for a cigarette and desperate for the loo. She hadn't been able to bring herself to use the tiny claustrophobic bathroom in the back and had been hanging on for the past half-hour. She thought of her disabled BlackBerry in her handbag. God knows what she was missing out on. Just one commission on a multimillion-dollar mansion would pay for a holiday to a five-star spa in Thailand and she could be up to her neck in floating frangipanis. Just hours from civilisation and Annie was already cursing herself for agreeing to come on this stupid, hairbrained . . .

At the bottom of the hill the King of the Road slowed and turned to lumber along the main drag of darkened souvenir shops, deserted mini-golf courses and fast-food outlets now firing up neon lights in the lengthening shadows. Annie reluctantly resumed her place up front and was instantly revived by the salty smell of the sea. She was back there as a child on Christmas holidays, sitting between her parents in the front seat of the Commodore. She clapped her hands with delight. 'Can we buy some prawns at the Fisherman's Co-op? There's a pub—let's go for a drink!'

The van stopped at a zebra crossing and Meredith noticed a surfer in a ludicrous pose. As if he was '*a hunk of burnin' love*'. He was sporting board shorts and a knitted beanie and carrying a parcel of hot chips. She was confused for a moment by his street mime, but then she remembered the artwork on display. No doubt the multicoloured jewels on *The King's* jumpsuit were glittering in the setting sun. What a sight they must look! Like the carnival had come to town. She ducked her head.

Annie cheered out loud at the surfie's salutation and was suddenly inspired by the sight of the steaming takeaway. 'Let's get fish and chips for tea.'

'For God's sake, Annie, you'll be wanting a game of mini-golf next!' Nina was horrified to hear herself regurgitate this nag. 'I mean—of course you can have whatever you want,' she said quickly, hoping no-one had caught her mother-hen peck, 'but we've got all this food in the fridge. I was thinking of maybe whipping up a grilled chicken salad.'

It was almost 7 pm and Nina had been awake since before dawn. In truth, about the last thing she wanted to eat was a salad. The thought of fish and chips was a delicious, greasy, salty, vinegary hug and Nina felt her willpower slipping off her like the transparent layers of a pickled onion. She looked at Meredith, hoping she would be outvoted.

'Gorgeous! Haven't had fish and chips for years,' Meredith enthused. Nina's shoulders sagged with gratitude. She slowed and parked alongside a papier-mâché shark hanging in a fishing net over the footpath.

Once the steamy, aromatic package of fried whiting, scallops and chips was in the van, the hunt for a place to stop for the night was on in earnest. Nina was driving and looking at the caravan park signs—*Lakes Haven, Lakes Ponderosa, Lakes Caravilla*. She peered beyond the thicket of tents, speedboats and four-wheel drives, trying to find a picturesque spot, but it was a pointless exercise in the gathering darkness. Garlands of fairy lights sparked into life in trees and very soon one spotlit caravan park entrance looked much the same as another.

Meredith and Annie were no help. They'd torn a hole in the paper fish-and-chips wrapping and were extracting tasty battered morsels. Like bloody seagulls, the pair of them, Nina thought with irritation. 'Look, let's just find ourselves a basic park and stop.' She turned into the next caravan park driveway and leapt from her seat.

Annie licked salt from her fingers as she watched Nina slide open the glass door on the tatty little prefab building that was the park's front office. 'Remind me again,' she asked, 'what the hell are we doing here?'

'We're having an adventure, apparently.' Meredith thought of her house back in Armadale. If she were at home she would be padding in silken slippers across her Tibetan wool rugs to the courtyard with a cup of chamomile tea.

Annie watched two grey-haired women in dressing gowns with damp towels slung over their shoulders shuffle along the path next to the van. They were nattering and swinging floral toiletry bags. 'Looks like a whole lot of pensioners towing caravans ticked the same box,' she said, fishing in the paper for another scorching chip. She imagined the scene at Jupiter's Casino. At almost forty, Annie was the elder stateswoman at these events. The younger female delegates would be ordering in sugary fruit cocktails and complaining bitterly that the spa was booked out. Annie, who always arrived a day early and indulged herself in every pampering treatment on offer, would have already tipped the barman to stash a bottle of Stoli under the counter and put it on the company tab. But there was no point in thinking about any of this, she reflected. This 'adventure' was already past the point of no return. They'd hit base camp. No doubt there would be a lot of tricky terrain to negotiate before they saw home again.

'Forty bucks for the night.' Nina climbed back into the cabin. 'A bargain, huh?'

'If you don't count the cost of the fuel . . .' began Meredith.

'There's no use talking about cost. We're going to have an experience money can't buy.' Nina waved the paper receipt. 'Now we're on lot 47 according to this . . . it's down this road here. Close to the toilet block.'

'God, I wish my mother could see me now.' Annie leaned between the seats at Nina's elbow. 'That was always at the top of Mum's agenda when we camped at Sorrento every Chrissy. "Brian, get as close as you can to the taps and the conveniences."

Jean's a nice country lady, of course, she still can't bring herself to say "toilets". Little does she know I first learned about sex in that caravan park. You can see right through canvas with a good light behind it. Kama Sutra shadow puppetry.'

Soon the RoadMaster was parked on a concrete pad underneath a gum tree, plugged in and humming with electricity. A bright and cosy nesting box for three hens who'd flown the coop. They'd scored a prime position—no campers either side. The standard-issue breeze-block conveniences were a short walk away through flower beds and, at the back of the van, the manicured lawn gave way to darkened scrubby bush.

Half an hour later Nina was stuffing paper wrappings into the plastic bin in the van and cursing herself for eating most of the fatty chips. She thought about breaking her promise not to use her mobile phone again. She shouldn't have agreed to the pact in the first place. Nina had a young family at home and they needed to hear from her. It was something the other two couldn't really understand. In the pool of light coming from the van's windows she could see Annie outside, now wearing a stylish pale-blue velour tracksuit and white ballet flats. She was sitting back in a canvas camp chair, on her third cigarette and nursing a champagne flute. Where does she think she is, thought Nina—*St Bloody Tropez*?

Nina fished for her phone, tucked it up her sleeve, stepped into the bathroom and called the home number. No answer. Then Brad and Jordy's mobile phones. No answer again. Where were they? In the lounge room, making some point by not picking up? Or had Brad taken the boys to Wanda's for their favourite meal of borscht with herb dumplings while her own maternal offerings sat unwanted—a pile of freezing bricks? She willed herself not to call her mother or leave any messages.

When Nina finally made her way down the van's steps she found Annie and Meredith both leaning back and surveying the starry southern skies. Neither of them could remember the last time they'd sat in a camp chair in the dark, so maybe they were having an adventure. Nina was mugged by the beauty of the rising moon, its edges hazy with a silver corona of salt and surf thrown up by the sea. The night was warm and clear.

'I'm trying to remember the last time I looked at the stars.' Meredith regarded the sequinned heavens. 'You know—really looked. Did you ever try to count the stars when you were little?' She held out her empty glass for a refill.

Annie retrieved the bottle of champagne from the shadows. 'There's about a hundred billion of 'em last time anyone counted, and between 56 and 250 million bubbles in a bottle of champagne—depending on which estimate you want to believe.'

'Someone counted champagne bubbles?' Meredith licked the rim of her Danish crystal champagne flute etched with stalks of wheat.

'When Dom Perignon first tasted champagne, they reckon he said: "Come quickly, I am drinking the stars." But then, he was pissed at the time!' Annie grinned and held up the bottle to Nina.

'Come on, Nina, have a champers.' Meredith produced another flute and they were all amazed to hear the fizzing of the bubbles in the quiet, even as they could hear the distant tumbling surf.

Nina found some absolution in her glass. She forgave herself for the chips . . . the piece of fish, two potato cakes and three fried scallops. It was the last meal of the condemned fat woman. That's how she'd think of it. The harsh words between her and Brad? That was understandable. They were both trying to navigate their way through this unfamiliar scenario. She'd never done this before—left her family to fly solo. Now, after weeks of planning all their lives to the last detail, she was on the road and travelling north away from everything she knew. She had wished for this for so long and resolved not to miss what was in front of her.

Nina kicked off her rubber thongs and dug her toes into the damp grass. Who, she wondered, was this anonymous woman, more than three hundred kilometres from all care and responsibility, listening to the surf pounding beyond the dunes?

'Here's to us!' Annie raised her glass. 'And to life on the open road.' A sultry breeze blew through the caravan park carrying the sound of tinkling crystal away to the shoreline.

The next breath of wind brought with it the unmistakable sound of Meatloaf belting out 'Bat Out of Hell'.

✷

'Good God, it's SO loud! It's deafening! Couldn't they turn it down?' Meredith was kneeling on the top bed, winding the van's windows tight against the assault of AC/DC's *Greatest*

Hits. 'Isn't there someone at that office who could *order* them to turn it down?'

'It's only half past nine,' Nina called from the sink, where she was calmly boiling the kettle for a cup of tea. 'They'll pack it in before long.' Meredith groaned and fell back with a continental pillow over her head. '*TNT* . . .' blasted its way through the open door.

'Fucking hell, it's SO loud!' Annie scrambled inside and slammed the door after her. 'So much for the eerie silence of the Australian bush! I need another drink.'

Nina wiped the counter with a tea towel. They were both looking at her as if it was her fault! Nina was accused on a daily basis of sabotaging the lives of her loved ones—of hiding socks and homework and sports gear with deliberate intent. A tiny mutinous voice urged her to abdicate and let the Forces of Chaos reign, but what would happen if she did that? 'Look, tomorrow . . .' she began.

'WHAT?' Meredith and Annie chorused. They couldn't hear her over the relentless thump of the music.

'Tomorrow we'll camp in the bush away from everyone! We really only have to bring the van into a campground once a week to empty the grey water and black water. The rest of the time we can park anywhere we like.'

Annie was puzzled. 'I know what grey water is, but what's black water?'

'Sewage. There's a canister under the toilet. You pull it out and you empty it into a—'

'Do NOT continue!' Meredith commanded. 'I've just eaten. That is enough to convince me to never use that toilet. If I don't use it, I won't have to empty it. I'd rather take my chances behind a bush with the ants nests.'

'*JAILBREAK . . .*' Another gust of wind blew Bon Scott's strangled cry for freedom through the gap at the bottom of the van's door.

'That's it!' Annie upended the bottle of red into her glass. 'I'm going to see where the fuck it's coming from.'

'Forget it, Annie.' Nina flapped her tea towel. 'It's no big deal. It's probably just a bunch of blokes on a fishing trip having a few drinks. Let's all have an early night. We've got a big drive tomorrow and—'

'I'm off to Camp Yobbo. I'll be back in a minute.' Another high-pitched guitar siren sounded as Annie wrenched open the door and plunged into the darkness.

'Take the tomahawk from the bottom locker,' Meredith called through a pillow. She'd clambered up the ladder to Annie's bed in a futile attempt to find some refuge from the noise. Nina caught the door and turned back to the counter. She didn't mind the music—she was used to the screech of guitars and drumbeats thumping through the kitchen ceiling. She checked her mobile. Still no message. She'd now rung Brad four times. His mobile and the home phone remained stubbornly silent. She ran through an alphabetical checklist of calamities that could have befallen her home and family, from 'Asteroid Impact' to 'Zeppelin Crash Landing'.

But there was only one real looming disaster: Brad would leave her for a skinny blonde football camp follower. She knew he would. If she were Brad, she would have left two years ago. Around the 85-kilo mark. Or maybe he was waiting until the boys moved out. By that calculation she had about five years of married life left until she was a clapped-out divorcee. Fair, fat, fifty . . . and forgotten. Like the rest of the dumpy discarded women living in her street.

Nina pulled the plug on the kettle and reached for a bottle of red wine. She thought of her new Patricia Cornwell crime novel stowed in her handbag, along with the family-size block of hazelnut chocolate she'd brought along for an emergency. That was the answer to her maudlin musings. In a moment she would be curled up in bed . . . except that her cosy corner was still in pieces. A jigsaw puzzle of cushions that would have to be assembled after she'd pulled down the table.

Bugger! It was always like this. This was her life. No matter how tired she was, there was always one more thing to do: a shirt to put in the dryer, a stack of mugs to wash, wet towels to hang up. Why hadn't she insisted on the top bed? It was her bloody van after all! What would Annie care? She'd soon be drunk enough to sleep outside on the concrete.

And then the noise stopped.

'Hooray!' Meredith sat up on the top bed and banged her head on the roof. 'Ow! Damn! Ow!'

Nina laughed, then apologised for laughing and then laughed again.

81

Meredith slid her gangly frame down the flimsy metal stairs with her hand nursing her outraged forehead. 'Yes, very funny! I'm glad I didn't get that ridiculous bed. I'd have permanent brain damage by the end of the week. And the stairs are impossible. Ow! Can you see a lump?'

Nina brushed at Meredith's fringe. 'Do you see him much?' she asked.

'Who?'

'Donald.' Nina took her drink and sat at the table. She popped a square of dark hazelnut into her mouth. 'Want some?'

Meredith waved away Nina's offering. This was what this trip would be like, she supposed. Every personal detail would have to be offered up for forensic inspection. 'Enough to know that he's apparently perfectly happy living in that dreary flat in the city by himself.'

'Do you think there's some woman involved?' Nina broke off another piece of chocolate. Meredith couldn't quite believe Nina had asked. Stuck in this sardine can, it wasn't only her physical space that was being compromised.

'No. I don't.' She batted Nina's question out of bounds. 'In some ways, I could have dealt with it better if there was. Apparently he disliked the colour I painted his den, and that was enough to walk out after twenty-eight years of marriage. He hasn't even got a den in his new place. I've no idea what I'm supposed to make of that.'

'What colour did you paint it?' asked Nina.

'*Mallard grey.*'

'You mean, like the duck?'

'It's a lovely soft shade,' said Meredith defensively. She'd had this argument before. 'It complements the whole cream-to-brown spectrum. I had cushions done in a *light rice* raw silk.'

'And what colour did Donald want it painted?'

'He wanted it left the same hideous dark green it had been for years. Apparently it reminded him of some old car he had before we were married. Honestly, there were bits flaking from the ceiling, scuff marks on the walls. It had to be done.'

'I know what you mean,' agreed Nina. 'You should see the walls at our place. Ten years worth of grunge from dirty footy boots and cricket balls. I'd love to have the place repainted.'

There had to be another woman, Nina immediately concluded. How many men of Donald's age—and he must be almost sixty—would leave to set up house by themselves? He was using the repainting of the den as an excuse. Nina might not have seen Donald for a long time, but she did know that Meredith had expertly organised his life for two decades. This new chick would be young, naive—probably an actress looking for a father figure. In Donald's line of work he met them all the time. There was no other explanation.

'Will he be at the wedding?'

'I imagine so. Donald and Sigrid were always close. Closer than . . . well, anyway, close. It's their *shared artistic vision*, apparently. Funny how it's ended up. He makes junk television; Sigrid's selling tat at the markets—last I heard, anyway. While I have my store full of beautiful things and Jarvis is dealing fine art.' It was indeed a strange turn of events, thought Nina as she noisily crunched another nut.

'Anyway, I hope he's happy. I suppose I'll find out soon enough, won't I?' Meredith turned and rummaged in an overhead cupboard for a glass. 'How do I get water out of this tap again?' Meredith perched her reading glasses on her nose and peered at the row of switches and dials on the panel above the fridge— AC current/DC current/gas—their operation was beyond her capabilities.

'You flick that red switch over the stove and it starts the pump.'

Meredith duly flicked the switch. The pump shuddered and water spluttered from the tap into the sink, splashing her shirt. Meredith jumped back. 'Damn! There's a knack to everything in this van. It all looks simple, but there're so many switches and keys and vents and dials. It's like being in a wretched submarine!'

Nina saw the door was now closed on the uncertainty she had glimpsed. It was as if, in Meredith's perfect, sunlit, art-directed home, there was a hidden room at the end of a long corridor crammed with heavy furniture. Nina figured that she had a while yet before she could get inside that space and explore. She was sure Meredith would be grateful for her expedition. After all, wasn't that what best friends did? Held hands and comforted each other as they poked in dark corners. Nina resolved to try again another time.

'Anyway,' said Meredith as she banged her glass on the chopping board, 'Annie's charm offensive seems to be working. She's probably downing vodka shots with the boys as we speak. Who cares? At least it's quiet.'

'She is drinking a lot.' Nina was encouraged by Meredith's disapproving tone. 'But it's such a big time in her life. You can see she's struggling with the big four-oh coming up and the idea that maybe she won't have kids. I can't imagine what it must be like for her . . . especially after that whole thing with the first husband. It's probably hard for her to trust any man ever again.' Nina surrendered to the chocolate and took another piece.

'I know it must be difficult, but she's . . .' Meredith snatched up a magazine and swiped at a rogue mosquito buzzing around her face. 'She's clever, she's capable and so well organised. And look at her! Beautifully turned out. Wonderful figure! She should be able to find another man. If she could just be . . . a bit less . . .' Meredith's thoughts were now consumed with obliterating the tiny pest. She thumped against the glass of the microwave and was rewarded with a black and bloody smear. 'HAH! Got him!'

'A bit less . . . ?' Nina was keen to hear what Meredith had to say about Annie's predicament, because she had her own theories.

'Well, that's it for me. Time for "lights out", Captain.' Meredith turned to go to her bed.

'What?'

'I can't help thinking I'm in a U-boat in the Atlantic in World War II—*I'll be down the back in my bunk, sah! Breakfast at 0700 hours!*' Meredith saluted and marched down the galley.

Nina laughed at her performance. Meredith was a surprise package, no doubt about that. Every time she was pegged as a regulation eastern suburbs matron-in-waiting, the old 'Mad Meredith' surfaced, waving a rubber chook on a stick. Nina congratulated herself on having a friend like that. However, why Meredith persevered with a frowsy frump like herself remained an international mystery.

After making up her mattress, a task which proved to be every bit as backbreaking as she had expected, Nina dragged on a threadbare cotton pyjama top and flopped into bed. She could only manage the opening page of her book—a particularly grisly description of an autopsy—before she started to yawn. She turned off the reading light and sang out to Meredith behind her drawn curtain: 'Nighty-night! Sleep well!'

'Goodnight!' Meredith called back, and then added: 'Oh, I can hear a frog. I can't remember the last time I heard a frog. Isn't that wonderful?'

The light behind the teal curtain extinguished, Nina cuddled her pillow in the dark. She offered a silent prayer to God to keep her family safe, and then cursed to find an uncomfortable ridge in the cushions that fitted neatly into her fleshy lower back. She rolled heavily to one side and then wrenched at her pyjama top bunched up under her armpit. A button popped off—typical! They would write that on her headstone, she supposed: *Here lies Nina Brown in a coffin two sizes too small. Typical!*

It was 2.15 am, Nina saw by her watch, when she was woken by the sound of Annie staggering through the door, falling up the steps, knocking over the ladder and swearing like a drunken sailor. Nina yelped as Annie stood on her hair, clambered over her and into the top bed.

Moments later Nina heard a mosquito buzzing in her ear. She woke to swat at it in the gloom and turned to see the van door wide open. Turning on the light, Nina was appalled to discover that the white ceiling of the van was carpeted with black mozzies. Thousands of them had invaded the RoadMaster, intent on making a feast of it.

'SHIT!' Nina hauled herself from her bed, slammed the door shut, grabbed a tea towel and flicked it at the roof, sending the bloodthirsty beasts into a frenzy. Down the back, Meredith's reading light snapped on.

'Oh my God, millions of mosquitoes!' she screeched. A couple of loud smacks against the wall signalled she'd joined the fray. The van rocked on its wheels, and it was soon obvious that a rolled-up copy of *Gourmet Traveller* and a damp tea towel were not up to the task. They needed chemical weapons.

'Grab the spray, quick! It's under the sink,' Nina called. Meredith found the can, pulled her nightdress over her mouth and carpet-bombed the van with noxious fumes.

'Go outside! Go outside!' she shouted muffled instructions and waved frantically at Nina, who dragged the bedclothes with her down the stairs. Moments later they were both standing on the wet grass, wrapped in a doona and shivering under the stars.

'What about Annie?' Nina asked.

'The hell with Annie. I hope she chokes.'

A frog croaked. Meredith picked up a rock from the grass and pitched it into the bush. The love call of the lonely amphibian was silenced.

✻

The next morning Ninety Mile Beach was cloudlessly, endlessly, brilliantly blue—from the top of the frame of Annie's vision, then down through sky and sea to the bottom of the picture, where her white feet, decorated with red toenails, were striding along beige sand. Way up ahead she could see Meredith, who was apparently power-walking to Byron up the coast; and some way behind Meredith was Nina, head down and arms pumping with exertion.

They hadn't woken Annie for breakfast and, judging by the silence which had greeted her hearty 'Good morning' and the careless slam of the door when they left for their walk, she was in trouble. And all of it over a few drinks! Well, that was probably an understatement. There had been more than a *few* drinks. She'd lost count after half a bottle of vodka, and that was on top of the champagne and wine she'd had before she made her heroic foray to investigate 'Camp Yobbo'.

And how wrong had she been about that? The camp of 'ferals' had turned out to be two youngish and personable blokes from the western suburbs of Melbourne, both officials from the Liquor, Hospitality and Miscellaneous Workers Union—the LHMWU. Which was fitting, considering that they had been exceedingly hospitable with their liquor. The 'miscellaneous' had turned out to be a spirited conversation about 'social justice', 'globalisation' and, when they discovered Annie was a real estate agent, 'working families' and 'housing affordability'.

They were driving to Darwin—the Top End—on a boys' own adventure and planned to catch at least one kind of every fish in the sea from Cape Schanck to Cooktown. One of them—was it Zoran or Matty?—had explained that playing the CD of eighties anthems was a time-honoured ritual to celebrate the life of the three-kilogram trevally they'd hooked from their tinnie. Annie remembered slow dancing to Australian Crawl, drinking, and, sometime in the early hours, kissing Matty. She also recalled that it was only the plastic pull-cord of a Mercury outboard motor digging into her shoulderblades that had made her stop and draw breath.

How had they come to be exchanging passionate kisses in that dark corner of a campground in Lakes Entrance? It was always like that on summer holidays, thought Annie. Sand under bare feet, salt on skin and the pulse of the ocean quickened the senses. Hearts and minds were loosed from their usual moorings. The universe was to be found in a tidal pool—the rhythm of life in the rush of water over rocks; grace and acceptance in the wave of the tentacles of an anemone; fate in the claws of a crab.

Annie kept up her brisk pace along the sand and saw the scattered debris of seaweed and the blanched bones of a fish stranded on the high tide mark. That's how she'd found Matty. He'd been thrown up on the beach like a shell—worn smooth and clean by the sea—and she had bent to pick him up.

But then, Annie had picked up many men over the years and taken them home. And like those shells collected on summer holidays when she was a child, during the drive back to the farm they mysteriously lost their pearly sheen. By the time she set her souvenirs on her bedside table they'd started to stink. The borders of her mother's garden at the farm were still decorated with sunburnt shells brought home by Annie from summers at the sea.

Thinking about the farm, Annie found herself wondering how her parents might judge Matty. Her mother would describe him as 'a bit of alright' and her father would pronounce him 'a decent stamp of a bloke'. A broad, burly sort of bloke who could haul haybales onto the tray of a truck from dawn till dusk, then charm the farmers' wives down at the local pub with his old-fashioned good manners. But then that's what they'd both said about her ex-husband, Cameron—and look how that had turned out.

Annie couldn't trust her instincts about men anymore. She remembered noticing last night in the firelight that when Matty laughed his features quickly fell back into calm and symmetrical order in his open, placid face, just a moment before she had composed herself. She felt him looking at her in this split-second—while her head was thrown back and her mouth open with the hilarity of it all—and caught him seeing something she wanted to keep secret.

Annie wasn't used to men trying to figure her out and didn't know that she liked it much. Mostly men unloaded their problems on her, as if they thought that she, unmarried and childless, could have no real worries of her own. As if her life was an empty, featureless plain. Thinking on all this had made her reach for another drink.

The exact sequence of last night's events was, mercifully, still a blur, but she did remember the kisses. Teenage summer holiday kisses. The kind of hot and salty smooches that had meant the two of you were going together. You were now a sandy, sunburnt young couple destined to be one, never to be parted . . . right through to Anzac Day. Although the names and faces had long since faded of the boys she'd fumbled with behind the caravan park toilet block or in the sand dunes, the promise of those kisses lingered.

When she'd finally made her way down the steps of the van this morning, it was as if the sandy-haired man in the red flannelette shirt, board shorts and rubber thongs had been an apparition. Matty, Zoran, the tinnie and the trevally had vanished. It was all too predictable. Just one more example of her crap timing.

Annie turned to see that the path of her footprints in the still cool, pale sand had been inundated by the lacy patterns of the tide. Her tracks had disappeared. And she found herself thinking of that silvery trevally and its bright, translucent, intelligent eyeballs, and wondering what it would be like when she was hooked from life and hauled over the side of the ferryman's boat. Would there be anything, anyone, any ritual to mark the fact that Annie Amanda Bailey had ever walked upon the earth?

She bent to pick up a fragile pink-tinged shell and felt the blood thump in her skull. The world turned upside down and suddenly the sea was where the sky should be. Annie heaved and vomited her insides onto the beach. She wiped her mouth and watched as the surf accepted her sour offering without judgment, sweeping the shore clean once more.

☼

Nina was hot. Boiling hot. She'd tied her sweatshirt around her hips, pushed the dripping frames of her sunglasses up on her head, knotted the laces of her sports shoes and hung them around her sweaty neck and she was still hot. Her calves were screaming with indignation. Her elbows, every part of her was protesting.

Nina turned to the ocean and could see spots in front of her eyes. Grey, worrying smears across her lenses that surely must be the harbingers of a heart attack. That's all she needed—to drop dead here on Ninety Mile Beach! Brad would have to drive all the way from Melbourne to pick up her huge, blubbery carcass and drag it home. If she did collapse right here, conservationists might try to roll her back into the ocean. She'd be in the news then: *Greenies Mistake East Malvern Housewife's Body for Dugong.*

Up ahead Nina saw Meredith pull up at some imaginary line in the sand and turn to march back down the beach towards her. Look at her, still lithe and fit—one of those portraits you saw in magazines under the heading: *Life Begins at Fifty: Four Women Tell.* Well, Nina could tell them life at forty-five, with an extra twenty kilos on board, was bloody hard going. Especially in sand. Even more so when you'd had about three hours' sleep and tried to wake yourself up with a huge bowl of muesli, a sliced banana and two cups of milky coffee. And then, stupidly, agreed to a walk along the beach. It was only 9 am but it was already hot and all was sand. Ninety miles of the stuff. Hateful, sinking sand.

Nina had woken at seven this morning. She immediately found her mobile phone and tried to call home, except her battery was flat. So she had plugged in her recharger and stayed in her scungy hard bed until the morning light hit the floor and revealed the corpses of a fallen militia of mosquitoes. She lunged for the dustpan and brush to sweep the dead down the steps. The rhythmic strokes soon restored Nina's peace of mind. There was nothing so calming, she thought, as watching the swipe of a damp cloth or the drag of stiff bristles restore order to a surface.

By eight her phone was fully powered. She dialled home. No answer. She then tried to call Brad's mobile. No response. Then she remembered that it was Sunday morning and, without her marshalling everyone downstairs for strawberry pancakes, bacon and maple syrup, they would probably sleep until midday . . . on Monday.

Nina turned to see the deep imprints of a lumbering, constipated brontosaurus behind her. She plopped her backside onto the beach. She was stuffed. Didn't have another step in her.

O, that this too too solid flesh would melt
Thaw and resolve itself into a dew!

It was the only quote from Shakespeare that Nina had ever memorised from her high school studies. She would bet that the

Bard had never intended for those lines from the *Hamlet* soliloquy to be used by a fat middle-aged housewife to berate herself for eating too many hot chips.

Lowering her sunglasses and looking out at the sea, Nina caught the shadow of a circling sea eagle against the bright rays of morning. She watched the bird's sleek form hover and then plunge, talons outstretched, to snatch a fish from just below the surface. The metaphor wasn't lost on Nina. She'd watched too much *Dr Phil*. Drawn too many cards from too many inspirational decks of wisdom. Stuck too many *O* magazine tear-out postcards on the fridge to miss the message. That's what she had to do—leave her earthbound, sweaty, lumpy body, fly to the horizon, dive and trust her instincts. She had to believe that, just below the seemingly impenetrable surface, there was a glittering prize waiting for her. Or was that just a line she'd nicked from a Danielle Steele novel?

In the meantime, The Journey Of A Thousand Steps had to start with the impossible trudge through the sand and over the bridge back to the van. She thought she might wait until Meredith passed her by. The last thing she needed this morning was a head girl urging her on with a lecture about the 'intense satisfaction of digging deep and pushing on through one's personal limits'. If Meredith tried that particular routine this morning, Nina might just have to drown her.

✸

Meredith slowed her pace at the spot where Nina was slumped in the dunes and gave her a hearty salute. Good on her for making it so far! It couldn't be easy to start an exercise regime with a punishing walk in the sand after an interrupted sleep. Nina was a good-looking woman, and even a few stray kilos couldn't disguise the fact.

Meredith had long been a subscriber to the old adage that, after a certain age, a woman had to 'choose between her face and her backside'. Nina was certainly carrying a bit of weight but her plump, round, unlined and pretty face was a testament to the saying. Meredith had no bum and the result was evident in the bathroom mirror—most mornings she saw that her face looked like the site of a landslip in Ecuador. She should tell Nina how attractive she was . . . and pass on the name of a decent beautician and hairdresser.

And she should tell Nina how much she enjoyed her company. She was a busybody, that was true, but she was also so . . . comfortingly motherly. Not that Nina would welcome that description. She had some 'self-esteem issues', that too was obvious. Too much daytime TV. Every time you turned on one of those mind-numbing programs, it seemed there was a woman on trial for some maternal misdemeanour or other. The accused would sit with tears rolling down her cheeks in front of a studio audience while husbands, friends and children all charging her with a range of female failings. Too overbearing, too undemonstrative, too tidy, too slovenly, too generous, too miserly. Mothers were to blame for everything these days, it seemed. *Motherguilt*—someone had even coined a name for the low-lying cloud of dread every woman had hanging over her head. It was a damn sight easier twenty years ago, when it was all men's fault.

Meredith stopped, turned her face to the sun and tugged her white singlet over the top of her navy jogging tights. She shuffled her feet so that her new sports shoes were perfectly aligned—toes and heels together. She stood tall, breathed in to lengthen through the spine, then out to engage the muscles of her pelvic floor and flatten her abdominals. 'Zip up and hollow,' she said aloud with some satisfaction. Perhaps Nina might also benefit from Pilates. She would give her that phone number too. The morning sunlight refracted through the water and infused Meredith's body with cleansing, invigorating energy. A walk along the beach was the perfect way to start the day. She hadn't done it in ages.

Last night's mosquito invasion aside, Meredith was surprised to find she was enjoying her campervan experience. She had woken this morning and surveyed the few square metres of her new domain—the modest row of wood-veneer cupboards over her head, the plastic domed reading lights and the expanse of synthetic curtaining—and felt a curious lightening of her load. If she had been in her own bed in Armadale, she would have been mistress of some five hundred square metres of pure wool carpeting, a hectare of raw silk curtains, hundreds of thousands of dollars worth of Italian furniture and German appliances, French cut-glass light fixtures, hand-painted wallpaper, a hundred-year-old hedge . . . and an empty den. She had to admit that, as much as she adored her home, there was something oddly comforting about being away from it—eating fish and chips out of paper, and living in a cheap plywood-and-aluminium box. Perhaps it was as simple as having nothing to dust.

'It's just one more thing to dust' was one of the favoured sayings of her mother, Edith. It was what she said when she was given a piece of Wedgwood or Belleek fine china for her birthday. It would be admired for the day, then sent straight to the 'good front room' and placed in the famous crystal cabinet. Meredith never saw any one of the precious items inside it used for any occasion in almost half a century. The family sat down in the kitchen every night and ate from plain white plates and ugly pyrex casserole dishes while a table setting fit for royalty remained behind glass. Even if the Queen of England herself had come to tea, Edith would not have surrendered the key to the crystal cabinet.

Striding along, right at the point where sand met sea, and relishing the painful strain in her thigh muscles, Meredith's pace did not slacken. She could see Annie up ahead and was determined to run straight past her. It would do Annie good to understand that her selfish act had cost both her and Nina a decent night's sleep. She didn't want to even think about what had transpired in the early hours at the campsite at the end of the caravan park.

Meredith was startled by a splash in front of her and saw that Annie had torn off her clothes and was diving, naked, through the aquamarine shallows and out through the breakers. She caught a flash of smooth white glistening thigh and was reminded of the Royal Doulton figurine of a mermaid she had once bought for her mother.

When Edith died last year and it had been left to her to pack up the contents of the old house in Camberwell, Meredith had dropped her father, Bernard, off at the nursing home and then returned to the house to find the key to the crystal cabinet. She had chosen a hammer from the neat shadow board in the garage, carefully laid newspaper on the Axminster carpet and then smashed every teacup, teapot, serving platter and gravy boat. The mermaid was saved until last. One blow had taken its head clean off.

Why had she even bought her mother that mermaid? she wondered. With her tight springy perm, permanently pressed slacks and neat blouse, there was no-one more unlike a mermaid than Edith. Now that she thought about it, she had never seen her mother wet. Not even from the bath, or the rain. Meredith was horrified to realise she was humming one of Edith's favourite songs, Rod Stewart's 'We Are Sailing'. She pounded all the way back to the caravan park in silence.

Eight

'Do you remember when we played here at the arts festival?'
Nina asked as the van trundled towards Mallacoota. The day
was still, and unseasonably warm. Nina was loving the drive
through the Croajingolong National Park to the sleepy coastal
town. She was deep in the Australian bush now. They'd all
been silent for a good hour, savouring the tangy smell of the
eucalypt forest.

'I know it was in the mid-eighties, but I can't remember a
lot more than that,' said Annie who, after a sheepish apology,
had finally been readmitted to her perch between the front seats.
In fact, a good many of Annie's memories of that decade had
sunk beneath a tide of drugs and alcohol. The places she had
been and people she had met now swam up to her like apparitions
from the Lost City of Atlantis.

'I first came to the Mallacoota Festival with Briony when
we were doing comedy,' said Meredith, who had wound down
her window to feel the breeze on her face. Both Nina and Annie

hooted with derision. The Epidurals! They'd forgotten about that time in Meredith's life when she had styled herself as one half of a comedy duo. Meredith had almost forgotten too. Had that insane woman with the hairy legs and armpits and spiky hair really been her?

The Epidurals had first met at their weekly mothers' group at a 'wimmin's space' on the first floor of the Fitzroy Food Co-op. Meredith's children were preschoolers then—Sigrid three, and Jarvis a baby. Briony had eighteen-month-old Artemis. The two had bonded over mashing lentils, pausing only to salute each other with organic carrot and parsnip juice. They were sure the vegetables were straight from the farm because the juice tasted slightly of dirt. Clean, pesticide-free dirt, they smugly reminded each other.

Briony always carried a small vial of Dr Bach Rescue Remedy in her wicker basket and would administer four drops of Cherry Plum Flower Essence on Meredith's tongue in the case of emergency, to 'restore emotional balance'. In the beginning Briony hadn't been sure that lentil vomit on an alpaca wool poncho actually qualified as an 'emotional emergency' but when Meredith began to hyperventilate, Briony thought she could make an exception in this one instance. After that, Meredith called for the Rescue Remedy even as she hauled her stroller up the wooden stairs to the 'wimmin's space', and Briony was happy enough to administer the dose. After all, it was about wimmin taking responsibility for their personal emotional, physical and spiritual well-being.

In the early eighties Meredith's husband, Donald, had been starting out as a filmmaker. He'd scored some work on *The Man From Snowy River*. In the dim kitchen at the rear of the tiny terrace in North Fitzroy Meredith had measured the seconds and minutes until he came home by the individual grains of couscous, barley and oats she ran through her fingers. She had spent hours boiling, steaming and rendering them into something the children would stomach. When the kids discovered corn-flakes at her mother's place she reasoned that corn was a grain after all, and was quietly thankful she'd found something they'd swallow. She didn't feel the need to mention this to Briony. One of Briony's favourite cautionary tales was about the scientific experiment with rats that fared better by eating the cornflakes box rather than its actual contents.

When, finally, Donald returned, with *Snowy* in the can and before pre-production started in earnest on *Crocodile Dundee*, he honoured his part of their bargain. During Epidurals rehearsals, he'd bring the kids along, asleep in the double stroller. He even laughed at the dick jokes. Meredith had loved him then. They were a team. She was a liberated woman and he was a Sensitive New Age Guy. Briony suspected that declaring themselves SNAGs was just another ruse men used to get wimmin into bed. Donald protested he'd never had the least desire to get wimmin into bed in his entire life. Meredith's comedy career had taken her on a round of dingy Melbourne pubs and clubs and once to the Adelaide Festival. She and Briony were routinely abused as 'a couple of hairy dykes' by the drunken hecklers from bucks' night parties. Standing at the bar after the show with their arms around each other's waists was a good way to fend off boorish pick-up lines.

They had abandoned the Epidurals after one particularly nasty review in *The Age*: 'The Epidurals is an apt name for this pair of die-hard feminists, because that's what every man and quite a few of the women in the audience were calling for after an hour of unfunny tampon, leg-waxing and armpit-shaving jokes. After a night crossing and uncrossing my legs during the put-downs of male genitalia, I knew an epidural wouldn't do the trick. The only way I would see this act again is under general anaesthetic. Utter rubbish!'

Meredith never forgot that public mauling and years later, when she heard this same critic on ABC radio hosting the afternoon show, she had logged on to the website guestbook and written anonymously that he was 'Utter rubbish!'. This had given her a great deal of satisfaction.

'So, do you ever hear from Briony?' Nina asked Meredith as the van purred along beneath a canopy of branches.

'She sent a nice card when Edith died. She's up in Cairns, running some mad tree-house eco village tourism thing in the Daintree apparently.'

'Well that apple hasn't fallen too far from the tree.'

'Meaning . . . ?' Meredith leaned forward to catch Nina's eye as she drove. Meredith knew exactly what she meant: that owning a swish interior decorating and homewares store was a long way from parsnip juice at a wimmin's co-op.

Nina blithely continued: 'Don't you ever look back and wonder what went—'

'What went *right*? Thank God Donald did so well in movies financially in those early days and was able to drag us out of that hovel in Fitzroy. Look at most of that old arts crowd now. You still see them hanging around the cafés, looking a million years old. Still renting. Poor as church mice, most of them. Thank God I left all that behind and made a success of myself for my family's sake. That entire era was an utter aberration, as far as I'm concerned.'

'You don't mean Sanctified Soul as well?' Nina was crushed. Being on the road and singing with the group was one of the best times of her life.

'A bunch of silly feminists singing black American, gypsy and protest songs? *A cappella*? It means "unaccompanied . . . without music". Stupid. Waste of time.'

'Oh, that's crap, Meredith!' said Annie. 'We had a great time. And out of all of us you were the one who was the most passionate about changing the world. Remember how you used to get stuck into me and Nina for wearing high heels?'

'She was right,' said Nina. 'I've got bunions now. They hurt like hell if I wear stilettos.'

'You and Briony would come to rehearsals covered in paint,' Annie continued. 'And you both used to brag about defacing almost every advertising billboard in the entire northern suburbs in the early eighties.'

'I used to watch out for those billboards,' Nina recalled. 'I remember going to work on the tram down Nicholson Street and getting this thrill every time I saw some half-naked woman in a lingerie ad covered in slogans. It made me think things were changing.'

'"Smash Sexism", "Adam and Even!" and "Use the 'F' word—Feminist". Wasn't that the sort of stuff you used to spray?' Annie asked with some amusement.

Meredith turned her face to the window. 'Actually Briony was the billboard specialist. I wasn't good with heights. I was better at the back of toilet doors. "Men put us on pedestals and then look up our dresses", that was one of my favourites. And "Feminism Spoken Here". I liked that one too. I used to carry a black texta in my bag.' She paused. 'I've got beeswax lip balm now.'

Annie laughed at the irony of it. 'Hah! Like to see you try to deface an ad for *Australia's Next Top Model* with lip balm.'

'Well, there you have it. In the end we didn't achieve anything really. Look at women in the media today—porn stars and princesses—that sums it up, doesn't it?'

'But at least girls today get to choose what they want to be,' Annie pressed on. 'That must have been the point. That must make it all worthwhile when you look back.'

'And what's Sigrid chosen? To get married at twenty-four!' Meredith huffed and planted her bare feet on the dashboard.

'You had Sigrid at twenty-five,' Nina reminded her.

'And that's what I'm saying—nothing's changed. I've told her she can do anything with her life, be anything she wants.'

'Maybe you should have been more specific,' Annie quipped.

Meredith's toes scrunched with annoyance. 'That's just a stupid punchline, Annie. You know what I'm saying.'

'Well, maybe she's rebelling,' Annie offered. 'The way you did with Edith.'

At the mention of her mother's name, Meredith turned her face back to the wall of trees flashing by her window. 'What's Sigrid got to rebel about? It's just damned stupid. She's doing it to punish me, that's all.'

'But that's what rebelling is,' said Nina.

The home truths were coming too thick and fast for Meredith's liking. She wanted the conversation to come to a dead stop. 'Neither of you has daughters. You just don't understand.'

Before Nina could open her mouth to protest, a road sign announcing they had arrived in Mallacoota came into view and Annie's memory was kick-started: 'I *do* remember! We all stayed in tents in Jaslyn's boyfriend's backyard. Ooh, he was gorgeous! A woodworker. Dirty nails. Smelled of linseed oil. We had quite a torrid secret affair during that festival.'

'What!?' Meredith and Nina were both appalled at the casual confession.

'You were screwing Jaslyn's boyfriend?' Nina turned from the road to look Annie in the eye. 'But we all had a pact about that, didn't we? Wasn't it strictly "hands off" each other's men?'

'Absolutely.' Meredith backed Nina. 'It was supposed to be a sisterhood that expressed women's solidarity, and part of that was being honest with each other, not letting men come between us. We were supposed to be beyond the "male gaze".'

Annie sputtered into her water bottle at the mention of the 'male gaze'. She hadn't heard that term in years and didn't know what it was supposed to mean . . . then or now. Something to do with being seen as a sex object, she supposed. Well that war, at least, was won. Didn't women these days have the right to view men in exactly the same way?

'Hey!' She shrugged off their disapproval and wrapped her arms around her knees. 'Like Meredith just said, it was a lifetime ago. Maybe it was an aberration. You don't think we still believe in all that "women need men like fish need bicycles" stuff, do you?' There was a long pause as everyone digested what Annie had just said.

'No we don't. But we bloody well should!' roared Meredith.

'Amen to that!' Nina pounded the steering wheel with delight, and to a rousing nostalgic rendition of 'Sisters Are Doin' it for Themselves', the mighty RoadMaster Royale rolled into town.

A $110 tank of petrol, a bucket of potato wedges, a packet of cigarettes and a bag of frozen bait later, and the RoadMaster was heading purposefully back out of town towards Genoa on the very same road.

They'd made a brief tour of Mallacoota and pointed out the landmarks they remembered. The town had been remarkably untouched by the past two decades. But they'd rejected the camping ground. Too crowded. Meredith wasn't keen for a repeat of last night and, besides, Nina had in her mind a virtual postcard of the place where she wanted to spend the evening: an isolated, shady flat clearing in the bush with a picnic table, a water view, kookaburras, wallabies . . . and no rock music or mosquitoes. Nothing less would satisfy her.

She turned off the highway and skilfully negotiated the van down various potholed dirt fire-trails leading to the South Arm of the Top Lake. Meredith peered ahead anxiously for low-hanging branches which would surely tear off the roof. Every scrape of gum leaves on aluminium made her jaw ratchet and tighten. The huge, unwieldy vehicle rocked alarmingly from side to side. In the back, Annie cursed and dived like an Arsenal goalie as books, sunglasses, mobile phones, bottles of suntan cream—and anything else that wasn't nailed down—slid off counters and crashed to the floor.

After a good twenty minutes of tortuous driving—during which Meredith and Annie both begged her to 'Stop! Here's fine!'—Nina turned the last corner and there it was: a deserted, picture-perfect spot on the lake's shore. Nina jumped from her seat and her expert survey revealed a wooden camp table, fireplace and a tidy pile of chopped wood. Even a well-maintained drop dunny. It was just as she had imagined. She gave the girls the 'thumbs-up' of approval and they climbed from the van with relief. They were treated to a raucous welcome by a tribe of kookaburras.

'Look, look! Wallabies!' Annie pointed to a thicket of scrub where they were being regarded in turn by inquisitive large brown eyes. She stepped forward and three grey furry heads ducked for cover, thumping through the crackling undergrowth to a safe distance.

'This is a wonderful spot. Gorgeous!' called Meredith from the sliver of pebbly beach just beyond a fringe of she-oak. Before her a still expanse of water reflected the afternoon sky and the hills of thick grey-blue bush off in the distance. There was not a sign of human habitation anywhere except, she smiled, for the giant, three-bed apartment-on-wheels that Nina was now reversing into a level parking place.

'Right! I'm going fishing. Who's coming?' Annie clapped her hands purposefully and started to load her basket with supplies. Cold chardonnay and a copy of the English edition of *Harper's Bazaar* went in first. She pulled on a pair of shorts and a singlet and slipped her feet into blue rubber thongs.

'Go for it, Annie! I didn't know you were a fisherwoman.' Nina opened the outside locker of the van and rummaged for her father-in-law's fishing rod.

'My dad used to take me out on the Goulburn River when I was a kid,' said Annie. 'It wasn't far from the farm at Tongala. You could still catch redfin, yellow-belly, all the native fish. But it's mostly just European carp now. Bastards of things!'

She kicked at the grass and jammed her fists into her jeans pockets. She was overdue for a visit to the farm, but knew what that would mean—more nagging from her mother about why she hadn't found a new husband, hadn't had kids. Still, Annie would have to face another round of it soon. Brian hadn't been well with his 'nerves', Jean had whispered down the phone the last time they spoke.

'The Worst Drought in 100 Years' was the headline in the *Kyabram Free Press* but it wasn't just the parched soil Annie had seen on her last visit home. It was as if her parents' youth and vitality were also evaporating before her eyes. They were in their mid-sixties, but seemed a decade older. Jean had refused to accept the envelope of cash Annie tried to press upon her, but she had been relieved to see that the $200 a week she later transferred electronically into the farm account hadn't been returned—although the simple reason for that might have been that Jean had no idea how to send it back.

Meredith slathered herself with sunblock, perched an improbable straw hat trimmed with cherries on her head, and traipsed off to join Annie by the water to chance her luck with the rod.

Nina turned the van's power supply to 'battery' and then spent some time sweeping the floor, straightening beds and restowing all the items that had come loose on the drive down the bush trail. Now what? She turned her attention to the campsite, fossicked for kindling and built a fire in the fireplace ready to be lit. She arranged the camp chairs, threw a tablecloth over the rough wooden picnic table and . . . now bloody what?

Nina realised that she had no idea what to do with herself. She should be settling back in a chair with her book and a glass of wine, enjoying the afternoon sun in this idyllic spot, but instead she found herself itching for some menial task to perform. She'd be stacking gum leaves into neat piles next.

She could hear Brad's voice: 'Christ, woman! Sit down! Relax!' But she was like a machine in perpetual motion—folding, wiping, washing, fetching, carrying. Fifteen years after the kids were born and she still rocked on her feet as if she was soothing a baby in her arms. It occurred to Nina that she'd hardly ever seen her own mother relax. She'd watched Wanda wait hand and foot on her father and brothers, and remembered vowing that her life would be different. This thought was enough to stop her at last. She was sitting in her chair with her book in her lap, dozing, when excited squeals echoed across the lake.

'A fish! Ohmigod, look, I've caught a fish!' Meredith came belting through the bracken dragging a plastic bucket with a still-flapping fish in it—as if it was the last thing she could possibly have expected to haul from the lake on the end of a fishing rod baited with a raw prawn. 'Annie says it's a black bream! A beauty! We can cook it over the open fire for tonight's dinner.'

'But I was going to do that chicken. I've got three fillets ready to go under the grill,' Nina whined. Meredith stopped and stared. Nina herself couldn't quite believe she'd said it.

The awful, silent moment was interrupted by the sound of an engine bumping down the track and two heads turned, alert as wallabies. With a loud grinding of gears, a four-wheel drive towing a tinnie with an outboard motor hove into view.

Nina and Meredith exchanged a glance—the idiots from last night! That morning, while Annie was still passed out in the top bed, they had been relieved to see them pack up and drive off. 'Hopefully, that'll be the last we see of those two morons,' Meredith had declared. Now, as she watched them stop the car, she groaned. There went the peaceful solitude of their perfect camp. She shoved her bucket of black bream behind the back wheel of the RoadMaster. Two door slams later and Annie's drinking buddies were crunching over the gravel towards the van.

'G'day! Great day for it,' the tall one with the black goatee called.

'Yep, sure is,' replied Meredith.

'Top rig! "King of the Road"! The only way to go. I'm Zoran. This is Matty.'

'G'day. Pleased to meet you.' Matty, the shorter, shaggy blond-haired one, scuffed at the dirt with his boots, nodded and offered his hand.

'I'm Meredith.' She stepped forward and pumped his palm vigorously. 'And this is my partner, Nina.'

Partner? Nina looked at Meredith with barely disguised astonishment. What sort of 'partner'? Fishing partners? Then she felt Meredith fumbling for her hand and noted her silly affectionate smile and raised eyebrows. Meredith couldn't mean that Nina was to play the role of her lesbian lover, surely? Meredith squeezed her fingers. Bloody hell! That's exactly what she meant.

After a secretive nudge from Meredith, Nina took her cue and greeted the boys in a low voice: 'Howdy.'

The owner of the goatee sneaked a look at his mate. 'You ladies here by yourselves?'

'Are you blokes here by *your*selves?' Meredith shot back. She'd always hated that question. The assumption being that, without a man present, women must be alone. She'd had a snappy comeback for it since the days of the wimmin's group.

'Yeah. S'pose we are,' said Matty. He spied the fishing rods on the grass. 'Anything biting?'

'Nup,' grunted Meredith. 'Been at it since dawn and haven't caught a thing.' Nina nodded dumbly in agreement. She was in awe of Meredith's improvised performance.

'Yeah? That's no good. We better push on for Eden then,' he said. 'Ah . . . before we go, we met this chick . . . er . . . woman in Lakes Entrance last night. Annie Bailey. You know her? She was travelling up the coast in one of these units.'

'Hmm . . .' Meredith rubbed her chin. 'Well, we've got a bit of a convoy going. We're expecting a couple more rigs like this to get here in the next hour. Six women on board, but there's no Annie with us. Sorry, can't help you, mate.'

'OK. We might get going then. Have a good one . . . *ladies*.' The tall one smirked through his hairy face furniture.

'No worries,' added Nina in a voice so ludicrously butch that Meredith pinched a roll of fat at her waist in rebuke.

The two men shuffled back to their 4WD, heads down, hands jammed in pockets. The engine roared into life and the tinnie trailer fishtailed in the gravel, throwing up a derisory cloud of dust. Meredith and Nina heard them explode with laughter once they figured they were out of hearing range.

'I still can't believe you did that.' Nina leaned over and slapped her thighs with merriment for the millionth time. 'You haven't lost your old Epidurals hairy-leg roots, Meredith. Aaargh!' She jumped to her feet. 'The smoke's in my eyes again!'

Meredith and Nina played another round of musical chairs to dodge the plumes from the open fire being buffeted this way and that by the cool breeze blowing in over the dark surface of the lake. Annie watched their futile manoeuvres in silence. As any bushie could tell you, you just squinted against the smoke.

It would soon change direction. And it kept the mozzies away. Not that any flying insect for a five-kilometre radius could have survived the noxious fumes from the repellent they'd doused themselves with.

'Actually, I thought the blond one was a real cutie.' Nina poked at the embers with a stick. A flurry of glistening red sparks swirled into the air and dissipated into the black void.

'Hey, are you cheating on me, girlfriend?' Meredith accused. And then they were laughing again. Meredith herself couldn't quite believe how she'd play-acted with Nina that afternoon. But then, selling homewares to women who already owned enough of everything required some level of improvisation and showmanship. She often felt that her domain behind the cash register at Flair was a performance space of sorts. She was astonished at how easily she'd pulled off the afternoon's charade with Nina and the rush of adrenalin she'd experienced. Her hands had shaken for a good hour afterwards.

Annie tightened her grip on her glass and stared into the flames. 'So what did this Matty . . . you know, the blond one . . . say again?'

'We've told you—over and over! He was looking for you. *Why* he was looking for you is what you haven't adequately explained yet,' said Meredith.

'Exactly!' echoed Nina. 'Maybe he had a glass slipper in the glovebox of the LandCruiser.'

'A pair of lacy size-10 knickers more likely,' Meredith chortled.

'Hah bloody hah,' muttered Annie.

'But honestly, Annie,' said Nina, 'what did you say they were? A couple of union blokes? If you keep wasting your time on—well, you're the one who said they were yobbos—how can you expect to find a decent man?'

Once again Nina had barged through the barrier into well-signposted personal space, but this time Meredith had to agree: 'Those two scruffy individuals were hardly what you'd call husband material. They were rejects, both of them. Undersize. Throw 'em back in the lake!'

Annie said nothing. She thought that perhaps Meredith and Nina had a point. There had been too many men lately. Too many anonymous fumbles in the dark after too many cocktails. And yet that kiss . . . she couldn't stop thinking about it. And Matty was trying to find her. What could that mean?

She couldn't remember if she'd made any promises. She had to stop drinking so much. And she would, right after she finished what was left in the bottle of merlot in her hand.

'Well, I'd better clear away these dishes.' Nina stood and snatched up her tea towel. It was almost like a security blanket with her.

'No. Sit down, relax!' Meredith pulled at her baggy shorts. 'Have another glass of wine and just enjoy the fire. Leave the damned dishes,' she ordered.

Nina did as she was told, took her glass and slumped back into her camp chair. She smoothed the tea towel over her thighs to dry it by the warmth of the fire. 'That bream was nice, wasn't it?' she finally sighed, fishing for compliments.

Meredith took the bait: 'Sublime, and I'll bet it's the first time anyone has cooked pan-fried bream with a white wine and tarragon sauce over this fire.'

Annie drained her glass, relieved that her love life was off the agenda. 'It was great. Truly,' she added. 'I'd like to see old Nigella whip that lot up in the middle of the bush. As my dad would say: "Top tucker!"'

Nina shuffled her feet closer to the glowing logs and purred with pleasure at the compliments. They almost compensated for the incinerated wooden handle on her good Le Creuset frying pan.

'I think there's another baked potato in there somewhere, if anyone wants one.' Nina scraped at the ashes with a stick. There were no takers. 'Well how about some lemon sorbet and vanilla wafers?' She didn't wait for an answer and was up on her feet again, heading for the van.

Annie kicked back in her camp chair and inhaled the comforting smell of seared eucalyptus leaves. 'I'm starting to see the sense in this whole mobile home thing,' she sighed. 'When Cameron . . .' she hesitated at the mention of his name, '. . . and I were first married we used to go camping in the Grampians in this crappy little leaky tent and live for days on muesli bars and chicken noodle Cup-A-Soup.'

Meredith was just about to ask after the infamous ex when there was a bloodcurdling cry from inside the van: 'OH NO! SHIT! SHIT! SHIT!'

Meredith and Annie scrambled to their feet, hurtled across the grass and piled up the stairs to find Nina standing in front of the fridge, her cheeks flushed, on the verge of tears. 'I forgot to turn the damned thing to gas and now everything in the freezer is thawed out! The lemon sorbet, the ice cream, a home-made passionfruit cheesecake, chicken satays, my bolognaise sauce, duck and orange sausages . . .' Nina was bent over, poking at soggy lumps of Gladwrap in the freezer compartment. She dumped a pile of plastic containers in the sink. 'Look at it! It's all ruined!'

'Christ, Nina!' exclaimed Annie. 'You scared the fuck out of me. I thought you'd been bitten by a snake or something.'

'Forget it. It's only food,' Meredith admonished.

Nina was aghast. '*Only food?* What are we going to eat for the next ten days?'

Meredith grabbed Nina by the upper arms and shook her. 'For God's sake, we're only an hour away from a Woolworths!'

Nina pouted and refused to be consoled. 'Well, we're just going to have to eat everything in the next twenty-four hours then . . . and that includes the chicken fillets I had for tonight.'

'Yes, of course we will.' Annie started back down the stairs. 'In fact, why don't we just stay up all night and eat the whole lot? Give me the chicken and I'll whack it on the fire now.' With that pronouncement, she left and slammed the door after her.

Meredith prised two plastic containers from Nina's grip. 'Look,' she soothed, 'just calm down. I'll pack this back in the fridge and we'll have another look at it in the morning. You put the fridge on the gas, or whatever it is you have to do, and let's have the cheesecake and sorbet now.'

By the flickering light of the fire, Meredith set bowls on the damp grass and scraped portions of gooey dessert into each one. In the shadowy darkness she couldn't see the quality of the china or the embossed leaves and berries, and it occurred to her that she didn't much care. She stared into the embers for a moment, then lifted her face to feel the caressing breeze from the lake.

'What the hell is wrong with that woman?' Annie huffed as she dragged another branch from the pile to set a blaze going again.

'It's just what she does,' said Meredith. 'She cooks. She provides food for her family. It's pretty primal when you think about it.' Standing barefoot under a vast and starry sky, in crumpled clothes with the smoke of a burning gum tree branch in her eyes, Meredith felt pretty primal herself. 'I can see why people enjoy roughing it like this.'

Annie almost choked on her wine. There was a $250,000 vehicle parked a bare four metres away stuffed with one thousand and one items. Meredith might have caught and cleaned a fish this afternoon, but without the $300 rod, the good Swiss cook's knife and Baccarat non-slip chopping board, she would have been up shit creek.

'I've got the gas on.' Nina appeared out of the darkness, a hand towel flung over one shoulder. 'So we'll have hot water for the dishes, and a shower if we want. I worked it out for myself, thank goodness, so I didn't have to ring Brad because we're way out of mobile range.'

'I thought we were leaving the phones off?' Annie challenged.

'We are,' fibbed Nina. 'I'm just saying, that's all. I mean, in the case of an emergency or something . . .'

'How would you have got on in the old days, do you reckon?' Annie kicked at a flaming log. She'd unearthed a pair of scuffed Blundstone boots from her wardrobe and brought them along. Their familiar, warm contours made her feel solid and earthed, like she'd slipped on her old self and was a straight-talking country girl again. 'Can you ever imagine yourself as the drover's wife in the old stringy-bark hut?'

'What?' asked Nina, who always seemed to find herself three beats behind any of Annie's musings.

'Like in the Henry Lawson story. How would you have coped with a shack full of kids and the drover gone for six months at a time taking sheep up the old Barcoo River?'

'I would have been fine,' Nina stoutly replied. She gathered her bowl from the grass and found her chair by the fire. 'After all, Brad's gone for most of the year with the football. I've done all the things that need doing around the house—I did the guttering and I built the carport. That's why—sorry I went a bit overboard—I'm so pissed off I forgot the gas.'

'So you're saying women need men like . . . ?' Meredith paused for a little crowd participation.

'Like this cheesecake needs ice cream,' Nina mumbled through a mouth full of passionfruit and melted lemon sorbet.

✿

After the bowls and cutlery had been cleared, washed and stowed by Nina, she took another look inside the fridge. Maybe the damage wasn't as bad as she'd first thought. The spag bol and satays could be refrozen without too much danger to human life; they could eat some of it for breakfast . . . Her inventory was interrupted by Meredith tapping on the flywire and beckoning her to come. They tiptoed back to their chairs in the dark.

Annie pointed to a pair of yellow eyes at the edge of the firelight: 'It's a possum. A little brushy by the look of him.' It was out to scavenge the remains of dinner. Annie found some leftover garlic bread in the ashes, unwrapped the foil and threw the delicacy by her feet. The three women watched, entranced, as one possum, then another, edged closer from the shadows and nibbled daintily at the morsels in their paws and then reached for more.

'They usually eat native fruits, flowers and leaves. I'd say that one's got a baby. Yep, there it is,' Annie whispered as a tiny head popped from a furry pouch to a lullaby of maternal coos.

'You know so much about the bush—you seem so at home here,' Nina observed. 'You ever thought of getting yourself a nice country bloke?'

Meredith winced—another clunker from Nina. Didn't she ever think before she opened her mouth?

'I did get myself a "nice country bloke", don't you remember?' said Annie. 'Cameron was from Quambatook, up our way.'

'Sorry. I forgot.'

'Quambatook!' Meredith leaned closer to the flames. 'What a fabulous name. Perfect for a paint colour. *I've done out the sunroom in a gorgeous quambatook.*' She was on a comic roll now, enjoying herself hugely.

She didn't get a smile from Annie, however. 'Can't imagine anyone wanting to paint their sunroom the colour of a muddy puddle at the bottom of an empty dam.'

Annie's morose statement silenced any further attempts at comedy from Meredith.

'Cameron and Patrick—that's his new "life partner"—have gone back, would you believe? They've taken over his family farm and are doing some biodynamic organic thingo.'

'It's pretty brave, him going back there,' said Nina. 'But it must be hard for you. Everyone knowing and everything.'

Once again, Meredith couldn't believe that Nina could be so matter of fact, but when she saw Annie wasn't protesting, she joined the interrogation. 'Do the natives know they've got a couple of gay greenies at the bottom of the paddock?'

'It's bloody awful,' Annie replied. 'Every time I go home to Tongala, I see someone who was at my wedding. I meet my cousins, and I think they probably want their cake forks back. I know Mum and Dad think I've made a mess of everything. They always wanted me to marry Lance from the property next door.' Annie had to smile to herself. She hadn't thought of creepy Lance, who liked to sleep with a poddy calf on the end of his bed, for many a moon.

'But you're doing brilliantly with the real estate,' said Meredith. 'Didn't you say you'll be able to branch out by yourself next year?'

'By *myself*—that's the thing, isn't it?' Annie tossed the last chunk of bread to the possums snuffling through the grass under the picnic table.

'You couldn't imagine yourself ever going back to the farm?' Nina pressed on.

'Hah! Sitting on the veranda looking out at a dust bowl and starving cattle? Not bloody likely.'

'But what about if you met some other country bloke? A straight one,' Nina hastily added. 'What if he came to live in Melbourne?'

'Never. You don't know country boys like I do. You should see my dad when he comes to town. He panics when he can't see the horizon. There's something about the flat country that affects their brains. I've seen Dad standing at the bottom of a hill having no idea what to do with it, except drive round it. It's like it doesn't quite make sense. Like the earth is playing some weird trick on him. My grandad went on a trip to the high country once and he said: "I had to get back home because my eyes kept running into mountains." You put a man like that in the city, they can't see far enough into the distance and it kills 'em in the end. Too many corners in the city.'

'Maybe you could take a city boy to the country then,' Nina persisted.

'Nah. It would be like putting a ferret in a round cage.'

'A ferret in a round cage?' The analogy was completely lost on Meredith.

'No corners to hide in, so they run around and around until they drop dead. City blokes don't do well in the country either.' Meredith found herself stopped in her tracks by Annie's argument.

'But what does that say about you?' Nina continued. 'You're from the flat country too.'

'Women are more flexible. I've been in the city a long time now. Plenty of possums live quite happily in the city. I've learned to adapt.'

As she said this, Annie reflected that when she had first gone to Melbourne—the fabled Big Smoke—at the age of nineteen, everything about it said 'freedom'. In those early years she'd found it—living in a shared household in Collingwood with an ever-changing roster of arty types, making lentil salads in the Whole Earth Café, singing with Sanctified Soul, travelling to festivals across the state. Then she'd met Cameron. He was working as a barman in Clifton Hill. They were both from the country and negotiating their way around city life. They'd fallen in love, married.

Annie had found them an old house in Brunswick. She had discovered a purpose in stripping the wallpaper and sanding the floorboards and a new job managing a vegetarian restaurant down the road. Meanwhile, Cameron had found himself 'a new gender identity' at a gay bar in St Kilda. When that life fell apart, Annie started again in real estate. She bought herself a smart apartment, designer clothes and snappy cars. At thirty-five Annie lifted her head from her desk, ready to find herself another husband. Only it seemed that all the 'good men' had been taken. Apparently they'd been won in some matrimonial ballot and she hadn't bought a ticket. For the past five years—apart from a few doomed short-term relationships—she'd remained depressingly single. Annie felt like she had been placed in a 'career woman' showcase, as if money in the bank and home ownership classified her as a luxury item few men could afford.

What sort of man did Annie want? Not one of those performers or musicians she'd flirted with in her early twenties—wimpy egomaniacs who couldn't even help her change the tyre on her pushbike. Not a city business type—spivs and spruikers. Poseurs who wore their sunglasses on their heads, their pullovers tied around their shoulders and, she wouldn't have been surprised, their socks tied around their ankles. Not a bloke from up home—farm boys whose flat-earth view of the world came from the back of a tractor. And definitely not a man with an 'alternative gender identity'.

With each passing year Annie couldn't shake off the feeling that she was like a marsupial with its paw caught in a steel trap—she couldn't go back, yet she was frightened to go forwards and experience even more pain. Annie didn't say any of this to Nina and Meredith. She was sick of herself and her predicament, and no amount of talking about it was going to help. Instead she sat and listened, finished the bottle of wine as Meredith and Nina talked recipes and home furnishings, and then she showed them the correct way to extinguish the fire. In the way only a farmer's daughter who'd been a volunteer for the district Country Fire Authority knew how.

That night a powerful owl kept watch over the RoadMaster as it glowed ghostly white in the moonlight. At various times each of the women woke in their bed to hear a deep and resonant 'hoot-hoot' and wondered where on earth she could possibly be. How far had she travelled? How had she ended up here?

☼

Annie pushed away her plate of scrambled eggs and duck-and-orange sausage speckled with fragments of carbonised bark. 'Blagghh! I feel like crap,' she moaned. She couldn't face food this morning. Another afternoon and evening of solid drinking had left her feeling fragile.

She lit a cigarette, ignoring Meredith's dire health warnings, had two puffs and tossed it into the fire. It tasted vile. She was almost forty now, she reminded herself. Time to give away childish things.

At the protesting squawk of camp chairs being folded, Annie winced. Meredith shook her head with shared exasperation. All hopes of a leisurely start had evaporated as soon as Nina had opened her eyes and realised it was Monday. A school day. By 7 am she had the fire blazing and a kettle boiling. By seven thirty she was rapping on aluminium and calling that breakfast was ready. Meredith had peered through the curtains and seen the campsite was still in shadow. The sun hadn't even crested the hills across the lake. She wished Nina to hell and back. Annie groaned and buried her face in a fallow pillow.

Nina had apparently decided that, if she expended enough frenzied energy here this morning, it would somehow get the boys out the door in school uniform in time to catch the tram at home in East Malvern. The beauty of the morning mist rising majestically from the water didn't rate a second look, nor did the crimson rosellas communing in the trees or the rock wallabies foraging in the dewy grass. They were all duly noted. Lovely. Time to move on.

'Will you tell us, please, what *is* the hurry?' Meredith pleaded as Nina scraped Annie's breakfast into the fire and it hissed its disapproval. She and Annie had cold backsides from sitting on the wooden bench, and badly wanted their canvas camp chairs back so they could warm themselves by the fire with their coffee.

Nina didn't stop to answer, but bent over the picnic table to clear butter, bread and a jar of her home-made raspberry jam. 'The sooner we get this all packed away, the sooner we can get moving. I've looked at the map and we've got a fair drive,' she announced and headed for the van.

'How many days till we're in Sydney?' Annie called after her. Once inside, Nina packed away the breakfast things and then checked her mobile phone. Dead as the proverbial duck. She had to get reception so she could remind Brad that Anton and Marko were going on the school excursion to Canberra tomorrow and run through the checklist of what they needed to pack.

Nina marched back to the picnic table with her road map. 'It's sixteen hundred k's to Sydney, roughly. If we just take it slowly we'll have two more nights camping on the beach. I thought we'd stop here . . . and here.' Nina pointed to the map without having any real idea of what was to be found beneath her fingertip. But it was all coastline and the names Bunga Head, Potato Point and Wreck Bay sounded promising enough. After all, who was she? *Captain Frigging Cook?*

Meredith, thankfully, didn't demand any more details. She was up for it, though she would have liked to stay exactly where she was for the whole two weeks. Maybe there was another wily black bream in the reeds waiting to be enticed by a tasty prawn. She could really become addicted to this whole fishing thing. It was a pity that they were driving towards Byron and everything that had to be dealt with there.

'If we're going through Sydney, why don't we stop and have dinner with Corinne?' suggested Annie.

Corinne! Her name reverberated in the silence as if a rifle had been fired across the lake. Annie turned, half expecting to see a flight of ducks take to the sky.

Meredith dumped her coffee cup on the splintery table. 'We are NOT going to see that tart.'

Annie was surprised at Meredith's vehemence. 'Oh, come on, it'd be fun. Even more of a reunion,' she cajoled.

'It could be the chance of a lifetime,' added Nina, who was thinking that their chances of getting Corinne to come to dinner were probably nil, but that she'd love to hear her dish the gossip on the people she read about in the glossy magazines.

'Are you forgetting how she double-crossed us?' Meredith stared at them both.

'That was twenty years ago!' exclaimed Annie. 'Time to move on, don't you think?'

'Yes, well, she certainly moved on . . . at our expense, I remind you. And you are NOT suggesting that we drive this vehicle into the heart of Double Bay, are you, Nina? We'd have our own postcode!'

'By the way, where *are* we going to stay in Sydney?' asked Annie.

Nina hadn't thought that far ahead, and had just assumed they'd find a park for the van . . . somewhere. Maybe overlooking Bondi Beach. She'd always wanted to go there. She wished she had the boys along for the adventure, to see the famed bronzed Aussie lifesavers and surfers.

On thinking about her brood, she checked her watch: 8.15 am. They should be getting out the door by now—if Brad wasn't still asleep and snoring. Had he taken the bread out of the freezer last night for their lunches? Had anyone remembered to feed the dog?

All these thoughts were stressing Nina out. It was ridiculous that she was away for so long. Why was she here, exactly? 'I'm sure there are plenty of places we can stop,' she said, annoyed by their questions. Why did she have to plan everything for everyone all the damned time?

As it happened, Meredith had been formulating her own plans. 'Well, if we're going right into Sydney, I think we should ditch the van somewhere, splash out and get a hotel room. I'll definitely be ready for a hot bath by then.' Annie smiled into her coffee. The woman entranced with 'roughing it' was already dissolving in a frothy honey-scented bubble bath.

Nina snatched up her map. 'Except that I don't have the money for that. It would probably cost us five hundred dollars each, by the time we take taxis everywhere. If push comes to shove, we can camp in Centennial Park.' She gathered the coffee, sugar and milk into her arms and stalked off. Meredith and

Annie watched her go. They were all tetchy, struggling to warm up in the chilly morning air, like the rest of the wildlife in the bush: Annie a bristling echidna to Meredith's imperious brolga and Nina's blundering wombat.

Meredith shivered and wrapped her scarf tighter around her neck. 'She's crazy. She can't be serious. Centennial Park? We can't turn up and block out the sun in one of the most exclusive neighbourhoods in the whole of Australia. I know quite a few people living around there. I'd never live it down.'

Annie agreed. 'What if we want to go out to some fab restaurant? Does she think we're all going to frock up inside that thing?' She jerked her thumb towards the van and saw that Elvis's ebony quiff was now shining supernaturally as the first rays of sunlight hit the side of the van.

'Maybe we should just avoid Sydney altogether. I've got nothing to say to that media slut, Corinne Jacobsen.' Meredith folded her arms in disgust.

Annie clunked her empty coffee cup on the table, astonished by Meredith's language, but even more alarmed at the thought of missing out on the oasis of shopping in the middle of their trek through the retail desert. After all, a woman was not a camel.

'We *have* to stop in Sydney!' Annie pleaded. 'All that stuff with Corinne? I'm sure she had her reasons for what she did. Forget it. We've all changed since then. Look at us. Look at Jaslyn! Who would have thought a hippie like her would end up in a war zone, but there she is in bloody Afghanistan!'

Meredith remained silent.

'Probably the only one who hasn't changed is Nina,' muttered Annie. 'Not that I think she realises that.' She turned to see Nina puffing as she wrestled the camp chairs into the locker at the rear of the van. They both watched as she swore and swung her leg back to give the chairs a mighty kick. Meredith's eyes widened and she jumped to her feet.

'Nina, don't! Be careful of my—'

A muffled tinkling of broken glass signalled a thousand dollars worth of Fabergé crystal glasses coming to grief. Nina gasped, covered her face with her hands and fled into the bush.

Nine

Apart from the well-signposted crossing of the state border, there were a few more clues that the RoadMaster Royale was now motoring through New South Wales. For one, the quality of the roads immediately deteriorated. This state was bigger, and there was apparently not enough asphalt to go round.

'The bigger the state, the lower the IQ,' said Annie.

'But that doesn't explain Tasmania,' Meredith deadpanned.

The road signs erected by the authorities had also changed. Instead of the Victorian nanny-state nags—'*Weary? A microsleep can kill you!*' and '*Tired? Take a powernap now!*'—the warnings were more sinister: '*Police now targeting speeding*'. Nina eased her foot off the accelerator. Brad wouldn't be happy if she copped a fine.

She was even more spooked that Meredith was staring resolutely out the window and wouldn't meet her eye, despite her earlier tearful apology for the smashed wedding gift and the offer of a cheque to cover the cost. Mercifully, k.d. lang was crooning from the CD player, doing her best to soothe frayed nerves.

They'd hit the Sapphire Coast. *A wonderland of natural beauty featuring pristine beaches, forests, mountains and waterways*, according to the pile of pamphlets Annie thumbed through at a service station just over the border.

Nina paid for the petrol, and then retreated to the shabby ladies' room and tried Brad's phone again. It was switched off. She was blinking back tears as she rang Jordan's phone, and tried to sound cheery as she left a message: 'Hello, darling. It's Mumma. Have Marko and Anton got their bags packed for Canberra? Tell Marko not to forget his asthma pump. And they need sunscreen. Tell your father to call me so I can make sure they have everything. Did you remember to hand in your assignment? Did you feed the dog? Don't forget to when you get home tonight. Bye, Jordy. I miss you. I'll call you later.'

Then she was scrabbling for rough paper towelling from the dispenser and scraping at her eyes. Nina peered at herself in the mirror splattered with dried soap and dead insects. 'You are pathetic!' she sniffed at her reflection. 'Just stop it! You're the one who wanted to take this trip. Grow up! Get a grip!' She splashed her face with water, retied her flyaway hair and returned to the van.

Catching the eye of Meredith sitting in the passenger seat, Nina saw her quickly look away. Nina's shoulders slumped. She wasn't good with conflict, never had been. She would just avoid talking to Meredith until she was in the mood to forgive.

In another hour they were approaching the sprawling coastal town of Eden. Annie attempted to thaw the ice between Nina and Meredith by sitting up front and parroting every fact she could from the tourist pamphlets on the history of whaling in Twofold Bay: '"One of the most bizarre aspects of the local whaling trade was the role played by pods of killer whales. From 1843 until 1930 they returned every year to Leatherjacket Bay and, after herding migrating whales into the bay, the killer whales cooperated with the whalers in their boats to attack blue, fin, minke and sperm whales. The killers harassed and snapped at their prey and threw themselves over the whales' blowholes."'

'Can you believe any creature could be so inhumane?' said Nina.

'They're animals, not humans,' snapped Meredith. '"Nature, red in tooth and claw". Ever heard that saying? Alfred, Lord Tennyson, I think you'll find.'

Annie poked her tongue out at the back of Meredith's head and continued reading: '"They were even known to alert the whalers to their quarry's presence by breaching and splashing in the bay in front of the whaling station. They were rewarded for their treachery with the lips and tongue after the whalers had killed the prey."'

'Isn't that awful?' Annie was genuinely appalled.

'When you think about it,' Meredith said, without turning her face from the passing undulating hills, 'it's not so different to what Corinne did to us.' Annie threw her pamphlets on the floor and retreated to a seat in the back.

The towns of Eden, Pambula, Merimbula and Wolumla were driven through in utter silence. No-one could even bring themselves to argue about what music to play. By the time the van topped the rise overlooking the little town of Tathra—the waves in the bay cresting into whitecaps blown by a stiff breeze, and the dusky timbers of the old steamer wharf warmed to orange by the autumn sun—Annie had had a gutful.

'This is fucking ridiculous!' she stormed as Nina parked the vehicle. 'I am going to make us all lunch and you two are going to sit here and work this out. Or else I'm getting off and hitching back to Melbourne.'

'I don't know why you have to swear all the time,' Meredith said primly. 'I really don't like it.'

Annie leaned forward into the cabin. 'Listen, Meredith. You swore as much as anyone in the old days. I'm sorry if it offends the new you,' she said in a tone that was anything but apologetic. 'It's the way I express myself and it's not because I'm an uneducated idiot with no vocabulary. *Zephyr, synergy, tryst, effigy*. There you go—there's a decent Scrabble score. I swear because I like to swear—and I swear the two of you are driving me FUCKING INSANE!' Twin door slams announced that Nina and Meredith had, like Elvis, left the building.

Alone at last in the humid cocoon of the van's interior, sunlight slanting through the venetian blind, Annie reached into the fridge for her first bottle of the day. She set out olives, cheeses, sliced ham, crab dip and pita bread on the table and stepped outside. Sitting on a fence rail in the shade of the van, she fired a cigarette and idly watched a young couple stroll up the street. He was wearing a T-shirt and board shorts, his feet were bare and he was carrying a blue cattle dog pup in strong, tanned arms. She was tall and lean with long sun-bleached hair, wearing a pink singlet and paisley peasant skirt. They were greeted by friends who patted the puppy and lingered to chat. Wandering further along, they waved at a car going by and then ambled into the supermarket.

Annie couldn't take her eyes off their leisurely parade. It was the way her family used to dawdle up the main street of Tongala. She knew everyone back home. And everyone knew her. All the scandals. Who had married who. Everyone's business. 'The ins and outs of a duck's bum,' as her mum would say. She recalled the time Grandad had warned her to be careful walking across the main street. 'Remember that terrible business when the youngest MacDonald kiddie got flattened by a milk truck!' When had that happened? '1947,' he answered, as if it were yesterday.

It was a genuine 'insert-your-name-here' moment. It struck Annie that what she needed was a sea change. Of course, she'd thought of it before, but never made any real plans. What was stopping her? She could live by the ocean—not in the flat dry country where there was no future, nor the sharp-edged city that had no past she cared to remember. Neither of them suited her. She could find a small property here. Grow herbs, fruit trees, vegetables. She'd always taken care of the kitchen garden at home on the farm. She would have a chicken run, grow a few fat lambs and maybe find a part-time job at the local real estate agency. She'd have a blue cattle dog pup and a horse, walk on the beach, camp out in the bush and maybe, just maybe, she could find a man to share it all with. And if she did, perhaps there would still be time for children. If that's what she wanted.

Annie ground out the cigarette under the toe of her boot. Giving them up would be easy when she lived by the ocean. She finally understood why she'd come along on this trip and why she'd drawn the Death card in that tarot reading. Annie had taken it literally at the time and had been keeping one eye out for broken bridges and steep cliffs. Now she saw it could also have been about the beginning of a new life. She could spring the trap and be free.

By the time the others returned from their solitary walks— Nina first, then Meredith—the bottle of wine was almost empty. When they were both sitting at the table, two sullen lumps of self-absorption, with really shitty windblown hair, Annie happily noted, she opened another bottle, poured three glasses and set them on the table. 'Right. Who's going first?'

Meredith surveyed the table setting and registered, in a nanosecond, that Annie had done quite well—although her napkin folding left a lot to be desired. 'I just want to know what Nina thinks she's achieving with all this ceaseless activity,' she said stiffly as she began methodically refolding her square of sky-blue cotton.

Across from her, Nina looked down at her rumpled lap and immediately catapulted headlong into a regretful explanation: 'I'm sorry. I know I'm being hopeless, but I haven't been able to ring home and . . .'

'It's two days, Nina,' Annie began. 'You're barely two days from home. What do you think could possibly have happened to Brad and the boys in that time?'

'Hah! Obviously you don't have kids,' Nina said carelessly. 'Oh, I'm sorry, Annie. I shouldn't have said that.'

'Don't worry, I'm used to it.' Annie shrugged off her condolences. Comments like that wouldn't worry her from now on, because she had a plan for a whole new life. 'But it's not like your kids are babies.'

'I know. It's just that I've never been away from them this long since they were born—apart from that time I had my veins done—and I've been trying to get them on the phone. I know we all promised but . . . anyway, there's no answer.' Even as she said it, Nina could hear her sons telling her she was 'Duh . . . retarded! We're not going to die while you're away, Mum!'

'In fifteen years? Never?' Meredith was incredulous. 'You mean you and Brad have never had a holiday—even a weekend away—just the two of you?'

'Brad always had football on the weekends . . .'

'What about the summer?' Annie wasn't about to accept Nina's pat excuse. 'He doesn't manage a cricket team as well?'

'We went away camping quite a bit. We even went to Fiji once. But the boys always came with us, so . . .'

'Forget all that,' Meredith spoke up. 'It's the constant nagging. Bossing us around. It has to stop.'

Nina had heard it all before. Brad was always telling her she was a nag. She grimaced into her glass. 'Actually, it'd make a good k.d. lang song. *Constant nagging* . . .' she sang.

Annie leaned over the table into Nina's face. 'Very funny! But you should hear yourself! You're driving us fu—sorry . . . nuts.' Uh-oh! She saw that tears were imminent.

'I know,' Nina snuffled. 'But if I'm not there for them . . .'

Meredith wasn't about to let a few tears put her off. 'What, exactly, could happen that Brad couldn't take care of?'

They just didn't get it, thought Nina. Everything could happen. Marko and Anton could be trapped in a horrible bus smash on the way to Canberra, and she wouldn't be there to drag them from the tangled metal. Jordy could take some party drug and fall into a coma, and she wouldn't be there at his bedside playing him his Red Hot Chili Peppers CD, even though all the medical staff said he was beyond hearing it. She wouldn't be the first thing he saw when his eyelids fluttered and opened. The dog could get out and be run over, and she wouldn't be there to scrape its flattened carcass from the road and bury it before the boys came home from football training. Brad could be in bed right now, undoing a lacy black balconette bra embroidered with rosebuds . . . Stop! She didn't dare bring any of this up.

'Nothing,' she said finally. 'But they're so useless without me, and I just want to make sure—'

'Enough!' Meredith held her palm up to Nina's face. 'Ring the boys when they get home from school, if you really must. Tell them you love them and then, for God's sake, just *let them be.*'

'And try to enjoy the trip,' Annie pleaded. 'You're the one who was desperate to come. If you haven't been by yourself in fifteen years, try to remember what you were like *before* you got married and had kids.'

Nina reached for a table napkin and blew her nose. 'What was I like? Tell me, I've forgotten,' she implored, looking up at them with big possum eyes.

Annie smiled and sipped at her wine. 'You? Hah! You were as sexy as hell.'

'I was a lot thinner then.'

'No you weren't!' said Meredith. 'Not much. You were the blonde, voluptuous one with the cleavage all the boys wanted to take home.'

'Why didn't someone tell me?'

Annie had to laugh at Nina's naivety. 'Because, duh, there were seven of us, remember? It was a fight to the death for the couple of sunken-chested SNAGs who were brave enough to chat up a femmo gospel choir.'

'And you're forgetting,' Meredith narrowed her eyes, 'Corinne had already screwed all the cute ones.'

Annie and Nina pelted Meredith with table napkins and cushions, and harmony was restored. Not quite note-perfect, but then, they were still in rehearsal.

✵

Soon enough they were back on the road and looking for the turn-off to the Mimosa Rocks National Park. Meredith had been studying the names of the local lakes and inlets on the road map—Wallagoot, Wapengo, Wallaga, Wagonga. The lyrical Aboriginal names sang to her like a lullaby. She was rocked back to the far-off days of her childhood and the tradition of the Sunday Drive.

When Meredith was a girl, it seemed every family in her street in Camberwell took to the road for a Sunday Drive. The ritual had been imported to Australia from Mother England in the 1950s, and the idea probably made sense over there. The average English family car usually had more windows, and was warmer, than the family home in Manchester or Leeds. Over there, it would have been a relief to get in the cosy car. In England there was also the concept of a 'destination', and something to see along the way. Within an hour the family would be at the seaside, touring a castle or pottering around a village's Ye Olde Curiosity Shoppe. They would make it back home in time for tea. In Australia you could travel all day, to nowhere in particular, and see nothing but flat, blasted country, shearing sheds, sheep and more sheep.

'I hated those damned drives,' said Meredith. She had her bare feet up on the dashboard again and was polishing off a packet of wine gums. 'Every Sunday morning after church, Edith would pack egg-and-lettuce or ham sandwiches, Kia-Ora 50/50 cordial, a great slab of madeira cake and a tartan thermos of tea into her wicker basket, and tuck it under her feet up front. Bernie would be running the FC sedan in the driveway, to warm up the motor. Kevin, Terry and I would fight over who got the window seats. Then we'd head out down Burwood Road, spot on eleven.'

Nina was scouring the roadside for the national parks sign and chuckling at the image of the Skidmores in their FC. In the old days, when they were travelling with Sanctified Soul, Meredith had often talked about her parents—Bernard Skidmore, the upstanding suburban dentist, and his faithful sidekick Edith—but Nina had never heard this particular tale before. Annie, still refusing to abandon her spot between the front seats, was enjoying Meredith's rave. In fact, she couldn't recall her ever being so expansive about her childhood.

'There were two options,' Meredith continued. 'A drive to a plant nursery in the hills—which wasn't too bad, because there was Devonshire tea to scoff on the way home—or Bernie would say, "Let's just see where we end up." And, truly, he would just drive till the petrol gauge read half-full and he would stop, and we'd have lunch. Do you know, it didn't matter where the hell we were—at a gravel truck lay-by, on a median strip with cars roaring by, in a roadside quarry. We would sit and eat our soggy sandwiches and drink warm cordial, while being attacked by blowflies, eaten by mosquitoes or poisoned by exhaust fumes. It was *beyond*!'

The idea of Meredith sitting on a pile of gravel by the roadside, eating a flyblown ham sanger, was, indeed, beyond belief.

Meredith popped the last wine gum in her mouth and bit down. She wasn't being quite as truthful as she might have been. She'd edited out that particular afternoon when she had kicked the back of her father's front seat and he had swung his hand back, slapped the side of her head and sworn furiously at her. He'd skidded the FC sedan to a stop in the gravel at the side of the road, got out, wrenched open the back door and dragged her from the back seat by the collar of her beaded green cardigan.

140

'You can bloody well walk home from here, Miss!' Meredith remembered her father's face up close to hers, snarling with anger.

'Sorry, Daddy. Sorry. I didn't mean it. It was an accident.'

Then he had driven off, up around the curve of the hill. Kevin and Terry hadn't dared to turn around to look at her. She remembered running up the asphalt road after the car, crying and wiping her runny nose on her sleeve, not believing they could have left her, terrified at finding herself alone in the bush. She also remembered her relief when she saw the familiar shape of the FC tail-lights up ahead. She had stood in the middle of the road, not able to go a step backwards or forwards, and wet her underpants.

'Filthy, filthy, disgusting girl!' her father scolded as he pushed Meredith into the back seat.

'Ee-ew, stinky Meredith!' Kevin and Terry had held their noses and complained as she wiggled her toes in her sodden white knee-high socks. Meredith had never forgotten that long, damp drive back to Camberwell, but what was the point in telling that particular part of the anecdote? It would only spoil a good story.

'When we got home, Bernie would get out of the car and say: "Wasn't that a fascinating day, children?" We'd probably driven two hundred miles. If we'd been in Europe, we would have driven through France, Spain and Portugal, and seen something worth seeing!'

The van rounded a bend and there at last was the sign to Mimosa Rocks National Park. A grey blur bounded across the road in front of the van.

'Look, a kangaroo!' shouted Nina.

'I can see it.' Meredith pointed. 'I can see it.' She was starting to think that, on this particular drive, she was seeing a whole lot of things she'd never seen before.

✿

After a short walk from the Mimosa Rocks campsite through the banksia trees, the wild beauty of Gillard's Beach unfolded like a pop-up picture in a child's book of fairytales. The pulsing surf had given birth to a luminous pearly moon suspended in endless twilight. Meredith couldn't quite locate the shade of the sky on her personal paint chart. It was a curious mix of *velvet cape*, *admiralty* and *prelude*. She gave up and named it 'beautiful'.

For Annie—sitting beside her on the dune and joining the peaceful communion—the years of viewing the sunset over vast, flat inland plains had in no way prepared her for the dynamic restlessness of the darkening sea. She was astonished every time she saw it. She was intrigued by the notion that she might be able to watch it every evening for the rest of her life.

Nina slammed the flywire door on the RoadMaster and flicked on the fluoro over the cook top. She paced the galley from bed to bed and scanned the iridescent screen of her mobile phone. When it finally showed she had coverage, she dialled.

'Jordan?'

'Hi, Mum.'

'Darling! I've missed you so much. How are you?'

'Good.'

'How was school today?'

'Gay.'

'Did you hand in your assignment?'

'Yeah.'

'Where are Anton and Marko?'

'Upstairs having a shower. They have to get up early tomorrow, if you haven't forgotten.'

'Have they packed everything?'

Silence.

'Have they?'

'Nah. They're goin' to the nation's capital in the nude.'

'Don't be a smart alec, Jordan, it doesn't suit you. Is someone there with you? I can hear voices.'

'It's the TV . . . oh, and a home invader in a balaclava who says if I don't get off the phone he's gunna waste me with a semi-automatic.'

Silence.

'Is your father there?'

'Nuh. He went out.'

'YOU MEAN YOU ARE AT HOME BY YOURSELVES? WHERE DID HE GO?'

'Dunno.'

'Jordan James Brown, this is your mother speaking. I will find your father and he will be back home soon. There's no need to be thinking about home invasions. Stay calm. Do you understand?'

'Not really.'

'What don't you understand, darling?'

'How you reckon you can still nag us from over the phone.'

Silence.

'What time did your father go out? Did he tell you why?'

'Dunno.'

'Did he say when he'd be back?'

'Nuh.'

'You just hold tight, Jordy.'

'Whatever.'

'I'll call back. I love you.'

Nina leaned against the cupboards as she felt her knees give way. Her face was instantaneously hot and her scalp was tingling with perspiration. She stabbed at the phone with rubbery fingers. Brad's number rang and rang, and was finally picked up. She heard a brief muffled greeting, and the phone went dead. She gasped—a short intake of breath so intense that surely the walls of the van would crumple and implode. Before she could exhale, she was dialling again.

'The mobile phone you are ringing is either out of range or switched off.'

'Oh my God. Oh my . . .' Nina dialled Jordan's number.

'Jordy, it's Mum.'

'Who?'

'THIS ISN'T FUNNY, JORDAN! Have you got Grandma Brown's phone number? And Baba Kostiuk's?'

'Why? What's wrong?'

'Nothing. Everything's fine. But if you need them, you know they are always there and . . .'

Nina could hear the line breaking up. Jordan's voice washed in and out on a gravelly tide.

'Mum? Mu—'

'Jordy? Jordy?'

The phone line spluttered, expired and that was the end of it. For the next half-hour Nina stood outside in the wind—under the banksia tree to the south, knee-deep in bracken to the north, east and west—holding the phone high and low. All was silent. There was no reception. She was six hundred kilometres from home—supposedly beyond all care and responsibility—but now reduced to a simple and terrifying helplessness.

She managed to at least get the van's lights and hot water going. Maybe she would be doing all these things without Brad from now on . . . now that he'd abandoned his family. When Meredith and Annie returned from the beach, they found her curled in a ball on the bed, bawling like a baby.

'So Brad's gone out—' Annie tried to make sense of it one more time—'and left the boys in the house by themselves?'

Nina snivelled and nodded her head.

'And you don't know how long for?'

Nina snorted into a tissue and shook her head.

Meredith slumped back into a seat with relief. 'So he's gone down the road to pick up a pizza for three grown boys who are apparently watching television and having a shower, and that's enough to reduce you to a blubbering basket case?'

'I can't get through.' Nina threw her mobile phone on the floor. 'Piece of shit!' She was immediately down on her knees, scrabbling under the table for the battery that had come loose.

Annie took her by the arm and hauled her to her feet. 'Look at yourself, Nina! This is . . . what can we say that hasn't already been said? They—will—be—fine.'

An hour later—after Nina had been more or less tranquillised with a plate of grilled chicken, a rocket-and-parmesan salad and two glasses of red—Meredith tackled her again. 'This isn't just about Brad and the boys, Nina. It's about *you*. Your constant fussing . . .'

'I do it all the time. I can hear all the crap coming out of my mouth, and I hate myself. I'm sorry.' And with that the tears sluiced down the spillway of her pink cheeks again.

Meredith shoved more tissues into Nina's outstretched hand. 'Now, don't carry on like this,' she said crisply. 'Being a nag's hardly the worst crime on earth.'

'What about being a fat, middle-aged pain-in-the-arse who can barely hold a conversation because she's been in front of her kitchen sink for fifteen years?' Nina's bosom heaved under her faded T-shirt.

Meredith looked at Annie with wide blue eyes. She didn't have a clue how to handle this abysmal level of self-hatred.

'Come on now, honey,' Annie crooned, 'we've come this far together and we're going all the way. What's this about? And I'm not just talking about ringing Brad or the kids to say goodnight. What's it really about?'

Nina kept her head down and honked loudly into her tissue, startling Meredith, who almost fell off her seat. 'I think Brad wants to leave me . . .' Nina whispered.

Annie and Meredith put their heads in their hands and groaned. Apparently Nina was worried about—in no particular order—being fat, stupid, old, a bad mother and, now, being dumped by her husband. What else could she possibly add to her list of woes?

'. . . and I'll bet he wants to take the dog.'

The moon was high when Annie stepped from the RoadMaster onto wet grass. She still couldn't bring herself to use the inside toilet. A stiff wind blowing in from the Tasman Sea tore the door from her hands and bashed it on the side of the van. She quickly secured it against marauding midnight pests.

She hesitated for a moment, adjusting her sight to the silvery threads of light woven through the banksia trees, and then saw that what she had thought to be tall clumps of grass were moving. She was standing in the midst of a mob of grazing kangaroos. They stopped for a moment, sensing her presence, and then bent their heads, intent on feeding.

Annie squatted, the blades of grass tickling the inside of her naked thighs. She looked to the heaving black sea. Luminous lashes fringed every wave, winking in the moonlight before crashing onto the shore and exploding with energy. How different it all was to the muddy, blank surface of the dam in the bottom paddock at the farm—that evil, unblinking eye that followed her everywhere. No matter how far she roamed.

Annie stood and pulled up her cotton pyjama pants. Her thoughts turned to Matty and she wondered if by any chance he could be standing on a beach close by, surrounded by kangaroos with fat pouches, looking at this very same moon, at this procession of black and silver waves and thinking of her. She had to find him and ask.

Dawn heralded an autumn day of still perfection. Nina tumbled down the stairs, mobile phone in hand, and saw she still had no reception. Not that it mattered. Who could she call at this hour? She dared not wake the girls after yesterday morning's effort. There was nothing to do but go for a walk . . . maybe a swim. She exchanged her phone for a towel and headed down the path through the dunes for the beach.

Nina chose a formation of yellow and pink sandstone rocks to aim for and padded across the sand. The sun was over the water now, blindingly bright and already warm on her skin. She knew she had to beat the urge to run back home and keep pushing onwards. Turning over last night's events in her head, she was sorry for herself. Sorry for immediately doubting Brad. Sorry for panicking Jordy. Sorry for losing it so badly.

Meredith was right. Looking at it logically, Brad had probably just gone out for a moment. Jordan had sounded fine and he was a responsible kid, even if he couldn't make his own bed or his breakfast. That was her fault. At sixteen she was crawling out her bedroom window with a bag stuffed with a tiny skirt and high-heeled boots to catch the tram into town, and getting in to see rock bands with a fake ID. Apparently she'd raised a kid who didn't even know how to use a toaster. The twins would manage. They always did. In truth, it seemed they'd hardly needed her since they could walk.

Nina reached the rocks and stripped down to her frayed floral one-piece. It had been a long time since she'd swum in the sea. For years she had covered herself with big shirts and hidden under the umbrella, watching Brad and the boys beyond the breakers, longing to be out there too. She always pleaded that she was scared of the water but it was the thought of the near-naked parade past the people sitting on the sand that truly terrified her.

This morning there was no-one to laugh at her dimpled thighs and plump bottom, and she ran—actually *ran*—across the sand and dived into the chilly frothing surf. No small hand to hold. No-one to watch out for. No-one to see her.

The water was cold and clear. Her body felt as light as a slice of peach floating in a glass of champagne. She dived to the sandy bottom and found a shell, grasped it and bobbed to the surface on a breath. She held it aloft and was—for one golden, fleeting moment—Botticelli's Venus, blown by the zephyrs of passion and attended by a goddess of the seasons. She twirled in the water just in time to see a huge wave bearing down on her. It whacked her across the side of the head, filling her ear with sand.

Nina stopped at the brick toilet block just up from the beach to rinse her feet under the tap. She was hopping on one foot and slapping the side of her head to get the sea water and grit out of her ear when that bloke from yesterday—did he say his name was *Matty*, or *Marty*?—came sauntering around the side of the building with a towel wrapped around his waist. Nina lunged for her sarong and clutched it to her body. She fancied he'd seen her pudgy stomach and had looked away in disgust.

'G'day again! Matty,' he said cheerily. 'Great spot! Nina, isn't it?'

'Yes. Hello. Hi,' said Nina as she scraped ropes of sodden hair from her face.

'How's your partner, Meredith, enjoying it all?'

Nina was flustered. He'd remembered their names—and the fact that they were supposed to be a couple. It was all highly embarrassing. Matty undid his towel to reveal red board shorts and began drying his bare, tanned, muscled chest in front of her. He did this so casually, so unselfconsciously, it was as though he and Nina shared a bathroom all the time. And—the thought flickered across her mind—that wouldn't have been an altogether bad thing. He really was a good-looking man.

'We're having a wonderful time, thank you. It really is so beautiful here.'

'Did you meet up with your convoy?' he asked, shaking his wet hair like a golden labrador. A shower of sea spray flew in a shimmering arc in the morning sun.

Nina was mesmerised. 'Pardon?'

'You said you had some other vans joining you. But I can't see 'em. Have they left already?'

'Oh! Oh yes, they headed off earlier,' Nina lied. 'We'll be meeting them a bit further up the coast.'

'In the Murramarang National Park?' Matty was now towelling his legs with long, languid strokes.

Nina couldn't help staring. 'Uh-huh.'

'We're heading that way. To the campground at Pretty Beach. Maybe we can all get together and have a drink at sunset.' He slung his towel across his shoulder and beamed at Nina.

'A drink? That would be ... great ... lovely. Meredith and I ...' Nina couldn't believe how absurd this sounded, 'we'll look forward to it.'

Nina thought that, even if she were a lesbian, Meredith would be about the last woman on earth she'd choose as a partner. She was way too bony. If she was going to take a female lover, she'd at least want her to have a bit of meat on her. Nina's eyes widened—she couldn't believe where this line of reasoning was taking her.

'Well, have a good one. See you tonight.' Matty turned and sauntered off, ducking a low-hanging branch. Nina watched him go for a long moment, appreciating the curve of his shoulders, and then hared off in the other direction, her sarong flapping against her wet white legs.

'There's no way we'll be watching the sunset with those two idiots,' Meredith said, tucking her hair into her towelling turban before attacking her grapefruit segments with a sleek teaspoon imported from Finland. 'And don't tell Annie when she wakes up. If she sees them again, I know what'll happen. She'll be off having sex with one of them in the sand dunes before we know it ... if she hasn't already. We have to save her from herself.'

Nina reached across the picnic table for a slice of toast and then stopped. A swim in the sea and a grapefruit for breakfast would start her day in the way she meant it to continue. She sliced the fruit, put a piece in her mouth and grimaced at its sourness. How anyone could eat this stuff unless it was covered in sugar . . .

'Actually, he seems lovely,' she ventured. 'He remembered our names . . . and the fact that we were a couple.'

'That's hardly a fact! No offence, Nina, but if I was a lesbian I wouldn't be choosing a partner who'd nag me to death.'

'Meredith!'

'Sorry.' Meredith poured herself an orange juice. 'But there is one fact, and that's that Annie doesn't know what's good for her. She should find a nice fellow and settle down. There are oodles of good men around. She's way too picky, that's Annie's problem.'

The screen door banged open. 'What's my problem?' Annie stood at the top of the stairs in a rumpled singlet and a fetching pair of cotton pyjama pants splashed with sunflowers. She scratched at her enviably flat tummy, smoothed her curls and blinked against the sharp light of morning.

'You sleep too much,' said Meredith airily, not skipping a beat. 'You're missing the best part of the day. Come and have some breakfast.'

'I think I might go for a swim first. It's stinking hot in this van. I reckon a dive in the surf will wake me up.'

'Wait a minute,' said Meredith quickly. 'I've just squeezed some orange juice. Have it while it's still cold.' She had one ear out, listening for the sound of a four-wheel drive leaving the camping grounds, but heard nothing.

'And have a grapefruit while it's still . . . er . . . fresh,' Nina stuttered. Meredith raised her eyebrows. Of all the people she could have had as an accomplice!

Annie hesitated, shrugged. 'OK then. Hang on, I'll just get my sunnies.'

When she had ducked back inside, Nina leaned across the table and hissed: 'This is awful. It's like we're the ugly stepsisters or something, trying to hide Cinderella.'

'That would only be true if that yob was Prince Charming. Which he's not. And if we were ugly. Which you might imagine you are, but I am *definitely* not.' Meredith thrust a cup at Nina. 'Now, pour the tea and shut up!'

Just then they heard the revving of a motor and a skidding on gravel. Meredith smiled triumphantly—the coast was clear. Annie stomped down the metal steps even before the cloud of grey dust billowing from the distant parking bay had settled.

'This is bloody annoying! I still can't find my good sunglasses. My Gucci ones. They cost me two hundred and ninety bucks.'

'You paid two hundred and ninety dollars for a pair of sunglasses?' Nina couldn't believe it.

'Pu-leeze, Nina! You can easily pay twice that much for a decent pair. I got them on sale,' said Annie irritably. 'I brought a couple of other pairs with me, but those ones are my faves. I hope I haven't lost 'em. God, I can't believe it's so warm already.'

'Why don't you go for a nice swim then?' suggested Nina.

Meredith kicked her shin under the table. Nina ducked her head, pushed her grapefruit aside, took a slice of toast and helped herself to jam and butter.

Ten

Annie was entranced with the tiny twinned towns of Tilba Tilba and Central Tilba as they slowly made their way up the main street for a mid-morning stop. Tumbling down the hill on either side were quaint wooden buildings, all with corrugated-iron roofs, painted wood spires and deep, shady verandas. The settlement couldn't have been more of a contrast to the string of flat, sunburnt coastal towns they'd just motored through.

It was dairy country, and that made Annie feel at home. Maybe she'd settle here. There were farms back up in the foothills that had a view of the sea. There were plenty of cafés and restaurants catering for the tourist trade, and a collection of art galleries and shops selling jewellery and hand-made clothes supplied by a tribe of local artisans. The bakery, lolly shop, general store and cheese factory reminded Annie of Tongala when she was a kid—back in the days when those shops were necessities, not just tourist traps.

The only blight on the delightful heritage streetscape was the RoadMaster Royale itself, which was bigger than some of the humble cottages they cruised past. It was as if an alien spacecraft had landed in Bag End, Hobbiton, Middle Earth. Meredith couldn't take her eyes from the rear-vision mirror, and cringed when she saw the patrons standing on the historic balcony of the Dromedary Hotel hoot and point at the Confederate flag painted on the arse of the vehicle.

For her part, Nina was feeling just fine. She'd retrieved a voice message from Brad from her phone at a servo some way back down the road: 'Hi, babe. Been trying to call you. Anyway, hope you're having a great time. The boys got off to Canberra OK. Anton couldn't find his cap, but I rang and Mrs Bogle's bringing a spare one from school. Um . . . the dog got out but Jordy caught him in next door's. Er . . . I'm really flat-out at meetings all day at the club, so you might not be able to catch me. I'll try again later. Love you. Miss you. Bye.'

One message from Brad and all was now well in Nina's world. However, she reminded herself, this trip couldn't just be about absent husbands, sons and fathers—past, present or future. She must remember to mention that to the others. It was about female friends being 'in the moment', offering each other '*a wise counsel and a trusting and deep constancy*'. That's what the article in the magazine had said. Was that happening yet? Were they having fun? Bonding, getting to know each other at a deeper level? Nina wasn't sure, but by the time they got to Byron she would make it happen.

Nina had spent years organising birthday parties, Christmas dinners, New Year barbecues for the family, school fetes, charity luncheons. She knew that you had to pay attention to the details—the food, drink, lighting, car parking, right down to having enough toilet paper and hand towels in the bathroom. It was all about 'stage managing' the occasion. If you did it right, everyone could relax and they'd all be having a great time before they knew it. Nina had observed this many, many times as she was up to her elbows in dishwashing water in the kitchen.

Anyway, Brad seemed to be managing at home, Nina reassured herself. She was looking forward to celebrating with a leisurely trawl through the shops and icing it all with a cake from the Tilba Bakery—a pretty vanilla slice of a building, which held a lot of calorific promise. And, Nina reasoned, she deserved a treat after the stress of last night.

Meredith insisted that they park out of the way in a side street. 'Imagine all these people coming to visit this National Trust heritage town, and all they can see is Elvis at Caesar's Palace?'

Nina urged the aluminium eyesore up a steep lane and edged it into a parking place. The effort brought her out in a sweat. Soon enough, however, the three of them were wandering in and out of the shops, Nina and Annie chattering like a pair of rainbow lorikeets: 'Oh, look at that, isn't that *gorgeous*?' 'What do you think—does this suit me?' 'You *have* to see this—it's *so* you.'

Meredith's expert eye dismissed most of the stuff she saw. Nanna-ware, she called it. She sniffed with disdain at gumnut earrings, padded coathangers and lavender sachets. 'Horrid. Awful. Junk. Most nannas I know would rather have white goods, thank you very much.' She picked up a wooden spice rack decorated with painted daisies and couldn't imagine anyone finding the time to paint such a godawful thing, and then anyone paying good money for it. Except perhaps the tubby woman in the stretch-knit slacks and Akubra hat, handing over her credit card for the matching egg cups.

Nina and Annie ignored Meredith's acerbic commentary and headed for a pile of vintage embroidered tablecloths. Annie inspected them and found the needlework to be nowhere near as fine as Nan Bailey's. She checked the price tags and had a new respect for her mother's glory box stuffed with embroidered fancies. If Annie could convince her mother to let her put them on eBay, the profits could easily fund a new water tank. She must remember to mention that when she called home. A wire stand crammed with real estate brochures next caught Annie's eye. There was a property, just for her, on page thirty—five acres, organic orchard, goat proof, chicken secure, creek water, vegie garden: $310,000. She was already hanging a hand-painted sign reading 'Annie's Farm' above the wooden gate.

Nina flipped through a clothes rack with a practised eye and found a navy-blue hemp shirt for Brad. But what could she buy for the boys? If it wasn't made out of plastic, or couldn't be ordered online, she knew they'd turn up their noses. She tracked down some fossilised mosquitoes inside chunks of amber. The thought that these 120-million-year-old insects from the Cretacean Age could one day be revived by scientists to suck human blood should give three teenage boys at least ten minutes of entertainment.

Nina was doing what she did best. She was a gatherer, trotting purposefully up the sun-dappled street with her woven dillybag over her shoulder. She had to notice, however, that hers wasn't the only tribe of women on the block. Everywhere she looked there was another group with their heads bent over a felt scarf or a pair of earrings. Nina looked on as four women shrieked with laughter at the fifth, emerging from a changing booth in a ghastly crimson goat-hair coat. They seemed to be having a better time than she was having with Annie and Meredith. Maybe she had 'friend envy'. Had Dr Phil ever done a show about that, she wondered?

Annie perused more real estate agents' windows in the main street. The tiny farm she wanted to buy was a poor cousin to some of the properties available: 'Only minutes from the pristine beaches of Mystery Bay, five hours south of Sydney, three hours east of Canberra'. She smiled to think that being three hours to the nation's capital could be a selling point. How far was Tilba from 'Bailey's Flat' at Tongala? She reckoned it to be about six hundred k's as the crow flies—a solid day's driving. This was the first roadblock in her path to freedom. She had no brothers or sisters and knew that one day everything would fall to her. With her father not well and the farm on hard times, that day could come sooner than she liked to think. Her hand-painted sign, threaded with ivy, creaked and crashed into the dust. Annie walked into the next shop and bought a handcrafted glass fruit bowl for her apartment back in Melbourne.

After an hour or so of shopping, Nina and Annie were done. They were now toting biodegradable eco-bags jammed with jars of preserved Burdekin plums, lemon myrtle tea sachets, packets of ground quandongs and tubs of mango moisturiser, macadamia-seed facial scrub and ti-tree-honey lip balm. Nina had found a hand-carved red-cedar spoon-rest she thought Wanda might appreciate, and had it gift-wrapped so Meredith wouldn't spot it.

Just as Annie and Nina thought Meredith might as well have been wandering the aisles of Target back in Melbourne, they heard her swoon: 'This is magnificent! Stunning!' They found her standing transfixed in front of an oil painting of a shimmering watery scene. A woman floated on her back, silvery hair spreading like jellyfish tendrils.

Everyone agreed that it was indeed 'magnificent', and would make a perfect wedding present for Sigrid. Meredith was convinced to have it when the gallery owner informed her it had been painted by a local artist from the hills back up behind Tilba, a 'rising star' who had recently been included in an exhibition in New York. Nina duly handed over a cheque for the artwork and it was bubble-wrapped with infinite care. It was only some way down the street that Meredith realised what she'd acquired . . . Another bloody mermaid.

✴

They were sitting at an outdoor table at Foxglove Spires under the vines—the van now parked across the road and stowed with their shopping—enjoying a coffee and a chocolate florentine after their organic pumpkin soup and ploughman's platter, when

Nina spluttered and showered the table with half-chewed biscuit. She stabbed her finger in the direction of the next table, where an elderly chap in a tweed cap was reading the *Daily Telegraph*. The front-page headline read: 'CORINNE BONED!' Underneath was a picture of the one and only Corinne Jacobsen, climbing into the driver's seat of her silver Mercedes Sports. She looked distressed, in a fetchingly tabloid way. Her eyes were hidden by huge dark glasses, her mouth was a glossy petulant pout and one shapely leg ending in a patent stiletto was revealed from the folds of a slim black trench coat.

'Shit!' Annie exclaimed so loudly that the gentleman gave her a withering look, stood and—after collecting his startled good lady wife, plus their wisteria shrub and pottery platypus— left. The newspaper was abandoned on the table.

Annie pounced. 'Fuck! They've sacked her!'

'Ner, ark!' Nina coughed and gagged again. A raisin had gone down the wrong way.

'I know, unbelievable! Listen: "After fifteen years fronting Channel 5's *Daylight*, television's veteran hostess Corinne Jacobsen has been axed."'

'*Veteran*? She'll hate that!' Meredith chirped happily.

Annie shooshed her and kept reading: '"Insiders say she is set to be replaced by her younger rival, popular newsreader Candice Byrne. Channel 5 boss Desmond Hyde confirmed last night that he was seeking a 'fresh direction' for *Daylight*, which has been struggling in the ratings. He denied Jacobsen had been 'axed', but said the network would not be renewing her contract. The normally chatty Jacobsen was tight-lipped as she left the set of the show yesterday morning, but friends say she is 'gutted' by the decision."'

'That's awful!' Nina had finally regained the power of speech. 'I mean, how old is she—forty-eight, forty-nine?'

'She'll be forty-seven next month! *Fresh direction*? It's bullshit! You see these blokes on TV who look a hundred years old. Double chins, nose hair, bald, eye bags—and everyone says they're "distinguished". Corinne still looks amazing. And she's a great interviewer as well . . .'

Meredith, however, wasn't buying it. 'Honestly, it's not that hard to get a reality show contestant to blab on . . . or some vacuous supermodel to prattle about her new skin-care range. And correct me if I'm wrong, but Corinne's played the game for years, hasn't she? With the Botox-brow, the collagen fish-lips. It's finally caught up with her.' She sat back and crossed her arms with satisfaction.

'Like it catches up with most women in the media in this country, Meredith,' Annie said tersely. 'Corinne battled hard to get where she is. Show a bit of solidarity—you used to be good at that.' Annie threw the newspaper on the table. 'Let's go! I'll get this one and meet you out front.'

Nina rushed to sandbag the horrifying silence. 'Poor Corinne! She'll be feeling awful. We really should go and see her in Sydney. We'll be there tomorrow night.'

Meredith grabbed her purse. 'I don't know why we'd bother. She's probably jetting to the Bahamas as we speak.'

Nina busied herself with gathering her handbag. She hated confrontation, but was determined to go on with it. 'You know,

Meredith, sometimes you can be so . . .' She searched her mind for the word—*bitchy? mean? callous? unfeeling? unsympathetic?*—and finally settled on the term that would cause the least offence: '*strong-minded.*'

'And that's a bad thing?' Meredith challenged.

Nina wanted to say yes, it was a bad thing. That it was no wonder that Sigrid had escaped as soon as she could, and never rang her mother. That it was perfectly understandable that Jarvis had moved a hemisphere away from her critical eye, and that Donald had probably taken up with another woman for exactly the same reason. If Meredith had been sitting in the hot seat on *Dr Phil*, they could have all lined up and told her. Dr Phil would probably have said something like: 'Y'all have legitimate concerns with this lady's behaviour as a wife, mother and friend. There's prob'ly been only one perfect child on the face of the earth and that was the baby Jesus. He grew up to "confound the elders". Meredith, what makes you so confounded certain about every darned thing?' But Nina wasn't Dr Phil.

'Well, only in that it can be hard for the rest of us,' she cautiously replied.

Meredith had heard this criticism before. 'Am I supposed to unlearn everything I know, not be who I am, not tell the truth, so that everyone around me can "keep up"?'

Before Nina could find the courage to answer, Meredith stalked off around the side of the restaurant towards the main road.

Annie was standing at the cash register, still tapping her foot furiously, when she powered her BlackBerry. There were eighty emails demanding her attention. Quickly scrolling down the screen she saw that they were mostly work related. One from a dreary country cousin who'd hit Melbourne and was looking for her; one from a boutique owner telling her the coat she'd ordered was in; a couple from male drinking buddies .at the conference. As she suspected, her social life wasn't exactly in full swing.

She tried Corinne's number. It was, not surprisingly, switched off. She left a message. 'Hi, honey, it's Annie from Melbourne. I am *so* sorry. I can't believe those bastards! I'm going to be in Sydney tomorrow night. In a bloody campervan, would you believe?! Don't ask. Long story. Call me and we can catch up.'

She bent to collect her bag and then, out of the corner of her eye, saw the silhouette of a Toyota LandCruiser towing a tinnie drive past the front window. She knew parts of that outboard motor intimately. She fell out the front door onto the street. 'Quick, quick! Get the keys! Let's go!'

Meredith and Nina, standing by the kerb, had already spotted the procession. In fact, Zoran had leaned out the window and waved 'G'day', and Nina had enthusiastically waved back until Meredith grabbed her arm. As the tail-lights of the trailer disappeared over a rise in the road, Meredith stalled: 'We're going already? I was thinking of having another wander around the nursery.'

'But I just saw them—those two blokes from Lakes Entrance. Didn't you say they were looking for me?' Annie tried to remain calm. She could hardly run up the street after them, screeching like some demented banshee. And, in truth, she didn't know what she would say if she caught up with them. 'Maybe they've found my sunglasses . . . my good ones . . . they cost me—'

'We know,' Nina interrupted. She couldn't stand the suspense. Why had Matty asked after Annie? Maybe he'd found her sunglasses, or maybe she'd been cast in a fairytale romance and this was true love. If this was a fairytale, Nina was the huntsman who had been ordered to take Snow White into the forest and couldn't find the heart to kill her. 'Come on,' she blurted. 'Let's go! Except . . .' she scrabbled in her handbag, 'I can't find the keys to the van.'

'They're in your hand,' Meredith pointed out. Nina jiggled the bunch of keys and took off across the road. The chase was on.

After they'd driven up and down the main street of Central Tilba three times, surveying the Dromedary Hotel car park and various side streets, Meredith finally called off the emu parade. 'They're not here. And let's face it, they're hardly likely to stop off for a string of handcrafted beads or a poster of the Dalai Lama,' she said as they drove past the Windhorse Buddhist Emporium . . . again.

As much as Annie didn't want to admit it, Meredith was right. The trail had gone cold. There was nothing for it but to push on. Her fate was fluttering in the breeze like the string of Tibetan prayer flags on the front veranda.

'Why don't we spend the night in the Murramarang National Park?' said Nina casually. She had to smile to herself. She'd kept this secret well. Little did Annie and Meredith know there was a surprise sunset cocktail party in the offing at . . . what was the name of that beach again?

Nina looked at her map and calculated they had roughly a hundred and twenty k's to drive. As soon as they cleared the town speed limits, she put the foot down.

✳

It was late afternoon by the time the van rocked down the Durras Discovery Trail into the Murramarang National Park. Meredith was really getting into the rhythm of life on the road now. It was simple. You parked, set up camp, ate, slept, woke, ate, took down camp, drove and . . . did it all again. She hadn't checked her mobile phone for three days and reassured herself that Caroline would cope with the store. She'd have to. Meredith had barely looked in a mirror, and was in the same outfit she'd worn yesterday. She could finally understand those women who took to the desert with a water bottle and a string of camels.

Annie had one eye out the window for the tail-lights of a trailer with a tinnie. It was a hopeless mission. There was a string of national parks up the coast to Sydney—they could be in any one of them. But then, she reasoned, she knew where Matty worked and could always call him back in Melbourne. Except she wanted to see him again with bare legs, his hair smelling of salt—not sitting behind a desk in a collar and tie. She remembered holiday romances from the past and the bare-chested boys she had watched swing from the riverbank on ropes hanging from the branches of peppercorn trees. They were mythical creatures—tanned, heroic—all worthy of endless romantic fantasies.

When she later saw them in the schoolyard in drab grey and navy blue uniform, clod-hopping shoes and hair slicked straight, it was as if they had fallen to earth. The spell had been broken.

Nina jammed on the brakes and everyone lurched forward. She peered at the map—Pebbly Beach, Pretty Beach, Merry Beach . . . For the life of her she couldn't remember which one was the venue for the surprise sunset cocktail party. Bugger! This was not like her—she had an almost photographic memory. It drove her family mad.

'I want to see the surfing kangaroos,' declared Annie, who had been reading the brochures again and become unofficial tour guide. 'They're at Pebbly Beach, so let's go there.'

Pebbly Beach? Hmm . . . that seemed to ring a bell with Nina.

'Surfing kangaroos? Surely not,' scoffed Meredith.

'That's what it says here,' Annie responded, shoving the brochure at her.

By late afternoon they were indeed marvelling at a mob of eastern grey roos grazing only metres from the shoreline at a wide and lovely beach. Only it didn't look like any of them were about to hit the surf any time soon. And it didn't look like Matty and Zoran would be joining them. The campground was full now and they weren't anywhere Nina could see. She was cursing herself. Maybe they were at Pretty Beach . . . or was it Merry? It was like trying to remember the names of the Seven Dwarves. Oh well, Nina sighed, Snow White would just have to wait a while longer for her prince.

After walking across the rocks and poking at various starfish and crabs in tidal pools, they returned to the van and set up camp. Meredith and Nina were both at the toilet block taking a shower and Annie was wrestling with the annexe when the phone call came from Corinne: 'Annie! You've called at exactly the right time! There's no-one in this whole Sydney rat's nest I trust anymore. I've got paparazzi camped outside the front door. I've had to take the phone off the hook. Malcolm's away in Europe. I'd love to see you. But you'll have to come here. No matter where I go, I'll be followed.'

The plan was simple. Nina would drive the RoadMaster to Corinne's place at Double Bay and go in the back gate; they would have dinner and park there for the night. 'I can't promise you much to eat. I can't seem to drag my sorry arse out of bed,' Corinne moaned.

Annie reassured her that the three of them would come and commandeer the kitchen. 'That'd be fab,' she sniffed. 'And it'll be good to see Nina . . . and Meredith. It's time we forgot about all that stuff in the past. Anyway, I need a bit of TLC from old friends. Maybe we can all get blind and sing a few gospel songs in honour of my demise.' Annie rang off and wondered how she'd break the news to Meredith.

After another five minutes of wrangling the stupid . . . fucking . . . ridiculous . . . annexe, Annie heard a nasty metallic snap and the ping of a bolt hitting aluminium. Now she would also have to break the news to Nina that she'd busted the annexe. Which one of her companions was going to be more pissed off with her was hard to gauge.

'There's no time to fix it before dark,' said Nina as, hands on hips, she surveyed the limp awning.

'A bolt snapped off. I heard it,' said Annie.

'Let's just roll the thing up for now and I'll ring Brad. This time I have to. We can't let it just hang there like that. I want to say goodnight to Jordy anyway.' Nina climbed in through the passenger door, found her phone and dialled.

'Hello?' The voice on the other end of the phone was young, tentative . . . and female. Nina heard a brief muffled conversation.

'Hello? Brad? Are you there?' she asked. The call was terminated.

Nina stared at her phone. She must have dialled the wrong number. She tried again. No answer. This did not make sense. She immediately dialled Jordan's number: 'Hello, Jordy, it's Mum.'

'Yep.'

'How are you, sweetie?'

'Fine.'

'Is Dad there?'

'He's gone away.'

'What? Where's he gone?'

'I dunno. Some chick was at our place crying. Dad went out with her.'

'What "chick"? Where'd he go? You're not making sense, Jordan.'

'I told you, I dunno. Talk to Baba Kostiuk.'

'She's there? What's she doing there?'

'Hello? Nina?'

'Mum . . . what are you doing there? Where's Brad?'

'Ah, Nina, you call at last. Brad had to go away for few days.'

'A few days?' Nina's voice had risen in her throat. It was the strangled squeak of a cartoon mouse.

'That's right. I have come here to be with Jordy. I will sleep in Anton's bed. You having a good time away from your family?'

Nina groped for some logic in her mother's words and, after speaking with Wanda for another five minutes, found none. A screech of frustration and a kicking of cupboard doors surprised Meredith and Annie, who were standing on the grass catching their breath after their exhausting grapple with the annexe. They were inside in an instant.

The next hour was spent in intense interrogation around the table, as if Nina was in a police interview room.

'You could have dialled a wrong number,' said Meredith. 'It could have been any woman who picked up his mobile from a table somewhere.'

Nina was unconvinced. 'But what was he doing out the other night, leaving the boys by themselves? And Jordan said there was some girl at the house . . . crying. He left with her and now he's away for . . . days . . .' The thought of it sent her scrabbling for a tissue.

'Has it occurred to you that the two facts might not even be related?' Annie was doing her best CSI impersonation. 'The girl at your place could have been some kid from down the street who fell off her bike. And, like Meredith said, the woman on the phone could have been . . . anyone. You're mounting this case against him without any real evidence, as far as I can see.'

With a lack of facts to be going on with, and the liberal application of spinach gnocchi whipped up by Meredith, Nina was finally coaxed off her windswept ledge. When the second bottle of chardonnay was opened, the cross-examination resumed. There were no grounds that anyone could discover for Nina's assumption that her husband was having an affair—no unexplained absences, no change in his personal habits, no odd phone calls. As Nina told it, their marriage was right on schedule on the same old track.

And then Annie put the big one on the table: 'How's your sex life?'

Nina paused, whimpered and wiped her nose. 'Well, you know. Fine. For people who have been married as long as we have and have three teenage boys in the house.'

'What does that mean?' asked Annie.

'That Brad's always up for it. But I'm so tired from everything, and it's hard to find time. And the boys' rooms are right next door, so . . .'

'So what?' Again, Annie didn't get it.

'They'd think we were gross! If Brad even kisses me in front of them, they pull faces.' Nina mimed hurling into the cheese platter Meredith had slid in front of her. 'If they heard us actually having sex? Erk. Boys! Maybe it would have been easier if we'd had girls.'

'Don't kid yourself!' Meredith snorted. 'If I'd had even the slightest notion that Edith and Bernie were going at it on the Axminster carpet, I would have killed myself. In fact, even thinking about it now makes me feel nauseous. Count yourself lucky you didn't have girls.'

'Everyone says that,' Nina replied.

'Everyone's right.' Meredith picked at a piece of camembert. 'I can talk to Jarvis about everything—I always could. But Sigrid? She's a mystery to me. I think she resented me going out to work. She never wanted to talk about herself—who she was with, what she was doing. And at twenty-two she was gone. Moved to Byron.'

Annie pushed the tissue box closer to Meredith's side of the table. This was threatening to be a soggy tennis match.

'I've only had the odd phone call and email since. Now she's getting married, and I've never even met the man . . .'

'Let's get back to Brad,' Annie intervened. She couldn't cope if the two women started weeping in unison. 'The only fact we have in front of us is that Nina has a husband who loves her and his family very much. He's hardly likely to be having an affair and bringing his mother-in-law in to cover for him! It must be some work thing, or something happening with his family maybe?'

'I've rung his mother. She hasn't heard from him,' Nina said, her head drooping into her hands.

Annie sighed; she was exhausted with it all too. 'We'll have to give him the benefit of the doubt, that's all.'

Meredith tore a tissue from the box, wiped her eyes and nodded. She was glad no-one wanted to linger on her own disappointments with Sigrid. She couldn't quite believe she'd brought up the topic.

They said their goodnights. Reading lights behind drawn curtains cast a blue glow through the cabin. As Nina assembled her bed she reflected that, if she had been in East Malvern right now, she would be standing by the foot of the stairs thinking about school lunches, sports gear, permission notes and pocket money. She would have been preoccupied, with no time to think about where her life was heading. And maybe that was a good thing.

When she climbed into bed with Brad, her mind would still be whirring with tomorrow's impossible timetable. He would sneak his hand onto her thigh, wanting sex, and she would brush him away, knowing the revulsion he must feel at touching her fat white Bratwurst legs.

'I'm tired, Brad. I've got so much on tomorrow.'

And he—dutiful father, loving husband—would kiss her cheek and roll over to sleep without protest. She loved him so much for his quiet acceptance of how things were with her. As he snored, she would look at his tightly muscled back and the long curve to his still-slim waist, and know that there would, inevitably, come a time when she couldn't refuse her husband anymore. And that time would only come because he would stop asking.

Now, as she climbed into bed and ran her hands across her flabby stretchmarked stomach, she knew she was in a land of regret way beyond the sweet and comforting balm of chocolate.

Eleven

Ulladulla, Nowra, Wollongong . . . almost three hundred k's up the Princes Highway and the RoadMaster Royale did not falter as it sped its precious cargo towards Sydney Town. Nina had the measure of the machine now—she merged like a maestro, changed gear, indicated, sped up and slowed down with a smooth and confident grace. She was grateful for the cylinders, valves and pistons that were acting in concert to produce such a seamless performance. She glanced down to admire her strong forearms conducting the vehicle with such skill.

By the time they reached Sydney's southern suburbs, Nina was weaving through the stream of traffic, imagining every car was a note on a musical score and she was conducting a big band—anything to stop herself thinking about home. She'd tried to ring Brad during the day and couldn't raise him. The last person on earth she would call was her mother. She knew that Wanda would put her through the mother of all interrogations with one aim in mind—to bully her into returning home. As confusing as things might be right now, Nina had no intention of taking that particular guilt trip back to Melbourne.

The three women were now, they reminded themselves, a long way from hearth and history, traversing places they had never visited before. And all of them, they reminded each other, were lucky to be women a long way from home.

When Annie had travelled to Paris in her twenties, it was the first time a Tongala Bailey had been to France since her great-grandfather had fought at Pozières in World War I. He had returned from that slaughterhouse to take up a Soldier's Settlement farm in Tongala in the 'Golden Square Mile'—the richest patch of farming land in Australia. And there he, and all the Bailey sons after him, had stayed. But they had not rested. They remained ever-vigilant, tight-lipped and upstanding against the spectre of the Dogs of War that might rise up and ravage the peaceful plains at any time. Photographs of relatives in uniform and medals in glass cases were propped above the Murray River pine mantelpiece in the drawing room. The Baileys were a cautious and frugal tribe and remained suspicious of the outside world. Annie was seen off to Europe with money and malaria pills, insurance, clean undies and her mother's tears ironed into cotton hankies. When she wrote home, she was careful not to mention that she had shared a bunk in a backpackers' hostel with a German boy.

As soon as she was able, Meredith had escaped the cotton-wool confines of the tidy, affluent suburb of Camberwell where she had grown up. She'd taken a perverse pleasure in sending

Bernard and Edith postcards from the most exotic locations she toured—Kathmandu, Istanbul, Casablanca—knowing that Edith would sluice an extra bucket of Pine-O-Cleen over the kitchen floor and that Bernie would drop another note in the contributions plate at St Mark's to finance the Lord's protection of her. When Meredith contracted dysentery in Bombay, she was almost proud of herself. Couldn't wait to write. Her parents had probably incinerated the postcard for the sake of hygiene.

Nina was determined that one day she would visit the graves of her forebears. Her mother and father had both come to Australia as teenagers after World War II. Untold millions of Ukrainian men, including her grandfathers and six great-uncles, perished in that conflict. It was the women left behind who had rebuilt the country. Nina had heard many tales of her great-grandmothers selling roasted sunflower seeds and bunches of home-grown herbs outside the Lvov cemetery, to provide for themselves and their families.

This was the mantra of hard work and self-sacrifice she'd been raised on. Whenever she looked at another pile of football jumpers to be washed and felt like complaining, it was her Great-Baba Magdalyna offering a bunch of sage flowers she thought of, or her Great-Baba Glaphira warming her hands over a mean and spindly flame. Nina imagined them huddling in shawls against a winter wind that blasted the earthly names from the tombstones of a multitude of angels. And with that she would reach, with gratitude, for the fabric softener.

✵

'We'll be in the middle of Sydney in an hour, but we still haven't decided where we'll stay tonight.' Meredith was getting antsy now. There was a deeply troubling blank in her travel diary.

'In Corinne's backyard in Double Bay,' Annie mentioned casually. She'd already told Nina, but had been avoiding giving Meredith the bad tidings.

Meredith took the news more calmly than they might have expected. 'Well, I suppose we'll be close to the shops in the morning,' was her only comment. She was prepared to countenance that Annie and Nina might be right, and that it was time to let go of the past with Corinne; but then, when she thought back to that night at the Athenaeum Theatre twenty years ago, the embers of humiliation glowed red hot.

It was to have been Sanctified Soul's 'big break'. Roscoe Fortune from Fortune and Associates—the most prestigious talent agency in the country—was coming to check out their act with a view to signing them. The gals were all excited about the possibilities. They hugged themselves and each other as they dreamed of tours to international arts festivals and a recording contract.

It might all have been a mirage, but Meredith sometimes checked the gig guides and saw that at least a couple of the *a cappella* choirs from those days were still together and had exactly the kind of career Sanctified Soul could have expected. While their little group may never have become world-famous, Meredith had spent years imagining how it might have been. She could have kept on performing—playing the odd gig here and there. She would not have sunk so much of her creative energy into interior design; she might have spent more time with the children. And if she'd done that, she would not be in this passenger seat right now, travelling north to a denouement she was dreading more and more with each passing traffic light.

Meredith's clients never really understood that she possessed the soul of an artist. Even as they admired the way she expertly coordinated their living spaces—creating a perfect stage on which they might perform—she knew they were thinking that they'd paid too much for something they could have done themselves. If only they'd had the time and energy.

Was it fair for Meredith to blame Corinne for the direction her life had taken? Probably not. But it had been a tipping point, and the tide of human history was often turned by one vain or stupid act. Corinne's behaviour was driven by a self-serving obsession Meredith still had trouble understanding.

Without Corinne, Sanctified Soul had lacked that one voice— that glorious, angelic, soaring top note—that raised them from the ranks of the mortal to a choir of heavenly angels. The most galling thing was that Corinne had known it and had campaigned to be given most of the solos. They had sung at Carols by Candlelight in the Domain one Christmas and Sanctified Soul, led by the tiny ethereal figure in the white satin pantsuit, complete with feathery halo, had been the stellar attraction.

'*There's a star in the East on Christmas morn*,' Corinne had sung, her voice ringing like a church bell across frozen fields.

'*Rise up, shepherd, and follow*,' they had replied in stirring, harmonious unison.

On that night at the Athenaeum when Corinne didn't show, Meredith had given herself the solo in 'Rain On Me'. One tiny uncivilised corner of her soul had hoped that she might eclipse Corinne and be noticed by Roscoe Fortune as the star on the top of the tree. They had taken their places on stage, without Corinne, and sung two numbers beautifully, until Meredith stepped forward for her solo in the light of the follow-spot:

'Showers of sadness cloud my soul.
When the sun comes out,
I look for the rainbow.
When night turns to day,
I long for—'

What? Meredith remembered the stark, horrifying moment as if it were yesterday. Was *yesterday* the word she was searching for? Or was it *today, another day, bygone days* or—Jesus help her—*hip, hip hooray?* She had faltered in that instant. Slowed, then stopped until the auditorium was silent and all she could hear was the rustling of scorched-almond packaging, and her heart, fluttering like one of the pigeons under the eaves. The performance had been a fiasco. The only thing that made it bearable was that Roscoe Fortune hadn't turned up either. Meredith had stopped to stuff her appalling purple gospel robe into a bin in Collins Street as she ran out of the theatre.

When she heard, barely a month later, that Corinne had moved to Sydney and was being represented by the very same Mr Fortune, she saw the whole scenario for what it was— professional sabotage. Corinne hadn't been in a life-threatening coma, nor was she actually dead, so she had no excuse that would mollify Meredith. And Meredith had never, ever, in all the years since, asked for an explanation from her. She didn't want to hear one, and it would be the same tonight.

✵

The likes of the RoadMaster Royale roadshow had rarely been seen in Double Bay. It wasn't so much the size of the unit that affronted the well-heeled inhabitants of postcode 2028—they were used to seeing giant cement mixers, cranes and pile-drivers in their winding, hilly streets. Anonymous Hong Kong bankers and home-loan moguls regularly hired massive mechanical hit-men to muscle in on a view of Sydney Harbour.

It wasn't that the tackiness of the paint job on the van particu-larly offended them either—Double Bay was Tacky Paint Job Central. If you ordered a coffee at a café in Cross Street, it would only be a matter of time before you spied a matron in a headscarf who was delusional enough to believe that, if she applied her Chanel make-up with a trowel, no-one would notice the three-day-old facelift scars weeping into the collar of her Valentino jacket.

However, what did give passers-by pause for thought was the sheer audacity of the driver who crawled around up and down Bay Street in the massive rig while a procession of luxury European cars stuck behind it honked their disapproval. After some time two women were observed jumping on board toting bags from Cosmopolitan Shoes, a glossy white cake box and a bunch of creamy tea-roses. By the time the interloper (the Victorian numberplates were the subject of much scathing comment) had moved off, there were at least three locals who were now running late to pick up their daughters from Piano, Ballet and Mandarin.

Bang on 6 pm, after casing the front of the house—a massive three-storey cream rendered pile surrounded by a high fence and screened by fig trees—Nina squeezed the vehicle up a skinny back lane. Annie was reminded of how she used to pull her stretch jeans over her hips with a coat hanger in the zipper. On either side of the lane faces appeared at sash windows. Some of them were the ladies of Double Bay—in towelling robes and hydrating face-packs, clutching the second or third gin and tonic of the evening and looking out for errant husbands—and some were nannies in peanut-butter-smeared tracksuits, clutching the fourth vodka of the evening and looking out for errant mothers. Then there was Corinne Jacobsen. She was in a black bra and panties, clutching a flute of champagne and training a pair of high-powered binoculars on the bougainvillea.

Annie jumped into the laneway and, as instructed, rang the bell on the back gate of Number Five. The intercom crackled with a voice that was suspiciously cheery.

'Annie, darling! You're here! Hang on—I'll be down in a minute.'

'She's coming down,' Annie announced through the driver's side window.

'I hope she's bringing a jar of Vaseline. We'll never make it through this gate.' Nina found herself, ridiculously, breathing in, as if that would help them squeeze through the gap.

'There's still time to go to a hotel. You can drop me off and come back here by yourselves,' huffed Meredith.

Ten minutes later and the RoadMaster was successfully manoeuvred between two stone gargoyles on either side of a wrought-iron gate. In another ten minutes an extension cord from the RoadMaster was running the length of a sandstone-paved courtyard and plugged into a socket in the pool cabana. Annie—juggling cake and roses—followed Corinne and was instantly swallowed by the vast glass-fronted entertaining area, which glowed like a human aquarium at the end of the garden.

Nina and Meredith had begged off to change shoes, tidy hair and apply lipstick. As Meredith exited the tiny bathroom in the van, Nina reached for her hand and gave it a tight squeeze. 'Please, Meredith, I am begging you. Can we just get through this without any drama?'

Meredith gave a tight, dry laugh. 'I can assure you I feel the same way you do. The sooner we're back in here, tucked up in our beds, the better.'

As they stepped from the van onto the mosaic patio, ragged black shadows swooped through the garden emitting high-pitched shrieks. Nina jumped in fright: 'My God! What was that?'

'Bats! Looking for the Queen of Darkness probably.' Meredith marched past the massive Balinese water feature towards the conflagration of dozens of blazing vanilla candles, and Nina hurried after her.

✵

'I can't believe you're here!' Corinne lunged at Nina, clutched her upper arms with bony fingers and kissed the air beside both her ears. 'How are you?' She cocked her head like a bright-eyed, blinking Indian mynah bird.

Before Nina could answer, Corinne rushed at Meredith and threw her tanned, sinewy arms around her midsection. 'And you too, Meredith. You look amazing! How long has it been?' The immediate response that came to Meredith's mind was *not long enough*, but Corinne had already moved on.

'And Annie . . . so that's four of us! We'll have to have a singalong later—*Jesus on the main line, tell 'im whachu wantttt*—' Corinne trilled as she turned to the travertine marble counter and splashed Perrier-Jouët champagne into two more flutes. She held them out to Nina and Meredith.

'Oh, this is amazing! And that thing you're travelling in on your hilarious expedition . . .' Corinne's mouth had formed a perfect puffed 'O', like a sugar-frosted Froot Loop. Meredith noted that her forehead was unmoved by the joyous occasion.

'It's a RoadMaster Royale,' said Annie.

'Five berth,' added Meredith.

'Four-cylinder, 2.2 litre Mercedes engine,' Nina stated.

'Well, here's to you and Mr Elvis Presley—*uh-huh*!' Corinne held up her glass and they all tinkled their hellos.

'So how's it been?' she asked and, again, before they could answer Corinne was on to her next thought: 'It must be *such* fun. Away from home, leaving all your troubles behind.' She grimaced and downed her drink in one gulp.

Meredith saw Corinne's hands shaking and raised her eyebrows at Annie. *Is this woman on something?* was the silent question.

Corinne poured herself another glass and turned to Nina, who was busy appraising the tiny size-8 figure that had been squeezed into a skimpy black-sequinned mini-dress. 'I see in the paper that Brad's still with the football club. How's he coping with all this latest crazy business?'

'Pardon?' said Nina. 'What "crazy business"?'

'You haven't heard? You really have been in the wilds, my darling! Haven't you been reading the papers?' Corinne rummaged through the pile of newsprint on the counter.

Nina was flustered and looked at Meredith and Annie, who both shrugged. They had no idea what Corinne was on about either.

'Here!' Corinne held up the back page of the previous day's *Daily Telegraph*—the very same paper that had featured her on the front. When they were sitting around the table at Foxglove Spires, none of them had thought to turn to the sports section.

'TABBY IN REHAB HIDEAWAY' screamed the headline. Nina snatched up the paper and scanned the story:

The Richmond Football Club is in damage control over the latest AFL drugs scandal. Team manager Brad Brown told the *Daily Telegraph* last night that Kyle 'Tabby' Hutchinson has entered a secret drug rehabilitation centre on the Gold Coast and is determined to work through his 'personal issues'.

On Monday Melbourne police formally charged the star Richmond midfielder with possession of a prohibited drug. He will appear in the Melbourne City Magistrates Court next week.

The Richmond Tigers issued a formal statement last night: 'The club is not in a position to make any comment regarding Kyle Hutchinson being questioned by police,' the statement said.

'The police have advised the club that they will detail the circumstances of the interviews at the appropriate time and until then no club official will be available to the media.'

However the *Tele* tracked down Brad 'Kingie' Brown and he confirmed that Hutchinson has checked into a drug rehabilitation facility 'on the Goldie'. Brown also said that both he and Tabby's fiancée, aspiring model Emma Pang, are with him at this secret location and that they were all united as he 'reviews some personal issues'. He declined to give any more details. The Tigers have now lowered the 'cone of silence' over the troubled star. All calls to team management have since gone unanswered.

Nina dropped the paper on the counter, snatched her champagne glass and fell back onto a stool next to the kitchen counter. Her beaded scuffs dropped to the floor. Annie grabbed the paper, and she and Meredith read the article with their heads together.

'I always told Brad that Tabby was going to be trouble!' Nina babbled. 'They've pinged him before on drug tests. I knew it was just a matter of time before the police found out.'

Meredith noticed that Corinne had suddenly engaged her intelligent little bird brain and was staring intently over her champagne as Nina prattled on: 'Brad's found coke, ecstasy in his locker. He's always been an accident waiting to happen.'

'Really?' Corinne took a casual sip of her drink and reached for an encouraging squeeze of Nina's hand. 'How awful! Why didn't anyone at the club say anything? Why didn't Brad report him to the police?' Corinne's line of questioning was way too forensic for Meredith's liking. Maybe the seasoned TV interviewer wasn't as out-of-it as she appeared. Time for a little diversion.

Meredith waltzed the length of the massive adjoining entertaining area. 'Corinne, I *adore* your feature wall!' She extravagantly praised the *lemon granita* 'velour' textured expanse, which soared a good two storeys to a glass canopy. The paint finish was *so* three years ago, and she couldn't miss the giant Warhol-esque portrait of Corinne above the white glass-tiled fireplace. Meredith had always thought that it was acceptable to hang one's ancestors in pride of place, but a picture of your own self—no matter how fabulous—was pushing the limits of good taste.

'And this portrait of you . . . !' As Meredith had guessed, her supplication at the shrine of Corinne proved to be irresistible.

'It's fun, isn't it?' Corinne was at her side in an instant.

'The whole place is brilliant!' Meredith surveyed the hand-painted silver orchids on white wallpaper, the mirrored chandelier the size of a Volkswagen, the black sculpted floor rugs . . . and thought that it all looked like an exclusive bordello—appropriate enough for a media whore like Corinne Jacobsen. She ladled on more compliments, and Corinne greedily lapped them up.

'We've just had it done. Malcolm brought the decorators over from Switzerland. They did our chalet in Gstaad and we adored it so much that we knew we just wouldn't find anyone in Australia who could do a better job.'

Meredith gritted her teeth. That was the first insult from Corinne, and she'd only been in the door ten minutes. No doubt there'd be plenty more to come. Meredith remembered that Corinne had been an expert at the sly put-down. She'd turned it into an art form.

'Meredith, you must go and have a look at the shoe sale in Georges, they've got all the big sizes left.'

'Meredith, would you like to borrow my lipstick? I know you have political issues with female frippery, but you look so washed out.'

The jibes always came in the guise of genuine concern, so there was no way she could reasonably complain.

'And are you still selling your kitchen utensils?' Insult number two. Meredith thought she might try to drink as much of Corinne's expensive champagne as was humanly possible.

☼

Nina bustled between the wooden butcher's block and the gleaming European appliances, and thought the word 'kitchen' was a crude term that didn't do the room justice. It was vast—as big as the entire downstairs of her house, she estimated. Shafts of light from the ceiling created a theatrical setting in which food was an afterthought. It was the same with the giant American brand-name fridge—as big as a shipping container and complete with rattling ice-maker and water dispenser. Nina had investigated and found precious little inside worth consuming. Luckily the van was groaning with supplies and she had the makings for cannelloni, garlic spinach and asparagus Milanese.

Wearing an apron had restored Nina's equilibrium almost as much as reading the story about Brad in the paper. She knew where her boys were now. Brad was on the Gold Coast, Jordy was with her mother, the twins wouldn't be home until Friday afternoon and . . . this was good champagne, possibly the nicest she'd ever tasted.

In between chopping onions and garlic and rinsing spinach leaves, Nina poured herself more bubbles. Annie was sitting at the stainless-steel dining table, listening to Corinne rehash the events leading up to her humiliating public sacking. Nina caught the odd filthy oath of revenge and saw Corinne's head drop on Annie's shoulder. There were tears. Nina chopped furiously, figuring that once dinner was in the oven she could catch up on the gossip.

For her part, Annie was smiling, nodding, making all the right sympathetic noises in all the right places, even though Corinne seemed oblivious to the fact that the names of most of the players in the drama were a mystery to her old friend. Annie caught herself wondering what she and Corinne really had in common anymore. They'd formed an alliance as members of Sanctified Soul, sharing a sneaky laugh about Meredith's sensible shoes. They'd both had rooms in that notorious share house in Collingwood for a while. But those times were long gone. Did Corinne just think of her as a comforting souvenir of the old days, not unlike the moth-eaten Strawberry Shortcake doll Annie had propped on a shelf in her bedroom back at the farm? She noted that Corinne hadn't asked after her parents, or indeed anything else about her life. The thought of this made Annie shift out of her reach.

Meredith had fled the kitchen and was pacing the other end of the room—appraising various objets d'art with an expert eye, idly flipping through fashion magazines and helping herself to more champagne. She picked up a silver-framed photograph of Malcolm the billionaire standing on the slopes next to . . . Was that the Duchess of York? What a self-satisfied, puffed-up old fool he looked with his stupid pink aviator glasses perched on his fat head.

By the time Nina laid the dishes on the table, no-one was particularly hungry. They picked at the food as they talked and drank, then drank some more. Nina unearthed a few nuggets of information from Corinne that would be a hit with her P&C committee—Candice Byrne, Corinne's younger rival on *Daylight*, had recently had a nose job and was secretly dating the weatherman; the high-profile host of the quiz show Nina loved was addicted to painkillers; and the late night newsreader was having an affair with the boss of the station. She was thrilled with the quality of the dirt dished at the table.

Meredith realised that she was well on her way to being 'tired and emotional', but she still had enough of her defences intact against Corinne's dark arts to wonder if all these revelations were designed to prise more information out of Nina.

Not to be left out of the boozy confessional, Annie owned up to a six-month affair with the married editor of the local newspaper. Corinne and Nina 'oohed' and 'aahed', and there was a round of salacious bedroom talk, during which Corinne revealed that she and her husband, Malcolm Pearson, the billionaire packaging tycoon, hadn't had sex in six months and she was feeling most neglected in the bedroom. It was all wildly indiscreet, even accounting for the effects of the champagne. Meredith watched Corinne through her glass.

And then Nina leaned forward and offered one of her own celebrity tidbits—'Tabby' Hutchinson had come to Brad and asked for an advance on his salary because he wanted to buy his girlfriend, the nubile Miss Emma Pang, famous swimsuit model, a new pair of breasts.

'Noooo! So did the club cough up?' Corinne asked merrily.

Nina had opened her mouth to reply, when Meredith finally spoke up, intercepting the ball right in front of the goal posts. 'Why didn't you turn up to the concert that night, Corinne?'

The conversation slid on muddy ground and cannoned into the boundary fence. Annie and Nina picked themselves up and groaned in protest: 'Meredith! Come on, forget it.'

'No. I want to answer that.' Corinne groped for her glass and stood, holding the edge of the table to steady herself.

'I didn't come that night because I knew Donald was going to be there.'

Annie attempted to head off the confrontation with a lame, 'What does it matter? Here, have another drink.' But it was too late—even she, pissed as she was, could see that.

'And what did Donald being there have to do with it?' Meredith inquired.

'You're not going to like this, Meredith, and I have tried to shield you from it all these years . . .'

'Go on, we're both big girls now,' said Meredith evenly. Annie and Nina shrank back into their seats. This was going to be ugly.

'Donald tried to rape me.' The word 'rape' was airborne. The spectators all breathed in and watched where it would land.

Meredith took the mark. She cleared her throat, sipped her champagne. 'Oh yes. And when was this exactly?'

'After rehearsal, the night before that gig. He drove me home and grabbed at me in the front seat of the car. Ripped my dress. So there you are, Meredith. That's why I didn't come. Deal with it.'

'That is an utter fabrication.' Meredith glared at her.

'Oh really? Is it?' Corinne turned to Annie, who had her elbows on the table and was rubbing her eyes as if she must have been dreaming this entire exchange. 'Annie? You and I were sharing a house together then. You'd gone home early that night. You remember how I came in the front door. How was I? Tell her.' Corinne stabbed the air in Meredith's direction. Her wide diamond-studded platinum bracelet glittered in a column of light.

'Yes, Annie, why don't you tell me. How was Corinne?'

'I don't want . . .' Annie mumbled into her hands.

'TELL ME!' Meredith was also on her feet now, and leaning halfway across the table.

'She was crying. She said Donald wanted to have sex with her . . .'

'And you believed her?'

'I . . .'

Corinne took two steps and stumbled. 'Are you saying I'm a liar?'

Nina grabbed at Corinne's arm and tried to pull her back into her chair.

'I'm saying,' snarled Meredith, 'you're a fake. Everything about you is manufactured—"As seen on TV"—and so is this pathetic fantasy. No wonder you're married to a man who made his money in cardboard.'

Corinne slammed her glass down and folded her arms. 'And you've always been jealous! You were the one who wanted to be a star, but you were never fucking good enough.' She didn't seem to be drunk now—every word was crystal clear. 'You thought you'd married a big-time film director. He's a sleaze merchant. The biggest joke of all is that he makes reality TV. He's the one who's a liar. He's had you fooled for years.'

Meredith jumped back and sent her chair flying. She smashed her glass on the floor. In a reflex action Nina was immediately on her hands and knees, searching for shards on the marble tiles.

'Did you know, Nina?' Meredith demanded.

Nina looked up, appalled that she might be dragged into the fight. 'Only what Annie said . . .'

'So you ALL believed Corinne's filthy lie! Well, FUCK ALL OF YOU! There—you must be pleased with my obscenity, Annie.' And with that Meredith turned and ran into the shadowy courtyard.

⁂

'She's a bitch. She always has been, and you both know it.' Corinne shredded the foil on another bottle with perfectly tended pearly fingernails.

'No she's not.' Nina was leaning forward on the table, her elbows on the stainless steel as the room spun in front of her.

'You don't even know Meredith anymore.' Annie rattled ice cubes into a glass from the fridge dispenser and topped it with water. She turned to see Corinne, champagne in hand, still bright-eyed and pacing.

'I know enough to know she put Donald through hell! He could have been in Hollywood now, making movies, if she hadn't been so selfish. All that effort . . . for fucking what? Selling French spatulas to bored housewives? Don's missed out on a lot of opportunities over the years.'

'You still see Donald?'

'We're in the same business. Hard not to. I've caught up with him a few times.' Corinne sniffed and pinched at her nose.

There was no doubt about it, thought Annie, when it came to drinking Corinne was punching well above her minuscule weight. Perhaps there was an intriguing explanation for her frequent sojourns to her fragrant upstairs bathroom. Nina was face down on the table now, and breathing like a draughthorse with a chaff bag over its head.

'It sounds like you've forgiven him for trying to rape you.' A blast of icy water had defogged Annie's brain. She was coolly surveying the crime scene. 'That's very big of you.'

'All that was twenty years ago. We've spoken about it. He's apologised. We were different people then.'

'But you're still furious with Meredith? Sorry, I don't get it.'

Corinne turned, her pupils two glittering pinpricks in the taut, pale canvas of her face. 'She's so high and mighty, as if she thinks she's better than everyone else. Taking the moral high ground. She was always like that and she hasn't changed. I saw her tonight pawing my things like some fucking know-all from *Antiques Roadshow*. I know what she was thinking.'

'What was she thinking?'

'That I don't deserve all this!' Corinne flung her arm to the ceiling. 'That I must have fucked my way to where I am. That I wasted my life on something stupid and inconsequential.' Corinne downed the contents of her glass. 'That's what everyone thinks, apparently.'

'And have you?'

'You're in real estate, you're forty, you're single. You tell me how our lives get wasted on meaningless shit.'

'You're pissed, Corinne.'

'Oh, truly! Why don't you all just piss off.' Corinne turned her back and swiped the bottle from the table. Annie shook Nina's shoulders.

'Come on, Nina, sweetie. We're going.'

Nina lifted her head. Straw-blonde hair was sticking out like the stuffing from a scarecrow. A string of saliva dangled from the corner of her open mouth to the sleeve of her cotton shirt. 'Huh?'

Annie hooked her hands under Nina's armpits and heaved her to her feet. As she steered Nina towards the door Corinne followed on spindly heels that peck, peck, pecked on the floor tiles. She would have the final word: that was part of her contract with the world.

'You might be content with the way things have turned out for you, but it's not over for me. Corinne Jacobsen's got plenty to say yet. You just watch.'

''Night, Corinne. Lovely to see you,' Nina slurred and waved a floppy hand. 'Thanks for having us.'

Annie, her foot on the bottom step of the RoadMaster, looked back to see stumps of candles flickering. She could make out Corinne, still restlessly pacing, a small black insect flitting among the flames.

✿

It was just on dawn and the bats were coming home to roost in Corinne's garden when Nina attempted to back the RoadMaster through the wrought-iron gates. She had an award-winning hangover. The pressure behind her eyes made her head feel like an overinflated basketball.

Annie was in the laneway, feebly calling directions in between leaning against the fence to cool her forehead on the sandstone blocks. It was while she was picking grit out of her eyebrows that the corner of the van collected a pillar and sent a carved stone gargoyle crashing to the ground. Nina climbed from the front seat and they both stood surveying the pile of pink sandstone rubble.

'Ah, stuff it!' said Annie. 'She won't be up yet. Let's just go—I'll ring her later.'

'Bloody hell, look at the van!' Nina gasped as she saw one side of the aluminium had folded like tinfoil. Annie shrugged. There was nothing that could be done about it now. Another five minutes of manoeuvring and the van had cleared the laneway and swung into the quiet street. With the tension of it all, Nina thought she might throw up on the steering wheel.

'Navigate me to Centennial Park and we'll stop there for the day and head off late this afternoon,' directed Nina. Annie reached for the street directory and saw that Meredith had organised her corner of the cabin perfectly: the road maps were neatly stacked under her feet; the tourist brochures were tucked into the compartment by her side; the glovebox held sunglasses, sunblock and packets of lollies, all tidily arranged on top of the elegant travel diary. It was Meredith herself who was a mess. She was still passed out, fully dressed, on top of the bed down the back.

Soon the van was parked under a Port Jackson fig tree at the edge of Centennial Park. From the front seats Nina and Annie watched a parade of early morning joggers, walkers and cyclists with iPods plugged in to their ears. They groaned in unison and headed back to their beds.

✻

A short taxi ride and Nina was sitting at the open window of a café overlooking Bondi Beach. A low, sodden canopy of cloud hung over the water, threatening to rip and dump rain for the first time since they had left home. She watched a freakish parade saunter past on the footpath in front of her perch—seedy derros swigging from bottles in paper bags; Goths wearing skull pendants and nose-rings; Japanese tourists toting dinky Gucci handbags and photographing everything in sight; half-naked yoga freaks with rolled-up rubber mats tucked under toned arms. It was 11 am on a Thursday, and she was in a foreign land.

In fact, Nina reflected, she could have been sitting in a booth at the Mos Eisley Cantina in a pirate city on the planet of Tatooine (*Star Wars IV: A New Hope*). She had to smile to herself, thinking of how the boys would have fallen about, laughing to be in on her 'spot-an-alien-life-form' game. At this moment she missed her sons—missed their passionate kisses when they knew their brothers weren't watching, their demands for one last cuddle after the lights were out, and their whispered declarations that she was 'the best mumma in the world'.

How had she landed at this particular breakfast bar at the end of the universe? Nina thought everyone must be looking at the chunky middle-aged woman in the oversized shirt and leggings, wondering why she was there. Except that no-one was paying her the slightest bit of attention—including the tattooed Maori waitress in the bikini top, shorts, cowboy boots and blue-black Mohawk—a refugee from the planet Aruza, if Nina

197

wasn't mistaken. Only she remembered that particular race of humanoids shared their memories via cybernetic implants, and Nina seemed to have been long forgotten.

The remains of Nina's 'brekkie with the lot' were slumped on the plate in front of her. She'd ordered refried beans, poached eggs, bacon, hash browns, mushrooms and crusty toast, thinking they might cure her hangover. Instead, she now had a bloated stomach to go with her mighty headache. Two cups of peppermint tea hadn't helped. There was nothing for it but a reviving shot of vodka in a Bloody Mary.

'There you go, dollface.' The drink was dumped on the bench and the plates cleared with a clattering efficiency that made Nina wince. She found a couple of painkillers in her handbag, gulped at the spicy, alcoholic tomato juice, crunched the celery and imagined it was all doing her good. Only it wasn't.

She watched the surfers in the distance. In their wetsuits on the flanks of the rolling grey surf, they reminded her of buzzing flies on the hide of an elephant. Nina thought of the morning when she had ducked under the aquamarine waves at Mimosa Rocks. It was a moment of exquisite freedom on this trip that she would never forget. But, in truth, the journey had mostly been exhausting.

For so long Nina had imagined being away from her 'boys' own' life of football, electric guitars and computer games. She would commune with treasured women friends and come to a deeper understanding of the feminine. *Women friends help us define who we are and who we want to be.* But now, when she saw Meredith and Annie close up, she saw they had no idea of who she was. As for who she wanted to be, Nina wasn't quite sure she knew herself, so how could they help?

Nina rolled the cool tumbler of juice between her palms. She had to admit that all the behaviour she had indulged in over the past few days—the crying and doubting and questioning—had been ridiculous theatrics. She should have known Brad had an important reason for leaving town while she was away. That was the thing about her husband, she thought, as she fished for the ice in the bottom of the glass—he was a simple, loyal soul. Could the same be said of her?

Nina sucked the chunk of ice, and then held it to her throbbing forehead. Had she said anything out of order last night? Nothing she could think of, specifically. And anyway, if she had, Corinne wouldn't tell anyone. Would she? Nina's stomach lurched and she could taste a vomity sourness in the back of her throat. She put up her hand to order one more for the road.

Annie chose three promising wisps of silk and jersey, and headed for the changing room. She pulled the curtain closed and dumped the clothes on the wooden floor. She hadn't seen herself in a full-length mirror for some days, making do instead with her unsatisfying waist-high reflection over sinks in caravan park shower blocks and the poky bathroom in the van.

A quick inventory came up with: red curls exploding into a bedraggled mop, puffy eyelids, cracked lips, jeans with grass stains on the knee, an orange tie-dyed singlet and a pair of scuffed suede flatties. Brilliant! Here she was in one of the country's most exclusive shopping strips—Queen Street, Woollahra—and she looked as if she was on her way home from the butcher's after buying cat's meat.

As the van had droned up the highway towards Sydney, Annie daydreamed about where she'd go and what she'd buy on her shopping expedition. There were boutiques in Paddington and Double Bay she'd read about in magazines, and been looking forward to ransacking for years. Now, racks of gorgeous clothes, display cabinets full of beaded scarves and jewellery, shelves of handbags and rows of fabulous shoes lay before her—an uncharted land brimful of treasures—and she couldn't find the energy to explore. It was all too hard. It was as improbable as Captain Cook traversing the globe to land in Botany Bay, and then deciding not to go ashore.

Annie reached to unhook her bra and fancied she could smell the sour tang of last night's alcohol seeping through her skin. Curse Meredith and Corinne and their pointless, stupid argument. What a bloody nightmare this trip was turning out to be. The term 'emotional rollercoaster' didn't do it justice. It was more like enduring a turn on the Mad Mouse—a tortuous, vertiginous ride that made you long to get off and feel firm ground beneath your feet.

Maybe they should just chuck it in. This trip was proving one thing: that all the crap Nina spouted about women's *special friendships* was just that—complete and utter shit. The only thing holding them together for all these years had been the memory of the sisterhood of Sanctified Soul—but a less saintly bunch of women would have been hard to find.

They were all fakes and liars back then. They had stood and sung about the 'oppressed women of the world'—while Briony seethed that the purple of their gospel gowns was the last shade she would have chosen; while they all saw the needle tracks on Genevieve's arms and told each other that it was her decision how she lived her life; while they all sang about the war in El Salvador, but Nina couldn't even point to it on a map; while Meredith and Corinne battled each other for the spotlight; while poor, dumb Jaslyn moaned about her faithless boyfriend and she, Annie Bailey, nice little country girl, was screwing him on the grass behind the tour bus. How had they ever thought they were improving the lot of women through their unholy alliance?

And two decades on, nothing had changed. Women still clawed and kicked each other for a prize no-one could identify or articulate. She had always thought that her female friendships were not much more than shallow gossip over an inconsequential cup of coffee. They were designed to look substantial and nourishing to other women but in reality were no more use than—what was it her father said?—'tits on a bull'.

Women friends were like that pair of comfortable rubber thongs you kept in your handbag for emergencies. As soon as there were no men around to admire your sexy stilettos, you could put them on and breathe a sigh of relief. But then you were inevitably reminded that you had ugly toes.

Annie left the velvet curtained changing booth behind her and idly chose a pair of dangly earrings, a studded handbag and a chain belt. She paid up and bagged the lot.

Looking out for a taxi on Queen Street, she watched two glossy women tripping by, arm in arm, with their heads together like a pair of prancing creamy ponies. Annie could not imagine wandering up this street with Nina and Meredith. They'd look like three old nags who had escaped from their horse float. Annie held up her arm and whistled; wearily picking up her shopping bags, she climbed into a back seat that had seen better days. Her arse dropped to the axle.

✵

There was no way to adequately prepare yourself for seeing the Opera House close up. Of course Meredith had seen it on television and once even from a car window, but she had never walked up the broad stairs fronting the promenade and stood underneath the massive, vaulted entrance. She read in her guidebook that more than a million tiles made up those graceful curves that looked to be billowing in the wind sweeping down Sydney Harbour. Although tens of millions of tourists had marvelled at this exact same fact, in exactly the same place where Meredith now stood, it was still—undeniably—a thrill.

Meredith smoothed her tan trench coat as it flapped at her legs and paused to watch the procession of a wedding party along the boardwalk. A long white tulle veil was being whisked away by the stiff breeze, and the tiny Japanese bride attached to it looked as if she might become airborne. Like a human seedpod. Her new husband gathered the fabric in his arms to stop her from flying off over Circular Quay and landing— *sprouting*—on the northern shore of the harbour.

A wedding! And what fine hopes did they have for their union? She was driving almost two thousand k's to witness the marriage of her daughter, but what was the point of it all? Meredith thought of Nina, fed up with the daily reality of domestic drudgery, and Annie, so tortured because she couldn't step onto the very same treadmill. But Annie—and Meredith should remember to tell her this—had already made it almost as far as forty. If she could just hold on a few years more—and those years would go by in the blink of an eye—then she would be at the same age most women were when their children left home. Annie, lucky woman, wouldn't be blamed for being a bad mother. And, even luckier, she wouldn't have to think back on that time when she had held a baby to her breast. She wouldn't be overwhelmed by the loss of the purest love one human could ever feel for another. Any way you saw it—from the point of view of a mother looking down at a baby, or the baby looking back at its mother—every joy was shadowed by its evil sister, sorrow. Kids left you, and took your heart with them.

Meredith muttered, 'Hah! Good luck!', and then wondered what she meant by that. Her mother Edith had been a champion bridge player. Edith had always said that success didn't so much depend on the cards you were dealt, but how you played them. If spades were the length of your leg, diamonds the brilliance of your intelligence, hearts the depth of your emotion and clubs the strength of your conviction, then Meredith had been given a good hand. But all her life she had felt Edith leaning over her shoulder and 'tut-tutting' as she had played her cards. Meredith had always thought her mother had nothing to teach her and yet, since her death, Meredith could not stop thinking about what she might have learned from the way her mother had lived her life.

Perhaps it was as simple as being satisfied with your lot. Meredith had never found that particular peace, and had always wanted something . . . more. She recalled one of her mother's favourite sayings: 'Happiness, Merry, lies not in getting what one wants, but in wanting what one gets.'

Meredith had always dismissed that timid notion. What had Edith got? Plain crockery, a tiny kitchen, a worn lounge suite and dreary carpets, and the boring man she'd married . . . her distant and taciturn father, Bernard the Dentist. How could that have been what Edith wanted?

That's why she'd bought her mother beautiful fine china. She wanted her to be surrounded by rare and precious things. Edith possessed the soul of an artist—something her husband and sons never appreciated, but Meredith did. It was revealed in the way she elegantly arranged flowers in a vase or in the lovely small watercolours of the garden that she painted and placed on the kitchen windowsill.

That figurine of a mermaid? Meredith had wanted Edith to swim away from all she knew. But had Meredith missed the obvious? When Edith was fifty she had three children who lived close by, six grandchildren and a devoted husband. So, her mother *was* surrounded by rare and precious things. Things money couldn't buy. Meredith, at almost the same age, had none of these. She had a house and a shop crammed with shiny, expensive stuff and had never felt more unloved in her life. She felt a wave of grief wash over her and found herself reaching for her mother's hand. 'I miss you, Edith,' she whispered.

Meredith had dreamed, for so many years, of what it would have been like to sing in the concert hall of the Sydney Opera House. Stepping into that soaring auditorium ribbed with ten thousand organ pipes this afternoon was like walking into the rarefied air in the heart of a seashell. Meredith curled up in the warm darkness of the back stalls, and then saw a young woman walk onto the curved stage way below. The woman stopped, threw her arms wide with the pure joy of being there and sang. Mimi's aria from Act 1 of *La Bohème*, if Meredith wasn't mistaken.

Listening to her sing now, unaccompanied—*a cappella*—tears slid down Meredith's face. Her mother's words came to her from the kitchen in far-off Camberwell, ringing like a wooden spoon on the sides of a mixing bowl: 'You can wish upon a star and make your dreams come true, but always remember that you have to choose your dream carefully. I'm sure you think that's a dull way to go about life, Merry, but I chose the dream of a daughter. Here I am, and here you are. One of my dreams came true.'

❊

Annie and Nina had been surprised to find Meredith sitting on a wooden fence railing, waiting for them, in front of the RoadMaster in Centennial Park. They'd left a note that everyone would meet at 2 pm to hit the road again, but they'd expected that by now Meredith would have been waiting for a taxi at the airport back in Melbourne.

They were speeding up the Pacific Highway, heading north for Seal Rocks—travelling a good hour, exchanging the odd comment on the slow traffic and various landmarks. No-one had brought up the events of the night before. In truth no-one knew where to begin with the post-mortem. Everyone always talked about freedom on the road. No-one ever mentioned that it was like being on jury duty: you had to stick it out in a small space together until you came up with a verdict on each other's criminal acts.

Then, in the rear-vision mirror, they saw that the clouds had burst over Sydney and the rain was bucketing down.

'I'm sorry for last night,' said Meredith. 'I behaved appallingly and I apologise.'

'Don't,' said Annie. 'I shouldn't have dragged you both there in the first place. You were right about Corinne. She's always been just out for herself.'

'She has this way of making you feel as if you're not quite good enough,' said Nina. 'Annie said she told us all to "piss off" in the end.'

'Did she? The cow!' exclaimed Meredith.

And with that the black cloud in the van also burst and they joined in a hearty round of Slagging the Hostess.

'Hope the skinny bitch gets washed down a drain into the harbour and gets eaten by a shark.'

'Did you get a load of that picture of Her Highness over the fireplace? *Fucking awful!*'

'Still, it was more animated than her face. How much Botox has she got in her head? And by the looks of things they transplanted the pufferfish lips as well.'

'She's shit on that *Daylight* show. And what's with the cleavage? People are trying to eat their breakfast for God's sake.'

'That husband of hers must be loaded. Could you ever sleep with an old toad like that?'

'Let me think . . . How much is he worth again?'

'She's doing cocaine.'

'Noooooo . . .'

'Trust me. Absolutely.'

'We smashed her stone gargoyle. Brad will go mental over the ding in the van, but it was worth it!' Nina was a little unsure of herself on this particular declaration.

Then it was time for some serious talk.

'You know, Meredith,' Annie mused, 'Corinne said her dress was ripped that night, but I didn't see it. In fact, the first time she ever mentioned the dress was last night. And she never said the word "rape" either. She said Donald had tried to come on to her so I just assumed . . .' Uh-oh! Annie had talked herself into a corner here. A fine mist clouded the windscreen. Nina began testing the windscreen wipers, as if she wasn't really listening.

'What did you assume?' asked Meredith.

Annie shifted her backside on her cushion, coughed and fidgeted. The thing was, back in those days Donnie Dalrymple kissed everyone, and his attentions were often accompanied by a sly bottom squeeze or a peer down the neckline. Genevieve, for one, had never been convinced he was a 'reconstructed' male. She'd bailed him up one night in a pub car park and told him a baseball bat to the balls might help him get in touch with his 'feminine side'. They'd all had a good laugh about it later (when Meredith was out of hearing) and that had seemed to be the end of it—until the accusation from Corinne that he'd tried to have sex with her. The group never sang together again after that.

'Well . . . Donald . . .' Annie squirmed again.

'Yes . . . ?' said Meredith, not taking her eyes from the road.

'He did have . . . an "eye for the ladies". I know he was supposed to be a SNAG and all that, but . . .'

Meredith decided to put Annie out of her misery. 'You're talking about the bum pinching and the breast ogling?'

'What?' Nina swerved over a line of cat's eyes into the gravel. 'Yikes! Sorry.'

'You knew about that?' Annie was astonished.

'Of course! Genevieve was right. That whole SNAG thing was wishful thinking. I always knew Donald was a bit of a perv, but that didn't mean he was going to go through with anything. Any woman who thought that we could suddenly breed a race of men who were immune to a good pair of breasts was fooling herself. Besides, I was watching him, and he damn well knew it.'

'Bloody hell,' Nina muttered.

'And I'll tell you who else I had my eye on . . . Miss Corinne Jacobsen chatting up my husband every time she thought I wasn't looking. Donald was in the film business in those days. She wasn't above offering him oral sex for a part in a movie. He used to tell me about Corinne's flirtations, and we'd both have a good laugh over it.'

'My God! So what *do* you think happened that night in the car?' Annie couldn't believe she'd waited almost twenty years to hear this.

'That she probably came on to him, he rejected her and, good little actress that she is, she faked being upset.'

Nina finished the story: 'And she had already hijacked Roscoe Fortune, so she used Donald as an excuse to us for not turning up at the concert.'

'Fuck me!' Annie shook her head in wonderment. The fact that Corinne had appeared in the Sydney newspapers on the arm of that greasy opportunist Roscoe Fortune, just weeks after, had never sat well with her.

'No—fuck Corinne Jacobsen!' said Meredith. She was getting the hang of this obscenity stuff again.

'But didn't Donald tell you?' Nina was puzzled. 'He must have known for all these years that he had something to do with her not turning up the next night.'

Meredith paused. Nina was right. Donald had listened for years as she raged about Corinne's callous double-cross. And he had always shared his stories about her pathetic come-ons. Why hadn't he mentioned that particular night? She'd been thinking about that all day.

'I don't know,' she said finally. 'I really don't know. Maybe, when we get to Byron, I'll find out.'

Twelve

'OI! THAT'S BLOODY DANGEROUS UP THERE!' The shout echoed across the Treachery Beach campground.

From all over, heads were popping out from tents and caravans to see what the fuss was about. A procession of holiday-makers in floral print shirts, damp bathers and rubber thongs strolled towards the RoadMaster. Men were nursing beers, women were wiping hands on tea towels, kids had frisbees tucked under their arms. They took up positions at a variety of vantage points to watch the show in the setting sun. The gyrating form of Elvis the Pelvis was an entertaining support act. What was the crazy woman doing up there anyway?

From her perch on the branch of a paperbark tree, Nina could see the site manager had driven down the dirt road on his trail bike. 'YOU SHOULD COME DOWN NOW!' He cupped his hands and called again.

'For God's sake, Nina, you're not a teenager! You'll kill yourself!' Meredith watched, horrified, as Nina, a good four metres up, inched her way forward on the high branch. Just a little way to go and she would be able to step on top of the van.

'Is she on the roof yet?' Annie called from inside. Meredith couldn't believe anyone could ask such a stupid question.

'Of course she's not! You'll hear her walking, like Santa . . .' Meredith saw Nina open her mouth to protest. 'Only a lot, lot thinner,' she added hastily.

'Bugger off,' Nina muttered under her breath to the assembled multitude as she shimmied further along the branch. That's all she needed—a whole crowd looking up the legs of her shorts to her ninety-kilo arse! Nina then surprised every onlooker with a graceful dismount from the branch onto the roof of the van. There was a smattering of applause.

'I'm fine!' She waved away their congratulations. This was child's play for Nina. She'd braved flying foxes, tree huts, rope swings and climbing frames with her sons when they were little. She was surprisingly agile for someone her size, and not in the least afraid of heights. She paused for a moment to take in a last view of the giant sunlit snowy dune behind Treachery Beach before it turned to grey in the gathering darkness.

Nina was determined to fix the TV aerial so she could catch the evening news to see if there was anything about Brad and Tabby. She was also keen to watch her favourite weekly quiz show, especially now she had the inside dope that the chatty host with the fake teeth was a pill popper. She'd always thought him unnaturally enthusiastic about the cookware in the festoon-lit prize palace.

Nina knelt down, peeled back a square of flywire and called through the open vent: 'Now pass me up that roll of wire and the electrical tape.'

'OK.' Annie duly passed the equipment through.

After some minutes of fiddling, calling for two clothes pegs, and fiddling some more, Nina had the aerial standing tall. 'Now turn on the TV and let me know when you get any reception.'

'It's still a bit fuzzy . . . That's better . . . No, it's gone snowy again . . . Oh, that's clearer . . . What'd you do then? . . . Leave it there!'

'How's that?'

'That's about as good as we'll get it, I reckon.'

'OK. Fine. I'm coming down.' Nina stood to see that she still had an audience. She couldn't resist a flourish and a bow, and laughed as she was rewarded with a few more claps and 'woo-hoos' of admiration.

'Careful coming down—it's getting dark,' called Meredith.

'No shit, Sherlock,' Nina grunted. She grabbed the branch and swung her legs across to the tree trunk. It was an impressive move. Only she slid down the trunk a lot faster than she'd intended, bare flesh scraping on rough bark.

'Ooooh,' exclaimed the crowd in a spontaneous, collective wince. It hurt like hell, but Nina was not about to give anyone the satisfaction of watching her limp in pain. She gave another jaunty wave when she hit the ground, and it wasn't until she was inside the van that she grimaced and clutched her inner thighs. 'Owww! Owww! That really stings!' On closer inspection the tender white skin looked as if someone had taken to it with a cheese grater.

'Honestly, I told you to be careful,' Meredith scolded.

'That was a really dumb thing to do,' said Annie.

Nina groaned. Who in their right mind would go away with a bunch of women? At least if she had been with the boys they would have laughed and kissed her better. Soon enough, however, her two nurses had her sitting up on the bed against a pile of pillows with a gin and tonic in hand and a bag of frozen peas between her legs. She wouldn't have had that expert nursing from her boys.

The television reception wasn't perfect, but it was good enough for Nina to see a female in a neat black jacket saying: 'And next on *Six Evening News*—insiders dish the dirt on Tabby Hutchinson. Cocaine and ecstasy found in his locker and how his girlfriend Emma Pang's breast implants put the Richmond Football Club over the salary cap.'

Then a young blonde in a low-cut black top saying: 'Emma and I used to laugh about it. She always reckoned that if the Tigers won the Premiership she was getting a "Double D", but if they were wooden spooners she'd probably have to settle for a "C".'

'Turn it off! Turn it off!' Nina screeched. 'Oh—my—God! Did I . . . ?' she appealed to umpires Annie and Meredith, who were sitting at the table, not moving an inch.

'I'm afraid so,' said Meredith.

'And did she . . . ?'

'Looks like it,' said Annie.

'The bitch!' declared Nina. 'The absolute lying . . . Oh hell! Brad will have a heart attack!'

'We should keep watching to see if she comes on,' said Annie.

'Of course she won't,' scoffed Meredith. 'Not the esteemed Miss Corinne Jacobsen. She'll have traded that juicy information, and I wouldn't mind betting she turns up on Channel 6 some time soon. She's handed them the scoop of the year.'

After advertisements for carpets, air conditioners and spa baths, the news resumed. The three women watched, wide-eyed, as Emma Pang's former best friend, Cheyenne Neck, appeared. She was overjoyed to be on the telly. Nina identified her from her diamanté heart-shaped nose-stud. Miss Neck had been a regular attendee at the wives' and girlfriends' lounge all last season. No doubt station management had thrown enough money at Cheyenne to compensate for the loss of her friendship with Emma. She was a good little performer. It was easy to imagine Cheyenne and Emma trading fluoro-wrapped tampons, nose candy and filthy secrets in the ladies' at the MCG.

There was the further promise that more of the grubby saga would be aired on *In Depth*, in its no-holds-barred entirety. *The whole, complete story. The full, total, absolute, uncensored truth—coming up, right after the weather.*

Nina had seen enough. She scrambled for the off-switch. The bag of frozen peas fell to the floor. With the heat coming from her body, Nina wouldn't have been surprised to find that she'd cooked an entrée of pea soup.

'Brad will have seen it,' she moaned, head in hands. 'He'll already be on the warpath, trying to find the idiot who leaked the story. Someone will get sacked. I'll have to ring him. Oh my God, he'll go ballistic!'

Annie and Meredith couldn't bring themselves to offer any sympathy for her predicament. It was Nina's well-documented lack of discretion—helped on by a bottle and a half of champagne—that had got her into trouble. It was a cruel way for her to learn the lesson.

'You can get phone reception up near the office,' was Annie's only offer of help.

Nina trudged up the grassy hill in the dark. She was shivering—whether from the chill wind blowing in from the South Pacific Ocean, or at the thought of what Brad would say, she couldn't tell. She huddled against the cold weatherboards of the wooden shack, the only light coming from the illuminated face of her mobile phone. As it rang, she prayed she would be put through to message bank. No such luck.

'Brad Brown speaking.'

'Hi, honey, it's Nina . . . it's me,' she stuttered.

'Babe! How's the trip going? I've been trying to call you. I can't talk long, I've got a crap situation happening here.'

'I know. That's why I'm ringing.'

'I'm on the Gold Coast. You've probably read—I'm in the middle of a total shit-fight. It's just hit national television in the worst way.'

'I know. It was me.'

'Sorry?'

'The story on the TV tonight about Tabby. It was my fault.'

'What?'

'I don't know how it happened, Brad, honestly. It just came out, and I didn't mean—'

'What *the fuck* are you talking about?'

'I told Corinne Jacobsen.'

'You did WHAT?! What did you tell her?'

'You know—about what you found in his locker and everything.'

'YOU ARE KIDDING ME! YOU ARE FUCKING KIDDING ME . . .'

'Like I said, I didn't mean to, it . . . just . . .' Nina's tears fell like hailstones on a corrugated-iron roof.

'Stop it! Stop crying! I can't stand it when you cry. Corinne Jacobsen?! You cannot be serious! What did you tell her . . . exactly?'

'That you found coke and ecstasy in his locker. That he wanted the money for Emma's implants.'

'Did you tell her about the gambling?'

'What?'

'Or the greyhound race-fixing stuff?'

'No, I didn't know about . . .'

'So, it was just the drug stuff then?'

'I don't know why I even said it.'

'YOU ARE AN IDIOT, NINA! YOU KNOW THAT? I can't believe that even you could be so stupid. This could cost me

216

my job. You realise that, don't you? How'll we afford the boys' school fees if I haven't got a job?'

Nina couldn't form a single word. The thought that the boys might have to be taken out of school was just—

'So, you spilled your guts to Corinne Jacobsen. Anyone else?'

'No . . . apart from Annie and Meredith.'

'JESUS CHRIST, NINA, SNAP OUT OF IT! You have to learn what "privacy" means. What "trust" is. What "secrets" are. I knew this would happen. You go away with two women—who, let's face it, you hardly know—and you tell them everything! You do it all the time! I've warned and warned you. Can you be trusted with anything? Now turn your phone off and keep your big mouth shut. I don't want to talk to you anymore. I'll fix it—like I've always fixed everything, while you've just been sitting on your arse, gossiping with your mother and making pancakes.'

'Brad—'

The line went dead. Nina's heart went dead too.

☼

Nina couldn't face the evening meal, and that hadn't happened for a long while. Even in the depths of her misery she thought that this was probably a good thing—the only good thing to come out of this whole disaster. She was supposed to be losing weight on this trip but, judging by the tightness of her waistband, she hadn't shed any. Her life—her body—were beyond her control.

This day (was it Thursday?) felt like the longest of her life. The journey north was beginning to take on the epic proportions of Frodo's journey with the ring. Right now Nina was on the bleak and freezing summit of Weathertop—the place where Frodo's heart was frozen solid by a stab from a Morgul-blade. She wished her boys were by her side to carry her away to the paradise of Rivendell, where she could be bathed and nursed and healed. Nina decided that sweeping the floor and repacking the cupboards in the van might soothe her ragged nerves.

'Pass me those dishes and I'll wash them,' she said as she struggled from her chair by the camp fire Annie had set blazing.

'Aw, come on, Nina, stay. Sit. Let's talk,' Annie pleaded.

'Annie's right. You need to debrief.' Meredith couldn't bring herself to say the word 'share'. The term had a fake, tinny ring to it coming out of her mouth. Nina slumped back into her chair.

'Don't,' said Annie. 'Don't torture yourself. It'll come right. Didn't Brad say he'd fix it?'

'How?' Nina replied miserably. The damage was done—she couldn't see any way out of it. The uninterrupted sound of the surf relentlessly pounding the beach beyond the dune told her that Annie and Meredith couldn't think of anything either.

Annie threw another fence post into the blackened iron fireplace. Her sneaky scavenging around the back of one of the permanent cabins at Treachery Beach Camp had turned up enough wood for tonight's blaze. No self-respecting country girl would ever fork out ten dollars for the measly bags of wood they were selling at the office. The dried-out post caught alight and the three of them stared into the flames as if they might find some answer there.

'Anyway, it's only football,' said Meredith.

Only football? Nina would have laughed if she'd had the energy. Meredith didn't understand that most of Nina's adult life had been ruled by goal umpires—the loathed men in white coats who adjudicated between the posts and semaphored success or failure. At any time during those years when he had played first grade, Brad was one whistle-blow away from despair. And when he was down like that, he wouldn't talk, wouldn't take any interest . . . in anything. He left the care of their sons, their house and their lives to her. Nina may have been a spectator, but she'd been in the game as much as anyone on the team.

Nina had nursed Brad's corked thighs, ministered to his bruised shoulders, massaged his knotted muscles—*glutei maximi* and *medii, gastrocnemii, tibiales, deltoids, pectorals, latissimi.* She could name every sinew, ligament and joint. She had more knowledge of the intricate workings of the male groin than any woman should ever have been expected to acquire. Nina inhabited the black-and-blue landscape of her husband's skin. It was more familiar to her than her own body.

Back then Nina had imagined that, when Brad retired, he might 'settle down', although she didn't quite know what that meant. Wasn't sure what she was wishing for. All she knew was that, every time her small boys heard that Richmond had lost a game, they would run upstairs to their rooms, dreading the slam of the front door that announced their father was home. And every time they did that, it was as if they were trampling Nina's heart underfoot. Brad didn't shout at her or the boys—Nina supposed she should be grateful for that—but his brooding, silent presence sucked the joy and light out of the house.

When Brad did finally hang up his football boots, things got worse. There had been the mandatory round of boozy testimonials and media tributes, but they were over within a month. Nina had hoped Brad might find a job with her father's food import business, in a sports store, an office or as a commentator. Instead, he had spent the next football season at home, refusing to find a job, watching the matches on television. He played and replayed the games, and raged at the screen. When the offer of the team manager's job came, Nina had surrendered, embracing Richmond Football Club as The Way, The Truth and The Light. Football was not a sport—it was a religion. That's what everyone said, and in Nina's house it was true. She saw herself crucified in a black guernsey, decorated with a martyr's yellow sash.

Brad would never understand what his football career had cost his wife. For nine months of the year there was never a weekend the family could call its own. She could never speak freely when she left the house. Brad had warned her that anyone she might meet would have their own team allegiances. In any seemingly innocent social situation, a West Coast Eagle, a Sydney Swan or a Collingwood Magpie would pounce on a crumb of a secret she might drop and flap back to a rival nest with it.

Nina now felt uneasy at any gathering outside the family. She couldn't trust herself. It was not in her nature to keep secrets . . . mostly because she couldn't tell what was a secret and what wasn't. A few times she'd confided in one of the mothers from school, only to be met by gales of laughter—that 'secret' had been on the news last night! So, year by year she had found her social circle dwindling. She now mixed mostly with the wives of other past players, who were in the same predicament—their husbands' old jealousies and rivalries haunted every conversation.

Now, as team manager, Brad was on call 24/7. The phone rang incessantly. Brad assumed she knew by heart the medical records and match performances of dozens of players; the names of the sponsors, the coaching staff and the board members; the history of the club and all the words of its song. And when, one by one, Jordan, Anton and then Marko had announced that they wanted to play for the Mighty Tigers one day, the final siren sounded for Nina—she could see her future stretching before her, divided into endless twenty-minute quarters.

'I once added up how many pairs of football boots I've bought,' said Nina. 'It was fifty-two. Just once, I would have liked to have bought a pair of pink slides with butterflies on them, or a pair of patent leather Mary Janes with a little buckle on the side. I wish the twins had been girls.'

'Oh, Nina,' Meredith scolded, 'you don't mean that.'

'Maybe you'll have grandchildren one day.' Annie kindly came to her rescue as she poked at the fire. 'All girls. You can buy as many pink shoes as you want.'

'I'm going to tell you a secret,' Nina announced, 'and then you both have to tell one too.' Annie nodded her agreement. Anything that might cheer Nina up was worth a try. Meredith was also glad for the diversion. She was huddled in her chair, wrapped in her *Rajasthani pink* pashmina shawl, her face warmed by the blaze and remembering her Girl Guide days. She had been just about to suggest they sing a hearty round of 'Ging Gang Gooley'.

'I want my own café,' Nina declared. 'I want to cook. I've got the whole idea in my head. There's an old bakery in Balaclava for rent. I could do big home-made breakfasts—Symyky fritters, grilled chicken and pork sosysky. Big stuffed rye and black bread sandwiches for lunches and precooked things people could take home for dinner. Real traditional Ukrainian dishes—potato pancakes with sour cream, boiled cabbage dumplings and meat dishes like kotlety, shpyndra, sicheniki. And for dessert I could do sweet little pampushky filled with poppy seeds and tossed in cinnamon. I'd have a long table down the middle, and smaller tables off to the side. I'd paint the whole room pink and call the place Nina's.'

There it was at last. Nina's secret cherished plan had made itself known. There was silence and Nina had expected it. She was sure that Annie and Meredith, both successful business-women, couldn't possibly think she had enough talent to make a go of it.

'*Prussian blue* would be preferable.' Meredith finally spoke. 'Better for the digestion. You get pink and all that heavy food, and it would be too much.'

'I know that place,' Annie added. 'It's been up for rent for a while. I reckon I could help you get a good deal on it. But that doesn't have to be a secret, Nina. It's a plan. A good one too. You should do it.' She reached over and clinked her glass with Nina's.

'I guess I've kept it secret from my mother and Brad. They can only see me at home with the boys. But they'd cope, wouldn't they? I could be back home in time to make their dinner.'

'They'd *have* to cope,' said Meredith. 'And it would do them good. Your future daughters-in-law will thank you every day of their married lives.'

Nina was thrilled with their votes of confidence. She sat back and nursed her drink. Her hands were trembling. She was already behind the counter ladling steaming borscht into bowls.

'Now it's your turn, Meredith.' Annie took up the wine bottle and filled her glass. It seemed to her that the flames of the camp fire flickered with an almost supernatural intensity.

Meredith leaned back in her chair. She couldn't remember ever seeing so many stars—an immense, broad canvas of glittering eternity, tonight as close as her own bedroom ceiling.

'I painted Donald's den that colour on purpose. I was sick of him being in there for hours talking on the phone, working at his stupid computer on his ridiculous ideas, leaving his toenail clippings on my pure wool carpet, taking up useable space. We'd run out of things to talk about after nearly thirty years and all I could see ahead was another thirty years of vacuuming around him, cleaning whiskers out of the sink, wiping his muddy boot prints off the parquet floors. To be perfectly frank, Donald had become just one more thing to dust.

'I spent weeks looking at paint charts trying to decide what colour would annoy him the most and, when I found a lovely grey named after a duck—*mallard grey*—that was it! Donald in his mallard grey duck den! I don't think he ever got the joke.

I've turned the room into a place for gift-wrapping. I believe Martha Stewart has just such a room, and now, so do I. You can't tell anyone I did it on purpose though. It's a secret. But I'm glad I shared it with you.'

Annie and Nina weren't sure whether to laugh or cry. To think that the dynamic partnership of Donald and Meredith—their shared artistic passion and determination to change the world—had come down to whiskers and muddy boot prints? And that Meredith had chased him out of the house as if she was taking a broom to trespassing poultry?

Annie disappeared from the circle of light and raided the haul of stolen scraps she'd stashed under the van for the fire. Her petty thievery from the nearby cabin woodpiles might be something she'd keep to herself. As she turned back to the fire with her arms full of offerings for the blaze she thought of what secret she might give up.

Annie could have come up with more hair-raising tales of illicit and outrageous behaviour that would have shocked her companions, but that wouldn't have been in the spirit of things. So perhaps, she thought, now was the time to trust her companions with her secret. Maybe this was the real reason she'd decided to come on this trip. To find a time to tell it and rid herself of the burden that seemed to be getting heavier with each passing year.

When the fire was stoked once more, Annie began. 'This is a strange secret, because I think I've kept it from myself more than I've kept it from anyone else.' She paused to consider how she might best continue.

'When I was eight, my six-year-old sister drowned in our dam.' In her mind's eye, Annie saw the flat oval muddy surface of the water blink in surprise.

'I remember Dad running up to the house with Lizzie in his arms and her long black hair dripping. The drops of water made little round marks in the dust. I remember thinking that even a black tracker would never be able to find someone who'd drowned and been carried away, because I watched the drops sink into the brown earth and disappear. Water's not like blood that stays there, and you can follow the trail.

'The last time I saw Lizzie was in Dad's arms—her hair was swinging and the sun was shining through the water. It was this beautiful rainbow spray. It's weird because I can't remember the funeral or anything else after that.

'When I was a kid, I was always trying to follow trails of water 'cause I thought they might lead me to Lizzie. Even now, when I see water dripping on a floor or a path, I have to follow the drops. It's silly, I know, but it's this compulsion. I have to do it, just in case . . . As if I'd find Lizzie in a bucket, or at the end of a garden hose!

'Every time I see a rainbow on a wet day I imagine that Lizzie might be at the end of it. I remember my mother crying endlessly for Lizzie—for years, really. And I think I made my mind up then that I never wanted a child of my own. I was scared to love someone that much and then lose them like that. I think I've only just realised it now. I know that sounds stupid, but driving away from everything has given me some sort of perspective on it all, I guess.

'I'm sure that's why I married Cameron. Deep down I knew he was gay, that he'd leave and we'd never have kids. And in some ways, I think I've chosen every man I've had a relationship with for the same reason. Every time I met a man who said he wanted kids, I ran away. And now I'm probably at the age where I might not get to have them . . .'

Nina and Meredith sat forward in their chairs. They began to protest that she did have time to have children, she could adopt . . . Annie headed off their sympathies. She'd heard it all before.

'No. Really. And I don't want you to feel sorry for me. I'm fine with it. I'm relieved to tell you the truth. I saw how my mother grieved after Lizzie left us, and I don't ever want that for myself. So that's my secret. And you're the first people I've told it to.'

Nina and Meredith could say nothing. As mothers, they had both lived with the daily dread of losing a child. They understood Annie had entrusted them with a precious secret. It was one secret Nina vowed she would always keep.

Annie let her mind reel back to her childhood. After Lizzie died she had always tried to stay close to her mother. She knew, even then, that with her father away with the cows in the paddocks all day, it had been up to her to fill the old house with the noise of childhood. If she could laugh loudly enough, play happily enough, catch her mother's attention—then perhaps Jean wouldn't notice Lizzie was gone.

Annie had sat at her mother's feet listening to the soft whirr of the sewing machine. She would trawl through the pile of fabric scraps and tack together small triangles or squares of stripes and florals to make dresses for her dollies. Everything was dutifully held up for her mother's inspection. Everything was extravagantly praised.

'Just lovely! You are a clever girl. One day, Annie my darling, you'll be able to sew for your own children. And you *must* have children. At least four. They'll all play together and watch out for each other.'

Annie thought of the small space by her mother's feet under the sewing table. She could smell the rich, dark tang of sewing-machine oil, hear the clunk of pinking shears on wood as they chewed through fabric . . . and her mother crying. Blizzards of linen and cotton threads had floated through the air and Annie had imagined she was looking out the window of a fairytale through falling snow. The swish of a satin evening skirt or a silky petticoat would drape and billow from above, falling and blocking her view. The curtain at the end of a play.

All over Treachery Beach Camp, through the branches of paperbark and ti-trees, Annie could see the twinkle of small camp fires. How many secrets were being shared tonight, she wondered. How many friendships were being forged in the heart of those flames?

'*Jesus on the main line, tell Him what you want,*' she sang softly.

'*Jesus on the main line, tell Him what you want,*' Nina joined the refrain.

'*Jesus on the main line, tell Him what you want,*' Meredith completed the trio.

'*You can call him up and tell him what you want.*'

✵

They were on the road early next morning. Nina wasn't saying much as she battened down the hatches for the day's motoring. She'd made a call to her boys, but she wasn't forthcoming on the conversation. She was quiet and that was unnerving. Meredith and Annie had become used to Nina's running commentary on all things domestic: 'The dustpan and brush go here. Hang that towel out to dry! Give that mat a shake!' Her silence was unnatural. The drone of her nagging was as much a part of their daily routine now as the annoying buzz of a blowfly over their breakfast bowls. A Nina who had given up nagging had given up on life.

The company was pushing on for Scotts Head, some two hundred and fifty kilometres north, for the night's stay. During the next hour or so in the van, as they headed into the blanched light of another hot day on the coast, there was no conversation. The drab twinned towns of Forster–Tuncurry—joined at the hip by a massive concrete bridge—passed by without comment. More dumped rocks. More fast food franchises. More cheaply built apartments. Another beachside paradise lost to bad planning and ugly development. What was there to be said?

By 10 am they were at the settlement of Taree, looking for coffee and diesel. Nina was standing at the counter of the BP service station when she caught sight of the front page of the *Daily Telegraph*.

'HUNTIN' CHEYENNE' screamed the strap headline in red: 'See Sports'. Nina snatched up the paper, turned it over and there, on the back page, was a grainy image that made her day.

The young woman in almost-focus was Cheyenne Neck. No doubt about it—snapped in the dim light of a toilet cubicle, the flash from a mobile phone camera had caught the heart-shaped stud in her nostril. She was bent over the toilet lid. What was that substance she was putting up her nose through a straw?

Meet Miss Cheyenne Neck, the woman who claims to be a credible witness to Kyle 'Tabby' Hutchinson's drug excesses. This photograph of her was taken in a toilet cubicle in a Melbourne nightclub some hours after the Richmond Tigers' recent heartbreak loss to the Sydney Swans at the MCG.

Ms Neck has made a string of sensational claims against the embattled Tabby Hutchinson—including that the Richmond team management covered up the discovery of cocaine and ecstasy in his dressing room locker.

Team manager Brad 'Kingie' Brown said last night the claims were 'a complete fabrication'. The further accusation that the star midfielder had approached the club for an advance on his salary to fund breast implants for his model girlfriend was also 'ridiculous', he said. 'Miss Neck is obviously troubled. She is at best misguided, at worst malicious,' he added.

Hutchinson's girlfriend, Emma Pang, also came to his defence. 'Cheyenne has been dating one of the Swans players since Christmas. She got dropped by one of the Tigers reserves players and I can only think she's done this to get back at him and the club,' said Ms Pang. 'I've got no idea where she would get this stuff. It's all just evil gossip,' she added.

Ms Pang also denied that she had undergone any surgical enhancement of her assets. 'Check me out in the April issue of *Zoo Weekly*. Have a look for yourself!' she challenged.

Hutchinson has been charged with possession of a prohibited drug and will appear in the Melbourne City Magistrates Court next week. 'The idea that his drug use was known about and condoned by this club is outrageous,' Brown said. 'Anyone who repeats this disgraceful lie will face swift legal action.'

Nina could have cried with relief. Instead, she executed a neat soft-shoe shuffle around the metal display stand of chocolate and grabbed herself a celebratory handful of Cherry Ripe and Crunchie bars. As she was heading for the cash register, Nina's mobile rang. She fumbled in her handbag.

'Hello, Nina Brown speaking,' she answered in her best professional tone, just as she had been trained to do.

'Did you read it?' Brad's mood was ebullient.

'Just now!' Nina was elated to hear him so upbeat.

'Not bad, eh? Now for Miss Corinne Jacobsen. We owe her one.'

'Oh, Brad, don't do anything that—'

'All's fair in love and war, babe! I love you, and this is war. As *Six Evening News* might say—*stay tuned*. You just enjoy your trip. The boys are fine. Gotta go.'

This time, when Brad rang off, he'd given Nina the Kiss of Life. She paid for her provisions with shaking hands and skipped back to the RoadMaster. Meredith and Annie read the newsprint thrust under their noses.

'So, this Cheyenne creature . . . was she telling the truth or not?' demanded Meredith.

'Who cares? Doesn't matter,' said Nina as she bit through the dark chocolate into a bounty of ripe sugary cherries.

'But she's like some sacrificial lamb. It's not really fair . . .' Annie complained.

'Hello? It's *football*,' exclaimed Nina, 'not tiddlywinks! There're millions of dollars at stake here—and my sons' education. You come between a footballer and a premiership and this is what happens. Shit is what happens. Maybe she'll have learned her lesson and get herself a nice panel beater.'

Nina joyfully revved the engine and roared off towards the Pacific Highway. She didn't tell them about Brad's oath to get Corinne. Who knew what he might come up with? The spectacle would not be for the faint-hearted.

Just up the road they sped past the iconic Big Oyster. It was no longer a restaurant, sadly, and now loomed over a used-car yard. 'Pick up a pearler of a deal!' Annie read aloud from the painted sign.

'It looks like a set of false teeth. So ugly!' Meredith physically recoiled from the window.

'The locals call it the Big Dentures,' laughed Annie, reading from one of her brochures.

Like every carload of tourists that ever drove past the massive concrete mollusc, they entertained themselves with a list of the Aussie Big Things they'd heard of: the Big Merino, the Big Avocado, the Big Potato, the Big Pineapple. The Big Dugong, Cod, Blue Heeler, Gumboot, Mosquito, Pelican, Earthworm.

'Why do people do it? What's the point?' asked Meredith. 'They should at least make them something most Australians can relate to around here—the Big Melanoma, the Big Cigarette Butt, the Big Police Speed Radar, the Big . . . Mac.'

'There *is* no point . . . and that's the point,' Annie patiently explained. 'You haven't been on a holiday in Australia unless you've had your photograph taken in front of a Big Thing.' They all vowed to pose in front of the Big Prawn at Ballina, just south of Byron Bay.

'So, how long will it take us to get to Byron?' asked Annie.

'We're right on schedule to land on Monday morning.' Meredith checked her travel diary. 'The wedding's on Tuesday, on the beach at dusk.'

'It's an odd day for a wedding,' said Nina.

'That's what I thought,' replied Meredith. 'Just another part of the mystery, I suppose. But I'm *so* looking forward to seeing Jarvis.'

The names Donald and Sigrid were notable by their absence.

Thirteen

It was mid-afternoon when the redoubtable RoadMaster pulled in to the Scotts Head Reserve Trust caravan park. This time Annie was nominated to front the site office. She jumped from the coolness of the air-conditioned cabin to the sandy path and was surprised to find the afternoon air so warm and oppressive. Thunderclouds were piling on the horizon—plump grey pillows arranged at the bedhead of bright blue sheets of sky.

A weary young mother with a sleeping baby in her arms and a pink bunny rug flung over one shoulder was behind the counter. As Annie handed over her credit card, she could see directly into the lounge room beyond, to where a television blared with cartoons. Two small children in school uniform sucking on icy poles were splayed on piles of dried laundry. The floor was an obstacle course of plastic toys. Annie could smell onions and garlic frying.

This unselfconscious view into the banality of family life fascinated Annie. Most of the houses she found herself in were empty or carefully tidied for public inspection. The casual scene in front of her was an aspect of humanity that was never on show in her modern apartment block in Port Melbourne. Were there any children in her entire street? She'd never noticed. Once more, Annie thought that she might have barricaded herself against the realities of life.

When the van was parked—close to the gas barbecues and near a small red-brick toilet block—Meredith and Nina busied themselves setting up the table and chairs in the sun. Annie noticed that the people at adjoining campsites were entirely oblivious to the fact that they might be observed. Folks lounged in swimsuits, poring over crossword puzzles; they emptied buckets of soapy dishwashing water onto the grass, towelled naked children. Human flesh was on display in all its lumpy, bumpy, hairy, hang-down glory. Annie was reminded that she had spent many summer holidays in just such a setting and, thinking back on it, she could only imagine that her parents made the drive from Tongala to the seaside every year for her benefit. How many times had they made sacrifices—driven long distances, spent time with families they didn't much like and saved their money to send her to boarding school—so that she might not miss her little sister?

Her mother's attempts at domestic order had always been sabotaged by sand. 'It gets into everything,' the mothers would complain to each other in the first days of the holidays. Soon they surrendered, and just dealt with the drifts of grit in shoes and beds and clothes. And soon the mothers would stop scolding about bedtimes and dirty feet—it was as if the sand burred the edges of their minds and reclaimed them into the dunes.

Then as now the fathers—divested of their overalls, their hard hats, ties and jackets—found themselves with more in common than they might have imagined. Tent pegs and tow bars, gas bottles and flywire. Li-los that wouldn't inflate, surf mats that wouldn't deflate, dogs that went missing, possums that had taken up residence in canvas annexes. There was something so comforting and democratic about it all—an Australia that Annie, living alone as she did, with her plasma TV screen and remote control lighting, had almost forgotten existed.

'I love it here,' said Nina, puffing after her exploration of the two beaches a short walk away through the banksias and paperbarks. 'Down there's Little Beach. It's this lovely cove surrounded by rocks. And just in front of us, over that dune, I think they call it Big Beach.'

Meredith shaded her eyes and took in Nina's heaving silhouette. 'Little Beach, Big Beach? The people round here didn't spend much time on naming things.'

'They didn't have to . . . a beach by any other name . . .' Annie smiled.

'There's a boat ramp and a gorgeous long walk we can take on the sand,' continued Nina. 'There're surfers on the point, and you can sit on these wooden benches and watch. Why don't we stay here an extra night? Then if we drive hard we can have one more night on the road and get into Byron on Monday morning. I'd like just one day when we didn't have to move.'

Meredith and Annie were more than happy to stay. They both had clothes to launder. Meredith fancied an afternoon in the sun working on her sudoku; Annie had all the latest fashion magazines stashed in her suitcase. They would linger in this glorious spot for two nights and their sojourn would begin with a swim.

✵

'Oh my God—look, dolphins!' Nina pointed to the spot where sleek forms were arcing and diving in the waves. The three women were up to their necks in the warm water just off Forster Beach. Nina had sought out the green wooden sign and found its correct name. With every hour she spent padding through paths in the dunes, her bare feet encrusted with sand, she was feeling more energetic. She had inspected tiny lizards skittering up tree trunks, crushed melaleuca leaves in her hands to smell their pungent aroma and sifted tiny shells through her fingers. She couldn't remember having done any of these things for years. The sea breeze was breathing life into neglected corners of her mind.

'I can see them! I can see them!' Annie squealed and swam towards the pod. Nina splashed after her.

Meredith turned and paddled back towards the beach—they looked like dolphins, certainly, but she thought they could also just as easily have been sharks. When her feet hit the bottom, she waded briskly back to shore.

Meredith laid her towel on the sand in the shade of a ti-tree, pulled on a gauzy beaded kaftan and surveyed the scene. Mothers were bent over, walking toddlers through the froth at the water's edge. Children dragged surf mats out to catch one more wave. A group of men stood at the top of the boat ramp, heads bowed in earnest discussion. The clouds had blown out to sea and the late afternoon sun slanted across the water, edging every ripple with amber glass. She counted the arrowheads of the Norfolk pines in the distance, black against the blue-grey hills behind. Eight of them. An auspicious number.

It was all just . . . perfect. Meredith retrieved her sudoku book and her pen, and stretched out on her stomach. Life was complete—she couldn't think of one more thing she desired. Her shop stuffed with must-have homeware items seemed a million miles away. She thought she must be experiencing something as simple as happiness.

When Annie and Nina joined her on the sand, they were on a high.

'They swam right under us!' Nina was breathless with excitement and exertion. She wrapped her floral sarong up to her armpits over her faded bathers.

'There must have been about six of them,' Annie babbled like a child. 'Dolphins, right under our feet—all around us. It was amazing!' She shook the water from her red curls and towelled her slim legs. In her black jersey bikini, fastened with golden rings, she cut an enviable figure.

'We're so far from Melbourne,' Nina marvelled. 'I've never been this far north. We're about halfway between Sydney and Brisbane. From here on in, it'll start to be more tropical.'

'Maybe we can buy mangoes and fix some daiquiris.' Annie flapped her towel and then arranged herself on it.

'There's a couple of small shops over there behind the caravan park.' Nina indicated behind her. 'Maybe I can get some steaks. Do you fancy a barbecue for dinner?'

The evening's timetable was drawn up and agreed upon—a last sunbake, a sunset walk on the beach, a barbecue, then Friday Night at the Scotts Head Bowling Club.

☼

They were becoming a harmonious trio now, working in concert. As the darkness dropped a thick curtain on the four sides of the gas barbecue hut, they had all pitched in—one turning steaks, one making salad, one assembling condiments and cutlery. They ducked under and over each other, Annie's lethal mango daiquiris in hand.

Praise was lavished on Nina's aged balsamic vinegar and Meredith's lovely table napkins—so much more *luxurious* than paper towels. Annie had flirted outrageously with the fishermen waiting next in line for the use of the barbecue. She happily tottered about in her bikini and a pair of black satin sling-backs, stopping now and then to shake the sand out of the toes.

After dinner they showered in the amenities block, tossing soap over the flimsy walls of the cubicles, handing bottles of shampoo underneath. They squeezed past each other in the confines of the van, and managed to pull together evening outfits and apply make-up.

It was about 8 pm when Annie, Nina and Meredith strolled into the Bowling Club dining room. After six nights on the road with just each other for company, it was exciting to be socialising. Annie was resplendent in one of her purchases from Toorak Road—a long paisley-printed jersey halter dress. She'd unearthed brand-new jewelled thongs to match. Her hair was pinned up in a tumbled confection of curls. She'd applied red lipstick and was wearing large diamanté hoop earrings. Tonight she turned the heads of most of the folk sitting at long tables wearing rumpled sandbagged T-shirts and scuzzy shorts.

Meredith was in a pristine cream scoop-necked top and had found the last pair of black linen trousers that weren't creased beyond recognition. Linen! Why had she ever imagined she would find an iron on the road? She vowed that on her next trip she would pack non-crush fabrics, and was surprised to find herself already planning another adventure. Her silver hair was still damp, but drying into fetching feathery layers. Her make-up created a polished portrait of beige-iness, a triumph given that she'd primped using a hand mirror under a bedside reading light. The ubiquitous pearls were in evidence—tonight in drop earrings and threaded on a white ribbon. She was an elegant apparition in this setting of painted brick, carpet tiles and fluorescent lighting.

It was Nina who looked like she belonged in the Scotts Head Bowling Club. She had found a perfectly plain powder-blue cotton shirt and worn it over three-quarter-length black pants. She refused to change out of her old scuffed black leather slides. Meredith had provided her with a touch of glamour—ropes of quartz beads and matching earrings. She hadn't been up to the task of blow-drying her hair in the tiny, humid bathroom, so her blonde frizz was tied back with a gold lamé scrunchie—even though Annie had threatened to tear the offending item off her head and incinerate it with her cigarette lighter. Make-up had seemed unnecessary, but Annie had commanded Nina to sit on the bed while she attacked her with mascara and pink lip gloss.

They found themselves a table, and then wondered what they might do around it. Talk? To each other? They'd done enough of that for now. Most folks nearby were carting meals to tables from the open kitchen servery. Sunburned children ran up and down the swirly, carnival-coloured carpet and threw paper serviettes. Annie got to her feet and beckoned Meredith and Nina to follow her around the corner.

The brightly lit bar was crowded and lorded over by three animated television screens. The walls sported lawn bowls and fishing club paraphernalia—trophies, ribbons, team photographs— so that the blokes gathered there might understand they were in some sort of shrine to all things male and conduct themselves accordingly. With all due respect. The low-ceilinged room was humming with conversation—that particular low and resonant drone punctuated by loud oaths and hearty guffaws that Nina knew so well from the bars Brad inhabited at the football club.

However, there was one indication that Nina was far from Tigerland. One TV was broadcasting a game of Rugby League— the enemy football code. On the field were two teams Nina had never heard of—the Manly Sea Eagles and the Brisbane Broncos.

Their jerseys were garish stripes of burgundy and gold; maroon and white, combinations that Nina thought were more suited to Melbourne Cup jockeys than football players. As she tuned in to the game, she saw the action was horrifyingly brutal.

Annie ordered drinks at the bar and returned with three glasses of white wine. Nina took hers with a mimed 'thanks' and then, mesmerised, found herself an empty seat at a table where she could see the screen. The two blokes she was sitting with were wearing red-and-green banded footy jumpers. They were oddly quiet during the game. They drank their beers steadily while wincing and muttering the odd 'fuck off' or 'fuck him' or 'fuck that'. The language didn't bother Nina—it hardly registered with her. During half-time she found the chance to introduce herself to . . . Johnno and Robbie, as it turned out.

'You're not enjoying the game much?' she ventured.

'Fucken Manly,' spat Johnno.

'Bronco deadshits,' added Robbie.

Again Nina wasn't fazed. The world of blokes held few surprises for her. 'So, I like your jumpers,' she said. 'Red and green. I don't know the team.'

'The colours are *cardinal* and *myrtle*. We go for the Rabbitohs,' Johnno grudgingly replied.

'Rabbits? They named a team after some *rabbits*?' The comment was out of Nina's mouth before she'd thought about it.

'Rabbit-*ohs*!' Robbie was clearly offended. 'After the blokes who used to sell rabbits in the streets of Redfern during the Depression.'

'Oh, that's . . . interesting,' was Nina's hopeless response. 'Actually, I'm married to a football player—Brad Brown.'

They both looked at her, clueless.

'Brad Brown. "BB". "Kingie",' she offered.

Still no response. Obviously more information was required.

'He used to play with the Tigers,' said Nina.

'Balmain or Wests?' asked Robbie.

'Pardon?'

'Balmain Tigers or Wests Tigers?' asked Johnno slowly, as if Nina was mentally challenged.

'The Richmond Tigers. AFL,' she said proudly.

'Fucken shit game,' said Robbie.

'Never heard of him,' added Johnno.

They both took their beers, got up from the table and walked outside to the balcony, where Nina saw them laugh as they puffed on their smokes.

Nina was thrilled by this casual exchange, utterly thrilled. It was the first time in almost two decades that she had been with people who hadn't heard of her husband! This called for another drink. She downed her wine and headed for the bar. Over in a corner she spied Meredith in the middle of a knot of men. Responding to Nina's wave, Meredith indicated that, yes, she would like a refill.

When Nina scooped up the fresh supplies off the bar and edged her way through the patrons to where Meredith was surrounded by admirers, she wasn't surprised to find the conversation was about fish. Meredith took the proffered drink, smiled at Nina and again bent her head to listen. Nina had nothing to add, so she left Meredith to it and went off to find Annie.

'. . . about ten snapper, a few morwong, a couple of samson—and all a decent size too,' a tall red-headed man was saying. 'And—you won't credit this—but a pearl perch, I reckon close on three and a half kilo.'

'Bulltwang! They don't grow that big. You're full of it, Meggsy!' roared his offsider. He squeezed Meredith's upper arm and leaned to whisper in her ear: 'Don't listen to him, love, he's a total crap artist.'

At the closeness of his lips to her ear and the smell of his beery breath, Meredith felt a rush of . . . something she hadn't felt for a long, long time. She looked up into his amused eyes that were deep blue tidal pools in his weathered brown face. Thick grey hair stood out in salt-stiffened tufts. Bill was his name. He smelled of the sea, and fish. Tiny translucent scales were caught in the cables of his Aran-knit jumper and Meredith fancied she'd been netted by King Neptune himself. She lurched on her white espadrilles.

'Whoops! You right there?' Bill threw his massive muscled forearm around Meredith's shoulder to steady her. She could feel the heat of him through her clothes. Meredith didn't object as his arm dropped to her waist. And stayed there.

'But your pearl perch—it's one of the most prized eating fish in Australia. Beautiful!' Bill enthused, to the agreement of his mates. 'Have you ever eaten pearl perch, Meredith?'

'No, I don't think I have.'

There was a murmur of disbelief and a shaking of heads at this sad confession.

'I'll have to take you out in the boat with me then and catch you one. Or maybe I should strip off and dive for pearls for you instead, seeing as you're a pearl kind of girl.'

Bill reached to finger one of the pearls threaded on ribbon and as his calloused hand brushed her left breast Meredith was aware that her nipples tingled. She quickly folded her arms.

'How long are you staying, did you say?'

'Just till Sunday morning.'

'Well,' he said, leaning in to whisper in her ear again over the noisy hum of the room, 'we haven't got much time to get to know each other, have we?'

✤

Annie stood on the outside deck of the club overlooking the smooth expanse of the bowling greens. The smoke from her cigarette curled under the eaves and then dissipated in the stiff breeze now blowing in from the beach.

She'd made a tour of the premises—inspected the carved wooden honour roll dedicated to 'Those Who Served' and the portrait of the Queen in a blue gown, a vase of kangaroo paw and wattle in evidence, and bearing the legend: NSW Women's Bowling Association, 1989. As she wandered between tables, she had felt every eye surveying her outfit and felt more and more conspicuous. Finally, she'd taken refuge on the bench outside, ignoring the sly appraisal of the blokes in football jumpers in a huddle down one end of the concrete balcony.

244

She was relieved to see Nina push her way through the double glass doors. 'I think I'll wander back to the van. I feel a tad overdressed.'

'I'll come with you,' Nina said, shivering in the wind. 'I'm really tired. I think I must have got a touch of sun today. Will I get Meredith?'

'Nah, leave her. That big bloke is all over her. She might get lucky.'

'She wouldn't. Would she?'

'I certainly hope so. She'll find her way back. Let's go.'

Annie and Nina walked the cyclone wire covered path alongside the greens, and back to the adjoining caravan park. They threaded their way through the dark—past open fires, hissing gas lamps, shadows on canvas—carefully stepping over tent pegs and guy ropes.

'I was thinking about a sea change to the country or the coast,' said Annie. 'But God, I can't imagine myself fitting in in a place like this! Look at me. I'm dressed like a freak. I reckon I'd hyperventilate if I couldn't buy new shoes once a fortnight. No barista, good bread or organic market! One restaurant. One bowls club. Two conversations—football and fish. What the hell was I thinking?'

Nina could see her point, but it wasn't the whole story. 'This town's tiny, but there're lots of other places on the coast that—'

'Forget it. It's all too far away from Mum and Dad.' Annie shook her head. 'I can't see myself going anywhere much until they're both gone.'

'But that could be another twenty years!'

'Yeah. I s'pose it would have been different if Lizzie was alive—we could have shared the load. It's weird when you think about it. All that feminist stuff we got into years ago, the independence and individuality we all banged on about, and how does it end up? Nursing your parents—making soup and beds, and rinsing undies. It mostly ends up being women's work. And it lands on you just when you start thinking of escape.'

Nina nodded. She dreamed of escape too, although over the past few days she had come to believe that the entire concept might be overrated. Wherever you escaped to, you were still there. On this trip, she reflected as she turned the key in the door of the van, they were travelling away from all they knew. What was appearing just over the crest of the road? The Big Nina, the Big Annie and the Big Meredith.

✵

The breeze chilled the places where Bill's tongue had licked at Meredith's bare breasts. The planks of the bleachers under her naked back were still warm with the absorbed heat of the day. She couldn't believe she was doing this—in a place that must have been the scene of a thousand teenage trysts. No doubt they would have laughed to see two middle-aged lovers desperately clawing at each other under the stars.

The moon was low and heavy in the sky, and over Bill's head Meredith could see a restless, endless sea of silver. She was entirely naked now and so was he. He lay over her, covering her body with a fleshy warmth that stopped the shivering. The heat from his body infused her limbs and she relaxed. Her fingers trawled across his hard, muscled back and found crusts of dried salty foam.

The waves were breaking on the rocks below and, as Meredith slipped out of her skin, they seemed to be breathing for her. A long, slow intense pulse of energy roared and peaked and crashed. Meredith was swept away into the depths. She was a mermaid swimming away from all she knew.

❄

'You had sex with that bloke last night, didn't you?' Annie was revelling in the exquisite pleasure of having her tormentor in the spotlight. There was no need for Meredith to reply—she was smiling like the cat that got the cream.

'Meredith, you only just met him!' Nina was aghast.

Meredith refused to surrender any information. She stood beside the flimsy camp table and stretched languorously. 'It's a divine morning. Who's coming for a walk?'

'It's past midday. We've been up for hours,' said Annie, making the point that she wasn't the only one capable of sleeping in and wasting the day.

'Just hang on a tick,' said Nina. 'I want to see what the weather's doing at home before I ring the boys. They're playing football this afternoon.' She collected the breakfast things and the remains of the fruit salad and ducked into the van. When she switched on the television to see the Saturday afternoon sports show, the panel discussion immediately caught her attention.

'It's probably a day Corinne Jacobsen would like to forget,' the young female ex-hockey champion in the red blazer was saying.

'Well, she hasn't commented yet so . . .' began the telegenic male host sitting next to her behind the desk.

'But, you have to say she's got a lot of fast talking to do if any of these reports are true,' the salt-and-pepper-haired elder statesman of the panel interrupted and stubbed his finger on the pile of newspapers in front of him.

'If you've just tuned in,' said the host, 'Logie-winning actress Tasha Bowen has this morning made sensational allegations that her husband—tennis ace, Mitchell Haddon—has abandoned her and their nine-month-old twins for the veteran former Channel 5 TV hostess.'

'She's almost twenty years his senior,' the hockey champ chick chimed in.

'Well, this one's definitely *not* "love-all",' punned the chirpy host. 'We'll be back with more—an exclusive interview with Tasha Bowen, and a look at the career highlights of Mitchell Haddon—right after the break.'

Time had stood still for Nina as she watched all this on the van's small television. Now she wrung her tea towel nervously. This was obviously Brad's handiwork. Tasha was the famous younger sister of Travis Bowen—one of Richmond's star wingers. By the time Nina had screeched for Meredith and Annie to join her at the table in front of the TV, and furnished them both with cups of tea, the sports show was back.

The three hosts efficiently summed up the allegation made in that morning's Sydney *Telegraph*, Melbourne *Herald Sun*, Brisbane *Courier-Mail*, Adelaide *Advertiser*, Hobart *Mercury*, Perth's *West Australian* and the Cooktown *Courier*. Corinne's affair with the twenty-seven-year-old tennis star had (allegedly) begun when he was the number two seed at the Australian Open that January. He had recently moved out of the marital home, citing a need for 'more space'. The space he had found was in Corinne's bed while the billionaire (with a special emphasis on the 'b') packaging tycoon Malcolm Pearson (her second husband, it was noted) was in New York working on a company takeover.

The evidence? That had been kindly supplied by the nation's sweetheart, Tasha Bowen herself. A blurry black-and-white nude photograph of Corinne in the shower, with the various rude bits blacked out, flashed up on the screen.

'Oh my God!' exclaimed Nina.

'Holy shit!' muttered Annie.

'Shoosh!' commanded Meredith.

'This is just one of the many photographs found by Tasha Bowen, and supplied to the nation's media,' intoned the host. 'And Tasha has agreed to speak with us from her hotel. Good afternoon, Tasha. Can you tell us about this photograph?'

'It's one of the ones I found on his computer,' said Tasha, her eyes brimming in a damning close-up. 'And I took his phone. He thought he'd lost it. I know I did the wrong thing, but I had to know for sure. There were lots of text messages on it from her. Nothing that, you know, you could say on television 'cos there might be kids watching.'

The panel members all nodded sympathetically, even though they had an urgent requirement for more information before the next break.

'Tasha, we know this is a very hard time for you,' crooned the host. 'Especially when your twins Violet and Daisy are so young...'

'Six months old! Hard to comprehend this sort of behaviour.' The crusty old ex-footy player crammed into his red blazer shook his head with genuine wonder. 'Tasha, do you think that this *alleged* affair had anything to do with Mitchell's much-criticised performance at the Australian Open this year, when he was bundled out in the first round by the unranked Russian?'

'Well,' Tasha sniffed, 'Corinne... Miss Jacobsen... *she* was there. She was there the whole time in the same hotel. Mitchell said that he couldn't sleep in our suite 'cos of me breastfeeding the twins and everything. So he took another room up the hall. I couldn't understand why he still looked so tired. Now... I reckon I know why.' The camera zoomed in to catch her tears.

'He should of won.' She sobbed. 'If he didn't want to do it for me and the girls, he could of done it for Australia.' She dropped her head, unable to continue.

This was possibly the worst news of all for Corinne. She'd already been branded a husband stealer, home wrecker and cradle snatcher. Now she'd done something far more reprehensible— robbed the nation of international sporting success. Her reputation was rubble.

In the van, Meredith was slapping her hands on the table in merriment, Nina was open-mouthed and speechless, while Annie cringed in the corner, chewing on a cushion.

The piece wrapped with an invitation to viewers to take part in an exclusive *Sportsdesk* poll: *Which Woman Would YOU*

Rather Be With? The choice was between a blurry image of the naked forty-six-year-old Corinne Jacobsen, taken with a mobile phone, or a glossy portrait of Tasha Bowen in a leopard-print bikini on the beachside set of her soapie series for the cover of *TV Week*. It was a no-brainer.

'I have to find my mobile and vote.' Meredith jumped from her seat and began rummaging through cupboards.

'Don't! You're being a total bitch!' admonished Annie. 'Poor Corinne.'

'*Poor Corinne?*' Meredith was scandalised. 'Shane Warne went down for less!' She stabbed her finger at the television. Annie could find nothing to say. Meredith had a point.

The weather report was halfway through when Nina's phone trilled. She fell downstairs and took the call.

'Did you see it?' Brad's tone was triumphant.

'Bloody hell! How did you pull that off?' Nina was genuinely in awe of her husband's powers.

'Bit of inside info from young Travis . . . Apparently the kid sister and the in-laws were waiting for hubby to come home. I talked her out of it. Convinced her that she was far better off financially if she nailed the prick.'

'She did that alright! And Corinne . . .'

'I told you I'd fix her too. Didn't win Best and Fairest over so many years for nothing!'

Nina smiled. It was an in-joke between her and Brad that the Best and Fairest title was won by rat cunning more than anything else.

'I've just gotta get Tabby through this court thing in Melbourne on Monday and I'll be back to my usual shit-fight. Jeez, I'm knackered with all this! I wish you were here. I just checked and the boys are off to footy with Dad, so it's all good at home. I'll see you soon then. Miss you, babe.'

'Bye, honey, see you soon. I miss you too. I love you.'

'Love you too.'

※

Annie was strolling to the beach under the shade of the paperbark trees for an afternoon dip when she was stopped in her sandy tracks by a sight she'd long given up on seeing again. There, on the boat ramp, was a LandCruiser with Victorian plates. Behind it two men were uncoupling a tinnie on a trailer—Matty and Zoran.

The last time Annie had spotted their rig was outside Foxglove Spires at Tilba Tilba. She hadn't set eyes on Matty himself since that first night at Lakes Entrance. She had been entertaining herself with daydreams about him, but time and distance had made her think that she was probably nurturing an adolescent fantasy. Well, she'd soon find out. She pulled the combs from her hair and shook out her curls, tugged her bikini into place and draped a beach towel over her shoulder.

As she came closer to the ramp, Matty stood up from behind the boat and Annie instantly knew he was no conjured fantasy. She stumbled on the fringe of the towel. In that moment he saw her.

'Hey, Annie! Annie Bailey?' he called and waved.

'Hi!' She regained her balance and waved back.

He was out from behind the boat in an instant, and coming towards her—a bare-chested, sandy-haired, muscled . . . *dreamboat*. Annie couldn't believe she'd come up with that word. It was out of some 1950s *Gidget* movie. And then he was standing in front of her smiling, and leaning in to kiss her cheek. Her nose touched his broad, suntanned shoulder. She was reminded of those passionate kisses in the dark, and her face felt hot.

'I've been looking for you. I've got your sunglasses,' he said with a broad smile. So that was it, thought Annie. She was thinking that might be the reason he was seeking her, but hoped it wasn't the only one.

'Great! I've been looking everywhere for them.' The words *and for you* popped into her head.

'Come on over—I've got 'em in the glovebox. You remember Zoran?'

Zoran turned to wave and grin, and went back to loading the fishing rods. Matty found the sunnies and pressed them into Annie's hands. He held her slim fingers for a moment—long enough for Annie to remember that his hands had cupped her bare breasts under her velour top.

'We're just about to go out for a session,' he said, taking back his hands and running them through his mop of sun-bleached hair. Annie guessed that he'd also remembered where they'd been. 'We'll trawl over a few reefs, after Spanish mackerel, so . . .'

Annie expected that his next words would be: *good to see you again—bye.*

'. . . you staying here?'

'With my friends, Nina and Meredith. In this bizarre giant motorhome.'

'I remember you said that. It's not the van with Elvis on the side?'

'Uh-huh,' Annie replied. 'Or should that be *uh-huh, uh-huh!*' She threw in a salutation from The King.

Matty got the joke and grinned at her. She noticed that his teeth were even and white. Perfectly formed, like the rest of him. Annie caught herself thinking that one could tire of such physical perfection. There had to be something wrong with him. In that moment she saw it—his ears were just slightly out of proportion. For some odd reason this made Annie feel better. Perhaps, she thought, because it was proof he was human after all, not just some figment of her almost middle-aged imagination.

'If it's the same van, that's weird.' Matty wrinkled his tanned nose dashed with freckles. 'Nina and Meredith, right? I've met them. We caught up with them in Mallacoota the day after I met you. They said they didn't know you.'

And then Annie remembered Meredith's ridiculous lesbian charade. 'That's because they were trying to . . . I know this sounds stupid, but they are pretty protective of me. I was down by the lake when you were there.'

'They don't like men, huh?' Matty nodded. 'That's cool—a lot of women like that don't like—'

Annie had to laugh. 'They're not lesbians! They just made that up.' She could see he was struggling to make sense of it all.

'So I guess that's why they turned down the invitation the second time to meet up with us at Pretty Beach.'

'What? You saw them *again*?'

'I ran into Nina at the beach showers at Gillard's. We were all due to have sunset cocktails at Pretty Beach.'

'Really? We stayed at Pebbly Beach that night.'

'Well, anyway . . .' Matty shrugged and grinned again. 'Here's an idea. We're staying at Lot 55, just next to the path over the dunes. So why don't you bring the ladies over around six, and we'll have those cocktails and make you dinner? Zoran's a top cook. And, hopefully, there'll be Spanish mackerel on the menu.'

'I'm sure the girls would love that. Although . . .' and here Annie thought she might entertain herself, 'do something for me. Don't let on you know they're not gay. I'd like to see them squirm for a bit.'

Matty laughed. 'I'm remembering now that you have a wicked streak in you, Annie Bailey. OK, deal. See you then.'

'Good luck with your fishing!'

✲

'I'm not staying long,' Meredith hissed. The sun was sinking behind clumps of ti-tree as they trailed through the campgrounds to Lot 55. 'I'm having one drink and then, I have . . .' she paused, trying to find the right term, 'an engagement.'

'Oooh! She's gonna bonk her mystery man again! You trollop, Meredith!' Annie nudged Nina. 'Your woman's bisexual. Can't keep her eyes off the blokes. Did you know that, honey? When do we get to meet this stud anyway?'

'They think we're lesbians!' Nina grizzled. 'How long do we have to keep this up?'

'Come on now, girls—hold hands, play nice,' sang Annie as she marched ahead with righteous purpose. 'Serves you right for lying to them back in Mallacoota. If you hadn't tried to interfere in my love life this wouldn't be happening.'

'Shut up, Annie,' said Meredith. 'This is completely embarrassing. We're having just one drink and then we're going. As for your "love life", someone's got to interfere sometime. You're not making much of a success of it.'

'Oh that hurts, Meredith! But I like this guy, so just do it for me. It won't kill you. He doesn't need to know my friends are total fake lezzo weirdos.'

'I met that Matty again,' Nina blurted.

'What!?' Annie turned and glared at her with as much fake indignation as she could muster.

'At Gillard's Beach and we were all going to meet up and have a cocktail party on the beach . . . only,' now Annie and Meredith were both eyeballing her, 'I got a bit lost.'

'So did you tell him *then* that you weren't a lesbian?' demanded Annie.

'Not exactly. He just assumed so . . .'

'You let your filthy lie follow us up half the east coast of Australia. So, serves you both right! You better start acting like a lovely couple.'

Annie trotted along, happily humming to herself. Meredith and Nina straggled behind her, arms folded like two sullen schoolgirls on a dreaded excursion. Up ahead Annie spied Matty and Zoran standing under the striped annexe of a handsome old-fashioned green canvas tent, complete with seven-foot wooden poles. They were dressed in clean shirts and cargo pants. As she came closer, she could see five chairs arranged around a camp table set with an ice bucket and plates of antipasto—dips, olives and bread sticks.

For a pair of 'yobbos', they were surprisingly domestic, thought Nina. They looked far more like a same-sex couple than she and Meredith ever would. Annie couldn't have chosen a gay man *again*, could she? She looked at Meredith who raised her eyebrows. She seemed to be thinking the very same thing.

After a hearty round of kissed 'hellos' and the acceptance of Annie's bottle of wine, Matty offered drinks. 'We have vanilla martinis, or would you like to start with your very impressive chardonnay?'

Zoran stepped forward and proudly explained the menu: 'Grilled eggplant and red pepper antipasto. This one's ceviche—raw snapper cured with lime juice. I caught the fish this afternoon, so it's about as fresh as it can get. Then the dips are beetroot and this one's basil and fetta. All home-made. Please, help yourselves.'

Nina was bug-eyed. They didn't seem like 'union thugs' or 'idiots'. She searched for confirmation from Meredith, who refused to look at her.

When they were all settled with drinks and plates of food, Matty gave Annie a secret, conspiratorial smile and began: 'So, you've been a little mischievous, hiding Annie from us.'

Nina and Meredith shifted uneasily in their chairs, coughed in unison, sipped at their martinis.

'Yes, they've been impersonating the ugly stepsisters, I'm afraid,' scolded Annie. 'Very naughty ladies indeed.'

'And Matty's been chasing Cinderella up the coast with a pair of sunglasses. Priceless!' chuckled Zoran.

'Still,' continued Matty, 'when you're in such a *close* relationship yourself, you want the best for your friends, don't you? So we forgive you. That's a brilliant rig you've got. You gals do a lot of travelling?'

Nina stuffed her mouth with bread so she didn't have to answer. This was torture.

'We get away whenever we can,' Meredith mumbled.

'And you're obviously both huge Elvis fans. Where'd you meet? At a convention or something?' asked Zoran. Meredith said nothing. Bugger Nina—it was her turn. Annie was pinching her own thighs, trying not to laugh—this was the best fun she'd had in ages.

Nina almost choked on her half-chewed lump of bread. 'Um . . . well, we've all known each other for about twenty years. We used to sing together in a gospel choir called Sanctified Soul. But Meredith and I only recently . . . got together.' She looked to Meredith for assistance. And found none. 'Didn't we . . . sweetheart?'

This was beyond excruciating. Nina wanted to run away and jump into the sea.

'That often happens, doesn't it, Zoran?' Matty turned to his mate. 'You're friends for years and then one day it just turns into . . . something else.' He reached for Zoran's hand and gave it an affectionate squeeze. Zoran ostentatiously blew Matty a kiss.

At the sight of Meredith and Nina exchanging looks and then turning back to Annie, their foreheads furrowed with concern and sympathy, Annie couldn't help herself. Her head pitched forward to her knees and she exploded with laughter. On her cue, Matty and Zoran saw the game was up and both fell about.

'Very, very amusing.' Meredith was stony-faced. Nina scowled.

'You should have seen yourselves!' snorted Annie. 'Oh God! That was the funniest thing I have ever . . .' She collapsed into giggles again.

'Sorry,' Matty apologised. 'Annie made us do it.'

'And you're not the ugly sisters at all,' added Zoran. 'In fact, if you weren't gay, I'd ask you to dance.'

He reached behind him for the ghetto-blaster, and soon Cyndi Lauper's 'Girls Just Wanna Have Fun' rocked out through the caravan park.

✷

Three hours later, Zoran and Nina had decided they must be related to each other. Her parents were from the Ukraine, his were from Slovenia. What were the odds of them meeting at the Scotts Head Reserve Trust Caravan Park on a Saturday night in April?

They'd had a true meeting of minds over Zoran's dry red Spanish mackerel curry and mango salad. Nina pronounced it the best curry she had ever eaten . . . in her entire life. Zoran had flushed with pleasure from the tips of his long skinny toes to the whiskers on his black goatee, and given her the recipe.

After that, they had fallen into a deep discussion about food and Nina's café plans, about life with immigrant parents, and politics in Eastern Europe. Nina couldn't recall anyone understanding her as completely as Zoran did. She talked with him for three and a half hours and didn't feel the need to mention her famous footballer husband once. This was another revelation. That question she had asked at the beginning of the trip—Who was this anonymous woman far from home, listening to the surf pound beyond the dunes?—she now had the answer to: she was Nina Kostiuk. Herself. No-one else.

Annie was some metres away, just beyond the banksias, rolling in the damp sand on the moonlit beach in a passionate embrace with Matty. Sand *did* get into everything, as her mother had once complained. They paddled, splashed, crawled, built a soggy sandcastle and kissed over its collapsing towers. They kissed and kissed again, lying at the water's edge with their feet in the foam and their heads tangled in seaweed. Annie was water-logged, sand-logged, lust-logged. Her jersey skirt was wet and heavy, her knickers damp, her hair coarse with grit, tiny shells were pressed into the soft flesh between her toes.

When the moon was at its biggest and brightest, Annie whispered to Matty that she wanted to spend the night with him in his tent.

'No.' He put a wet finger to her lips. 'No. It's not right tonight. Not with the others here. Not now. Let's wait.'

☼

By shifting, random scraps of moonlight Annie and Nina peered at the lock of the RoadMaster's door. Annie jiggled the key and pronounced it locked from the inside. Nina cursed herself for handing over the main key-ring to Meredith earlier in the evening. She must have secured the latch from the inside.

'Oh no!' groaned Annie. 'I'll bet Meredith and her bowls club fuck buddy are in there!' She threw herself into a flimsy metal camp chair and checked her watch: 11.30 pm. She was tetchy and frustrated. She lit a cigarette, which she thought was ironic, considering that her libido was stranded at high tide.

There was no cloud and the onshore breeze had turned into a fair wind. Nina's teeth were chattering. They were both sleeveless. Annie walked to the end of the van, near to where she imagined Meredith's bed must be, and put her ear to the thin aluminium wall.

'I can't hear anything. They're probably unconscious from too much rooting.'

'What'll we do?' whispered Nina.

'Well, when I was a boarder at good old Girton Grammar in Bendigo, you had to leave your shoes out the front of the door if you had a boy inside your room. Can you find any?'

Nina scavenged in the shadows. 'Just this.' She held up a garment for inspection in the dim light from the park's power pole. It was a thick, cream-coloured Aran-knit fisherman's jumper.

'OK then,' said Annie. 'At least you can wrap that around yourself to keep warm. We'll give her ten more minutes . . .'

There was an urgent 'ding' from Nina's handbag. She scrabbled through the debris inside and found her phone. The text message read: 'Luv U Mum. Miss U. Cum home soon. Jordy. XXX.'

Nina's heart melted. Her eldest, darling baby boy was thinking of her. 'Isn't that gorgeous?' She allowed herself a nag-free moment of pure maternal love. 'Although he should be in bed by now. You know, it's the weirdest thing. I was just thinking, back there while I was talking to Zoran, that finally . . . finally, I might be the old Nina. Not "wife" or "mother" or "daughter", just me . . . And now look! It's like the boys have sensed I was somehow drifting away from them.'

'Remember the Force, Luke!' declared Annie, throwing her cigarette into a bucket under a tap where it hissed and died. 'Remember the Force.'

The front door banged open. A hairy hulk of a man barged down the stairs, grunted, 'Night,' and sprinted for the car park in front of the surf club.

'It's a Wookie!' cried Nina.

'And he's just shagged Princess Leia!' yelled Annie. 'After him, Han Solo!'

✵

They moved on from Scotts Head early that morning with bruised hearts. Annie was thinking about Matty. Meredith was mooning over Bill. Nina, unusually for her, had stayed curled in her bed complaining that she wasn't feeling too well as the camp was packed up. She drifted in and out of sleep dreaming she was protecting her three baby boys from the Attack of the Poisonous Curry Pot Noodles.

They were in for a long drive that Sunday. Angourie was Annie's choice of destination. Her brochures raved about the legendary surf, the famous Blue Pool, the Yuraygir National Park and stunning beaches. She had to see the place and, if they stayed there for the night, it would put them within easy striking distance of Byron Bay. They could make a stately procession into town on Monday morning, in good time for the wedding the next evening.

However, they weren't too far down the road before Nina skidded the van to a halt in the gravel at the side of the road. The fiery mackerel curry had done its work. She leapt from the driver's seat and flew through the cabin to the toilet. A series of graphic explosions and low groans propelled Annie from her seat at the table, gagging, with her hand over her mouth.

After emptying half a can of vanilla-scented room spray in the cubicle, Nina emerged clutching her stomach. 'Must be the chillies,' she said weakly. 'We don't usually eat anything too spicy at home. The boys don't like it. Oops! Hang on. Here I go again.'

Annie stood at the side of the road puffing at cigarettes and surveying empty paddocks while Meredith inspected the wild-flowers in a damp drain. Twenty minutes later it was plain Nina was not in a fit state to drive. She was in agony. She lay down on Meredith's bed in the rear of the cabin, within easy reach of the bathroom.

There was no way Meredith wanted to brave the stink of the toilet, but she suddenly realised that her need was equally pressing. A stinging hot stab of pain in her bladder sent her sprinting up the stairs and into the loo. The eye-watering experience told her one thing—she had an attack of cystitis to equal Nina's diarrhoea. A few minutes later she emerged, pale-faced and shivering. She considered saying: 'I usually don't have any sex at home—I don't like it,' but decided that might be too much information. 'I might sit up the back here with Nina. I'm not feeling too bright myself. Chillies probably. Are you OK to drive, Annie?'

Annie, apart from the usual crashing hangover and a nasty sand rash on her knees and elbows, was feeling fine. 'No worries! You two just get comfy there in the back and I'll get us to Angourie in no time,' she sang, impersonating the jovial leader of a Japanese tour bus. Meredith and Nina vowed to strangle her—when they felt up to it. With a protesting crunch of gears, the RoadMaster lurched onto the highway with Annie at the wheel. For the next leg to Coffs Harbour, Nina and Meredith wobbled up the galleyway and took turns in the stifling, stinking loo.

As she looked for a chemist and a place to park the hulking van, Annie made a cursory tour of Coffs. Her survey of the place confirmed what she had suspected—that there was a direct correlation between the number of old blokes in whites at the lawn bowls club and the amount of rocks dumped on the beach. The locals up and down this part of the coast had spent a life-time battling the ocean with their earth-moving equipment—

building sea walls, marinas, groins, harbours, breakwaters, boat ramps, docks and piers. They apparently considered it their patriotic duty to divert the rivers and thwart the tides. The bowls club was packed this morning and the Coffs Harbour front was a fortress of massive boulders.

A packet of Ural urinary alkaliniser crystals and Panadol capsules for Meredith; a box of Lomotil anti-diarrhoea tablets for Nina; and cigarettes, hot chips and a can of Coke for Annie. Then, suitably medicated, they were soon heading north again, past the Big Banana.

As she cruised the highway in the driver's seat, Annie was enjoying herself hugely. She was playing her favourite Black Eyed Peas *Monkey Business* CD and joyfully puffing on her fags—the smoke streaming out the partly open window in satisfying, elegant ribbons. In the back, Nina and Meredith, lulled by the drone of the engine and the gentle rocking of the cabin, were both, mercifully, asleep.

Annie thought back on last night. Was it her heart that was bruised, or her ego? She decided that Matty had rejected her. He could have found a way for them to have sex last night if he'd really wanted to. He could have moved Zoran out of the tent or dragged a sleeping bag out on the grass under the stars. She wasn't used to getting knocked back and didn't like it one little bit. There was something about Matty that was way too self-possessed and controlling for her liking.

She had Matty's phone number in her mobile and the promise of a dinner date back in Melbourne, but was now thinking that she might just pass on the offer. She decided there just wasn't that spark between them—that 'certain something' that would sweep her off her feet. And that, she realised, was what she was hoping for—a king tide of emotion that would wash her up into her future, so that she wouldn't have to dog paddle anymore.

They were six hundred kilometres north of Sydney now and well into subtropical climes. The Pacific Highway had turned inland and the dense dark-green of sugar cane plantations stretched either side on fertile river flats.

Annie drove into South Grafton and saw that, if she followed the highway, she would bypass Grafton itself. However, the chance to see the mighty Clarence River was not to be passed up. With the Murray River now reduced to muddy puddles in some stretches because of the drought, she longed to see a deep and fast-flowing waterway. This was big river country and the brochures she had been reading promised broad, shiny expanses plied by gaily painted houseboats. She grabbed the map, balanced it on her knees and made the decision that she would drive into Grafton proper.

From there, Annie calculated, she could drive out of town and follow the western side of the Macleay River up to Lawrence. A ferry would take them back across the river and they could head directly to the coast and Angourie. With her travelling companions still dozing, Annie was thankful she was able to make all these decisions without the usual tiresome discussion and negotiation.

The RoadMaster slowed to crawl across the bridge over the Clarence. Annie, entranced with the river's lazy, serene majesty, ignored the agitated toots of the drivers behind taking in the magnificent vista of the Confederate flag on the wide backside of her vehicle. She drove slowly through the gracious city of Grafton and admired the generous plantings of its famous jacaranda trees, its handsome Victorian buildings and spacious streets. Then she headed out of town along the road that hugged the western bank of the river.

The land here was a sodden, sandy sponge all year round and through it the water surfaced in a thousand random puddles. The early afternoon sky was overcast and everywhere Annie looked, mirrors were glinting with a grey sheen. She wished that her father could see this place. That he could feel the moisture seep into his bones and be restored. Annie wiped at her damp forehead. The warmth and humidity melted the boundary between skin and air, making it hard to tell where her skin ended and the air began. She was dissolving into the landscape.

Reluctantly leaving the close embrace of the Clarence behind, Annie steered the van some way inland towards the settlement of Lawrence. She would find the meandering river there again and load the van onto the ferry for the crossing. Clouds were now hanging low on the horizon and Annie drove her sleeping cargo into a sensuous autumn mist. A flurry of moisture smeared the windscreen. For the first time since the RoadMaster had left Melbourne, the wipers were put to good use.

The road ahead was a beaten belt of pewter through the fabric of soft grey fog. Jewels of flashing red and blue lights pierced the gloom. Annie slowed and could make out the word 'Detour' on a bright yellow sign.

The rain was really coming down now. Drops, fattened on the peaks of the mountains to the west, exploded on the glass in front of her face. Peering through the deluge, Annie could vaguely see a shiny tangle of wet metal and the ghostly forms of people wading through ankle-deep water. She leaned out of the window to speak to a police officer in a see-through plastic shroud.

'Truck crash!' He cupped his hands to shout against the wind. 'Where you headed?'

'Angourie,' Annie shouted back. A gust tore her voice away. The rain was driving almost horizontally through the open window and soaking her shirt-front.

'Could take hours to clear. You'll have to take the detour up through the Summerland Highway, and then double back down through Casino.'

'Casino?' Annie was sceptical. She knew the lay of the land by now. 'That'll take all day!'

'You could probably camp here overnight in this thing.' His index finger stabbed a hole through the fog. 'As long as you get right off the road and don't become a traffic hazard. Otherwise, if you want to get to the coast tonight, Casino's your best bet.'

Annie gave a thumbs-up and wound the window tight. According to the map, there was another way to go. She could skirt The Broadwater, go up through Tullymorgan, and then rejoin the Pacific Highway somewhere between Jacky Bulbin Flat and Mororo Road. They should make Angourie in time for a walk on the beach at sunset. She waved her thanks to the plastic-wrapped form of the man in blue and moved off.

Staring through the pelting rain, Annie drove slowly and found the signs she was looking for. She congratulated herself that she was doing well in handling the big machine. And why not? After all, she'd been driving the tractor on the farm since she was ten. The roads were flat, shining panes of water; in the rear-vision mirror she saw the van was leaving a fair wake in its path. She could, she reflected, be steering an old-time paddle-steamer up a river in the Congo.

'Where in God's name are we?' Meredith climbed into the front seat, rubbing her eyes and pulling at her rumpled clothes. She wiped a patch of moisture from her window and squinted through it. 'I can't see a damned thing, and it's absolutely bucketing down.'

'There was a truck crash back a bit, so I'm negotiating my way around it.' Annie threw the map to Meredith and pointed. 'It's that bit there.'

Meredith found her reading glasses and stared at the damp square in front of her, turning it this way and then that, as if she was trying to decipher the runic symbols on an ancient scroll.

'Annie, we're in the middle of nowhere! The Pacific Highway's miles away. How did we get here?'

'Just help me, alright?' Annie was in no mood for one of Meredith's lectures. The van's air-conditioning was still at full bore and Annie, in her damp shirt, was now feeling chilled to the bone. 'We're on the Lawrence–Tullymorgan Road, and so I'm thinking this left here is the Tullymorgan–Jacky Bulbin Road.'

Annie slowed and swung the van into the track on the left and headed north again.

'Hang on!' Meredith shouted, her face pressed against the foggy window. 'That sign said Mangrove Creek Road.'

'Shit! Did it?'

'You've missed the turn-off. The map says it was back a bit.'

'Are you sure?'

'Well, just let me get a handle on this.' Meredith peered at the map again. 'Yes. I'm right. We're headed the wrong way. You'll have to stop and turn back.'

'I'll find a place to pull over.'

The rain intensified. The wipers were slashing at the water triple-time, but it was making no difference. Annie could barely see the road in front of her. What she could see was that either side was hemmed in by dense vegetation. 'Jesus! We're in the mangroves!'

'That would explain why it's called Mangrove Creek Road.'

Annie drove another few kilometres. 'There's nowhere to turn!' She was feeling panicky and claustrophobic. The impenetrable dark green walls were as high as the roof. From her perch in the driver's seat she couldn't see through them or over them although sometimes, through the driving rain, she could make out tortured black tangled roots emerging from brackish water.

'The sides of the road are just swamp. I don't want to put this thing into a ditch. Maybe if I just keep going a bit further, there'll be a right turn so we can get back onto the other road.'

Meredith bent over the map again. 'There're no turn-offs on this road. It looks like it's a dead end.'

'What?! Give me that!' Annie turned to grab at the map.

'LOOK OUT!' Meredith yelled as a flash of white skittered past the windscreen.

Annie turned back and wrenched the steering wheel hard right. The RoadMaster did as it was bid and swerved off the road. It faithfully and purposefully dropped its front wheels into the fast-running water channel. The beast tipped, and planted its snub nose deep into the mud.

Annie and Meredith lurched towards the windscreen, saved from smashing through it by their seatbelts. In the rear of the cabin, the toilet door was flung open and Nina fell out onto the floor with her knickers around her ankles. She slid right down the length of the cabin on a slippery slide of raw sewage.

The motor hissed and died. Again, it was hardly what you'd call a *Thelma and Louise* moment.

Fourteen

It was difficult to know who was most startled by this turn of events. Annie and Meredith up front, with their feet jammed against the windscreen? Nina, in a crumpled heap by the table? Or the bald-headed white ibis, now winging its way back to its nest in the Everlasting Swamp? It was, for all of them, a close call—although, as Meredith, Annie and Nina considered their plight, they couldn't see how it could have been much worse.

The van was tipped at a thirty-five-degree angle, its back wheels barely on the edge of the road. Black, viscous water was already seeping through the cabin doors and pooling on the rubber matting in the foot wells under the dashboard.

The slick of sewage that had slopped over the rim of the shallow toilet bowl had stopped running, and was now soaking into various squares of carpeting and floor mats. Every loose item on every bench—cameras, sunglasses, books, the chopping board, binoculars, shoes, sunhats and plastic baskets of sunscreen, pens, lip balm and moisturiser—had been dashed to the floor.

To add to the carnage, when Annie had last raided the fridge she hadn't secured its top latch, so that the appliance had spewed its insides through an open, lolling door. Eggs, milk and fruit, split plastic containers of leftover bolognaise sauce, olives and camembert cheese, had all been vomited up and were marinating in a stinking stew. Outside, the rain was steadily drumming on untold millions of mangrove leaves. A biblical multitude of mosquitoes had been disturbed and now smelled an opportunity.

Nina cried first. That was understandable. She had been sitting on the loo, doubled over and clutching her writhing gut; she'd had no warning they were driving pell-mell into disaster. She had been violently upended from her plastic perch, bashed her head on the sink and then been unceremoniously ejected into the cabin, landing on her bare arse. She was wailing with pain and indignity in equal measure.

Meredith was the next one to crack, although it wasn't outright weeping. Nina thought it sounded more like the whimpering of one of Anton's guinea pigs.

Annie willed herself not to cry. Couldn't. Shouldn't. Wouldn't. Instead she unbuckled her seatbelt and fell forward and the gear stick jammed into her ribs. 'Fuck!' Annie knew that she'd never been so precise in her employment of the expletive in her whole life. 'Fuck, fuck, fuck!'

'For God's sake, do you think swearing's going to help?' Meredith sniffed. Her reading glasses might have been smashed, but her sense of outrage was still intact.

'I think I might have broken something,' moaned Nina. She suddenly had an image of herself as Shelley Winters in the *Poseidon Adventure*—everyone thinking that she was too fat to make it—but her heart would go on . . . and on. Or was that *Titanic*? Amazing, she thought, how leading ladies had become younger and slimmer, but more buoyant during the past quarter of a century.

Meredith also unbuckled her seatbelt and extended her palm to brace herself for the drop against the hard dashboard. Nina might be seriously injured. She had to assess the situation.

She clambered between the front seats to the cabin behind. 'Where does it hurt?' She gently placed her palm on Nina's shin, which looked to be bruising already.

'Everywhere. But I think my ankle copped the worst of it. Ow!'

'Can you move it?' Nina obediently wriggled her toes and turned her foot. 'Well then, I guess that means it's not broken,' Meredith diagnosed, drawing on some rudimentary medical knowledge from Girl Guides. 'Let's hope it's just a sprain. My God, it reeks in here!'

'The first thing we'd better do is try to ring roadside assist.' Annie reached into the glovebox. 'I'll get the number. It's in the folder. Let's hope there's reception out here.'

Annie found her BlackBerry and mumbled a silent prayer to the God of Telecommunications but there was, predictably, no coverage. They were, as Meredith had already helpfully mentioned, precisely in the middle of nowhere and way out of mobile range.

'My God, what are we going to do now?' gasped Nina. It was a very good question and no-one had any good answer for it. There was a long silence between them as the rain steadily beat down—and then, instantly, ceased.

Annie located a road map, opened the driver's door and jumped down to the roadway. The low cloud was clearing fast, and the heat of the afternoon sun was already evaporating the moisture and raising a plume of steam from every broad, thick leaf. The light was refracting through dripping water, creating a shifting mosaic of silver and gold. Annie immediately thought of Lizzie, and the old familiar feeling of loss, on top of everything else, had her blinking back tears. She shielded her eyes from the bright shards of reflection to peer at the map.

The estuary was a jigsaw of channels, lagoons, sand bars and alluvial islands—Oyster Channel, Rabbit Island, Shark Creek, Crystal Waters. Fish, prawns and oysters spawned here. Waterbirds nested. Insects swarmed in the silvery grey, oily mud. It was the sounds Annie was most amazed by. Water was running fast in the channel by the roadway; beyond that, in the thick density of mangrove leaf and root, frogs chorused, birds called and the air hummed with buzzing creatures—every living thing had been invigorated by the fierce tropical storm. Along the road in both directions there was nothing to see but more mangrove trees.

Meredith's head emerged from the door, but the brutality of the light and steaming humidity sent her reeling back inside. She stood gripping the corner of the kitchen benchtop as one horrifying thought pushed everything else from her mind.

Crocodiles! There would be crocodiles submerged in the vile, stinking swamp. Meredith had seen enough Hollywood disaster movies to know what came next. At nightfall a huge monster of a thing would emerge and pull them one by one, screaming, to a gruesome death. Nina, with her swollen ankle, might hold them all back, and so would have to be sacrificed first.

'Annie! Come back inside,' Meredith called. 'There could be anything out there.'

'I know,' Annie called back. 'You should come and have a look. It's like the mud is moving. It's incredible.'

'Crocodiles!' screeched Meredith, stumbling back and tripping over Nina's prostrate form.

'Ow! Careful! My ankle!'

'There are no crocodiles!' Annie shook her head in disbelief at Meredith's amateur theatrics. 'We're way too far south for crocodiles. I meant crabs! There're thousands of 'em, everywhere.'

Meredith slammed the van door with annoyance. Here she was, in the worst predicament she could ever recall being in—apart from that time she had dysentery in Bombay—and Annie was narrating a fascinating nature documentary.

Inspecting the vehicle for damage, Annie was surprised to find none. Not from this accident anyway. There were various scrapes in evidence from Nina's misadventures. The front of the RoadMaster was lodged solidly in the mud up to its bonnet but seemed to have, like Nina, suffered a mighty indignity more than anything else.

Elvis was still singing. The reflective jewels on his jumpsuit were sparkling in the sunset. However, the light was dimming fast. In another moment it would drop behind the trees and be gone. Annie estimated that in a scarce half-hour all would be pitch-black. There was probably a farm a way back—but how far? It could be ten kilometres. Annie didn't care to make the walk alone in the dark. Rescue looked to be impossible until morning, but there was not one flat surface inside the van they could sleep on. It was time to accept their fate and set up camp on the road for the night. The first thing they had to do was to get Nina outside and wash the shit off her.

Meredith had been itching to say what was on her mind since she had woken earlier that afternoon and found that Annie was delivering them into a wilderness. As it turned out, the opportunity to savage her pig-headed travelling companion soon presented itself.

Nina had suffered the humiliation of standing out on the roadway nude, on one leg, using Meredith as a crutch. Annie washed her down with cold soapy water from a bucket. She couldn't remember suffering such mortification since the twins were born and she'd sat in a kiddie playpool in the maternity ward trying to ease her labour pains. Meredith and Annie conducted themselves with quiet professionalism as she moaned and she was grateful for that at least.

They had all worked together by the van's dim interior lights to throw out the stinking matting and ruined foodstuffs, sluice down the floors of the van with disinfectant and pack away some of the items catapulted in the crash. After that, they'd sat outside on the road on camp chairs, plastered with insect repellent, and shared a candlelit supper of cheese, salami, dry biscuits and a jar of gourmet jalapeno dip. Annie had made a head start on a bottle of Margaret River merlot.

Another round of Nina's medication had done the trick and her stomach felt easier. Meredith had gulped down enough Ural to catch her cystitis before it travelled to her kidneys and caused any more discomfort. Now, at the rear of the vehicle, work continued by the light of a torch balanced on Nina's knee. A decision had been made to erect a makeshift tent over assorted bedding in the event of another storm rolling in during the night. They swatted at an infinite cloud of insects attracted by the torch's piercing blue glow.

'What's Brad going to say?' Nina moaned as she watched Annie and Meredith work up a sweat dragging mattresses out of the front door in the still-humid evening. To Annie, it seemed that Nina had said this a hundred times and now, enough was enough.

'Who cares what Brad bloody well says?' she snapped, and then sucked her index finger where the sharp edge of a blue plastic groundsheet had sliced her skin.

Meredith let go of the broom she was balancing and it clattered on the roadway: 'Well, that's exactly the comment you would expect from someone who's single. But some of us have families to think about.'

Annie pointed an accusing bloodied digit at Meredith. 'And what's that supposed to mean?'

Nina groaned and dropped her head on her folded arms. A storm was rolling in all right—a nasty female tornado, right in front of her at ground level.

'It means exactly what you think it means.' Meredith was defiant, and leaned into the shaft of torchlight to catch Annie's eye. 'If you weren't so damned selfish, you'd be considering someone else's feelings instead of thinking about yourself all the time. If you did that, you might have a relationship and not be so bloody mean and miserable.'

Annie was stunned by the ferocity of Meredith's attack, and could only manage: 'I beg your pardon?'

'It's too late for manners now.'

Annie hurled the plastic sheeting she was holding to the ground. 'Yes, and I've noticed the joy your marriage has brought you, Meredith. Let's face it, you've spent your entire life doing exactly what you wanted to do. And while you weren't looking, your whole family buggered off. You don't even know who your own daughter is marrying. Fuck you!'

Meredith crossed her arms and marched furiously into the darkness just beyond the torchlight. Fear of snapping crocodiles propelled her back towards the side of the van.

Nina, sitting in a camp chair, concentrated hard on the throbbing pain in her leg to take her away from the hideous reality she was facing. 'C'mon now,' she pleaded, 'we're all tired. Let's just—'

'And look at Nina!' continued Annie. 'Trapped at the kitchen sink for years. You think I want a life like that?'

Nina opened her mouth to defend herself, and then decided she was in too much pain to go on with it.

'It seems to me, Meredith,' Annie spat, 'that the whole bullshit about women "having it all"—all that feminist crap you and Briony spouted back then—was just a way to get you out of the sheer boredom of motherhood. You've got no right to judge me and how my life's ended up. I'm the one who's independent.'

'Independent my backside,' snarled Meredith. 'Half your waking hours are spent looking through an empty bottle, your mouth like an ashtray, trying to remember who you slept with last night.'

It was Annie's turn to stomp into the safe anonymity of darkness. Meredith shouted at her retreating back: 'YOU'VE MADE A MESS OF YOUR LIFE JUST AS MUCH AS WE HAVE!'

That pronouncement hung limply in the air while they each paused to consider it. The noise of nameless life roiling in the mud, and a distant rumble of thunder, stopped any thought of going on with the argument for now.

'Let's just get this tent up. I really need to lie down.' Nina sighed. She was too weary to bother with her usual 'look over there' routine. There was, after all, no 'over there' to look at. Beyond the small pool of light coming from her torch, the night was utterly black. The moon was obscured by a scarf of stray cloud, and seemed reluctant to show its face in this company.

Nina hung her head. She had thought they'd come to some understanding over the past few days, that the three of them were beginning to find a true connection—and at the first test the whole elaborate construction had shattered. If this was the *touchstone* of female friendship she had longed for all these years, Nina had no use for it.

✻

It must have been about 9 pm, although it felt much later. They were bundled, fully clothed, in their beds on the side of the road. Annie was wrapped in a doona and lying on a random collection of cushions assembled from the seats around the van's table. She had angled her head so that she was looking out from under the plastic sheet and into the heavens. She sought the constellation of the Southern Cross in the night sky. There it was! Ever since she was small, Annie had felt comforted by the sight of those four stars and the tiny pointer and it was the same tonight. She wasn't so far from home as long as the Southern Cross was in view. The air was cool and damp. Under her feathery cover, Annie was as safe as a baby white ibis under its mother's wings.

She considered what Meredith had said—that if she weren't so selfish she would have a partner by now. This trip was showing her just how singular she had become. For years now she had only had herself to please in her one-bedroom flat and she called that 'independence', but now she could see the years of solitude stretching before her and couldn't find much joy in the prospect. But then again, the challenge of 'sharing'— if this trip was anything to go by—seemed equally daunting. Maybe she was already too old to change.

Meredith and Nina were lying side by side on a double mattress. They were both comfortable enough, despite the stifling closeness under the sagging plastic cover. Nina was nibbling at a block of chocolate and crunching hazelnuts in Meredith's ear. Nina's shin and ankle were still throbbing, but she liked to imagine that the sugar was going some way to ease the pain.

Meredith was appalled at her harsh words to Annie and had been stung by her equally barbed response. It was true, she had always had an excuse for not being at home—store inventory, trade fairs, trips overseas to locate new stock—and she had let her family stray. She wasn't sure why she'd done it. If she hadn't seen Sigrid for a year and a half and didn't know who she was marrying, it was her own fault and no-one else's.

Meredith made a heroic effort to keep her worst nightmares at bay. Crocodiles were probably the least of her worries. She retrieved a small torch and her novel from her handbag and attempted to read the tiny print in a small circle of illumination. Although, after rereading the same dramatic passage for the fifth time, she realised that this particular tale of bloodthirsty Nepalese insurgents in the foothills of the Himalayas wasn't bringing her any comfort. She closed her book and clicked off the light. The night instantly moved in to smother her.

'I'm sorry, Meredith,' came Annie's disembodied voice from the darkness. Nina stopped crunching chocolate to hear what might come next. Meredith rolled over and could make out the lump of Annie's bedding just a few feet away.

'You know something?' Annie continued. 'I've never really had any close female friends. I've had the chance to have them, I've known lots of great girls, but I just let the relationships slide. And I know it's been hurtful when I haven't returned calls or sent birthday cards, and I've been thinking about that on this trip. Why do I do that?

'Now I think I know. You remember what I said about not wanting kids because of Lizzie dying? I think it's the same with the women in my life. I've somehow thought that if I got too close, depended on them, they might be taken away from me.

'I've got male friends. I'm comfortable with men. But I know I can be distant with women, and critical. So, I'm sorry. Being here with you on this trip has been one of the best things I've ever done with other women, and I'm glad Nina made me come.'

Nina realised she'd been holding her breath while Annie spoke. She waited for her usual comic sign-off of 'Hey, just kidding' and heard nothing.

Beside her, Meredith sighed deeply. 'Thanks,' she mumbled. 'I'm sorry too. I think I started it.' Annie's heartfelt confession had touched her and she now felt she wanted to make her own. 'You're right about the whole female friend thing.' Meredith rolled onto her back. 'I'm the same. I have plenty of acquaintances, of course—women who come into the store regularly, and a few I play tennis with—but not anyone I could call a *real* friend. You know, tell everything to, who'd give me advice.

'I never really had the time for friendships. I've always some-how thought that one day, when I wasn't so busy, I'd do all that. As if friendships might be something to reward myself with for all my hard work. But in the meantime I've gotten old. And every time I think about making friends, it seems harder and harder.'

Meredith paused here to fight down the heaving tide of unhappiness rising in her chest that threatened to spill into tears. 'I neglected my kids too. I'm not even friends with my own daughter. The thing that worries me most is that they'll have children, and I won't see them. And then what will it have all been for?'

Nina groped under the covers for Meredith's hand, found it and squeezed. 'That won't happen,' she whispered.

Meredith squeezed a silent 'thanks' in return, but continued: 'It's exactly what *will* happen. Sigrid's in Byron, Jarvis will be in London . . .'

Meredith felt Annie swiping in the darkness for her other hand and reached to catch it. 'Don't forget, Meredith,' she said, 'that you did give them life . . . and inspiration. They'll always respect you for following your dream. And by the time they have kids, you'll be able to leave the shop and go visit. You've left already, and for all anyone knows you could be walking with Jarvis and pushing a stroller through Notting Hill right now.'

Meredith snorted: 'I wish I was!'

'You'll make it work,' added Annie.

'Do you think?'

'I'm sure of it,' Annie comforted. 'It's the same for you, Nina. That's why you have to open your café.'

'It's funny'—Nina tucked the remains of her chocolate under her pillow—'I'm worried that if I just stay home for all the boys' lives, they'll imagine that's all women can do—wash sheets, make pancakes and wait on them.'

Meredith was sure of herself on this point: 'They'll be flat-out finding a wife, if that's what they're after. Girls these days can't even make toast!'

Annie agreed. 'Life's changed so much since our mothers were young. I see young women at work all the time who have no idea what it'd be like if some man said they couldn't follow their hearts.'

'And maybe that's just as well.' Meredith continued the thought. 'Why should they care? It's what we wanted for ourselves and our daughters, isn't it? To be able to choose how we live our lives.' The thought that her own daughter was doing exactly that made Meredith pause. 'Although, they'll never know how liberating it was not to give a rat's about shaving your legs. I adored the old "mohair stocking".'

Annie laughed out loud. 'Jeez, I haven't heard that expression for years!'

'What about you, Annie?' asked Nina. 'I always feel so awful when I hear myself going on and on about my family and then remembering you don't have one . . .'

'I love hearing about your life!' Annie propped herself on one elbow. 'Don't you ever think I don't! I think you're amazing the way you run your house and the store and care for everyone the way you do. If I was just surrounded by other single women moaning about not being married, it wouldn't be much of a life, would it?'

'What about a husband?'

'Marriage? I don't know. But I would like someone to share my life with. Stand next to me. I just have to keep believing there's someone waiting for me, that's all.'

'I'm sure there is,' stated Meredith. 'I'm positive.'

'You know what I just realised?' said Nina. 'None of us has sisters . . .' And then the realisation of what she had just said made her sit up. 'Oh God! I mean, you know . . . apart from Lizzie. I'm so sorry, Annie, I didn't mean . . . Oh Jesus, I'm so bad. I just never stop and think.'

At the sound of her dead sister's name said aloud by someone after so long, something inside Annie's heart gave way. She gave voice to the charge she had levelled at herself every day for more than thirty years: 'It was my fault. I was supposed to be looking after Lizzie that afternoon.' And then Annie was gulping down tears that threatened to drown her, right where she lay.

Meredith was now sitting up too, clutching at Nina's arm. 'No, no . . .' they began.

'Mum told me to watch her. But she was always running off and I was looking for her in the hay shed and the chook shed, in the garden . . . and I . . . I just couldn't find her . . . and all that time she was . . .'

Annie turned her face into her pillow and wept. Meredith and Nina held each other, listening until the muffled sobbing slowed.

Nina cried in sympathy for her friend. 'How sad for you. To blame yourself all this time for something that couldn't possibly have been your fault. I love you, Annie.'

Tears slid down Meredith's face too as she spoke. 'What a dreadful thing to have happen to you. I can imagine you as a dear little girl, so full of life and joy. To have all that stolen from you. You deserve to find peace and love in this life, and if I can help you find it, I promise I will. I love you too.'

Annie's chest shuddered, slowed and calmed. She saw the great eye of the dam flutter and close its lid over the stagnant depths. She could hear the water rushing past her ears in the nearby channel. It swept her thoughts along with it away into the creek and she slept.

✾

The moon was high when Meredith was woken by a rustling in the thicket of mangroves not far from her head. For one moment there she imagined she was back home in Armadale listening to Donald on the other side of the bed, snoring to beat the band. Then she took in the ghostly form of the RoadMaster shining in the moonlight, and remembered where she was. Nowhere.

The rhythmic squelching of mud nearby was accompanied by a low grunting. It was a sound Meredith could not identify. She sat bolt upright. It came from an animal. A big one. That could mean only one thing—crocodiles! She leapt to her feet, dragging the doona with her, hit her head on the broom handle and brought the plastic sheeting down.

'Annie! Nina! I told you! They're out there,' she babbled. 'We've got to get inside now!'

Nina flailed her arms, still dreaming she was beneath a life raft in the mid-Atlantic, and trying to find Leonardo DiCaprio among a floating tangle of wooden planks, dead bodies and chunks of ice. She cleared the plastic and stood unsteadily, gulping air and thanking Almighty God that she still lived.

Meredith was frantically wrestling with the front door of the van when Annie woke from a deep sleep and couldn't remember where the hell she was either. At that moment the roar of an engine cut through the night and the camp was blasted with blinding floodlights. Meredith, Annie and Nina stood shielding their eyes, transfixed like proverbial rabbits.

'What the fuck are youse doing here?!' came a voice. Deep, male and rough as guts.

'Three little suckling pigs by the look of them,' chuckled another male voice.

Annie thought of the stories of horrific abductions and murders in the Australian outback and felt for the broom handle. Then Nina saw the silhouette of a gun in the headlights and screamed as if to wake the dead.

✿

Annie peered through the flywire of the front door at the mud-splattered monster LandCruiser ute parked in the driveway under the porch light. Cigarette smoke curled out of both windows.

Trevor Baum, macadamia nut farmer, appeared at her elbow and thrust a cup of hot coffee at her. 'Here you go. You're lucky they saw you before they started blasting. Bloke next door got his quad bike shot last week. He'd parked it by a tree and gone off for a leak and . . . Boom! One stuffed petrol tank.'

Annie grinned at the tale and gratefully sipped at the strong, milky brew.

'But those blokes do a bloody good job. Feral pigs are a real menace out here. You should see the friggin' mess they make. They wreck everything. Go and have a look before your van gets towed in the morning and tell those idiot animal rights greenies back in the city.'

'I'm from the country. I know what you're talking about.' Annie nodded in agreement. 'City people have got no damn idea.' She slurped her coffee and turned to see Meredith down the hallway cradling the telephone.

'Hello. Is Sigrid there? This is her mother speaking.' Meredith heard her own voice echoing down the telephone line—absurdly formal, considering she was barefoot and wearing an Aran-knit fishing jumper over a singlet and a pair of shorts.

She paused to bestow a good-natured grin upon Mrs Bev Baum, who was blinking, watching her as she stood on the synthetic caramel-coloured carpet. The reproduction Swiss cuckoo clock on the wall chimed an accusing eleven o'clock.

'Mrs Dalrymple?'

'Yes.'

'I'm Charlie! I can't believe I'm talking to you. Sigrid and I are getting married in less than forty-eight hours.'

Meredith held the phone closer to her right ear and jammed her finger in her left. She must be mistaken—she thought she'd heard the young woman on the other end of the line say she was marrying Sigrid.

'I'm sorry?' said Meredith. 'Who did you say you were?'

'I'm Charlotte Newson, but everyone calls me Charlie,' the girlish voice burbled on. 'We are *so* looking forward to you being here. There's not that many mothers who would be able to deal with all this. Siggie reckons you've been great. I'm looking forward to breakfast before the wedding. That means we can spend the whole day together. We've got so much brilliant stuff planned. My mum's here too. You'll get along fine. It means so much to us that you're coming.'

'Is Sigrid there?' Meredith repeated the question—it was all she could think to say under the circumstances.

'She's asleep. I can go and get her if you like, but I'm sure you know she's pretty grumpy when she gets woken up.'

'No, no, that's fine, just leave her,' Meredith stuttered.

'Are you sure? Can I give her a message?'

It was a female voice, Meredith was sure of that now.

'Just tell her that I was hoping to get to Byron tomorrow afternoon, but that I've been . . . delayed. It looks like I won't be there until the early evening, or later.'

'Fine. No problem. I'll tell her. We're picking up Jarvis from Ballina airport in the morning. Don—Mr Dalrymple—got here yesterday. Do you want to speak to him?'

'No, no. That will be fine . . . er . . .'

'You can call me Charlotte if you want, but I'm much more of a Charlie, to tell you the truth. Imagine k.d. lang—but with curly blonde hair.'

Meredith could not imagine any such thing.

'Well, we'll see you tomorrow then. Call us the minute you get into Byron.'

'Bye, bye then,' Meredith whispered. She hung up the phone and stretched her hand to the flock wallpaper to keep upright.

'Would you like a cup of tea? You look a bit peaky,' offered Bev, tugging at the belt of her lavender chenille dressing gown. 'Are you alright?'

'I'm fine, really, just . . . fine. Fine,' replied Meredith.

Annie clapped her hands for attention. 'Well then, we'd better be off. We've left our friend Nina out there at the mercy of the crabs. Thank you *so* much for the use of your phone. You've both been *so* kind.' Annie edged her way back to the front door.

'Are you sure you don't want to stay? We've got a spare bedroom. And there's the couch . . .' Bev indicated a small floral two-seater now occupied by a hulking, panting rottweiler.

'No, really. Like Meredith said, we're fine. We've got everything we need for the night. Thanks again.'

'Here's some nuts.' Trevor shoved a cardboard box of macadamias in her direction, and then adjusted his scrotum through his scarlet satin boxer shorts. 'One day they'll be one of the nation's prominent sources of bio-fuel, because their smoke-point is one of the highest of any—'

'Thank you!' sang Annie in a desperate attempt to fend off the recitation of the remainder of Trevor's 101 Handy Macadamia Nut Facts.

She turned and bolted, her thongs slapping on the concrete front steps and down the path to the ute. She threw the box of nuts into the back and hauled herself up on the metal truck-tray, dragging Meredith up after her.

'Are youse right?' came the yell from the driver's window.

'Hang on tight ladies!' came the courtesy safety warning from the passenger's side.

With an ostentatious skid on the gravel that tipped the truck sideways and threatened to chuck both Meredith and Annie head-first into a rock garden populated with plaster jabiru, they were on their way. The vehicle blasted out the driveway and pelted back down to the dead end of Mangrove Creek Road.

Were they having an adventure *now*? The rush of damp night air blasted Annie's curls from her scalp as the truck barrelled down the track. She knew that she, definitely, was. Annie couldn't recall the last time she'd shared the back of a LandCruiser with a massive dead feral pig as she headed into the depths of a mangrove swamp at midnight.

'Yahoooo!' she screamed, and punched a hole into the dank darkness.

Meredith, standing next to her and gripping a metal bar, was silent. Pig blood was dripping onto the tray of the truck and she could feel the disgusting stuff, still warm, on her feet. The putrid smell of the dead brute made her sick to her stomach. Her hair felt as if it was being torn out, root by root, in the whistling wind. Her mind was paralysed, still back in the muffled hallway of the Baum farmhouse. All she could hear was the insistent 'bong, bong, bong' of a fake cuckoo clock chiming the death of a long-cherished dream.

✵

'Can I get you something, Davo? Chook?' Nina was hobbling around the illuminated campsite, imagining she was back in her kitchen and able to rustle up a nice cup of tea and freshly baked Anzac biscuits for a couple of visiting Mormons.

In fact, what was on offer was half a bottle of merlot, hazelnut chocolate and the remains of a jar of jalapeno dip. The two men standing in silhouette in front of the headlights of the giant humming 'pig-rig' looked like they'd much rather sit down to a supper of fried evangelist and beer.

From what Annie had gleaned, they were professional pig shooters from the nearby town of Coaldale. The ugly, bristle-haired, seventy-kilogram boar hanging upside down off the metal frame was destined for dog food. It had been shot through the head with a bolt action Winchester 243 rifle. Annie had been excited to inspect the gun. She'd been handy with a rifle on rabbit-shooting expeditions back home. Nina could only marvel at Annie's ease around these rough blokes who made the average AFL player look like a schoolboy.

'We're right! No probs!' Davo spat into the dirt. 'We might head back home. There's another huge bastard out there some-where, but he's well gone now.'

'Are you sure?' asked Nina as she nervously tried to peer beyond the wall of dense vegetation. 'I don't know how we'll get back to sleep knowing it's there.'

Chook moved to put Nina's mind at ease: 'A bloody sight better than you would having us going at it with the rifles. Sometimes we have to slit their throats to finish 'em off, and they squeal like netballers.'

Davo leaned forward to slap his jeans and laugh heartily at this image. Nina clamped her hand over her mouth in horror.

'So,' Chook continued, 'youse all set then? The roadside assist will be here first thing. They'll probably put the whole rig on the back of a truck and cart you into Maclean. Fix the old "Heartbreak Hotel" on the spot.'

'Heartbreak Hotel! Good one!' Davo pointed to the Elvis decal on the side of the van and guffawed again. Obviously Chook was the wit of the outfit and had Davo in his thrall.

'Can we give you some money?' Annie offered. 'You've been to so much trouble for us. We really appreciate it.'

'Nah! No way, darlin'.' Chook waved her away with a meaty hand.

'Well, at least let me give you these.' Annie reached into the shadows and handed over two bottles of champagne.

Davo examined a label by the LandCruiser's headlights. 'Fuck me! French! The missus'll think it's Christmas!'

'If I come home with a dead feral pig and champagne, I might even get a root out of it,' Chook deadpanned.

Davo laughed again. 'Come on, you stupid bastard—let's get goin'.'

The two men climbed into their rig, slammed the doors, revved the engine and executed a neat three-point turn in the gravel. It was the kind of turn the disabled RoadMaster Royale had no hope of making on the narrow road. They paused long enough for Chook to lean out the window. 'Relax! The worst that can happen is that the mozzies get ya, and the crabs and spiders finish ya off. Night, ladies!'

Over the throaty surge of the ute's engine, Davo's high-pitched staccato laugh could be heard echoing through the swamp. The tail-lights receded and the camp was once again plunged into darkness.

There was one more sound that could now be heard over the orchestra of frogs croaking, mosquitoes buzzing and nameless creatures burrowing through the inky muddy slop, and that was Meredith's low and heart-wrenching sobs.

✲

'It doesn't mean you won't be a grandmother,' said Annie. 'In fact, there's a lesbian in one of our offices who's got twins. They did it with artificial insemination. The kids have got two mothers and a father. It all works. They're a great family.'

Meredith heard only one word out of this entire speech—the word 'lesbian'.

'Or they could adopt,' Nina helpfully added. 'Oprah's done lots of stories about female couples who have adopted kids, and I admire them. I really do.'

Who knew what time it was now on Mangrove Creek Road? The moon had dropped and was just peeking over the top of the trees. None of them imagined they would get to sleep any time soon. This was an emotional emergency and it was all hands on deck.

Besides, the spectre of a giant feral pig crashing through the undergrowth was enough to keep them awake until dawn. They were now all piled into the same double bed for reasons of safety—Meredith and Annie up one end, and Nina down the other end with her bad ankle hanging off the mattress onto the road.

'It's my fault,' sniffed Meredith.

Annie elbowed her in the ribs. Nina kicked at her shins with her good leg.

'OK, OK! I know it wasn't my *fault*.' Meredith honked into a tissue. 'But at least I could have seen it coming. I'm such an idiot— I just assumed that "Charlie" would be, you know, a man!'

'There wasn't anything that tipped you off when she was growing up, or when she moved out of home?' asked Nina. Annie was glad for the question. She was dying to ask the same thing, but thought it was too intrusive. She was coming to appreciate Nina's blithe disregard for social boundaries. Although, if she could just shift her arse over a bit . . .

'No. No. She didn't bring many boyfriends home as a teenager. But now I look back and wonder whether I just didn't notice anything unusual because I was always too preoccupied with the store. The last time I was in her place in a flat in Balaclava, she was living with a girlfriend. But I didn't give it a minute's thought.'

'And why would you?' said Nina.

'And what does it matter anyway?' added Annie.

'Because I could have been there to talk it over with her. To tell her that I loved her, no matter what. She couldn't trust me. That's what I keep thinking about. I couldn't care if she smuggled heroin, she's still my daughter . . . OK, if she was a heroin smuggler, I might mind. But, truly, I just want her to be happy.'

'And I'm sure she *is*,' Nina enthused. 'She's decided she wants to get married. Doesn't that tell you she's found a great love? And that she believes in it so much that she wants to declare it to the world, even if some narrowminded idiots might disapprove? She's invited you to be there to witness the occasion, and isn't that a wonderful thing any mother would be grateful for?'

'That was good, Nina,' whispered Annie.

'Thanks.'

Meredith groaned, rolled over and dragged the doona with her. 'I suppose it'll be some godawful ceremony. Some white witch in a tie-dyed skirt chucking rose petals into the bloody ocean. Then we'll all go back to someone's carport for wholemeal pizza and cheap white wine in plastic cups.'

Nina, used to sleeping with a man who hogged the bed-clothes, hauled the doona back over her hips. 'It couldn't be worse than *my* wedding! I was hugely pregnant. I decided to lace myself into this corset so I didn't show so much. I flaked out during the vows and then spent the reception hurling in the dunny.'

Annie laughed. 'What was your wedding like, Meredith?'

'Registry office and a counter lunch,' she admitted. 'Then we got on the *Princess of Tasmania*, sailed overnight in the worst storm in twenty years and stayed at a pub in Launceston. We didn't have two beans to our name.'

'If I get married again, I'll have seventeen bridesmaids and fly to Paris. You can both be matrons-of-honour. I'll choose the dresses. I've always liked teal,' Annie teased Meredith, who squealed with satisfying disgust.

'Just what I've always wanted,' Nina sighed. 'To be a matron-of-honour. Can't they find a better name for it like, lady-in-waiting or . . . something?'

'You'll be waiting alright—you still reek!' Annie reminded her. Nina whimpered and pulled the bedcovers over her head.

'Is she doing it to get back at me for working?' Meredith asked.

'You know something?' said Annie. 'For once this isn't about you. It's about what Sigrid wants. Did you become some radical feminist comedienne just to get back at your mother? . . . On second thoughts, don't answer that.'

'I did, I suppose. But it didn't really work. There were a couple of times when I was onstage and looked down to see Edith sitting in the front row. She pretended she didn't get any of the jokes. Bless her.'

'Your mother was the best.' Nina poked her nose over the edge of the doona. 'I remember her bringing a plate of pikelets to a Sanctified Soul concert. She loved you. She was so proud of you—no matter what.'

'But how would you feel, Nina, if one of your boys was gay?' Meredith persisted.

Nina laughed. 'If Jordy came home and said he was dropping out of footy to go to ballet school, I would be the happiest woman in the world! And that's not to say I haven't met plenty of gay footballers.'

'Ooh! Who?' whispered Annie.

'Oh, there's this full forward who plays for . . .' Nina pulled up short at the white chalk mark on the grass. 'Sworn to secrecy, sorry.'

'So, what do I do when I get to the wedding? What do I say?'

'You just kiss everyone and hand out presents,' Nina advised. 'That's what Oprah does.'

'And think of it, Meredith—when you're eventually parked in a nursing home, there'll be two daughters to come and visit, not just one,' said Annie brightly.

'Oh, great! That's cheered me up.'

'And we'll come and see you too,' added Nina. 'I'll pluck the hairs on your chin . . .'

'And I'll change your incontinence pads.'

'Hah! You two will be sitting right there next to me.'

'No we won't,' laughed Annie, 'we're younger than you. You might not have cared about us during the past twenty years, but you're *really* going to need us over the next twenty!'

'I have enough money. I'll hire professional care.'

'Do you really think we've made a mess of our lives?' asked Annie.

'Who hasn't, in one way or another?' sighed Nina. 'But that's what friends are for. It's just good to have someone who knows you well. Someone who believes in what you're aiming for, encourages you to go for it, but still loves you even when you miss the mark.'

'Amen to that, sister,' agreed Annie.

'*Ging gang gooley, gooley, gooley whatcha . . .*' sang Meredith.

'No, no! Stop!' shrieked Annie and Nina.

'I need to wee,' said Meredith.

'So do I,' said Nina.

'Let's all go together and that way we can watch out for feral pigs . . . and crocodiles,' said Annie.

The three friends joined hands and tiptoed into what remained of the night.

Fifteen

By mid-morning the next day, around a café table in the small town of Maclean, the 'Long Night of the Mangroves' was already being shaped into a legendary tale that would be told and retold whenever the three of them were together—although each was desperately trying to edit out the parts that did them no credit.

'You can't tell anyone about the bit where I skidded down the floor on my bum,' pleaded Nina.

'Only if you leave out the stuff about the crocodiles.' Meredith eyed them both.

'Or tell anyone that I missed the turn-off,' Annie bargained.

'But you *did* miss it!' Meredith and Nina accused.

A pot of tea for three was delivered to the table along with a plate of Danish pastries. They fell on it like scavenging ibis.

'How long until the van will be ready, did they say again?' asked Meredith through a mouthful of apricot jam and pastry. They had all watched the paralysed RoadMaster being slowly winched onto the back of a massive truck early that morning. They somehow felt they'd let it down and clucked in unison to see it so helpless, its nose caked with mud. Perhaps Nina's father-in-law was right, it did have a 'personality'. Even Meredith felt they'd somehow sullied the good name of The King.

Annie checked her watch. 'It's the "electrics", so they reckon it could take a good few hours. We probably won't get away till mid-afternoon, and then we've got to get the ferry. And it's about one hundred and sixty k's to drive after that, so that will get us into Byron . . .'

'At sunset,' calculated Nina, who had already devoured her apple Danish and was reaching for something with custard. 'And the wedding will be twenty-four hours later.'

'Well, let's just get there and not tell anyone we've arrived till tomorrow morning.' Meredith reached for the teapot.

'Don't you want Jarvis and Sigrid to meet us at the caravan park tonight?' Nina was astonished. Monday morning had come into view as she watched the children waiting in school uniform at the local bus stops—she was missing her boys. However, by the time she had reception on her phone, they were at school. Brad was at work—in the Melbourne Magistrates Court with Tabby Hutchinson, she had remembered—and she couldn't raise any of them.

'No, no! We need time to get ourselves looking presentable,' Meredith pleaded. 'For God's sake, look at us!'

They turned to study their reflection in the café window, and a more sorry trio would have been hard to find on the entire eastern seaboard. Meredith was a ragbag of stained and crumpled linen. She'd washed her feet by the side of the road, but fancied she still had traces of dried feral pig's blood between her toes. The thought of it made her feel ill.

Nina looked equally hellish. She was wearing a blonde haystack on her head which would have happily made do for a waterbird's nest in the swamp. Her leggings and T-shirt were filthy and she imagined she still smelled of sewage, despite repeatedly dousing herself in disinfectant. She needed a hot shower in the worst way. Mercifully her ankle was moving freely, the injury not as bad as she'd first thought.

'Photo!' declared Annie, jumping up from the table and pressing her BlackBerry on a passing waitress.

Meredith and Nina recoiled in horror. Annie jumped behind them, tugging her stained singlet and muddy-edged sarong into place and grinning for the snap. The resulting image had both Meredith and Nina begging Annie to wipe it from existence, but she merely laughed and hid the device behind her back. The thought occurred to her that she might just keep the picture for blackmail purposes.

If this was Annie being a friend—Meredith and Nina looked at each other and frowned—they could not imagine having her as an enemy.

'So we've got about five hours to kill, girls. What'll we do?' asked Annie.

A midday screening of *Spiderman 3* at the Maclean cinema helped to pass the time until the van was ready. They were the only patrons in the place.

'I quite fancy Toby Maguire, especially in that lycra suit.' Annie leaned to whisper in Nina's ear. 'Although Kirsten Dunst's a bit of a spunk too.'

'Shh!' admonished Nina through a mouthful of Malteesers. 'Don't even joke about being a lesbian. Not now. Think of Meredith. And you can't have filthy thoughts about Spider-man. Just as well you haven't got any kids, you're not fit to be a mother!'

'What?' Meredith leaned and whispered, even though there was no-one in front or behind to disturb.

'Popcorn?' Annie passed the bucket to her and she and Nina dissolved in giggles.

They were behaving like bloody silly schoolgirls, the pair of them, thought Meredith as she clenched her buttocks with annoyance.

✺

By three o'clock that afternoon they were on their way to Byron Bay. They had made the crossing over the Clarence and the RoadMaster Royale, now hosed down and beaming in the sun, was charging up the Pacific Highway.

The van's interior had more or less been restored to order. They'd burned incense sticks to clear the stink of disinfectant. The tiny bathroom had been irradiated with Lily of the Valley spray and barricaded against further use. They would have to find a man to empty the sloshing canister of 'black water'. Meredith had already generously offered the services of her husband, Don.

'You still haven't told us about your mystery man from the bowling club.' Annie had taken up her usual position between the front seats.

'Bill?' Meredith chewed nonchalantly on a wine gum. 'Best sex of my life! He's got a huge penis. I had three orgasms in a row, and I had no idea I was capable of such a feat.'

Nina almost ran the van off the road again.

'He's going to come to Melbourne, and I am going to have sex with him in every room of the house. I might even ask him to take me in the courtyard.'

'Fuck!' Annie muttered.

'Exactly,' said Meredith.

'Is he married?' asked Nina. She seemed to think that everyone had the same regard for the sanctity of the institution that she did.

'No idea. Didn't think to ask. Don't care.'

'Do you think Donald's got a girlfriend?' Nina continued.

'I sincerely hope he has,' Meredith replied. 'I trust it's someone with a lot of patience in the bedroom department. You know, I sometimes used to do sudokus in my head while he was going at it for . . . hours, it seemed. I was quite good at it. I get my talent for numbers from Edith. I wonder if she ever played bridge in her mind while she was having sex with Bernie.'

Meredith's musing silenced everyone for a good few kilometres.

'My sex life needs a makeover,' Nina declared as she was overtaking a milk tanker on the highway. 'I've decided that I have to get over being so selfconscious. After three kids, this is my body. Get used to it!'

'Absolutely!' agreed Meredith. 'But remember that it's *you* who has to get used to it, not Brad. He's a very attractive man, and he would have had a lot of opportunities around the football club if he wanted to get off with some young thing. But he loves you! And why wouldn't he? You're a sexy woman. That Zoran would have raced you off on Saturday night if he'd had the chance.'

'No!' Nina squealed. 'He's young enough to be my—'

'Toy boy?' interrupted Meredith. 'You're not as old and unattractive as you think you are. The first thing you should do is put a lock on your bedroom door, to keep those sons of yours out.'

'Yeah,' Annie piped up. 'Let me tell you, Nina, of course they're repulsed by the idea of you and Brad having sex. They're teenagers, that's their job. But that's no reason to stop doing it. Anyway, they're probably too busy lusting over pictures of Paris Hilton.'

'Don't, don't! Marko's still got a Spiderman doona!'

'And Spiderman's shagging Kirsten Dunst, don't forget!' laughed Annie.

'*La, la, la, doo, doo, doo!* Not listening!' Nina stuck a finger in her ear.

'So, this brings us neatly to the question of Matty.' Meredith offered Annie a lolly.

'I've gone off him a bit.'

'That's only because he wouldn't bonk you on the first night!' charged Nina. 'You know, Annie, at last you might've met a decent old-fashioned guy who wants to romance you.'

'And you're so suspicious of men who don't want to fall into bed with you in the first five minutes . . .' Meredith took Nina's cue for some plain talk. 'You should give him a chance. I liked him. He's not "Mr Excitement", sure, but there's something so . . . dependable and kind about him. He's lovely to look at too. Don't let that man slip through your fingers so easily.'

Annie shifted her bottom on her fallow pillow. 'Maybe . . .' she mused. 'Maybe . . .'

They stopped at Ballina, piled out to have their photo taken in front of the Big Prawn, and headed off again.

'WELCOME TO BYRON BAY'.

The headlights of the sturdy RoadMaster Royale lit up the road sign and Meredith, Annie and Nina whooped with joy. They'd made it! Two thousand kilometres, nine nights, millions of mosquitoes, one black bream and a dead feral pig later . . . and they had arrived.

Old Swivel Hips was gyrating under the streetlights as they all sang loudly: '*Well, it's one for the money, Two for the show, Three to get ready, Now go, cat, go!*'

'Here, turn here!' called Annie. 'First Sun Holiday Park—this is the place you booked, isn't it, Nina?'

Nina swung the vehicle off the main street, halted at the park's boom gates and jumped down from the driver's seat. This was a ritual she was well used to by now. She handed over the forty-two dollars in cash at the fluoro-lit site office and in return received a pin code for the toilet block and a campsite number.

Soon the van was cosily parked between two rigs of equal bulk in pole position right in front of Main Beach. The RoadMaster heaved, sighed and settled into the grass. Nina plugged into the electricity grid and the unit hummed with cheery hospitality.

Nina, Annie and Meredith ran to the wooden railing edging the ocean and leaned over it to breathe in the salty breeze sweeping across Cape Byron. It was dark by now, but the sound of waves crashing on the beach below was exhilarating enough. At the end of the beach, just out of sight, the lighthouse blinked a cautious welcome to the most easterly point of the continent of the Great South Land.

The first stop was the shower block, and the second the laundry. With spirits restored by washing powder, body gel, shampoo, conditioner, deodorant, moisturiser and a change of clothes, the company was in the mood for a celebration.

Meredith had set the table on the concrete apron of their campsite and laid it with a good Irish linen cloth. Nina had thrown together a platter of tinned vine leaves, salsa dip, jars of pickled asparagus, marinated fetta and a packet of water cracker biscuits she'd unearthed from a cupboard. Annie had fetched the second-last chilled bottle of champagne from the fridge. They stood around the table and raised fine crystal flutes etched with stalks of wheat.

'Well, girls, we did it!' cheered Nina. 'Here's to us. To Byron or Bust!'

'Can anyone join in this celebration?'

Nina swung her head at the sound of the familiar voice from the shadows.

'BRAD! Ohmigod, Brad!' she cried and made a leap for his open arms. 'What are you doing here? How did you know I was here?'

'He rang while you were still in the shower.' Annie grinned.

Brad stepped into the light, his arms thrown around Nina and his head bent to kiss her neck. Annie looked at Meredith. Did Nina have any idea of how lucky she was to have such a big handsome husband holding her tight? Meredith laughed and threw her hands up in disbelief. Nina's long-winded campaign of whingeing and complaining had apparently been vanquished by a cuddle and a kiss.

'I knew you'd be here tonight,' said Brad. 'Isn't the wedding tomorrow?'

Nina's answer was to burst into tears.

'Not exactly the reception I was expecting,' he laughed.

'Did you bring the boys? How are they? Are they here?'

'Nup, they're at home with Mum. It's just us, so grab your things, we're staying at "Rae's on Watego's" tonight. The Mirabella Penthouse.'

'You're not serious?' Nina gasped. The hotel was rated as one of the Top 25 in the world by *Conde Nast Traveller* magazine. Nina had tucked the fact away after reading about it in the dentist's rooms while she was waiting for Jordan to have his braces removed. The idea that she might stay there one day had been an impossible dream.

'Yep! Come on. We're having dinner overlooking the beach. And tomorrow, you're booked into the spa. You could do with a bit of pampering after your adventure. Did you have an adventure?'

'Oh, Brad, you have no idea!' Nina sniffed.

After kisses all round, and promises to meet for a pre-wedding drink back at the van the next day, Nina and Brad headed off.

'Wasn't that wonderful?' Meredith dabbed at her eyes with a tissue.

'You old softie, Meredith,' teased Annie.

'I never said I wasn't the romantic type,' she sniffed with indignation. 'It's just not something I care to display to all and sundry.'

Annie's BlackBerry rang. She snatched it up from the table and briskly walked to the back of the van. Meredith noted that she was waving her arms and then calling: 'Over here!'

Before Meredith could make sense of what she was up to, another head appeared around the corner out of the darkness.

'Hello, Mum.'

'Jarvis! Oh, my . . .' Meredith stood, overcome with emotion, unable to move.

Jarvis, tall and slim like his mother, walked to her, slipped his arms around her waist and kissed her cheek. Meredith laid her head on his chest and sobbed heartily.

'How did you know where I was?' she asked, snuffling into his shirtfront like a baby rabbit.

'I took the liberty of nicking your phone and ringing Don.' Annie was triumphant.

'You weren't that hard to find,' said Jarvis. 'Confederate flag—rather nice touch.'

Meredith noted that Jarvis now had a trace of an English accent.

'Siggie's booked us a table at a Thai restaurant down the road,' he said. 'We can sit outside. It's brilliant to be back home! I've missed Australia and I've missed you too, Mum.'

Meredith howled some more and, after grateful kisses for Annie, she and Jarvis were gone too.

Annie took up the bottle of champagne, settled into a camp chair and propped her feet on the table. 'Excellent! More for me!' she said out loud before proceeding to drink the lot. She was relieved to be alone, at last.

✵

Nina stood naked on the wet tiles of the bathroom floor. Her husband, up to his neck in bubbles and rose petals in the bathtub, whistled a low note of appreciation. She reached for the towel.

'Don't,' he whispered. 'Let me see.'

Nina breathed deeply to hold in her stomach. She placed her hands on her full hips and twirled slowly. The candlelight shone on the damp white skin of her rounded bottom and the glistening curves of her breasts.

'Look at you. Just look at you,' he said in wonderment. 'How beautiful you are. I can't believe you are my wife.'

311

That night, as the light of the waning moon stole in through the open balcony doors to caress the rumpled bedsheets, Nina remembered who she was. She was the wife of Brad; mother of Jordy, Anton and Marko. And, she reflected, that had bestowed upon her more happiness and contentment than any woman could expect in this world.

✿

'You've always been an inspiration to me, Mum,' said Jarvis. He leaned in towards the candlelight and sipped at his lemongrass tea.

Meredith marvelled again at how handsome he was. He was just twenty-two and, to her, still a boy. His thick, straight dark hair and fine bones had come from her side of the family. There was her mother Edith in the elegant arch of his eyebrows. His luxurious lashes, brown eyes and full mouth were Donald's.

She thought of her husband with a twinge of guilt. Perhaps she hadn't always been as charitable to him as she might have been. After all, he had been a good father. And married for almost thirty years. Men got less for murder, she reminded herself.

'I should have been there for you more than I was. I can see that now,' said Meredith quietly.

'No! Don't be ridiculous.' Jarvis waved her away and Meredith recognised her own imperious gesture. 'I loved hanging around the shop—all that great stuff you imported. I think I inherited my taste for beautiful things from you. You'd be depressed to see my hovel in Shepherd's Bush, although I do have Egyptian cotton bedsheets. But one day I mean to be sitting pretty in Holland Park, and you'll be impressed then.'

'I'm impressed now,' said Meredith emphatically.

'I know you are, but you know what I mean. You were always driven to make a success of yourself. I'm the same, and I'm proud to have inherited that from you.'

'Thank you, darling. That means more than you know. But I don't think Sigrid thinks of it that way.' Meredith was slightly ashamed to be fishing for reassurance from her son on her mothering abilities, but couldn't help herself.

'Sigrid's always had a chip on her shoulder,' shrugged Jarvis. 'Who knows why? If you'd been at home 24/7 baking cakes, I don't think she would have turned out any different.'

'What about this wedding tomorrow? Is she doing the right thing?'

'I like Charlie. You'll like her too. This is right for Siggie at the moment. It's her life, she's in love and that's all that matters, isn't it?'

Meredith nodded. It was all that mattered—she had to keep that in view.

'How did you get to be so smart?' she asked him.

'And good-looking?' he added.

'And full of yourself!' Meredith swatted at him with a napkin.

'It was just a matter of choosing the right parents. After that, everything was simple.'

Meredith reached her arms out to her son. He shifted to the next seat so she could hold him. Meredith breathed him in. Every memory of their lives together was in that smell. From the day he was born and she first cradled him; when he had fallen and she had set him on his feet again; every time she had sneaked an illicit teenage cuddle. Her heart was full, she wanted nothing more than to hold him like this forever.

'Hey, don't get all soppy on me now.' He laughed and unwrapped her hands from his neck. 'Save all your tears for tomorrow.'

Jarvis held his mother's hands and looked into her eyes.

'Mum, there's something else you should know. Dad's brought his new girlfriend with him.'

'Oh?' Meredith gulped. It stung a little bit, but not as much as she might have expected.

'Her name's Tania, she writes for a TV magazine and her pearls are fake.'

Meredith had to laugh. Jarvis was her son, no doubt about it.

The sun came up on Main Beach at Byron Bay on a late April morning that was almost unnaturally still. A steady parade of surfers had stood on the cliff, murmured their insults to the ocean and turned away in disgust.

For Annie, now measuring the length of the broad beach in long strides, the temper of the water was perfect. The peaceful wash and delicate transparent curl of sea onto sand was utterly calming. The rhythmic 'plip, plop' of the tiny waves was a relief after the battering from the natural elements and the emotional tsunami she had experienced all the way up the coast. It was a fine day for a wedding.

Annie stopped to shrug off her T-shirt and shorts, down to her bikini, and dived into the water. It was, as Nina had promised—it seemed a lifetime ago now—deliciously warm. She crested the surface and turned back to see the sweep of the town above the low dunes, and was surprised at how low-key it all was. Here and there the tops of roofs peeked above a scrub of ti-tree, melaleuca and native palms. There was nothing much to see and, after the profusion of ugly edifices in towns strung all the way up the coast behind them, that was a blessing.

It was the drama of the mountain range behind that drew Annie's eye. The highest peak was Mt Warning, an extinct volcano named by Captain Cook. Annie had read up on the place last night and loved its Aboriginal name—Wollumbin, the Fighting Chief of the Mountains. The cover of lush sub-tropical rainforest painted a dark-green silhouette that held the promise of a verdant valley and a rushing creek. Maybe that's where she could find Annie's Farm.

Walking back to the van she saw that Meredith was up and about, pacing the grass by the railing.

'They're coming to get me in a minute. Wish me luck, Annie. Christ, I'm so nervous!'

Annie put her arm around Meredith's shoulder. 'You'll be fine. Remember what Nina said—just smile and give presents.'

'Oh, that reminds me, I must get that painting. A mermaid! Sigrid will think her mother's gone mad.'

With the painting by her feet, Meredith adjusted her pearl earrings and tugged at the jersey skirt she was wearing. Annie noted with some amusement that it was one of her own purchases from Toorak Road.

'I hope you don't mind—it's one of yours. You've got so many beautiful things. Everything of mine's crushed beyond recognition,' Meredith twittered. 'In fact, would you mind if I borrowed a dress for the wedding as well? I was thinking of that long jersey one you wore at Scotts Head—I've got a black lace cardigan that would look lovely with it.'

'It's yours,' said Annie, pleased that Meredith could now see the sense of her emergency shopping expedition.

'How do I look?'

Annie appraised Meredith and didn't hesitate with her compliments. She always presented well, but this morning, smiling broadly from under her cherry-trimmed straw hat, she looked tanned, relaxed and especially vibrant. 'Gorgeous! You look just gorgeous. Too young to be the mother of the bride.'

'Two brides today!' grimaced Meredith. 'Can you believe it?'

'Now—'

'I know, I know. I'm getting an extra daughter. That's how I'm going to think of it.'

At that moment the bride and bride peeked around the side of the van.

'Fucking hell!' exclaimed a young woman who surely must be Sigrid, thought Annie. She remembered telling Nina that she wouldn't recognise Sigrid if she fell over her, but the truth was that she was a Skidmore. There was no doubt about it. She was blessed with the same long, lean limbs as her brother and the quizzical deep furrow at the top of a long, straight patrician nose was pure Meredith.

Annie's nostalgic appraisal of Sigrid halted at the jewelled piercing in her left nostril. Annie had to smile to herself—and wait until Meredith saw it! Sigrid was holding hands with someone who actually *did* look like k.d. lang with curly blonde hair.

'Muuum! What's with the daggy Elvis-mobile? Typical! I knew you wouldn't come by plane. You've always had a crazy streak in you. I told Charlie she better watch out, I take after my mum.'

And that, Meredith reflected as she leaned forward for a kiss, had made the whole journey with The King worthwhile. She wished her mother, Edith, could have been here with them both. She might have brought a plate of pikelets along for the wedding reception.

✲

It was early afternoon and the main street of Byron Bay was buzzing. Nina now understood, as she trawled through shady arcades and under low verandas, why everyone wanted to visit the town. Its hippie origins were still in evidence. The tang of patchouli-scented incense wafted from doorways of shops offering organic food, herbal remedies, fruit juice, Balinese knick-knacks and original artworks.

In the shade of giant Norfolk pines, holiday-makers and locals sat at tables on the footpath. Barefoot surfers—glumly commiserating with each other on the lack of swell—stood, arms folded, leaning against walls and scowling at the parade of backpacking blow-ins carting dreaded boogie boards.

Nina—fresh from the spa with glossy pink fingernails, and sleek blow-dried hair—poked through the racks of clothes in one shop after another with increasing desperation. She had barely an hour and a half before they had agreed to meet back at the van to frock up for the wedding. Brad trailed after her, patiently holding her handbag.

Nina smiled wanly at him, not wanting to ruin the day. She stopped at the window of one particularly upmarket boutique. Did she dare go in? She always imagined that the shop assistants in these kinds of places were secretly laughing at the delusions of a dumpy mother-of-three who imagined she might find anything to fit her.

'Go on, go in!' Brad urged. Nina stepped inside onto cream carpet and almost immediately saw The Dress—a long, floaty sky-blue confection of loveliness. Its three-quarter length sleeves were edged with tiny silver beads, and the same beads decorated the low, scooped neckline. Nina checked the label and her shoulders sagged—a size 16.

'Just try it on,' said Brad. Nina gathered up the dress and stepped behind the curtains, willing it to fit her. She slipped the fabric over her head and, for once, found that she didn't have to drag it down over her hips. It slid and fell in a sensuous silky puddle around her pink toenails.

Nina looked in the mirror and couldn't believe it. She'd lost weight. Quite a lot of weight, in fact—maybe three or four kilos. She wiped a tear from her eye, and offered a silent thanks to Zoran's Spanish mackerel curry.

✸

Annie was standing at the foot of the Cape Byron lighthouse, staring up at the white expanse of tower, when Matty called her name.

'Annie! I knew you'd be here.' He looked up and shaded his eyes from the afternoon sun to share her view. 'It's a pilgrimage. You can't leave Byron Bay without visiting the lighthouse.'

'I thought you were heading north to Cooktown, chasing red emperor.'

'I am. But I realised that I had bigger fish to fry here in Byron first.'

'That's an awful joke.'

'I know. I've been telling myself not to say it to you for two whole days.' Matty stood next to her and took her hand. 'Let's walk out to the point,' he said.

Their eyes were at the same height, Annie noticed, as they strolled along the path to the lookout. She wondered if that might mean they shared the same view of life.

At the bottom of the cliffs on either side the ocean stretched forever. On a wild and windy day they might have been blown to the heavens, but the morning's calm had lasted into the afternoon and all was peaceful and still. The waves traced even, graceful arcs on the surface of the water—as if the gods had dropped a pebble into a pond a thousand miles away.

'It's beyond beautiful. I'll bet most people who come to Byron think about staying forever,' said Matty.

'You don't?'

'I'm a boy from down south. I couldn't leave everything behind to live here. I'll come up for a holiday, but it's not home. I'll go back.'

'Where will you go back to?'

'Mum and Dad live in Daylesford in Victoria, just near the lake. Mum hasn't been well and my brother lives in New York, so . . . it's just me. "You have to cut your coat according to your cloth," as my grandmother used to say.'

'My mum says "bloom where you are planted",' said Annie.

'See your aphorism and raise you one: "let the sun shine on your face and the shadows fall behind you".'

'Shit happens.'

'We should stop this now, it's getting silly,' said Matty.

'Que sera, sera.'

'A mystic hangs a fig leaf on a eunuch.'

'What does that mean?' she asked.

'Fucked if I know.'

Annie laughed and turned to look at him. She searched his eyes for . . . something. Was it clues to a painful past, a needy present or a troubled future? Annie could see nothing. Just a calm, simple kindness there. His eyes were the same soft, dusty brown as the earth she knew so well, and a silent declaration came to her, unbidden, from somewhere she couldn't name: *I'm home*, was what Annie Bailey thought.

✸

It was twenty years ago when they had dodged over and under each other in the poky dressing rooms at the Athenaeum Theatre, but Meredith could not remember being as nervous about the performance that night as she was now.

Meeting back at the van to prepare for the wedding was probably a mad idea—especially since Nina had left Brad cooling his heels in an expensive luxury penthouse suite—but they all felt they owed the RoadMaster Royale their presence . . . for reasons they couldn't quite articulate.

They were on the road again. That's what it was. Just like in the old days. Although, back then, they weren't sharing lip gloss and champagne. Instead, they had swigged from Briony's flask of vile blackberry and echinacea tea (good for the throat), been given a painful reflexology foot massage by Jaslyn and had their hair serially tortured by Corinne armed with tail comb and hair spray.

Annie remembered discovering Genevieve that final night, hiding behind a heavy velvet curtain, puffing on a joint. Annie had crammed into the smoky hidey-hole and shared a few illicit drags.

'Are you nervous?' Annie had asked.

'Nah,' Genevieve had replied. 'I just reckon it's good to be alive. We're all going round just this once, I reckon. We should suck it all down while we can, sister. One day we'll look back and know that we were never more brave and beautiful than we are now. So let's just get out there and show 'em what we got.'

Nina, Annie and Meredith leaned against the railing at the top of the cliff. The afternoon sun was dropping below the mountains behind. The vast ocean, polished to a brilliant pink-orange sheen, heaved and rolled. Waves broke and frothed with apricot-tinged foam. The wedding party was gathering below on the beach.

Nina turned her back on the scene and held her crystal flute of champagne high to capture the last rays of the sun. 'I'd like to propose a toast . . . to Lizzie Bailey. I think she's the one who brought us all here.'

'To Lizzie and her beautiful sister,' agreed Meredith.

'To sisters, lost and found!' Annie held her glass aloft with a steady hand. The sound of tinkling crystal drifted out over the ocean. On the wind's inward breath came the insistent pounding of pagan drums.

☼

'Red rose petals for passion, white for purity, yellow for friendship and pink for joy,' Galantha intoned as she flung the petals from a wicker basket into the ocean. Her tie-dyed skirt washed in and out around her bare, bangled ankles. 'We call on the winds from the four corners of the earth to bless this union made by the Goddess Aphrodite.'

'So mote it be,' the assembled multitude bowed heads and replied in reverent unison.

'Dear Lord, spare me!' Meredith groaned in Annie's ear.

'Fuck me sideways.' Annie rolled her eyes.

'Isn't it lovely?' sighed Nina as she dabbed her eyes with a tissue and leaned back to find that familiar, fragrant place for her head on Brad's chest.

'Sigrid, Charlie...' Galantha addressed the happy couple. 'As you give love, so will you receive love. As you give strength, so will you receive strength. Together you are one—apart you are less. Ever love, help and respect each other, and know truly that you are one in the eyes of the gods and of Wicca.'

With the seal of a passionate kiss Sigrid and Charlie were pronounced to be wed.

An archway of flaming torches stuck in the sand illuminated the throng who were dressed in rainbow colours and chattered like a flock of parrots. The newlyweds posed this way and that in response to calls of 'over here, over here!'. Drums beat out a wild tribal rhythm, bells clanged, Tibetan finger cymbals chimed. Meredith reflected that the wedding photos would be a far cry from the blurry happy snaps of the Dalrymples outside the bluestone Melbourne registry office all those years ago.

Sigrid stood front and centre—tall and effortlessly elegant, like her mother—in a cream raw silk shirt tucked into white cotton drawstring pants. Charlie stood next to her in a champagne silk petticoat slip, tiny pink rosebuds threaded through her blonde tresses. Meredith held hands with Jarvis and next to him was Donald, alarmingly tanned and sprightly, holding hands with his new squeeze, Tania, who was complaining that her cyclamen satin high-heeled sandals were being ruined by the saltwater tide.

Brad's arms encircled his wife's waist. He was smiling broadly, standing a good head and a half taller than the rest of the multitude. Nina was already making plans for escape back to their suite for another night of passion—her sitting astride his naked, muscled thighs as the waves pounded the shore and the sea breeze blew at her back.

Annie too was swept away by the joy of it all. She was laughing—mouth open, curls blown into disarray by the wind—when she had that sense again that Matty was looking at her. Then she caught sight of him standing at the top of the cliff, just beyond the flash of the cameras. That solid silhouette, two feet planted firmly on the earth, that she thought she might always recognise, wherever, whenever she saw it.

The photographs made, the wedding party and guests piled into a convoy of cars. On a slamming car-door and honking-horn tide of happiness the guests headed for the hills. Brad, in the driver's seat next to Nina, made a stop in front of Matty, who was dragged into the back to sit between Annie and Meredith.

'*Swing low, sweet chariot,*' crooned Meredith as she reached her arm around Annie's shoulders.

'*Comin' for to carry me home,*' Annie leaned to kiss Nina's cheek.

'*Swing low, sweet chariot,*' Nina threaded her fingers through Annie's.

'*Comin' for to carry me home,*' they sang in perfect, glorious three-part harmony.

A hundred pairs of hands clapped with admiration as the trio tumbled from the makeshift stage under the carport. The floor was scattered with the last frangipanis of the season. The beams were strung with Buddhist prayer flags, Hindu talismans, batik sarongs and bundles of dried herbs.

Had they ever sung together before? If they hadn't, they certainly should do. They were really wonderful! It would be a shame if they were ever to break up! Could they be booked for a school fundraiser? A birthday party? They were asked these questions over and over again as they were plied with slices of cold wholemeal pizza on paper plates and plastic cups of white wine.

'We used to sing together, but it's a long time ago now,' said Nina.

'A lifetime ago,' agreed Annie.

'But we just got back together, for a reunion tour,' Meredith added.

Sixteen

Annie sat back in her seat and thumbed through the in-flight magazine. Brad and Nina were sitting in front—her blonde head on his broad shoulder. Beside her, Meredith had taken out her novel and it was sitting on her lap, unopened, because she couldn't tear herself away from the window—looking down at the coastline, she was amazed to see how far their travels had taken them.

Annie tucked the magazine back in the seat pocket and turned to Meredith. 'There's something I forgot to ask you.'

'Hmm?'

'You were going to talk to Donald about what happened that night in the car with Corinne. Did he tell you?'

Meredith rummaged for her sunglasses. They were flying above the clouds now, and the light was startlingly bright.

'Yes, he did. After he'd had too many pineapple daiquiris.'

'And?'

'He'd been having an affair with Corinne. For all those years we were in Sanctified Soul, apparently. All that time when the children were little.'

'No!'

'That night she gave him an ultimatum. She wanted him to leave me and the children, and marry her.'

'Fuck me! I can't believe it.' Annie stared at Meredith, who stared straight ahead, sunglasses masking her emotion.

'He told her he was staying with me. They had a huge fight in the car. He swears that he didn't try to rape her—she was the one who hit him. I can only think that she invented the story to cover the fact that she couldn't deal with seeing him again.'

'That makes sense, I guess. But it was an incredible thing to accuse him of.'

'I'm sure she wanted to hurt him. From what he told me, she was unbearably disappointed. They really did love each other, so he said.'

'It's strange, isn't it? Even the other night, when she could have thrown it at you, she never mentioned it.'

'Yes, I know.'

'Why, do you think?'

'I'm not sure. Maybe because she couldn't stand to admit, even to herself, that she'd lost him to me. Pride, maybe.'

'So that means that you and Corinne shared . . .'

Meredith slid her glasses to the top of her head. 'I know! We were both in love with Donald. Can you believe it? Maybe deep down I knew, and that's why I hated her so much.'

'And do you still hate her?'

'No, not really. I've got a beautiful son and daughter . . . Two daughters now. I don't need anything more.'

'Anything from the mini-bar today?' asked the flight attendant. Annie hesitated. 'No, I don't think I will, thanks.'

'Good for you,' winked Meredith. 'We'll both have tea, thank you, but do you have any china cups? I'm allergic to plastic.'

'I'll see what I can find, madam.'

Annie placed her hand over Meredith's on the armrest. 'It must be devastating for you to find out after all this time.'

Meredith squeezed Annie's hand. 'There's no point in being angry about it now. I'm sure there were others over the years. I'm glad for him, in a way. He probably knew that once I'd had the children and established the business, I didn't really need him anymore.'

'Like a fish needs a bicycle . . . ?'

'Maybe. I wonder if Edith felt the same about Bernie.'

Brad leaned over from the seat in front. 'Meredith? Annie? Nina's dad's bringing the Odyssey to the airport. There'll be room for you both. Do you need a lift?'

'Thank you, Brad, but I don't think I'd fit,' said Meredith. 'I've got that damned mermaid painting, remember?'

Nina peeked between the seats. 'I can't believe they didn't like it. What did they say they wanted for a wedding present anyway?'

'Glassware.'

'Oops!'

'How about you, Annie? Are you right?' asked Brad.

'Yeah,' smiled Annie, 'I'm fine. I'll make my own way back home.'

'OK. Well, looks like we're all set then.'

And, for now, they were.

Acknowledgements

This book has been inspired by my beloved father, Graham Frederick Brown. Dad has never been able to resist the lure of a long drive. He is a trusted guide, a loving and faithful companion on my life's journey.

Once again I am in debt to the back-seat drivers at Allen & Unwin—Richard Walsh, Annette Barlow, Alexandra Nahlous and Jo Jarrah—they have been brilliant navigators on this particular trip!

As ever, my husband Brendan has helped me 'stop, revive and survive'. Thanks too to my dear little speed humps Marley and Maeve.

And finally (at risk of over-extending this analogy), much love to my dear lollipop lady, Hilary Linstead.

Happy trails!